THE WRONG WOMAN

O. J. MULLEN

Boldwood

First published in Great Britain in 2024 by Boldwood Books Ltd.

Cover Design by Head Design Ltd

Cover Photography: Shutterstock

A CIP catalogue record for this book is available from the British Library.

Paperback ISBN 978-1-83617-919-1

Large Print ISBN 978-1-83617-920-7

Hardback ISBN 978-1-83617-918-4

Ebook ISBN 978-1-83617-921-4

Kindle ISBN 978-1-83617-922-1

Audio CD ISBN 978-1-80415-499-1

MP3 CD ISBN 978-1-78513-361-9

Digital audio download ISBN 978-1-83617-916-0

Boldwood Books Ltd
23 Bowerdean Street
London SW6 3TN
www.boldwoodbooks.com

To my wonderful wife, Christine, the real brains of the outfit and very definitely The Right Woman

PROLOGUE
1998

Shouting wakened the tiny figure in the bed; he rolled over, rubbed the sleep from his eyes and stared at the ceiling. Angry voices weren't new: six-year-old Jonathan McMillan had grown up hearing them; they scared him. He buried his head under the duvet, put his fingers in his ears and tried to blot them out. Like many children his age, Jonathan was afraid of the dark, so a lamp was left on to keep the monsters in his young imagination at bay. As he slept, the superhero figures he'd got from Santa Claus – Batman and Robin, the Hulk and Captain America – stood guard on the bedside table and, underneath, his collection of DC and Marvel comics sat in a neat pile on the floor. Jonathan couldn't read them, not yet – his mummy did that – but he was happy to just look at the pictures. Tonight it wasn't Doctor Octopus or the creatures hiding in the bottom of the wardrobe that had disturbed him. It was his parents fighting downstairs.

He scrambled out of bed to the landing and sat on the top step, afraid to go further, his little body trembling inside the Spider-man pyjamas while the two people he loved most in the world screamed at each other.

His daddy called his mummy a name Jonathan didn't understand, something smashed against the wall and she yelled back. For a moment, there was silence and the boy thought the row was over: he was wrong – it was only beginning. His mummy was talking, saying something he couldn't make out. Whatever it was sent his daddy into a rage and he roared, 'You fucking whore!'

The child heard the slap of skin on skin, then his mummy crying, and a silent tear, the first of many, slipped down Jonathan's cheek. Suddenly, the glass door in the lounge shattered and his parents fell through it into the hall, locked together, his father's hands round his mother's throat, her punching him until he let go. They sensed their son on the stairs and drew away from each other, red-faced and panting.

His daddy said, 'It's okay, son, it's okay. Be a good boy and go back to bed.'

Jonathan stayed where he was, sobbing so hard he almost couldn't breathe. His mother had known this moment would come and dreaded it. Now it was finally here, witnessing her little boy's distress without being able to comfort him was even more terrible than she'd imagined; her heart was breaking.

The lies didn't come easily but were spoken gently, quietly, asking the child to believe them. 'Go back to bed, sweetheart. Everything will be okay. Everything will be all right.'

Lifting her coat from the hall stand sent him out of his mind. He ran to her, begging, 'Please, Mummy, please don't go!'

She knelt beside him, so close he could smell her perfume and see the purple bruise around her eye. She held his shaking body tight. 'Darling, I have to. I'm sorry.'

'No! No! Take me with you! I want to go with you!'

She glared over his shoulders at her husband. 'You can't, Jonathan. I want you to come with me but you can't.'

'Why? Why can't I?'

She faltered. 'It... isn't possible.'

His father yelled at her. 'Tell him why! Go on! Tell your son why you can't take him!'

'Peter, don't do this... He's just a child.'

'He deserves the truth.'

'Peter, for God's sake don't...'

He grabbed the boy and spoke to him, his voice cracking with pain. 'Son, listen to me. There's a man in a car at the end of the street. She's going to meet him. It's not just you she's leaving, it's both of us.'

Jonathan didn't understand what the words meant, though they terrified him; he clung tighter to his mummy's legs. She buttoned her coat and spat her contempt at her husband. 'You bastard. What good did that do?'

'At least he knows.'

'It doesn't change anything.'

The boy pressed his back against the door, barring it with his outstretched arms, screaming his anguish while the warring adults towered above him. 'No-o-o! No! Don't leave me! I love you, Mummy!'

His mother hesitated, wanting to scoop him up, wanting to whisper reassurances as she tucked him into bed and kissed him goodnight. Except it wouldn't be true; the man she was running to had made it clear he wasn't prepared to raise somebody else's child.

He wanted her and only her.

She defiantly lifted her trembling chin as waves of sadness welled up inside her. Her son sobbed, wild-eyed with sorrow. 'Please, Mummy. Please don't leave me. I'll be good. I promise I'll be good.'

It took all she had not to give in.

From across the hall covered in broken glass her husband goaded her, playing on the guilt she was suffering, every word meant to wound. 'What kind of woman leaves her child? What selfish, soulless bitch does that? You're not fit to be a mother. If you walk out that door I'll make sure you never see your son again. You hear me? Never!'

She balled her fists and rounded on him. 'You think this is easy? You think this is what I want? I should've done it long ago only I didn't have the courage. This is my chance to be happy, maybe my last chance. Threats and emotional blackmail won't stop me taking it.'

She picked up the suitcase Jonathan had watched her wordlessly pack that afternoon. When he'd asked, 'Where are we going, Mummy?' she'd searched for a reply.

'Mummy has to leave.'

'Why?'

She still didn't have an answer for him, at least, not one that would do either of them any good. 'Don't worry, I'll visit you.'

It sounded inadequate and it was.

Jonathan asked, 'When?'

Her lipstick had smeared and she'd lost an earring – a detail the boy would remember for the rest of his life. 'Soon, very soon.'

She hugged him, tenderly brushing a strand of fair hair from his tear-stained face, and forced a smile that disappeared before the words were out of her mouth.

'Cross my heart and hope to die. Do as Daddy says and go back to bed.'

'No! No! I want to go with you! I want to go with you!'

She looked at her husband and shook her head. He moved between them as she opened the door and stepped into the cold night air. Jonathan raced upstairs and stood on the bed watching her walk towards a future without him. Eventually, he lay down and cried himself into a sleep torn by nightmares even all his superheroes together couldn't fix.

The boy outgrew the Spider-man pyjamas; the comics and action figures ended up on the shelves of a charity shop, replaced by Nintendo and Super Mario, and the world kept turning. It was years before he lost hope and stopped waiting for the woman who'd given birth to him to make good on her promise.

She hadn't then and wouldn't now.

PART I

1

GRAPEVINE ADVERTISING AGENCY, BOTHWELL STREET, GLASGOW

Tony's voice cut across the room when she came through the door. Every head turned in Julia's direction exactly as he intended. 'On behalf of myself and your grateful colleagues, let me say how much we appreciate you breaking into your busy schedule to be here! Glad you could join us, Julia!'

'Sorry, Tony. The traffic...'

Tony Connors, the founder and MD of Grapevine, one of Scotland's foremost boutique advertising agencies, was wearing a beige linen Raviet, more at home on an August day in Nice or Portofino than a muggy morning in Glasgow, over a T-shirt and jeans, and looked younger than his fifty-one years. Tony usually managed with a light, if cheeky, touch, understanding that creative people were a special breed who danced to a beat only they could hear. But when he was making a point his sarcasm became a blunt instrument that rarely missed its mark. Julia found a seat near the back, too flustered to notice the man standing beside him. Tony dredged a half-smile from somewhere and continued what he'd been saying before the interruption.

'If you're curious about where Ellis got his suntan, I can tell you. He's spent the last decade in South Africa. Cape Town's loss is our gain; he comes with the best references I've seen and a track record that blows most of us out of the water. He could've gone to London. Ogilvy, Sum, or any of the big players down there would snap him up. Instead – don't ask me why – he decided to return to his native land.'

Somebody shouted 'Cue the piper', and everybody laughed.

Julia couldn't see Ellis's face until he lifted his head and his eyes held hers in an intense stare that made her uncomfortable.

Tony let the laughter die before he went on. 'Okay, okay, maybe that was a bit over the top.' He hooked a thumb in Ellis's direction. 'But I'm serious when I say Grapevine is fortunate to have landed this guy. I'll be giving him the tuppenny tour, so you'll have the chance to make the case for the defence.' Tony paused and scanned the crowd. 'One more thing. He's only just arrived in the country. Give the poor fella a break and save the salt-mine stories for later, eh? He won't believe you. I've already told him you're the best-paid bunch of scruffs in the city.' He clapped his hands. 'Okay, people, let's get at it. It's Monday, anything can happen.'

* * *

In Julia's office, the Scottish roll-out of a new range of loans and mortgages, the latest offerings by one of the major banks, lay on her desk where she'd reluctantly left it on Friday night. The campaign had been signed off and was ready, apart from a few details that had still to be agreed. She'd considered coming in on Saturday morning to finish it but suggesting that to her husband would've started another row and spoiled the weekend; their careers stole enough from their lives without giving up more.

She'd been introduced to Rob at a party, seen his blue eyes, and known he was the guy she'd been waiting for. Now they were married and had recently moved into their first real home together after renting an over-priced shoebox. Rob was with the Galloway, Bartholomew and Figgis firm of architects based in Park Circus. Building was booming again and he was up to his eyebrows with client meetings, site meetings, meetings about meetings; it seemed to never end and Julia wondered how he coped with the pressure.

She was a senior accounts manager at Grapevine, a job she loved but that came with more stress than she wanted. Her team got together every Monday to go over the schedule for the week ahead and tidy up outstanding pieces of business. Calling the two people she managed a 'team' was stretching it a bit. Ravi and Olivia were typical of the talented people Tony took on – young, bright, full of ideas and enthusiasm, who didn't mind working odd hours at short notice to meet the deadlines glorified sweatshops like advertising agencies were known for. Ravi was Ravi Malik, a gangly, six-foot-tall twenty-three-year-old who made self-deprecating cracks about his height before anybody else could. His specialism was graphic design and Julia hadn't worked with many better. He was irreverent, football mad and easy to get along with; she liked him and laughed at his daft jokes. Olivia Hassel was the same age but could hardly have been more different, a petite, quietly spoken graduate of Strathclyde University's Business School capable of thinking on her feet and distilling a product's USP into a few sharp lines.

This morning, they were in good form, sharing matey chit-chat about the weekend. Ravi brought Julia in. 'And were you dancing on the tables anywhere we'd know? Please don't tell me the police were called. I'll need more coffee to handle that.'

'No and no, Ravi. Now, if you don't mind, can we cut the comedy and do what we get paid for?'

She snapped like a humourless prude and wished she could take it back. Normally, she gave as good as she got but for some reason the familiar banter had irritated her. Ravi and Olivia were up for it, which meant it was her.

As they were about to begin, Tony breezed into the room followed by Grapevine's star recruit and Julia got her first real look at Ellis Kirkbride: with carefully cultivated designer stubble, collar-length dark hair flecked with grey at the temples, he was more handsome than he'd seemed from a distance. Of course, the suntan helped. He had a Mulberry leather satchel and a camera slung casually over his shoulder, which confirmed her opinion he was a poser. When he saw her, he ran a hand over his jaw and Julia felt vaguely uncomfortable for the second time.

Tony said, 'Sorry to break in unannounced. Please tell me we aren't interrupting anything too important.'

Tony Connors was a busy man. It was unusual for him to take a personal interest in a new employee; there had to be a reason. He said, 'I need a word, Julia,' and threw a fake smile at Ravi and Olivia. 'You guys should grab a quick break away from this slave driver.'

He grinned as though he were joking. In fact, with his characteristic lack of subtlety he was reminding the two juniors how unimportant they were, tactlessly signalling they weren't part of the conversation. Julia didn't disguise her annoyance. 'Was that really necessary, Tony?'

He feigned surprise. 'Was what really necessary, Julia?'

'Shutting them out like that.'

'Is that what I did? Then please apologise on my behalf. Assure them it wasn't my intention to put them down, that they're valued and valuable members of Grapevine whose contribution... blah, blah, blah. You know, the standard guff. And the answer to your question is yes, unfortunately it was necessary. I'm doing the rounds, introducing Ellis to everybody and their granny. A waste of time because he won't be working with them. But he will be working with you. I'm bringing him onto your team. Effective immediately. He can use Sylvia's old office until we sort something else out.'

He held up his hand to stave off her objections. 'And, yes, yes, before you say it, you're right, you ought to have been consulted. No argument.' He shrugged indifferently. 'The boss took an executive decision, what can I tell you?'

Julia swallowed her anger. This wasn't the first time the MD had undercut her. Tony's off-the-cuff style was famous – anybody who was unhappy with it was welcome to close the door behind them on their way out. Her mouth set in a line that left no doubt about her feelings. 'You mean *you* took an executive decision.'

Tony didn't notice or, if he did, he didn't care. 'Correct. I mean *I* took an executive decision.' He stepped back and studied her reaction. 'Are you saying you aren't okay with Ellis joining you? Because now's the time to get it out in the open.'

'Will it change anything if I'm not?'

He made a you-know-better-than-that face and pursed his lips. 'How long have you been with Grapevine, Julia?'

'Too long.'

'Me and you both. Then I'm surprised you need to ask.' The MD leaned over the desk to emphasise his point and there was fire in his eyes. 'It won't change a damned thing, but you can lie to yourself that you stood up to the Big Bad Boss if it helps. When word gets out your street cred will be sky-high and I won't tell if you won't. Here's the deal: the jungle drums are saying we're going to be asked to pitch for one of the biggest inner-city developments in a decade.'

'The Waterfront?'

Tony shook his head. 'No, I didn't waste my time on that.'

'Why not?'

Instead of answering, he glanced away. When he brought his attention back, irritation pulled at the corners of his mouth and there was an edge to his voice. 'Because I wasn't prepared to spend money on a window-dressing exercise for Glasgow City Council. Let's just say there were people involved who had a lot of influence with certain well-placed individuals and leave it there.' He paused. 'If it's true – and there's no reason to think it isn't – this one is different.'

'What makes it different?'

'They'll be inviting us. It's a prime chunk of business but it won't be easy. Winning will depend on us being at the top of our game. Guaranteed we'll be up against big-dog agencies from Edinburgh and London, maybe even further afield. To beat them our ideas will have to be better, stronger, more creative than anything they come up with. Can we do it?' He nodded slowly and answered his own question. 'I think we can. In fact, I'm sure of it.'

Tony was serious and Julia started to understand where he was going. As he stood beside his new boss, Ellis Kirkbride's expression revealed that what he was hearing wasn't a surprise to him – he'd already been briefed. Old-school male chauvinist that he was, Tony had elected to tell a guy who'd got here five minutes ago before he'd told her. Julia bit her lip in anger and tried not to take it personally. Complaining would label her a touchy female expecting special treatment because she was a woman, displeased when she didn't get it. The MD's abrasiveness when he felt he was being second-guessed ruffled feathers. In his own words, he couldn't have given a 'tuppenny damn' which snowflake he offended. Today it was her turn.

Tony carried on. 'So I'm keen to throw everything we have at this. And by everything, I mean you two. The brightest and the best Grapevine has – our very own dream team. Ellis couldn't have arrived at a better moment. I've seen what he's done, what he's capable of, and it's nothing short of excellent; his input and experience will be invaluable. Putting you together makes sense. I'm excited, and it isn't too often these days I can say that. Trust me, it'll be great.'

* * *

Julia drove the Mazda Rob had bought her for Christmas through the early-evening traffic from her office in Bothwell Street to the West End flat in Hamilton Drive. 'Manic Monday' might have been coined for the 'racket' – one of Tony Connors' descriptions – they were in: it had been a stressful one and she was mentally exhausted.

When she got home she hurriedly undressed, threw on a grey track-suit top, navy-blue leggings, a pair of white Lululemon Blissfeels and a sweatband to keep her hair off her face. Running had started as a way to keep fit and push back against the long hours behind a desk. Her favourite route followed the River Kelvin, crossing the bridge on Belmont Street near Glasgow Academy, taking the fifty-three steps – she'd counted them – down to the other bank and past the stone and brick ruins of the North Woodside Flint Mill, demolished before she was born. After a challenging day at Grapevine – was there any other kind? – this tranquil place in the heart of the city energised her and revived her spirit. On early-morning jogs she'd seen roe deer grazing at the water's edge, more grey squirrels than she could count and even a red fox returning to its earth from a night's hunting.

Her mobile rang; she fished it out of her pocket and saw she had a message from Rob. Her husband was a laid-back guy, easy to be around, but his electronic communications were famously curt: this one was no exception.

> Got the client from hell. Working on. Don't wait up.

Julia wasn't surprised – they were both workaholics, call-offs were par for the course. She'd lost count of the unused concert tickets, the meals that had gone in the bin, the dinner reservations cancelled at the last minute because one or other of them couldn't make it. She'd even been late for their wedding anniversary due to 'something coming up' at Grapevine. Though Rob could hardly complain, he wasn't pleased. They'd had words and slept in separate rooms. Julia had tossed and turned knowing she was wasting what should've been a lovely night. Rob hadn't fared any better and as dawn broke over Glasgow he'd slipped in beside her. Julia had tried to whisper, 'I'm sorry.' He'd put a finger against her mouth, his lips had brushed her neck and she'd moved towards him. Afterwards, lying in each other's arms, they'd made a promise to re-evaluate their priorities.

The intention was sincere but, of course, it hadn't happened and was never going to – they were always too busy.

The WhatsApp made Julia question for the zillionth time how they were living their lives. In the early days of the relationship, filled with the recklessness and wild optimism that came naturally with being in love, every other conversation had been about them and what they were going to do. West End flats or climbing the corporate ladder weren't important; having children barely got a mention. There was time for that stuff. Plenty of time. No, they were going to travel until they'd been everywhere, seen everything there was to see and felt the warmth of the sun on their faces in strange lands they'd struggle to pinpoint on a map. Sod the future; the future would take care of itself. All that mattered was right now and fantasising about what was to come. Night after night they'd lie awake into the small hours talking in excited whispers about opening a beach hotel in Kerala and sleeping under the stars in hammocks strung between two shady banyan trees; endless balmy evenings spent with sea salt on their skin, eating jumbo prawns fresh from the Indian Ocean served in a fragrant coconut curry broth, toasting their good fortune with palm toddy.

Most important of all, they'd be together.

Where had that dream gone?

Julia sat on the grass feeling lonely and alone: here she was, surrounded by peace and beauty while Rob was stuck in some stuffy office with people he didn't even like, not sure when he'd be home. It wasn't fair. It wasn't right. And it was time they did something about it.

She replied to his message with a sad face and three kisses. Suddenly, Julia didn't feel like running any more and started walking slowly back to the empty flat.

* * *

They sat across from each other, together but not together, the woman holding the tiny espresso cup delicately between her fingers watching her companion slumped in the leather armchair staring at the phone as if it were somehow responsible. Her name was Michelle Davidson, a thirty-one-year-old redhead who was single by choice, a state she was perfectly happy with and didn't care who knew it. She wore a black Karen Millen pencil dress and high heels that took great legs to the next level. Understated pearl earrings were the finishing touch on an outfit that looked as though the elements might have instinctively been drawn together. From the moment Rob Sutherland had taken her hand and introduced himself in his office in Park Circus the attraction had been there on both sides. Now they were about to go to the room he'd booked that same afternoon he seemed less sure: he'd messaged his wife and his conscience was bothering him. Nothing out of the ordinary so long as he got a grip on himself and started acting like a man. Infidelity always brought guilt, though in her experience it arrived after the sex, not before.

Michelle heard resentment in her voice and hated herself for it. 'I'm not liking what I see and doing my best not to take it personally.'

Rob sat up straight like someone who'd joined a conversation after it had started. 'I've no idea what you're talking about.'

'Don't you? Well, for starters, your face.'

'What's wrong with my face?'

'You look as if you're going to cry.'

'Don't be ridiculous. It has nothing to do with you.'

'And is that supposed to make me feel better? Would it shock you to know it doesn't? Boy, you've got making a woman feel good about who she is down to a fine art, haven't you?'

'I'm sorry, Michelle, that was clumsy.'

'Then at least we agree on something. Given the subject, I'm not certain it's a good basis for a relationship, even a very brief one. Perhaps we should finish our coffees and go?'

The suggestion caught him off guard. 'Go? Why would we do that?'

She sighed. 'Because this is supposed to be fun, otherwise why bother?'

'It is. I mean it will be. Julia and I tell each other the truth. Lying takes a bit of getting used to, that's all.'

Except it wasn't all: the mood was slipping away and Michelle didn't have the energy to pull it back. 'Look, we've been too hasty, rushed this and made a mistake. It isn't the first time and it won't be the last. Let's quit while we're behind, eh? Apart from my bruised ego there's no harm done.' She glanced at a passing waiter, then back to him. 'I assumed you'd been here before. I thought you could handle it.'

He turned the mobile off, slipped it into his pocket, and replied with a surprisingly forthright confession. 'I haven't done this before, Michelle, which is why I'm struggling and making a fool of myself. I've spent most of the day thinking about you. About us. Now—'

'We're actually here... you're having doubts?'

'No, no doubts, it's just...'

She leaned forward. 'You're not comfortable with the deception. I understand and I'm glad you told me. Most guys wouldn't be secure enough to admit it. They'd pretend this was something they did every other day, until their performance told a different story. It says a lot about you.'

The compliment wasn't appreciated; it was Rob's turn to take offence. 'Does it? Does it really? What does it say?'

'That you're honest.'

Rob laughed. 'Honest? You're joking, aren't you? If I was honest I'd be at home instead of about to go to bed with a woman I hardly know.'

Michelle tried not to feel insulted; he was spooked. 'You're worried about hurting your wife. I like that. It restores my faith in the shitty society we live in. We both have our reasons for being here. People need different things from a relationship. That's why open marriages exist.'

'That isn't us.'

Michelle could've pointed out that he was here with her but let it go. 'You have a partner and I'm not looking for one. Julia won't find out. As long as we're careful there's nothing to be worried about. Where does she think you are? What did you tell her?'

'I said I was working late.'

'"Working late." Okay. Not very original but okay. Will she believe you? Isn't she supposed to be smart?'

'She will and she is, the smartest lady I've ever met. No offence.'

The smile froze on the red lips. 'None taken but if Julia's so wonderful the question is why are you here with me?'

'Because I'm not wonderful. I'm also not smart – we're round the corner from my bloody office, for Christ's sake. All it needs is somebody from work to spot us together.'

'So... we're not happening?'

'We're happening, all right, just not here.'

2

He'd kissed Michelle in the car park one last time before following her tail lights back to the city. She'd put her arms round his neck and for a second he'd considered taking her back to the room. She'd said, 'Okay, crunch time. Shall I call you or will you call me?'

'I'll call you.'

'You'll call me? In other words—'

'Careful, your insecurity's showing.'

'You forget, I've been here before. "I'll call you" can be guyspeak for don't expect to hear from me again. Why did God have to make men so predictable?' Rob remembered the cynicism in her voice from the conversation in the Hilton as she added, 'And that's why I'm not married. Quite frankly, it would be boring and I don't do boring.'

'You've picked the wrong men.'

'Really?'

'Yes, really. When I tell someone I'll call – a woman, a man, anybody – I mean I'll call. It isn't complicated.'

Michelle stepped back to get a better look at him. 'And that's a promise, is it?'

'That's a promise.'

'God help me, I almost believe you.'

This woman had everything – looks, intelligence, sensuality, even a jaded way of seeing things he found attractive. In a word, she was nice, and more vulnerable than she'd seemed to him at the beginning of the evening when she was the one making the running and he would have called it off. Yet, she wasn't wrong: in spite of her obvious attributes he wouldn't be calling her. The sex had been good. Better than good, the sex had been great, actually, though not great enough to risk his marriage. Good, great or somewhere in between, it wouldn't be repeated; his nerves couldn't stand it. Early in the conversation she'd said something that had stayed with him.

'I assumed you'd been here before. I thought you could handle it.'

A sour smile played on Rob's lips – he couldn't and there was no point pretending he could. At this rate he'd have a heart attack and be dead before he was thirty.

On the drive home he'd gone over what he'd tell Julia if she was waiting for him, rehearsing his annoyance over the weight of his imaginary workload, defaming his boss and the endless demands of Planning.

By the time he got to a deserted Hamilton Drive he'd almost fallen for it himself.

* * *

Rob turned off the ignition and listened to the engine as it cooled in the night air, knowing he had only himself to blame for the sinking sensation in his stomach and his elevated heartbeat hammering in his chest. The faith he'd momentarily had in the fiction created to cover where he'd been and what he'd actually been doing had been short-lived. Now it seemed like something a child would invent and for a while he wasn't sure if he had the courage to get out of the car. He bent forward and rested his forehead against the steering wheel, close to despair. This could have been avoided. Except, instead of recognising the folly Michelle represented, he'd given in to temptation, and here he was.

For all her undoubted charms he didn't love her and never would. Young, free and single, she could do what she wanted with whoever she wanted; her risk was no risk at all. The same couldn't be said of him: life had rules, and everything, every act of omission or commission, had consequences. He didn't deserve to get away with what he'd done. If he did he'd be a lucky boy, a very lucky boy indeed.

Rob cut the self-pity short; it was useless and changed nothing. Being sorry after the event or because Julia might find out and leave him wasn't regret in any real sense. He was supposed to be a loving husband but when the test had come he'd failed spectacularly. The opportunity to honour the vows they'd made to each other had been there, yet, with clear knowledge and full consent, he'd abandoned them for Michelle's arms. It was too late for sackcloth and ashes. *Mea culpa* was a feeble cop-out and using the fact he and Julia hadn't exactly been firing lately was pitiful. Better to admit, at least to himself, what had really happened and be done with it: a woman – and not just any woman, a sensuous lady well aware of her power – had made a move on him. Pathetic and weak, he'd let his animal instincts make the decision.

He got out of the car and crossed the street, relieved to see the flat in darkness – of course, that didn't mean Julia was asleep. If she was waiting for him the chances of her believing the fairy tale he had ready were slim. His wife knew him better than anyone on earth; she'd suss something was wrong and it would all come out. The thought of discovery made him shudder. What a bloody idiot he'd been. Michelle was a beautiful woman, a wonderful lover. Tonight had been everything illicit sex was supposed to be – exhilarating, satisfying, dangerous – fine so long as it didn't become a classic example of how to screw your life up.

If his wife was awake, other than lie, what could he do? Telling the truth would destroy her, it would destroy them, but asking her to blindly accept he'd been working only added insult to an injury she must never discover.

Julia was the centre of Rob's universe, his everything; cheating on her had been the last thing on his mind when he'd taken the sapphire and gold ring from the little box in his pocket and put it on her finger in the sun-washed gardens of the Taj Mahal. He could still see the joy on her face. A special memory tainted. Remembering that moment brought a fresh wave of shame.

So much for extravagant romantic gestures.

* * *

Rob closed the front door quietly and slipped off his shoes, praying his wife wouldn't hear the old floorboards groaning under his step. At the sink, he poured a glass of water and drank it in two gulps while the silence around him roared. Tomorrow – or more accurately, today – he had a site meeting in Ayrshire at eight o'clock and another in the afternoon out in South Lanarkshire. Somewhere in between he'd get back to writing the report he'd been roped into presenting at the end of the week to the senior partners. Suddenly, the sheer normality of his life before tonight seemed a precious thing and he swore at himself for being a damned fool to jeopardise it with a one-night stand.

He undressed on the landing and eased the bedroom door open half expecting to see Julia in bed reading a book. In spite of the water he'd drunk, his mouth was dry, though his palms and the back of his neck were sweating. Before he'd left Michelle Rob had showered to remove any trace of her. When he'd come out her smiling comment hadn't amused him. 'You said you hadn't done this before.'

'I haven't.'

'So how come you know the rule?'

'What rules?'

'Rule, singular. There really is only one.'

'And what is it?'

'Don't get caught. Get that right and you don't need any more.'

The lamp was on at his side of the bed; the novel she'd been reading had fallen from her exhausted fingers onto the duvet when her attempt to stay awake finally failed. In repose his wife looked like an angel, innocent, without guile of any kind; Rob tried to imagine her doing what he'd just done and couldn't.

He got into bed and turned out the light. Sleep was a million miles away; he lay with his hands behind his head, thinking of something to do for his wife, something that would make her happy and salve his tortured conscience. Under the sheets the warmth of Julia's body was like a summer's day. Rob wanted to be close to her; lingering remorse forced him to keep his distance.

3

Julia's fingers reached across the bed searching for her husband, not finding him. She slowly opened her eyes and saw he wasn't there. If he hadn't come home something was wrong. Julia shot a worried glance at the clock on the bedside table and relaxed when she realised it was 7.10. Rob had mentioned a site meeting in Ayrshire. 'Darkest Ayrshire', he'd called it. Panic over – her workaholic husband, darling man that he was, had left without waking her. Julia was glad nothing was amiss, though she couldn't help feeling disappointed. In their hectic lives, mornings had become the time when they talked, drank their favourite Jamaican Blue Mountain coffee in bed and made love before going their separate ways to work. It would've been nice if he came through the door with two tall Americanos and a couple of almond croissants and got back in beside her; it seemed an age since they'd been together with nothing to think about but each other.

At first she didn't notice the folded rectangle of paper on the pillow. Rob was always leaving little messages for her around the house, probably imagining they went in the bin, unaware his wife kept them in a battered tea tin that had belonged to her grandmother. This would be the latest addition to the collection. Years down the line when she was old and grey she'd read her love letters from the past and relive what they'd found all over again.

The note was short but very, very sweet.

Love you to bits
    R xxx

With Rob already gone there was no point in Julia hanging about the flat. It made sense to get a start on the day before anyone else arrived. Twenty-five minutes later she'd showered and dressed and was getting into her car. In Bothwell Street she grabbed a cappuccino from Pret A Manger and took the stairs rather than the lift to her office.

Ellis Kirkbride was standing in the centre of the room studying the marketing material for the campaign her team had been working on pinned to the cork board covering most of the wall. He was wearing a black shirt, black cords under an orange body warmer, and white Nike Air Max 90 trainers with the distinctive Swoosh on the side. Her marketeer's instinct homed in on the logo. His arms were folded across his chest and as she watched he reached out to straighten a leaflet, tilted his head to inspect what he'd done, quietly mouthing something she wasn't able to make out. A criticism? Julia couldn't say but, for sure, the new guy wasn't short on confidence. This was her space; he had no business being here unless she invited him and absolutely none when she hadn't.

Julia coughed theatrically to get the unwelcome visitor's attention. Ellis turned and smiled, not remotely bothered by being discovered. 'It's yourself. Didn't realise you were there.'

Her reply was tart. 'Didn't you? This *is* my office or at least it was the last time I checked.'

He ignored the rebuke and pointed to the wall. 'I see you've been busy. Has the client approved it?'

Julia wasn't in the mood to discuss it. 'Not yet.'

The answer set him off on a stroll down memory lane that might've been intended to come across as empathy. He said, 'Whenever this sort of remit used to land on my desk, I shuddered. Banks and building societies are the worst companies to work with, expecting us to take dull products and somehow – Christ knows how – make them sexy. Not going to happen. It isn't possible. You've gone down the tried and tested "We're here to help" route. Very wise, if you don't mind me saying. I would've done the same. It's not true, of course. These people aren't in the business of "helping" anybody except themselves. Then again, this is marketing. What's truth got to do with it, eh?'

It hurt Julia to admit he was right: they'd spent weeks hashing out concepts trying to come up with something, anything, that wasn't so obviously done to death. With the deadline running out they'd given up on originality and compromised on a revamped version of every financial service campaign since the dawn of time, trusting that a modern twist to the graphics would carry the themes. It wasn't their finest hour and Julia would've preferred Ellis Kirkbride hadn't seen it.

If he'd respected her space and stayed outside the office until she got there, he wouldn't have.

Ellis took a last look at the stuff on the wall and turned to face her. 'Tony's told me great things about you. I'm looking forward to working together.'

'Let's hope we can.'

The negativity took him by surprise. 'Well, of course we can, why wouldn't we? What do you mean?'

'I mean, he obviously rates you, which is fine, but I'm a team player, are you?'

'Am I a...? For sure. Absolutely. We have to be able to think, to use a cliché, outside the box. Nobody, certainly not me, has a monopoly on ideas. Every marketing project is a problem searching for a solution. The doorman can come up with the strapline so long as it's effective.' His eyes stayed on her. 'Why on earth would you think I'd be anything else?'

He sounded sincere; Julia felt herself mellow. 'My sentiments exactly. As for what's on that wall, you're right. It was a dog when it arrived and it'll still be a dog when they sign off on it. Bog-standard stuff. But it's the clients' money – if they're happy, who are we to disagree?'

Ellis nodded. 'Tick the box and move on. For the record, I like what you've done with it. It's... solid.'

'Solid or stolid?'

He laughed. 'A bit of both, I'll give you that, but hey! Look, I can only imagine what was in your head when Tony gave that big build-up, then dumped me on you. If it had been the other way round, boss or not, I'd have had plenty to say about it.'

'I did, you were there. He doesn't care whose toes he steps on. Grapevine is his own little kingdom he rules like a benevolent despot.'

'One treasonous word and it's off with your expense account.'

She laughed. 'Close enough. When His Majesty makes a decision, that's it. Obviously he's made his mind up about you. The intro...'

Ellis ran a finger through the stubble on his jaw and grimaced. 'Yeah, it was embarrassing. I wanted to shout "For fuck's sake, Tony, I have to get along with these people. They'll hate me before I've even started. Give me a break!"'

Julia reassured him. 'Nobody will hate you, though I'm curious: South Africa's the other side of the planet, what took you down there?'

'It's a long story.'

'Give me the short version.'

'I'm not sure there is one.' He aimed a mock-accusing finger at her. 'You're not backward at coming forward, are you?'

The rebuke was mild but Julia felt it. 'I'm sorry, it's none of my business. Forget I asked.'

Ellis's smile didn't make it to his eyes. Julia was on the point of saying something else when the phone on her desk rang. Tony Connors could be a man of few words when it suited him. This was one of those times. He said, 'Julia? My office. Now. Is Ellis there?'

'Yes.'

'Bring him with you.'

* * *

It was a typical morning on the West Coast of Scotland – sunshine and blue skies ruined by a chill wind blowing from the Firth of Clyde, ruffling the hair and ruddying the cheeks of the group of serious-looking men with Rob. Above, the quiet drone of a Ryanair jet on its descent towards Prestwick Airport broke into his thoughts as he pretended to listen to the contract manager explain how the environmental challenges of the site were being overcome to turn featureless land into an enclave of expensive properties enjoying magnificent views across the water to the island of Arran. Rob had been to scores of meetings exactly like this one and could recite by heart the bullet points on the manager's list. From time to time he nodded to give the illusion of somebody who was interested in what was being said.

In fact, he couldn't have cared less.

He'd lain awake most of the night racked with guilt, staring at the ceiling until dawn's early light washed over the city. Now, standing in a scrubby field with salt air nipping his eyes, he remembered the uncertainty in Michelle's voice – 'Shall I call you or will you call me?' – and the untruth that had come so easily to his lips. He'd lied to bring the shameful episode of betrayal and monumental stupidity to a close and send her on her way as gently as he could; whatever he'd said, whatever promises he'd made, they wouldn't see each other again, at least, not like that.

Two hours earlier when he'd scribbled the note and left it on the pillow next to Julia that had been his sincere belief.

Rob felt his face flush and knew it had nothing to do with sea air because, mistake or not, against all reason he wanted to repeat it. Over and over and over again.

* * *

Given his position in the company it would've been reasonable to expect Tony Connors' office to have a view of the river. It didn't and, even if it had, the MD was too busy to spend valuable time admiring it. Today, wearing a black double-breasted pinstripe suit with a white open-necked shirt, he might've been a successful hippie who'd traded peace and love for stocks and shares. There was no tie; that would've been too straight. Julia guessed he was having lunch with one of his female friends and hoped the girl would enjoy whatever over-priced wine Tony ordered.

He waited for Julia and Ellis to sit down, rested his elbows on the desk and steepled his fingers in front of him before he began. 'I assume you've guessed why you're here.'

Julia said, 'The development you talked about?'

He clasped his hands together and nodded. 'The jungle drums were spot on. It's official. We've been asked to pitch.' He tossed a folder on the desk. 'I'll have this copied myself and over to you in the next hour. When you've read it I want you to start working right away. I've already block-booked Meeting Room 1. Keep the blinds drawn and the door locked. Initially, it'll be just the two of you. Once you tie down the grabber we'll involve whoever else we need.'

Tony saw the disbelief in their eyes. 'And before you start thinking I've gone all James Bond on you, remember: this is a big deal. Grapevine is small, just twenty-three people not including the cleaners. What you generate is intellectual property, in other words: gold. Protecting it is our responsibility. At the end of the day, ideas are what this business is about; let's not give somebody an advantage, eh?' The MD wasn't quite finished. 'Two more points: don't discuss what you're doing with anybody, and don't leave stuff lying around.'

He turned to Julia as she was about to speak. 'And yes, that includes the rest of your team. I appreciate it doesn't sit well with you but that's how it has to be. Before you give me a hundred good reasons why it can't, hear this: I don't care what you have to farm out. Clear the decks.'

Ellis asked, 'What's the remit?'

Tony leaned back in his chair. 'What it's always about: identity.' He reached for the folder and lifted a glossy A4 sheet with an artist's impression of a sleek building rising into a cloudless sky and pushed it towards them. 'Imagine this thing of beauty in gleaming glass and steel. High-end retailing and hospitality on the lower floors, luxury apartments from there on up to the penthouse suites.'

Julia caught the excitement in Tony's voice and said, 'Nice.'

Her reaction fell a long way short of his expectations; he barked his displeasure. 'Nice! Is that the best you can do? Christ Almighty. Aren't you supposed to have vision? Then, use it. Imagine this in the centre of the city and you're looking at the future of Glasgow, people.'

'Wow! That isn't the Glasgow I know.'

'Exactly, Ellis, it isn't the Glasgow any of us know. Not yet, though it will be.' He tapped the picture with his finger. 'Two more are in the pipeline. Approved and ready to go. And that will only be the start.

'The concept isn't new – far from it – but the project is a public/private partnership, in this case the city council and Campbell Coleridge Ltd – a bunch of councillors who know sweet FA about anything and an award-winning builder with a track record that goes back a hundred years but, in a marketing sense, hasn't taken on anything like this. It'll change the face of the city and have a huge profile. Failure isn't an option; it has to succeed.'

They sat in silence, letting what Tony had told them sink in until Ellis said, 'So what specifically is the brief?'

'Simple. Glasgow's about to have a new landmark – actually, three new landmarks. As of now, the project doesn't have an identity. Our challenge is to create one, one that has the name on everybody's lips. People have to be drooling at the prospect, buying bloody lottery tickets hoping they win enough to be able to afford even the lower floors. Aspirational living is the name of the game. So give me a concept head and shoulders above anything the other agencies come up with. You've got three weeks.'

'So no pressure, then?'

Julia would've laughed, except it wasn't a joke.

4

When she got to her office she shut the door and stood with her back pressed against it. Tony Connors was a demanding boss who accepted nothing less than 100 per cent from everybody, including himself, dismissing problems with a wave of his hand and the mantra 'Merely a challenge to which we shall rise'.

But this was different and he'd been open about how much it meant to him. His ego had decided the outcome of the pitch he'd tasked them with delivering: success was the only option. Grapevine wasn't a gig for the faint-hearted – Tony had never intended it would be. He was at the centre, driving the company forward – in some respects a trailblazer, in others a dinosaur; the last of his kind who'd jokingly, though not inaccurately, described himself at a Christmas staff party after he'd had a few too many as Don Quixote on acid. Despite his boorishness and casual misogynism – not unusual in the male-oriented realm of advertising – Julia enjoyed working for him. Today's meeting had left her spooked: being trusted to work on such an important pitch was a compliment, yet she was unhappy at having to exclude the rest of the team. As always her first instinct was to call Rob – the centre of her universe: husband, lover, partner and, above all, her friend; the person she relied on when life got too much. From the moment they'd met, just being together had been magical; changing her name to Mrs Sutherland was the easiest decision she'd ever made and three years on there were no regrets apart from the time they seemed to be spending apart.

Julia called him again with no better luck, swore quietly to herself and walked to the window. Outside on Bothwell Street people rushed about their business while a double line of cars waited for the traffic lights to change. The familiar scene calmed her and Julia settled down to read the contents of the folder. From the overview on the first page she immediately understood Tony's enthusiasm. He hadn't exaggerated; the project was a very big deal. A few of the building atrocities of the late 1960s and 1970s, when 'cheap' was sold as 'modern', were still standing, concrete blots on the landscape that, with the benefit of hindsight, should never have been allowed. The images she was looking at were very different, though in their own way just as controversial: a sharp and futuristic mix of styles that at first glance she wasn't sure she liked. Her husband was the architect in the family. Julia couldn't say if the development was progress, but it would certainly alter the character of the city centre and wouldn't be short of detractors. She and Ellis were about to work up a marketing strategy for the first step in this massive regeneration programme. A lot more than Tony Connors' ego and Grapevine's status in the business depended on getting it right – not a thought she wanted to dwell on.

The phone rang on her desk: Rob. He sounded irritated and distracted. 'Sorry, I was in another meeting. Honestly, it's the same every day in this place. Don't know how we're expected to get anything done. Most of them are a waste of bloody time when I could be doing something useful.' He caught himself whining and paused. 'Okay, rant over. What's happening in your world?'

Her husband was usually unflappable, taking everything in his stride. When things didn't go to plan, Julia would scream and use language her mother wasn't aware she had in her vocabulary. Rob didn't let things get to him; his reaction was to joke about them. Complaining was out of character and made Julia frown on the other end of the line.

'Rob. Is everything all right? You sound...'

'What?'

'I don't know... stressed.'

'I'm fine. Some days are harder to get through than others.'

'Tell me about it. In case you've forgotten, I work for Tony Connors.'

'He's lucky to have you.'

'I'm not sure he would agree.'

'Tell him if you want to be under-appreciated you can stay at home.'

Julia laughed. That was the Rob she knew and loved and her concern melted.

'How was Ayrshire?'

'Cold. Remind me never to buy a house near the sea.'

Julia laughed. 'I wouldn't worry too much about that. Where we are is great, if only we were together more often to enjoy it.' Her voice softened to a whisper. 'I missed you this morning.'

'Pleased to hear it.'

'No, Rob, I'm serious. I can't tell you how disappointed I was when I found you weren't in bed with me.'

'Believe me, Julia, dragging myself out at stupid o'clock isn't my idea of the good life. I'll make it up to you when we get home.'

Julia bit her lip, suddenly reminded of why she'd phoned. 'Put a pin in that promise. I'll collect on it later.'

'What's the problem?'

'I have to work late.'

'How late?'

'Late enough, I'm not sure. Grapevine's been invited to pitch for a prestigious piece of business. Tony is mustard-keen on winning it. I'm afraid it's going to be my obsession for the next few weeks. Sorry, baby.'

'Now who's disappointed?'

Julia detected a trace of resentment but when Rob spoke again it was gone. 'Got to hand it to old Tony, he can definitely spot talent. Whatever the pitch is for he couldn't have anybody better on it than you.'

'Then, you forgive me?'

'How could I do anything else? This morning it was me who spoiled the party. Tonight, it's your turn. I'll survive... somehow. Remind me how the microwave works again, will you?'

'You know very well how it works.'

He kept the joke going. 'Mmmm. Maybe I do and maybe I don't. We're about to find out, aren't we? Is Tony actually going to do some work for a change or is he leaving that to somebody else?'

'It'll be me and Ellis, Ellis Kirkbride.'

'I haven't heard that name before.'

'He's new.'

'And Connors teams him up with you on a landmark project? What's this guy's story?'

'I don't know much about him but apparently he's lived abroad and done some great stuff in the past. Tony really rates him.'

'It certainly sounds as though he does. What's he like?'

Julia hesitated without knowing why. 'Ellis? He's okay, I suppose. A bit of a bighead but all right once you get past that.'

'Is he good-looking?'

'I haven't really noticed.'

'I don't believe you.'

'Let's just say he's all right and leave it at that, shall we?'

'I'm taking that as a yes.'

'Rob Sutherland – is that jealousy I'm hearing?' Julia giggled, picturing him grinning down the line.

He played along. 'Jealousy, no. It's what I'd call proprietorial self-interest.'

'In other words, it is jealousy.'

Rob didn't disagree. 'I'm taking care of what's mine like any husband.'

Julia saw a chance to make a point. 'As I recall you weren't taking care of much this morning. In fact, if Ellis had been handy he—'

'If Ellis had been handy I'd have pummelled his ugly face to a pulp.'

'He doesn't have an ugly face.'

'Not yet. He will have when I'm finished with him.'

They laughed, for a moment as close as they'd ever been; Julia hated to be the one to end it. 'No need to worry about him or anybody else. All I'll be doing tonight is drinking lukewarm coffee and trying to come up with ideas that don't stink the place out.'

'When will you be home?'

'As soon as I can. Promise. Look, we talked before about sorting out our priorities. You and I should never be last on each other's list. All too often – like now – we are and it isn't right and I'm certain that's why we've been arguing lately. Maybe it's time to actually do something about that before we lose sight of each other.'

'It isn't intentional, it creeps up on us, slowly, when we aren't expecting it. "What were once vices are now habits", to quote the Doobie Brothers. And I'm absolutely with you on this. The situation deserves more than a conversation.'

'Thank you, Rob, that's what I hoped you'd say, but the Doobie Brothers? Where did they come from?'

'A rock band my father used to listen to.'

'In that case let me give you a tip: if you want people to get what you're saying keep your music references to the twenty-first century.'

'Message received and understood. I'll bear it in mind.'

'I love you.'

'And I love you, Julia. Hang up or we'll be here all day.'

One of his talents was the ability to make her laugh. At the end of a night they'd behave like teenagers playing a silly game about which one would be first to say goodbye. And here they were again. She closed the mobile with his words singing in her head, refreshed and renewed: Tony Connors had money, a reputation among his peers that was second to none and a string of leggy girlfriends twenty-five years younger than him. None of it came near to what Julia had at that moment.

* * *

Rob stared at the mobile on his desk, the phone he'd used to speak to Julia less than an hour ago. He'd had his lies ready in case she questioned exactly what the hell he'd been doing until one in the morning; it hadn't been necessary.

He'd said, "I love you, Julia" and despite the fact they'd been getting on each other's nerves, it was true. The paralysing fear of getting caught mixed with self-loathing was still with him. If the opportunity hadn't fallen out of the sky Michelle and the hotel bedroom would've remained secret, a regret never to be repeated. Except it had, and while a part of him despised what he was considering, another part urged him to make the call, knowing where it would lead.

The voice in his head was sly and persuasive, though it stopped short of asking what he had to lose: Rob knew the answer. Everything. He'd got away with it once: why was he even thinking about going there again? Before he'd met Michelle, being unfaithful to his wife hadn't crossed his mind. Julia could've had anybody; fortunately she'd chosen him. Only a fool would risk losing her.

He swallowed hard, realising he was that fool, his throat suddenly dry, heart hammering in his chest as he punched in the number. 'Michelle, it's me.'

Her reply was spoken with the satisfaction of a woman who understood men better than they would ever understand her. She said, 'Hi, Rob. What took you so long?'

5

The cartons stained with soy sauce had been pristine when Ellis returned from the Shanghai Teahouse with them in a brown carrier bag. Julia liked Indian food better and would've preferred samosas and curry but when he'd suggested Chinese she'd said yes. Hunger hadn't helped the creative process and they'd fallen on the sweet-and-sour pork, steamed seabass with chilli jam and roast duck in plum sauce. Now, the boxes and forgotten grains of cold fried rice were strewn on the table in the middle of Meeting Room 1.

Ellis sat with his feet up, sipping a can of Diet Coke, studying the scribbles on the whiteboard in the corner, not liking what he was seeing. At twenty minutes after eight o'clock they'd been on it for hours with nothing to show for their efforts. In the beginning, fired up and ready, they'd believed finding the gold they were after was only a matter of time. Since then, as every theme was explored and dismissed as uninspired or uninspiring, the mood had dipped. Experience told them the first session often produced the 'big' idea. From that point on it was only a matter of tailoring it to the brief. Without it, they had nothing.

He shook his head and stabbed a wooden chopstick at the whiteboard. 'We're over-thinking this. I mean, at the end of the day, what is it?

Just a marketing plan for another inner-city building project, no different from work we've both done before. It shouldn't be this hard.'

Julia leaned back in her chair, arms hanging languidly at her side; she felt bloated and regretted finishing the last of the duck. 'God knows why Tony's so hot for this one. After decades in the business. I don't get it. Maybe he's settling a score.'

'Professional or personal?'

'How the hell would I know?'

Ellis lifted his legs off the table. 'Or perhaps the truth is right in front of us and we're missing it.'

'Really, like what?'

He shrugged. 'Could be our boss is going through a mid-life crisis. It's either obsess about this or buy himself a Harley-Davidson and a one-piece black leather racing suit.'

Julia giggled. 'Next stop a ponytail?'

Ellis made a gagging noise in his throat. 'God, I wish you hadn't put that image in my head. When I see him that's what I'll be thinking. His pep talk has backfired. Tony's "Anything can happen" has subconsciously drained our energy. I couldn't come up with a decent idea if my life depended on it.'

'I feel the same. Look, we have the product in front of us. Let's go back to basics and start with the audience. Who are they?'

'We've already done this, Julia.'

'Then we do it again. Describe the target market in a couple of words.'

He sighed, reluctant to go over old ground. 'People with money.'

'And what do they do with their money?'

'Buy expensive stuff.'

'Why?'

'Why? Because they can.'

'More.'

'Buy expensive stuff...' Ellis teased out the thought in his head '...to... impress their friends.'

'Exactly!' Julia jumped up, suddenly animated. She raised a hand and counted selling points off on her fingers. 'This development is expensive, stylish and slap-bang in the city centre. High-end living that makes a statement about who you are and what you've got – the bricks-and-mortar equivalent of thumbing your nose at anybody who didn't think you'd amount to much. What you're buying is an address that says, "Fuck you!"'

'You're right.'

'To some people that's important; it matters to them.'

Ellis shouted, 'That's it! That's bloody it!'

'That's what?'

'The strapline, we've got it.'

He dived across the room, lifted a blue felt-tipped pen and wrote in capitals on the whiteboard 'WHEN THE ADDRESS MATTERS' and stepped back to let her see. 'When the address matters. All the reasons you'd buy boiled down to four words that will be on every ad, every hoarding, every sign, every brochure. Julia, you've done, it, you're a bloody genius.'

Ellis moved in beside her and held his mobile up in front of them. She realised what he was doing and tried to stop him. 'No, please, don't take a picture, I'm a mess.'

His arm snaked round her waist and drew her closer. 'You're nothing of the kind, you look gorgeous. Now say cheese!'

* * *

The pub was busier than Julia had imagined it would be on a Tuesday night. But what did she know about pubs these days? She could scarcely remember the last time she'd been in one – on a Tuesday or any other evening, come to that. When she went out with Rob it was usually to a restaurant or a concert and that hadn't happened much recently. A month after they'd met he'd taken her to his local and introduced her to his friends, pleased when they'd winked at him to show they approved of his new girlfriend. She'd done the same with her friends until they'd discovered they didn't need company and in fact would rather it was just the two of them. Completely natural – love's young dream and all that – but without realising it they'd become set in their ways and started taking what they had for granted.

Ellis was at the bar deep in conversation with the barman; they were both smiling. Julia conceded she'd been wrong about Ellis Kirkbride, ready to dislike the guy before he'd opened his mouth. Tony Connors could take the credit there. Tony could be charming when it suited his purpose, but his man-management skills were poor. His clumsiness rather than anything Ellis had done had shaped her opinion.

Ellis came over with their alcohol-free red wines and a couple of packets of crisps. 'Only smoky bacon, I'm afraid. It was that or haggis and black pepper.'

'Good call.'

He tossed them on the table and sat down. Julia said, 'Does zero tolerance take a bit of getting used to after South Africa?'

'No, they're pretty close to that themselves. I'm not a big drinker, never have been, so it doesn't affect me. But it's true what they say about Chinese grub. An hour after you've eaten it, you're hungry again. I am, anyway. What about you?'

'No, not really. I'm too excited. For a while I was starting to think we weren't going to crack it and didn't fancy telling Tony. Now we have to hope he loves the concept as much as we do.'

Ellis threw half a handful of crisps into his mouth and waited until he'd eaten them before replying, 'He will.'

'I wish I had your confidence.'

'Confidence has nothing to do with it. It's brilliant.'

'So we take it to him tomorrow and get his reaction.'

'I'd rather hold off. It needs more work. We'll do a big reveal after we've put flesh on the bones.'

Julia overruled him. 'No, we give him the concept because that's what he asked for. Bat the ball to him and see how he responds.'

'Oh, that's bold.'

'Or foolhardy. He might hate it and we'll be back at square one.'

'I promise not to say I told you so.' Ellis lifted his glass. 'Tony said I'd be working with the best. I'm happy to report he was right. Great job, Julia. Cheers!'

Ellis leaned forward in his chair and changed the subject. 'Okay, you've shown me Julia the Professional and I'm impressed. What does the other Julia do when she isn't behind a desk?'

Julia pushed a strand of wayward hair from her face. 'That's a question I keep asking myself.'

'And the answer?'

'Is not very much, unfortunately.'

Ellis sipped his wine and set the glass down. 'I find that hard to believe. You and your husband – Rob, isn't it? – must have interests apart from working.'

'We have, or, more accurately, we *had*. Before we got married, travel was our big thing. There are so many places we haven't been to and I assumed we'd be going to more of them.'

'I'm with you there. So why aren't you?'

Julia played with her wedding ring and shot him a sad smile. 'Now we can actually afford to go, we haven't the time.'

'And whose fault is that?'

She wanted to say Rob but that wouldn't be true – they were both absorbed in what they did. 'Rob's job is demanding and you know what Tony Connors is like. It isn't healthy and I don't mind admitting it.'

'So what's your response? What do you do?'

'I run.'

'Excellent! Where?'

'Anywhere, really. At the moment every evening on the banks of the river near our flat. It's quiet, a lovely spot, and after a hectic day at Grapevine it helps me unwind.'

'Does Rob run too?'

Julia laughed. 'If you knew him you'd understand how funny that is. My husband's too busy with AutoCAD; he doesn't do running.'

They nursed their drinks until Ellis said, 'You've been honest with me. It's only fair I'm honest with you. You asked about South Africa.'

'I really didn't mean to pry.'

'No, no problem, I'll tell you. A woman, what else? We met when she was here on holiday and fell in love. Or more accurately, I did. Three days after she went home I was on a plane to the Western Cape.'

'And?'

He shrugged. Julia expected him to leave it at that or reply, quite rightly, that it was none of her business. Instead, he fidgeted with his hands and concentrated on his shoes. When he spoke his voice was so quiet she had to strain to hear the words. 'Turned out she already had a boyfriend. Actually, not just a boyfriend, they were engaged. Me showing up was, shall we say, not part of the plan.'

'How awful for you.'

'It was.'

'Sounds as if you had a lucky escape.'

Ellis made a face. 'That's one way of looking at it, I suppose.'

* * *

Fifteen Months Earlier
Nettleton Road, Clifton, South Africa

Ellis Kirkbride watched an orange sun turn the horizon lava red as it disappeared into the ocean. Dusk came quickly here; darkness wouldn't be far behind. Below, in the garden edged with gently swaying palms, couples high on alcohol, cocaine, or both, leapt into the saltwater swimming pool fully clothed, squealing like the idiots they were. This was how the other half lived, the fortunate few with more money than they could reasonably spend in twenty lifetimes. Ellis filtered them out and forced his attention back to the view: from the villa's whitewashed terrace the Atlantic stretched to the horizon and beyond, four thousand kilometres, all the way to the frozen coastline of Antarctica.

He leaned his back against the French windows and stared at Sasha and her new playmate. She was still flirting with the blond Australian, her face flushed with laughter and wine; she seemed to have forgotten Ellis was there and didn't notice he'd been photographing them. An overweight politician he'd seen on TV came over and offered a pudgy hand. Pieter Dekker had probably checked himself out in the mirror before he left Constantia or whatever affluent suburb was home and decided he looked okay. Several large brandies later that wasn't true: the man was sweating and he was drunk. His clipped accent, softened by an expensive education, was noticeably slurred and under the dark-blue blazer he'd loosened the Leopard Creek tie that informed anybody who cared about such things he was a member of one of the most exclusive golf clubs in the world.

With the assertiveness of the truly pissed, he got straight to the point. 'You know, I've been coming to these shindigs for years. Usually, I'm on nodding terms with just about every bugger but I haven't seen you before. I didn't catch your name.'

'I didn't give it.'

Ellis looked past him to Sasha and the Aussie dancing to a corny Chris de Burgh song, her arms round his neck, moving as one, and the same fury that had brought him from Scotland to South Africa stirred in his belly.

Only yesterday, Ellis had been on a stool in the dimly lit Waterfront bar near his flat, cradling a bottle of Castle lager between his palms, reading the sports pages of the Cape Times, *when he'd become aware of a woman observing him and decided to play hard to get just for the fun of it.*

That had been the plan until he'd gazed into her eyes and seen his future.

Sex had been as intense as anything he'd ever known – she hadn't been able to get enough of him and he'd struggled to keep up. In the early hours, they'd finally rolled apart and gone to sleep in each other's arms, and he'd been sure that, at last, his search was over. She'd refused to reveal anything about herself apart from her name – Sasha – adding mystery to her undoubted allure. And Ellis was in love.

This morning, she'd invited him to the party, teetering on the verge of a strop when he'd said he'd rather spend the night just the two of them. To please her he'd agreed: this was how she'd repaid him. Across the room her new man was kissing her and Ellis ground his teeth.

The drunk was blathering brandy fumes and bad breath over him. He pointed to the camera round Ellis's neck. 'I'm guessing you're either with some society magazine – one of those glossy rags nobody reads – or you're an associate of Lance, am I right?'

Ellis had no idea what the hell he was on about. 'Who's Lance?'

'Lance Ackerman, our host. This is his place. What do you make of it? Pretty photogenic, I imagine.' Dekker leaned in and dripped poison onto the imported Italian marble floor. 'Of course, he doesn't actually own it. It's registered with one of his companies. Same with the properties in London and New York.'

Ellis wasn't interested in this clown's gossip; his brain was on fire with

Sasha's faithlessness. Pieter Dekker didn't notice and carried on. 'Or am I wrong?'

'Wrong about what?'

'You being an associate. Lance has his fingers in so many pies it's impossible to keep up.'

Over his shoulder Ellis scanned the guests for Sasha and her new friend. They'd disappeared and his mouth tightened. He ran a finger down the stem of the champagne flute he was holding and took his frustration out on the unlucky Dekker. 'Here's a suggestion. Why don't you fuck right off?'

Sober or drunk, the politician was used to being lionised. He held up his hands and stepped away. 'Wow! Steady on. No need to be offensive. If you want me to go, I'll go.'

'Do. And take your halitosis with you.'

Outside, the crowd around the pool had thinned; those who remained still made plenty of noise. Some of the women were naked now, their wet bodies glistening in the light from the villa. Ellis dug his nails into the stone balustrade until the pain in his fingertips forced him to stop and closed his eyes. When he opened them again there was a yellow moon in the sky and, below, the woman who'd writhed beneath him was arm in arm with the Australian on their way to the beach.

It had only been a day, yet with Sasha he'd felt safe, surer than he'd ever been that he'd found her. But like the others she'd deceived him and betrayal had consequences, as she was about to find out.

He clenched his fists, fighting back tears, cursing himself for making the old mistake of trusting a woman. The special one was out there, somewhere, waiting for him; he had to believe that was true or there was no point in going on.

* * *

The path fell steeply down the grassy embankment in a series of well-worn stone steps. Moonlight washed the white hull and sleek lines of a bluewater cruiser moored to the jetty. Ellis slipped off his shoes and moved carefully along the wooden landing, listening for sounds that would tell him they were on board. All he heard was the gentle lapping of the ocean and he smiled humour-

lessly to himself: discovering them so soon meant it would be over too fast and that would be a pity.

The silhouette of Lion's Head mountain, stark and magnificent, dominated the nightscape as Ellis scanned the beach. Further along, two figures clung to each other at the water's edge, their drunken laughter carrying on the warm air.

Fifty yards from them he picked up a gnarled piece of driftwood and weighed it in his palm – the Australian would never know what hit him. Sasha was in his arms, unaware of the danger until he dropped to the sand.

She saw Ellis and fell to her knees, blubbering like a child. He tossed the driftwood into the sea. 'You told me you loved me.'

'I do love you, I do! He... he forced me.'

Ellis shook his head sadly. 'Sasha, Sasha, he didn't. I saw you.'

His hands tightened round her beautiful neck and squeezed until the light went out of the eyes that had held his future. Her would-be lover was unconscious, face down in the sand. When he came to he'd have to explain how a moonlight stroll on the beach had ended in tragedy: Ellis wished him good luck with that.

The tide lapped at his shoes as he moved round the bodies, photographing them individually and together from different angles.

He knelt on the sand to take a close-up of Sasha's face and felt a tear slip down his cheek.

Click!

In life, the girl he'd known had been a vibrant, exciting woman.

In death, some might generously have described her as peaceful – Ellis saw only ordinary.

He started towards Cape Town eight kilometres away, already considering his next move. Out over the ocean a jagged flash of lightning scarred the sky; a storm was coming. He wouldn't be here to see it. In five hours he'd be on a plane. In another twelve, in Kuala Lumpur or Hong Kong.

After that...

* * *

Ellis continued. 'And to be fair, that's what I've told myself ever since, though it didn't feel it at the time. I was gutted and would've packed my bags and left, except I liked the little I'd seen of the country, so I stayed, determined to make a go of it. Last I heard she'd split from the fiancé to marry some tour operator and was living on the coast at Plettenberg Bay with their two kids. I hope she's happy. Sounds as if she might be.'

'Quite a tale. Any regrets?'

'Well, I would've preferred not to make such a bloody fool of myself. Apart from that, no, not about SA. Loved it, still do.'

'So why come back?'

He slipped his hands into the body-warmer's pockets and thought about his response. 'I'd done well considering how badly it had started for me. I had a good job, a nice flat in Observatory on the slope of Table Mountain. *And* I had money in the bank. I suppose it just seemed the right thing to do.'

'Like chasing after that girl?'

'Yeah, very like that.'

'Why?'

'I'm not sure, it just did. South Africa had been good to me, yet it never really felt like my home. God knows, Scotland isn't perfect. But I understand it – does that make sense?'

'Absolutely.'

6

Michelle lay naked on the bed watching Rob get dressed, wondering if this was the right moment, deciding to go for it anyway even if it wasn't. She said, 'I've something to say and I better say it now, otherwise I probably never will.'

He stopped buttoning his shirt, sensing she was going to tell him she didn't want to see him again, that for her the affair was over. 'Unless I need to know, don't.'

'No, no, it has nothing to do with you.'

'Then why?'

'Because it's a confession. When you rang me this morning I asked what had kept you, remember?'

His eyes traced the swell of her breasts. 'How could I forget?'

'It was an act. The truth is, I wasn't expecting to hear from you again.'

'Really? I'd never have guessed.'

'Yes, really. From the start it was obvious you hadn't done anything like this before. You weren't...'

'Cool? Is that the word you're searching for? If it is, you're right. That wasn't how I felt then and it isn't how I feel now.'

'What a nice thing to say. I was going for relaxed but cool's as good an adjective as any. For some men cheating on their wife wouldn't have been a big deal. You were different. You hadn't made up your mind about it, and I was sure you'd say you were going to call it off because you hadn't convinced yourself you wanted to be with me. Maybe you still haven't.'

'Are you asking me or telling me?'

'Neither.'

Rob sat on the edge of the bed and took her hand. 'And if I haven't, how would you feel about that?'

She thought for a moment before answering. 'Honestly, I'd envy your wife and I can assure you that isn't my usual reaction. Too many women are with the wrong guy. The lucky ones don't know it. Yet. But they will. So before this goes any further let's establish the rules: I'm not deceiving myself. I'm well aware of where I stand and my expectations are nil. Sooner or later this will run its course. Eventually, even the hottest affairs do. I might even be the one to end it.' Michelle squeezed his fingers. 'I was going to add and you'll go back to your wife, but that wouldn't be true because you'll never really have left her, will you, Rob?'

* * *

In the car driving home Michelle was in his head. They'd been together a grand total of twice and already she'd accepted the inevitable, that there was no future in it, telling him how it would be, her words born from experience: the Other Woman was clearly a role she'd played before. But he'd detected no bitterness. Sex wouldn't be enough. They'd go their separate ways – her, likely to some new lover, him, back to his wife.

She was wiser than he'd realised, giving him a way out if he wanted one.

He turned on the radio and turned it off again when a rock anthem filled the car, starkly aware of his choices. An image of her naked, red hair cascading onto her skin, rose in front of his eyes and the decision was made.

Julia hadn't put a time on how late she would be working so Rob was relieved to find she still wasn't home. He'd showered at the hotel. Now, he switched on the TV, slipped a pod into the coffee machine and went through to the bedroom to change his clothes. Later, when he heard her key in the lock, the coffee cup on the table beside him was empty and he was slouched on the sofa as though he'd been there most of the night.

She burst into the room and he got up to greet her. She said, 'Sorry I'm so late, Rob, were you asleep?'

The lie was out before he could do anything to stop it. He faked a yawn and smothered it with his hand. 'Almost. How did it go?'

Julia shucked off her coat. 'Great. Eventually. I'd love a coffee.'

'No problem, I'll make one.'

He kissed her and noticed wine on her breath and reacted. 'I thought you were supposed to be working?'

'We were, we went to the pub to celebrate.'

'Celebrate what?'

'For some reason Tony's mad keen about this commission. God knows why, but he is. I was dreading having to report it wasn't happening and for a long time it seemed as though it wasn't going to.'

'I'm hearing a but, Julia.'

'You are.' She put her arms round him and held him tight. 'Rob, it was the most incredible thing. Just as we were ready to admit defeat a concept arrived so obvious it was hard to believe we hadn't thought of it.'

'But you have so that's great.'

'Yes, we bloody well have. In fact, we think we've cracked it.'

She sat in an armchair and took off her shoes, bubbling away: full of it. 'Of course, we'll have to see what Tony makes of it. It wouldn't be the first time he's sunk a solid idea with his characteristic sarcasm. But, fingers crossed.' She beamed at him. 'Ellis says I'm a genius.'

'He's got that right. What's this guy like to work with? Wasn't he supposed to be a bit of a bighead?'

'Mmmm. I'm kind of sorry I said that now. My nose was out of joint because Tony palmed him off on my team without bothering to include me in the conversation. Tonight, honestly, he couldn't have been more open. We were hitting our heads off a wall, getting nowhere. I suggested we go back to basics. We'd already been over the thing a dozen times – most people would've torn their hair out. Ellis was fine about it. In fact, though the breakthrough came from me, he saw how we could make it fit before I did, yet he gave me the credit.'

Rob said, 'Why am I not surprised it was you?'

Julia acknowledged the compliment, the second of the day, with a quick smile. Whatever she was involved in, Rob could always be relied on to be cheering her from the sidelines. 'Everybody wants to be the one with ideas that fly. This time it was me. Tomorrow, who knows? What I said about Ellis didn't come from a good place. Forget it.' She nodded to confirm her opinion. 'Want to hear what we've got?'

'Of course, absolutely. First, let me get that coffee.'

'And while you're making it, I'll jump into the shower.'

He brought a cup for each of them and settled down to listen. Julia came back wearing the white bathrobe she'd bought from a beach trader on their second-last evening in Sri Lanka. Rob had kept out of the negotiations, listening to them haggle, both enjoying the cut-and-thrust of bartering while a warm breeze rustled the palm trees and ominous clouds gathered on the horizon over the Indian Ocean: a storm was coming to paradise. The woman's age had been impossible to guess. Rob re called her gold tooth and the near-perfect English she'd used to separate Julia from her money by assuring her the garment was 100 per cent Egyptian cotton.

It didn't matter if it was or it wasn't: Julia looked amazing in it. She sat in the lotus position on the couch radiating an energy he hadn't seen lately. Bubbling with enthusiasm, breathlessly telling her tale, she seemed to glow. Rob wondered if this Ellis character had something to do with it and felt a stab of jealousy and shame – a bloody cheeky thought considering what he'd been up to a couple of hours earlier.

When Julia finished speaking she scanned his face for approval; Rob didn't let her down.

'It's strong. In fact, it's very strong. To my mind it doesn't matter who you're in competition with, the poor buggers don't stand a chance. And I'm not just saying that, Julia, I mean it. My one piece of advice would be to not let Tony see it before you have the whole campaign fleshed out and ready.'

'Ellis said the same.'

Rob hid his resentment behind a smile. 'Did he? Well, he's right. When Tony does see it, it'll blow him away.'

'We can only hope. Ellis has some ideas.'

The name rolled off her tongue so easily she could've been talking about someone they both knew, an old friend perhaps, rather than a man who, until yesterday, had been a stranger.

In the pit of Rob's stomach jealousy morphed into lust as he imagined his wife's body under the soft material. 'I bet he does.' Julia missed the tawdry implication. 'Ellis sounds like a smart guy.'

She innocently agreed. 'He is. Very smart.'

'Should I be worried?'

His tone made her look at him and she realised he was serious. Julia rounded on him, her cheeks flushed with anger. 'If that's supposed to be a joke, it isn't funny.'

'You did notice he was good-looking.'

'Glasgow's full of good-looking guys. And I notice them, of course, I do. What the hell does that prove, except I'm not blind? Why would you be worried? Because he's a man, is that it?' She threw her arms up in frustration. 'Lord protect us from the fragile male ego! I really don't know what to say. Where you work is full of women. Should that worry me, Rob? Should I be quizzing you about where you've been and who you've been with?'

He stuttered a reply. 'Of course not. Don't be silly.'

'Then, what's got into you?'

Rob defended himself. 'Well, your team isn't involved, it's just you and him.'

'So what?'

'You went to the pub. I smelled alcohol on your breath.'

Julia had done well to hold onto her temper but it was starting to slip. 'It was alcohol-free wine – I'm not a fool, Rob. I'm surprised you didn't get onions and garlic and ginger and...' She sighed, exhausted by the futility of arguing over nothing, and spoke slowly. 'We shared a Chinese takeaway, which, since we're working, Grapevine paid for. Or they will when I put in my expenses. Rob, this isn't like you. What's happening here?'

His answer was to pull her to him and kiss her. When it ended, he kissed her again. 'Maybe you're right. Maybe I am jealous, and who would blame me when my wife's with another man?'

'Not "with another man". Don't be so dramatic. He's a colleague. I only just met him. Ellis Kirkbride has nothing to do with you and me.'

'Yes, but—'

Julia put a finger to his lips. 'Shhh. Don't spoil it. We haven't been spending enough time together and we've only ourselves to blame. I meant it about being disappointed when I woke up and you weren't there, because I wanted you.'

Rob untied the robe and let it fall from her shoulders. 'Well,' he said, 'I'm here now.'

7

On a Tuesday night, Glasgow was quiet: few cars and fewer people. The centre of the city was sophisticated and cosmopolitan, awash with designer-clothes outlets, cafés and coffee shops on every corner. It had changed from how he remembered it – the same couldn't be said for him. Returning from Africa had always been the plan. In fact, he hadn't wanted to leave Scotland and would've stayed if he could've been certain of the outcome. He took a left into an almost deserted St Vincent Street with heavy rain bouncing off the pavement, obscuring his vision. And suddenly, for Ellis Kirkbride, it was as though he'd never been away.

He switched on the wipers and peered through the windscreen, visualising Julia's face in the Mazda fifty yards in front, imagining her eager to tell her husband her great idea. Ellis smiled a humourless smile. Encouraging her to believe it had come from her amused him. She'd been so easily persuaded to take the credit, though they both knew it wasn't the truth. Her contribution had been a throwaway comment, nothing more. He was the alchemist who'd seized on her base metal and turned it into gold. But in that moment he'd felt her warm to him and for that alone giving her kudos she hadn't actually earned was a small price to pay.

At traffic lights on Great Western Road near Kelvin Bridge the rain stopped. Ellis found himself directly behind her, closer than he'd wanted, and drew back in his seat so he wouldn't be recognised. He hadn't known Julia existed until he'd seen her arrive late on Monday morning – was that really only yesterday? – and felt the familiar heat in his groin and the gnawing in his gut. Their first encounter hadn't been promising. Tony Connors was her boss and a bully; standing up to him, aware she'd almost certainly lose, had taken spirit. Ellis appreciated it even if he was against what she was doing. The MD's heavy-handed introduction had meant she'd decided he was part of a conspiracy to undermine her authority. If the positions were reversed Ellis would have felt the same way.

Getting a female to change her mind was no easy thing. When they took against you, you could run into a burning building to save their baby and they still wouldn't like you. By teaming them up the MD had unwittingly done him a favour and while winning her round was the challenge, appealing to her vanity with the strapline was the solution. Not forgetting the ace he'd played so many times before: the honest heart betrayed. Women lapped that stuff up and had to know all the juicy details. Julia was no different. He'd seen it coming before the meeting with Tony Connors, when her curiosity had revealed itself with a question as predictable as it was tedious. Why had he left Scotland? Ellis had waited for the right moment to deliver his reply, the pained reluctance of how he said it honed by experience: he'd fallen in love with a girl and gone after her; she'd deceived him and broken his heart, but like a brave boy he'd come to terms with it and moved on – the sympathy that particular tale evoked never ceased to amaze him.

The Mazda's right indicator winked and Ellis sensed they were nearly at her home. Julia stopped outside a row of identical buildings, unaware of the car pulling in further down the street. She climbed the stone stairs, turned a key in the lock and closed the front door behind her. In the bay window the curtains were drawn and Ellis smothered a pang of disappointment: seeing inside would've been fun. He settled for picturing the scene in his head – her husband standing to greet her as she came into the room; his wife rushing into his arms. And they'd kiss.

A streetlight illuminated Ellis's tanned face. He'd balled his fists and pulled away.

* * *

The basement had no windows but the privacy it offered came at a price few would be willing to pay. It was cold, the kind that seeped to the bone and made a sane person want to be somewhere else; the air was stale, heavy with damp, and it was hard not to feel claustrophobic. From a trestle table the vanilla arc of an Anglepoise lamp threw shadows on the discoloured plasterboard an amateur had nailed to the porous brick wall, masking it without treating what he was covering up, and an uneven tide mark ran the length of one side. The space was small but more than enough for what Ellis needed it for. He took off his shirt, popped the ring-pull on a can of Tennent's lager, then dropped into the only chair and switched the computer on. The screen seemed to pulse with a life of its own as he rewatched an old TikTok video he'd found of females in swimsuits dancing to a rock song. Behind them, under a cloudless blue sky, a white beach followed the curve of a bay. Ellis had been to that stretch of sand many times. Sasha's face was partly hidden by wraparound tortoiseshell sunglasses but he remembered the eyes that had bewitched him in a grungy waterfront bar. She broke from the group, ran towards the camera and stuck out her tongue. The gesture, playful and cheeky, incensed him.

Suddenly, he was pounding the desk, yelling, 'You bitch! You bitch! You're not laughing now!'

Above his head on the dull plasterboard, underneath her dead face, a line of Asian females smiled seductively for the camera in a series of 10 x 8 close-ups crudely affixed with Blu Tack. Ellis didn't remember their names or even where he'd met them. Malaysia? Thailand? Vietnam, maybe? Kuala Lumpur had been just the first stop on a year-long tour of the region, staying in seedy low-rent flats rented by the month, sleeping during the day, going out at night, while he figured out his next move. He'd become a familiar face in Bukit Bintang, and in Cintra Street when he'd eventually moved up-country to Penang. In Bangkok's Nana Plaza and Patpong it had been the same story. Sometimes he'd been out of his head on *Yaa Chud*, the poly-pharmaceutical mix of drugs, illegal yet easily purchased over the counter. Mostly, he'd been straight, aware of exactly what he was doing and why.

Prostitutes weren't his thing, though the advantages of using them weren't in doubt. There were no lies, no false promises or deception. All that mattered was how much.

Suddenly, the parade of smiling doll-faced women offended him. Ellis reached up and tore them from the wall. Why had he held onto them? The photographs of Sasha and the Australian on the beach, one dead, the other unconscious, represented justice; the others were an admission of weakness, a catalogue of loneliness that should've been destroyed before he came to Scotland.

He'd been devastated by Sasha's betrayal, by how she'd abandoned him at the first opportunity. Of course he'd sought solace; it was natural. Quitting South Africa so hastily might have been an overreaction but, with the police probably already searching for the unidentified man at the party in Clifton, it had been smart. Even smarter was selling his property in Rondebosch long-distance through an estate agent in nearby Claremont and insisting the proceeds be paid in US dollars into a Malaysian account; that clever little move meant he'd got out of the country without sacrificing everything he'd worked for.

He slumped in his chair, turned the computer off and sat in the darkness trembling with rage. What he was doing couldn't go on: unless he accepted how it had ended in Cape Town and let it go, this would always be how seeing her affected him. He put the can to his lips and drank; after a few mouthfuls he started to feel better. Ellis had had the same conversation with himself over and over again.

He'd had a good day – a great day, all things considered – why spoil it?

He remembered the selfie taken in the meeting room, dug the mobile out of his pocket and scrolled to Gallery. The photograph painted a picture that wasn't the truth – of course it did, they were marketeers, for Christ's sake! Illusion was their business. The two people in the shot appeared to be friends. They weren't – not yet – but they would be. Very good friends, indeed. From the phone's screen he smiled at the camera while, beside him, Julia held back, less sure. Ellis didn't blame her. They'd only just met; how else should she feel when she had a husband and probably thought she was in love with him? Winning her trust would take time; rushing it would have her running for the hills and he'd be back to hating the woman on the beach who'd proven herself unworthy. This was different. He hadn't been searching; Julia Sutherland had come to him.

Ellis finished the lager, crushed the can and tossed it into the corner, feeling better. Cape Town was the past; Glasgow was where his future lay. He hadn't been certain but now he was. The signs were good, although instinct urged him to take it slowly. All he had to do was keep a hold on his emotions. If he did, to paraphrase his new boss, anything could happen.

Ellis took a last look at the image. They made a handsome couple. He said the word out loud. 'Anything.'

8

What a difference a day made: Julia had been upset with what was going on – or, more specifically, what wasn't going on – at home, while at work her boss had publicly undermined her position. Twenty-four hours later those worries had been blown away; everything was fine in the Sutherland house – if Rob hadn't had another early-morning site meeting to go to they would probably have made love again – and the guy Tony Connors had foisted on her had turned out to be really nice. Julia was so happy even being stuck in a rush-hour traffic jam on Woodside Road couldn't bring her down. She caught herself singing along with an old Rihanna tune on the car radio and was back in a time when all she had to think about were boyfriends and lipstick and RiRi. The star had opened her show at the SECC with 'Only Girl (In the World)'. A teenage Julia more excited than she'd been in her life had been as close as she could get to the front.

Julia liked what she did at Grapevine. In spite of Tony's tendency towards megalomania he gave his creative people plenty of leeway and understood talent couldn't be turned on like a tap. Sometimes, the muse refused to visit no matter how nicely she was asked, exactly why the breakthrough the previous night was so satisfying.

Julia edged forward until she was almost at the lights and said the line out loud, writing it in the air with her free hand. 'When the address matters.'

Yeah, it was a killer. Tony was going to love it.

* * *

Yesterday, she'd found Ellis in her office assessing her work and been angry. Today, she was pleased to see him. He was standing in the middle of the room wearing a tan leather jacket that was obviously expensive, slim-fit jeans and a sky-blue T-shirt that highlighted his eyes. The clothes were stylish, worn with ease. Time had gone into putting the outfit together, and while the finished result might seem casual, the thought behind it certainly hadn't been: Ellis Kirkbride was dressed to impress.

He greeted her warmly. 'Good morning, good morning, good morning. And how are you today?'

'I'm good.'

'Still buzzing?'

'You better believe it.'

'Me, too.' Ellis handed Julia a polystyrene cup and a brown paper bag. 'Double-shot cappuccino and an almond croissant. Got the same for both of us. Sorry if it isn't what you'd order.'

She took them from him. 'No, you're wrong, it's exactly what I'd order. How did you know that?'

'I took a chance. Call it a lucky guess.' His dark eyes settled on her. 'I couldn't sleep. All I could think about was the campaign. And I discovered something about myself.'

'Oh, yeah, what was that?'

'I'm at my most productive at three o'clock in the morning. What did you do last night?'

Julia's reply wasn't the truth. 'Rob was waiting for me. I had a bath and went to bed.'

'Did you tell him our – your – idea? What did he think of it?'

'He was impressed, reckons it's on the money. But before we go any further let's you and me get one thing straight. I asked if you were a team player, remember?'

Ellis grinned. 'I thought that was your give-the-new-guy-a-hard-time routine.'

'You were wrong, it wasn't. Every contribution, great or small, takes us nearer, creating something we can put our names against. So there is no *my*. There is no *mine*. Not on this team. The only pronouns we use are *our*, *ours* and *we*.'

The grin disappeared; Ellis sipped his coffee – Julia was serious and he was listening. She stopped speaking and waited for his reaction. When it came, it surprised her. 'Does Rob realise how fortunate he is to have you to come home to?'

The question was rhetorical but it was too personal. He sensed her discomfort and hurried to undo the damage. 'That came out wrong. What I meant was, does he realise he married a smarter-than-average woman?'

Julia heard the apology and forgave him. 'Oh, I expect he has some idea. God knows I remind the poor man often enough. For what it's worth he agreed with you about not telling Tony the concept until it was all there.'

'Did Rob change your mind?'

'Not at all. We both think it's good. The alternative is to waste weeks on something he rejects and put ourselves under real pressure. Let's trust our judgement.'

Ellis finished his coffee and started to leave. At the door he stopped; when he turned he was smiling. 'As I said, you're the boss.'

* * *

Julia waited for Tony's reaction. Next to her, Ellis sat with his arms folded across his chest; he seemed relaxed. They believed they'd given the MD exactly what he'd hoped for, a concept that summed up the essence of the new development and delivered it to the heart of its market, though with the mercurial Tony you could never be certain. In a few acidic words he might expose a weakness they hadn't identified and brutally trash their work. He'd done it before, as others could attest, and it wouldn't be the first time somebody had left his office humiliated and in tears after he'd eviscerated the presentation they'd spent weeks on. Tony could be a monster but he had a feel for what worked and what didn't and was rarely wrong.

The founder of Grapevine was confident he'd seen everything there was to see. A lifetime in the advertising business had taught him that great ideas were as valuable as diamonds and almost as hard to mine. His impassive expression gave nothing away. Finally, he said, 'And that's it? Four words?'

Julia braced herself to face the inevitable storm of scathing criticism. She'd led the meeting from their side. If their boss wasn't convinced, it would be because she'd failed to sell it to him.

Ellis hadn't spoken. Now he did and there was a confrontational edge to his voice too clear to miss. 'Not just four words, Tony. You told us to come to you as soon as we had an outline. "When the address matters" is more than just a marketing slogan, it's the whole thing.'

Tony steepled his fingers and slowly shook his head. 'I don't like it.'

Ellis's frustration boiled over. He shot out of his seat and towered over his boss. 'You aren't serious, you can't be! When Julia came up with it I wanted to jump up and punch the air. I thought you'd—'

The MD didn't let him finish. 'I don't *like* it, I fucking *love* it! Throwing you two together was a masterstroke even if I say so myself. And I do.'

On another day Julia might've been irked. Not today; they had an Okay!

A relieved Ellis said, 'So we go with it, yes?'

'Absolutely. It's brilliant and you won't hear me say that too often.'

Julia said, 'And I can bring Ravi and Olivia in?'

It was an honest try, yet it failed. Tony acknowledged it and tilted his head. 'Sorry, Julia. It puts you in a difficult position – I get that – but until the gig is actually ours it's better to keep this between the three of us. Do you want me to speak to Ravi and Olivia?'

Julia accepted she'd lost. 'No, no, I'll deal with it.'

Under the desk Ellis squeezed her hand. In the excitement she didn't notice. He said, 'Amazing! Result! But looks like another late night for us. Will Rob mind or will he see it as the price of having such an amazing wife?'

It was a special moment, he was on a high, his eyes were shining and Julia regretted what she was about to say. 'Listen, I'm really sorry, I can't work tonight. Rob's expecting me home. If we're chasing a deadline staying on isn't a problem, but dropping it on him at the last minute isn't fair.'

Ellis didn't let it go. 'It's only nine-thirty in the morning. He'll have all day to get used to it.'

He was pushing; she didn't like it and replied sharply. 'Allow me to know my husband better than you. If I think it's short notice, so will he. And he'll be right.'

Tony was smart enough to not get involved. Struggling to get a hold on the brief was one thing – that wasn't the case here: the campaign was off to a flying start. He held up his hands. 'Sort it out between yourselves. I don't care how we get there so long as we do. Your enthusiasm is appreciated, it really is, Ellis, but it's Julia's decision.'

Julia's heart had gone out to the charming man who'd confessed to making a fool of himself over a woman; he wasn't in the room. Beside her was a sullen, dull-eyed stranger, a petulant child, angry at not getting what he wanted, and she was alarmed by how quickly the atmosphere had changed – one minute they had a green light from Tony Connors and were elated, the next at odds over a triviality. Bickering in front of the boss was embarrassing, not at all how this was supposed to go. They'd cleared the first hurdle, they should be celebrating; instead, the meeting was ending on a sour note.

Tony pretended he hadn't noticed. 'So, again, great work. Keep it up and Grapevine's pitch will take some beating. Before you go, Julia, I need to run some figures by you.'

Ellis left hurriedly, without a word, and avoided looking at them. When he'd gone, Tony said, 'He's upset and I can't blame him. There was a time when I had that hunger, the kind that eats you from the inside and makes you hard to be around.'

'And were you a bully if somebody disagreed with you?' She shook her head. 'Don't answer that, Tony, I think I can guess.' She pointed to the door. 'You saw how he behaved. That isn't "hunger"; he's only just got here. I can't work with that kind of intensity. Even if I could, I'm not sure I'd want to.'

Tony shrugged. 'Ellis believes you and he are on a roll and wants to keep going while you're hot. What's wrong with that?'

Subtlety wasn't one of the MD's skills – by identifying with Ellis Kirk-bride he was actually criticising her. Julia's cheeks flushed; she snapped at him. 'Are you questioning my commitment, Tony? Because, if you are, my resignation letter can be on your desk in an hour.'

Tony sighed his exasperation. 'Oh, for Christ's sake, woman. Nobody's questioning anything. I'm saying I understand the guy's disappointment, no more than that. What you're doing is working for him and he doesn't want it to stop. Why should that be so difficult to get your head around?'

Was this an apology, an explanation, or a dressing-down? Whatever, Julia wasn't impressed, but falling out with Tony was a losing strategy unless she was serious about resigning from the agency.

'It isn't. In fact, I completely get it. Because most days I'm at my desk before anybody else arrives and still here when they leave. It's called giving 100 per cent. Obviously you haven't noticed.'

'Julia...'

She talked over him: he'd had his chance to support her and blown it. 'I feel the same about my marriage. It comes first and always will, Tony. My husband deserves notice his wife won't be there when he gets home. Or is that too much to ask?'

The MD came round the desk and spoke with more honesty than she credited him with having. 'It shouldn't be and it isn't. You're absolutely right. More than one lady who refused to compete with my work has gone out of my life. Believe me, the loss was mine. And if you ever tell that to anybody I'll strangle you with my bare hands. I'll speak to Ellis.'

'No, I'm leading the team, I'll speak to him.'

'Fair enough, but bring him back on board. Grapevine needs both of you.'

9

Ellis hadn't gone far. In the staff toilet on the second floor he gripped the sink's cool rim and stared at his reflection in the mirror, overwhelmed by a loathing that twisted his features until he was almost unrecognisable. Africa was behind him. Glasgow was supposed to be a fresh start, a clean slate, a new beginning far from the disappointments of before. Discovering it was none of those things shocked him.

Julia had belittled him in front of Tony Connors and, blind fool that he was, he hadn't seen it coming. The error wasn't new; he'd made the same mistake in Cape Town and understood the consequences. They could've been talking and getting to know each other. All it would've taken was a call to Rob – Ellis hadn't met the guy, but saying his name out loud made him feel sick – to tell him she'd be late. Not days or weeks or months, just a few hours. Instead, she'd chosen to humiliate him. Tony had asked her to stay behind, probably so they could laugh at him.

Tears of rage ran down his cheeks; he couldn't stop them. Ellis balled his fist and crashed it into the face staring back at him. He looked dully down at a bloodied hand that might have belonged to someone else and he gritted his teeth as the first wave of pain arrived.

* * *

Julia hadn't seen Ellis since he'd marched, stone-faced, out of the meeting, leaving her to suffer Tony Connors' excruciating off-the-mark platitudes – one of these days he'd go too far and she'd tell him in no uncertain terms what he could do with his job. His behaviour would get him into trouble; he'd come up against a female who wasn't prepared to let him get away with it and have his picture on the front page of the *Daily Record* after the tribunal found against him. Julia would be long gone before that happened. Ellis was the surprise – maybe Tony' extravagant praise had gone to his head, but he'd seemed so nice; it had been fun. Which made his truculent-schoolboy performance all the more disturbing.

She was at her desk and didn't realise anyone was there until a sixth sense told her she wasn't alone. When she lifted her head, Ellis was leaning against the frame of the door with one hand behind his back. At first, Julia thought he was drunk. It was possible – his reaction when he failed to get his own way didn't bode well.

When he spoke she realised she'd misjudged him. 'I'm sorry. I'm an insensitive idiot. You were well within your rights to put me in my place. Please forgive me.'

There was a sadness to him that made Julia reluctant to punish him any more than he was punishing himself. She stopped what she was doing and smiled. 'Don't be silly, there's nothing to forgive. We disagreed. So what? In a dynamic environment like Grapevine it happens all the time. Where have you been? I was worried.'

'I haven't been anywhere. Just walking feeling sorry for myself. I bought a sandwich and couldn't eat it – the pigeons in George Square were happy to help me out.'

'Are you angry with me? Because if you are we need to talk.'

He stared abjectly at his shoes. 'I'm ashamed to admit I was but I'm not now. Have you told Tony you can't work with me, that you don't want to?'

'No, of course not. Why would I do that? You're keen to a fault. I wish there were more like you around here.'

'So I'm still on the team?'

'You're still on the team.'

He produced a bunch of flowers from behind his back, wrapped in purple cellophane and tied with lilac ribbon. Through her surprise Julia recognised red long-stemmed carnations, white gypsophila, orange and lavender gerberas and yellow freesias. 'These are for you. I selected them myself.'

'Oh, they're beautiful. You shouldn't have.'

'Yes, I should, and again apologies for being such a boor. I was going to get chocolates and didn't in case you were on a diet.'

Julia gave a look of mock disapproval. 'Are you suggesting I need to lose weight?'

'Absolutely not, you look terrific, but with women you never know.'

As he passed her the bouquet she noticed a red line of ragged skin across his knuckles that had started to bruise. 'That's nasty, what happened to your hand?'

Ellis had his answer ready. 'Oh, that, don't ask. It was my own fault. I wasn't paying attention and caught it in the car door.'

'Ouch!'

He made light of the injury. 'Yeah, and it wasn't easy. Took me three attempts before I got it right.'

'Is it sore? It looks it.'

'At the time it was bloody excruciating. I thought I'd broken it. Now, it's just painful and stiff.'

'Then why don't you leave it today, put some ideas together and we'll knock them about tomorrow?'

Ellis changed the subject to something that didn't require inventing things that hadn't happened: the pitch was common ground. He said, 'Tony loved what we've got. Isn't that great? I never doubted it, I knew he would, that's why I was so anxious to push on. But it's only the beginning. There's more where that came from. Thanks for your concern but I won't go home. Now, where were we before I rudely interrupted?'

10

Rouken Glen, ten miles from the city, was Michelle's favourite spot, serene even in winter when the duck pond was a sheet of ice and a bitter wind blew snow off The Boathouse café's roof. She came here when she needed to think or sometimes just to lose herself in its simple beauty. Today, she was blind to it and could have been anywhere. She sat in her car, stunned by what she'd discovered about herself and uncertain about how to react. She'd had affairs and knew how they went. Most smouldered for a while – the old 'across a crowded room' cliché – before catching fire, then followed a familiar pattern that, so far, hadn't altered: at the start the sex was great – on occasion, sensational – but it was short-lived. Without a deeper connection, passion ran its course and petered out, and when one of the lovers called time on the adventure the other was quietly relieved.

With Rob Sutherland it had exploded the moment they'd seen each other; an affair was a no-brainer. Rob was an attractive man. That he was married wasn't a concern. Morality had no place in the equation; affairs by definition meant at least one of the players had a partner, wife or a husband, otherwise subterfuge would be unnecessary.

Michelle was here because since last night Rob was in her head and she hadn't been able to shake him loose. Ridiculous, yet there it was.

They'd slept together a grand total of twice, still in the 'great sex' stage, but already it felt different from anything she'd known and she was having doubts, doubts that had stayed with her into the small hours and brought a revelation that had been like a blinding light: if Rob ended it right now she'd be utterly devastated. Facing up to that inconvenient truth hadn't been easy and she still wasn't comfortable with it.

She was financially independent, and when she needed a man, well, if you looked how she looked they weren't hard to find.

Michelle did what she wanted, when she wanted, with whoever she wanted!

Millions of women would take that deal. It was a nice life and she was satisfied with it. Or, at least, she had been until a couple of days ago. Suddenly, it wasn't enough.

In the cold light of day she knew she was falling in love with Rob Sutherland.

In love? Her? How the hell had that happened?

She played with a wayward strand of hair, twirling it absently round her finger. They'd agreed to cool it for a while and it made sense, except Michelle didn't feel like cooling anything. Chasing a man didn't bother her – it was the twenty-first century! She lifted her mobile and punched in his number, so anxious she was barely able to breathe. He didn't answer and for a few desperate seconds she thought he wasn't going to.

Then he did. Before he could speak Michelle blurted out, 'Rob, it's me. I know what we said but can we meet tonight? Please say yes.'

* * *

Across the city in the gently curving crescent of nineteenth-century town houses that was Park Circus, Rob's mobile vibrated on his desk. A part of him hoped it wasn't Michelle, another part ached to hear her whisper his name. He recognised the number and hesitated, afraid of where answering would take him. Rob had had his share of girlfriends, he liked women, but wasn't by any stretch of the imagination a philanderer. He hadn't been okay the first time he'd been with Michelle and still wasn't. There were no excuses for what he'd done – what he was doing – and

Rob didn't try to find any. Deceiving his wife was one thing; deceiving himself was something else entirely. Julia was wonderful; this wasn't about her. So what was it about?

The answer was shockingly obvious: making love to Michelle felt different because it *was* different and in the deepest part of him he could admit that even the sleazy skulking around, on edge in case they were seen, was exciting.

Lust, impure and simple. It wasn't complicated.

* * *

Ellis was furious with himself. He'd misjudged the situation and been slapped down in front of Tony Connors. The bouquet on Julia's desk was an open admission of that error and though she'd appreciated the gesture all it had required was an apology. As far as she was concerned the subject was closed but the misstep gnawed at Ellis's gut and if he continued to push too hard too soon he'd lose her completely. His contrition had gone over well. Now, he had to stay cool, give her time to forget the incident, and let things develop. Tony Connors was a clown who was convinced he'd hooked a talent and wouldn't have cared if Ellis had been the Devil incarnate – so long as he delivered, the horns and hoofs could be overlooked. Tony wouldn't be a problem.

* * *

Julia bent a carnation towards her and breathed in the spicy fragrance that reminded her of cloves. In Tony Connors' view, Ellis was hungry, champing at the bit to nail the brief. If he'd caused offence it was incidental and unintentional. Perhaps Tony was right; perhaps she'd overreacted. Ellis had been generous, given her credit for creating the headline and, of course, it would've been good to keep the momentum going as one possibility revealed another. Nobody wanted that more than Julia but, with his new-kid-in-town zeal, Ellis hadn't considered their circumstances: he was unattached, she had a husband, an important difference.

Besides, she had plans for this evening – catch a butcher on her way home, buy sirloin steaks or lamb chops and actually cook for them. Afterwards they might even pick up where they'd left off last night – wouldn't that be nice?

Her phone rang, startling her out of her daydream. As soon as she saw it was Rob on the line she knew she wouldn't be needing the steak. He seemed far away, whispering as though he didn't want to be overheard; Julia heard chatter in the background. 'I'm in a meeting that's just about to start. At the last bloody minute a client has decided they don't like the design they've approved months ago and want it amended. It's always the same with these people – they sit on their hands and expect us to drop everything when they screw up. I'd tell them where to go except this isn't the only build of theirs we're on. There's too much money involved to tell them to fuck off and get real.'

Julia swallowed her disappointment and tried not to sound like a nagging wife. 'Oh, baby, that's rotten. Never mind, we can eat later.'

'Sorry, that won't work.'

'Why won't it?'

'Because I'll be late.'

'How late?'

'No idea.'

'But we said... we agreed... didn't we?'

Rob's tone softened. 'Yes, we did and, again, I'm sorry. There's nothing I can do about it. Don't wait up.'

'No, I won't, Rob. I won't wait up.'

Julia went to the window and faced an uncomfortable truth: if they weren't careful they would drift apart. Below, in a busy Bothwell Street, afternoon traffic backed up at the lights. In a couple of hours the people in the cars, in the shops and offices all over the city, would go home to their husbands, wives and children. Julia envied them.

She gave herself a shake – feeling sorry for herself wouldn't make it better. All they needed was more time together. When she got home she'd go for a run and spend the rest of the evening searching Skyscanner for flights to India the way she should have ages ago.

As for Ellis, she'd bitten his head off for suggesting they stay on, believing she was spending the night with Rob. Now she felt foolish.

* * *

Michelle gazed at the swans gliding on the water – serene on the surface, underneath paddling for all they were worth. The analogy didn't please her. Waiting for a man wasn't something she was used to or intended ever to get used to. Rob had been surprised to hear from her and, despite the unmissable intensity of her words, hadn't committed to anything more than a promise to call back, and again, Michelle asked herself what the hell she was doing with this guy. An extra-marital coupling was how some people reinforced their own self-worth. She wasn't in that crowd, never had been, and never would be.

Affairs were about sex – with her in control. She smiled a sardonic smile: the Michelle of old, the woman she'd believed herself to be, wouldn't have been in this situation. Not in a million years!

Michelle tossed the mobile onto the passenger seat. It wasn't too late. When Rob got back to her – assuming he got back to her – she'd say she'd changed her mind, three nights in a row was pushing it, and take the reins back into her hands.

Rob Sutherland was a lucky man – if he didn't get that, she had no use for him.

Her mobile rang; she picked it up half expecting him to give a dozen reasons why meeting tonight wasn't possible. Days from now she'd receive a text telling her he loved his wife and was ending the affair.

It didn't happen.

Rob spoke quietly and Michelle heard an urgency in his voice that was a match for her own.

'Okay,' he said, 'we're on.'

11

WHEN THE ADDRESS MATTERS was an eye-catching top line, great as far as it went, though by itself not strong enough to carry a multimillion-pound inner-city development. Ellis had seen outlines of the finished buildings, slap-bang in the centre of Glasgow, and they were certainly impressive. The brief was to create an intrinsically Scottish identity that would make them irresistible. Exclusivity was key but it needed to be packaged properly. Ellis was very good at his job but, good or not, as soon as he started he realised the essential spark wasn't there and he had an awful thought: the other night might've been a fluke. After a fruitless hour he gave up and put his feet on the desk.

Grapevine was a means to an end, no more, a foothold on a new life far from the mess he'd left behind in South Africa. He'd planned on giving it a year or two before moving on. To where, he hadn't decided. Meeting a woman, especially one like Julia, wasn't part of the plan and it would help his cause if he came up with a substantial idea they could finesse together.

It was time for a new approach.

* * *

'Got a minute?'

'Sure?'

Julia looked happy to see him and Ellis smiled. 'Am I interrupting?'

'If only.'

He searched her face for a trace of animosity and found none.

She said, 'Let me guess, you've had a flash of genius and can't wait to impress me with it, am I right?'

He answered with flattery. 'If I remember correctly, genius is your department. No, the opposite, actually. Everything I come up with has been done to death and I can almost hear the confidence draining out of me.'

Julia put down her pen and gave him her attention. 'Then you're doing better than I am. My mind's an absolute blank; last night must've been somebody else. And I should have listened to Rob; telling Tony was bloody stupid. Far too soon.'

Ellis anticipated the rest and said it out loud. 'Because now he's expecting us to blow his socks off with something super fantastic and we have sod all.'

'Sod all is right. Okay, we're only at the beginning but...'

She left the thought unfinished – they knew the rest. Ellis saw an opening and said, 'Flair doesn't just show up when you snap your fingers. Sometimes, no matter what you do, it isn't there. Which is why two heads are better than one.' He groaned. 'Oh, Christ. Listen to me. Now I'm speaking in clichés.'

'Assuming the heads are switched on. Mine isn't.'

'So what do we do?'

Julia sighed. 'Leave it for now and start fresh.'

'Sounds like a plan. Just as well tonight isn't a goer.'

There was no reason not to tell him the truth, so she did. 'Yeah, turns out it could have been. Rob called me, he's working late.'

'He's working... boy, that man of yours certainly puts in the hours.'

'Too many. We both do.'

'Well, I haven't any plans. Why don't we just keep going to see if we can find a spark?'

Julia wasn't against it. 'Okay. Let me check in with Ravi and Olivia. They deserve a bit better than they've had so far, don't you think?'

Ellis didn't share what he thought.

* * *

Julia sensed the mood across the hall the minute she walked in and damned Tony Connors under her breath. In a couple of ill-chosen sentences the bloody fool had damaged a relationship she'd worked hard to forge. Reminding Ravi and Olivia of their status had been clumsy and unnecessary. Unfortunately, without knowing the backstory, they'd misunderstood the situation and taken being excluded as a slight. Julia didn't blame them; she would've reacted no differently, especially as a guy who'd only just joined the company seemed to be welcome. Bringing them back onside would take skill – this was as good a time as any to start. But it wouldn't be easy with young people who, day in and day out, were willing to go the extra mile for Grapevine. Or maybe it was her they did it for. Either way, they'd been wounded and it was Julia's responsibility to help them get over it.

They saw her and kept their heads down. Olivia's mouth tightened while Ravi stared at his computer screen and Julia realised this might be more difficult than she'd thought.

She started with a question and was met by silence. 'How's it all going?'

When no one answered she addressed the problem head-on. 'Listen, guys, trust me, I understand how you feel. This isn't how I work and you know that. We're a team. We've done—'

Ravi interrupted. 'Real teams stick together.'

Olivia added, 'And everybody gets treated the same.'

Julia cursed Tony again; he'd really screwed this up. If she wasn't careful these two would resign and she'd have to start again. 'Come on, don't take it personally. Tony can be a pain. Believe me, I've been on the wrong end of his boorishness more often than it suits me to remember.'

Olivia put into words what Julia had asked herself more than once. 'You could easily get another job. Why stand for it?'

'Because, despite his faults – and he certainly has more than his fair share – he's not the worst boss in the world. If I ever actually needed him he wouldn't be hard to find. The same would go for anybody at Grapevine.'

Ravi gave a laugh that told Julia it would take more than an empathetic little speech to convince him. 'He doesn't even know our names.'

Julia said, 'That's just him. It took him six months to remember mine.' She sighed. 'Okay, I can't let you in on what's happening or the three of us will be out on the street, but something's in the pipeline and it's a big deal, or at least it could be. Tony's paranoid about a leak and overreacting. It goes without saying I have every confidence in you two and, in case you're wondering, after you left we had words. I wasn't impressed with what he did and said so. But, at the end of the day, whether I agree or disagree, he's the boss; it's his decision. For the moment he only wants me and Ellis working on it.'

'You mean Mr Fucking Fantastic?'

Ravi's description made all of them laugh and they were back on the same page. Julia said, 'He isn't so bad when you know him a bit.'

'Once you get past his big head? Don't defend the arrogant prick.'

'He doesn't need defending. He's a colleague, a member of our team. Don't blame Tony Connors' behaviour on him. None of this is his fault.'

Olivia said, 'So what do you want from us?'

'Give Ellis a chance and bide your time. If this works out the way I hope, I'll need your input. Can you do that?'

Ravi and Olivia exchanged a look; he answered for both of them.

'For you. We'll do it for you.'

* * *

Ellis Kirkbride couldn't make out everything that was being said. What he could hear angered him. Julia was apologising to Ravi and the girl, showing weakness. This was business: sentimentality had no place; explanations were unnecessary. In the cut-and-thrust of advertising, bruising fragile egos wasn't a consideration, nor should it be.

Ellis had only just arrived but it had been long enough to notice how

Ravi acted around Julia. The guy was smart – he'd give him that much – making himself acceptable with his corny chat, pretending he was a friend when, in fact, he wanted to be her lover. She seemed unaware of the designer's motives, which made her, at best, a naïve fool. Unless she was quietly encouraging him.

He silently chastised himself. Had he learned nothing?

Could he really have forgotten what females were capable of?

His eyes drifted to the cork board and the marketing materials he'd generously described as 'solid'. That had been a lie – they were lacklustre, bloody boring. Ellis wouldn't dream of putting his name to such bog-standard stuff.

The rage that had travelled with him from the other side of the world rose in his chest. He fought against an urge to tear them down and rip them to shreds. With an effort he made himself calm down. Not because he was wrong about Ravi – he wasn't wrong and in due course that guy would get what he deserved. No, because he'd heard Julia defend him to the other two when it would've been easier to go the popular road, side with them and bad-mouth him.

That meant something, didn't it? Ellis was careful not to get ahead of himself. If his last experience had taught him anything it was not to rush. Given time Julia would discover what he'd realised when their eyes had met: that at last they'd found the right one.

* * *

At twenty minutes past seven, Rob Sutherland appeared, carrying his briefcase. He seemed fresh, rested and ready for the day ahead, very different from the man who'd skulked home at midnight. What architect was still at his desk at that hour? Ellis was convinced Rob was cheating on his wife and he intended to get the proof. Last night he hadn't been able to tell much about Rob except he was tall, taller than he'd somehow thought he'd be. In the car, Ellis ran his fingers through the stubble on his chin, assessing how Julia's husband would look to people who didn't know him. This morning he wore a dark suit and a crisp white shirt with a blue tie, every inch the upwardly mobile professional. He walked to his car with purpose in his stride, a guy with somewhere to go and something to do when he got there. Women would find Rob handsome – obviously, Julia did. He could probably be charming, too, when it suited him.

The silver Peugeot pulled away from Hamilton Drive to be swallowed by the early-morning traffic on Great Western Road. Ellis started his engine and allowed himself a wry smile: Julia's man was feeling good about himself, wasn't he? He'd got away with it, or believed he had, which wasn't quite the same thing.

She hadn't mentioned which firm he worked for or where their offices were. Ellis was about to find out: wherever Rob Sutherland was going, he was going with him.

At the second set of lights, the Peugeot indicated to go right and joined a tailback of vehicles from the beginning of Woodlands Road to the motorway and the city centre. About halfway along it turned right again, accelerated to the top of the hill and disappeared. Ellis hammered the steering wheel with his clenched fist. He'd spent the night in his car; losing him wasn't an option. By the time he was able to follow, the car was nowhere to be seen. All he could do was drive around hoping he'd spot it. This part of Glasgow had originally been where wealthy businessmen lived with their families. Over time most of the impressive town houses had been converted to offices. Ellis frantically scanned the streets and was about to give up when he saw the Peugeot parked outside a former town house in Park Circus. Rob Sutherland would be inside, at his desk, a man with nothing but his job on his mind.

The name on the brass plate at the side of the front door read:

Galloway, Bartholomew and Figgis
Architects

He had him.

PART II

12

SIX WEEKS LATER

Julia leafed through the glossy printouts Ravi had given her the previous afternoon, frowning in spite of herself. The ads were good – no surprise; everything he designed had aesthetic value – except they weren't talking to her the way she wanted. Julia asked herself why and immediately found the answer. Hogmanay was about people celebrating yet there were no actual people in the frame. Even the strapline, which had been Ellis's contribution, missed the mark. Very obviously being shut out had killed Ravi's flair and, while it was easy to empathise with the designer, he'd better get it back again and soon. Meantime, Julia didn't relish telling him she didn't like what he'd done.

Her negative reaction wasn't only about the ads; she had other things on her mind. Lately Rob was spending more and more time at work to the point where they'd almost become strangers living in the same house. The truth was, they hadn't followed through on getting travelling again, shaking themselves out of the rut they were in. And then there was the so-called 'project' talked about in whispers as though it was the only commission Grapevine had ever been involved with. Julia blamed Tony Connors and his obsession with winning it.

They'd made the pitch three weeks earlier in the City Chambers to a committee of eight. In the taxi on the short journey from Bothwell Street to George Square, Tony had been upbeat, more animated than Julia had seen him in a long time, doing his best to relax them.

It hadn't worked but it had been a decent try.

Before they'd been ushered into an airless room to give their presentation, the MD had had one final message for his marketing stars. 'Remember, it's Thursday, anything can happen.'

Whether 'anything' *had* actually happened was unknown because they'd heard nothing, and, while it was comforting to believe no news was good news, Julia was disappointed with her own performance: nerves had got the better of her. She hadn't been at her best and had fluffed her lines.

Thankfully, Ellis had jumped into the breach and rescued the situation with a statement powerful enough to be a headline marketing slogan and a performance that could only be described as flawless. The architect's artist's impression of the buildings had been soulless. The sharp images Ellis had worked up built on the original drawings but he'd cleverly embedded the clan crests in the wall at the entrance beneath the names The Cameron, The Buchanan, The Fraser and The Wallace, and decorated each sparkling chrome and glass foyer in an elegant light purple – the colour of heather – decked in the appropriate tartan.

Corny, yes, but stylish, and very definitely cool.

Ellis had unveiled it with the confidence of a man in no doubt it was a winner. 'This, gentlemen, is what money gets you.'

His delivery, unlike her own, had been unhurried and assured, hammering home the key notes of their proposal. When it had ended, Julia had searched the faces of the committee for a clue about how the presentation had gone and found none.

The MD had made only one comment to her as they'd waited outside for a taxi to take them back to Grapevine. He'd gazed at the statue of Sir Walter Scott on top of the column in the centre of the square and spoken out of the side of his mouth. 'Told you he was good.'

He hadn't meant Sir Walter.

Julia wished the ground would open up and swallow her.

From then it had been business as usual, or, more accurately, what had become the usual: Ravi and Olivia across the hall and Ellis now with his desk in what had been 'her' office.

Ellis clearly considered the others beneath him in the food chain and acted accordingly, barely acknowledging Olivia's existence. Ravi wasn't so fortunate. Overnight he'd become the focus of his ire. Julia didn't get why Ellis had taken against him, though he definitely had. The New Year's Eve stuff was the latest issue to draw his caustic disapproval. The previous day he'd scanned the proofs, damning them with faint praise. 'Very nice. Very nice, indeed.'

Today's criticism was less about the images and more about the guy who'd created them. Ellis stopped what he was doing and waited until Julia noticed he was staring at her. She said, 'What? What is it?'

'Ravi.'

'What about him?'

Ellis shifted his attention to the window and paused, reluctant to say what had to be said. 'You've seen the Edinburgh layouts – you tell me.'

Julia guessed where this was going and defended her designer. 'I agree they aren't quite right, if that's what you mean, but I like them.'

'Of course you do.'

The implication offended her. 'Meaning what, exactly?'

'You're allowing your feelings to get in the way of your judgement.'

'Don't be ridiculous. Feelings? What the hell are you on about? As for Ravi – he's one of the best I've worked with.'

Ellis ran a finger slowly over the desk and inspected it. 'He's got a thing for you.'

'He's what?'

'Oh, come on. All the jokes, the asides. Julia this, Julia that. There's a reason they don't happen with anybody else,' he scoffed. 'And the way he looks at you. Don't ask me to believe you haven't noticed.'

Julia was too stunned to be angry. She said, 'I haven't noticed because it isn't true. You're imagining it.'

She felt her temper rise and struggled to keep it under control, damned if she'd give ground when he was being obnoxious. 'Actually, I strongly reject your insinuation.'

Ellis pursed his lips and processed her words in silence. Her outraged response confirmed everything he suspected. When he finally spoke he didn't sugarcoat it. 'I'm sorry to hear that, from you especially, because we've both been in this game long enough to know there's a huge difference between pictures that are pretty to look at and marketing that does what it's supposed to do. Sell! If the client's bright – and some of them are – you have to figure out their criticism in advance and be prepared to meet it. Know where the threat to what you've produced and are asking them to approve will come.'

'And you told Ravi that?'

'Yes. Because it's better to be honest and, really, I didn't feel I had a choice. What he's produced would be better framed and hanging in a gallery, preferably somewhere I didn't have to see it.'

'That's unfair.'

'Is it? The world's knee-deep in graphics people. Ravi's all right so far as it goes, but at this level, I'm sorry, he just doesn't have it. I expect a leader to spot weaknesses in their team and address them. That you haven't, with respect, speaks volumes.'

Julia got to her feet. 'How dare you?'

Ellis wasn't intimidated and carried on. 'He isn't good enough to hold a creative position here, not if Connors is serious about Grapevine being a major player. I've a good mind to—'

Julia's phone rang before he could expand on what he had a good mind to do. She answered it and listened; the exchange was short and one-sided. At the end of it Julia said, 'Okay,' and turned to Ellis. 'Tony wants us in his office. Right now. As for your "observations". You're entitled to your views. Doubt my professionalism again and I'll fire you on the spot. Understood?'

* * *

They made their way to the meeting with Ellis still smarting from being put in his place. He'd challenged her judgement, openly questioned her behaviour and would be lucky not to have a formal complaint lodged against him.

In the corridor outside Tony Connors' door Ellis stepped in front of her and held up his hands. 'Please listen to me.' He sighed and stared at the floor, his jaw silently working to find the words. 'I seem to be apologising to you every other day and here I am again. I had no right to speak to you like that. It was uncalled for.'

From the look in her eyes and her clipped reply Julia wasn't in a forgiving mood. She fired back at him. 'Is that your version of admitting you were wrong? Because in my book, after what you implied, it doesn't come close to acceptable.'

'Yes, it is. I'm truly sorry if it falls short. But I'm not wrong about Ravi and I believe you know that. This isn't personal—'

'Really? It certainly sounds like it.'

Ellis's frustration got the better of him. 'Well, it fucking isn't! How could it be? I hardly know the guy. It's his work I have an issue with. Come on, Julia, admit it. The best that can be said of the latest graphics is that they're okay. If it was a Tourist Board advert for scenic Scotland that might well be good enough. Only it isn't, it's a flagship event worth millions to the city, which means what we present has to be absolutely spot on, not some clichéd stock shot that's been used before – and to better effect – a dozen times.'

His objections weren't coming from a good place and Julia was unimpressed. 'Developing a concept has to start somewhere. It takes time, or have you forgotten? That's all Ravi's doing. Getting away from the blank page. Throwing stuff out to get a reaction he'll take onboard in the next generation.'

'So you don't think there's anything in what I'm saying?'

'Frankly, no, I don't. The New Year project is a work in progress. What we begin with won't be what we have at the end; it never is.'

Ellis held up his hands. 'Okay, you're the boss. I just hope you're right.'

'I am.'

The exchange had been short and heated. Ellis was breathing hard. Julia remained unmoved. For her, the subject was closed, yet she was conscious of a sour note it would take time to get over. And despite his apology the intensity of his anger when she'd disagreed with him had unsettled her.

13

Tony kept his head down and didn't make eye contact until Julia and Ellis were seated opposite him. When he was ready he scanned their faces, his expression blank, stern even, and Julia feared he was about to deliver disappointing news.

Tony steepled his fingers, and shoehorned himself into the picture. 'Well, I was right, wasn't I?'

Julia barely smothered her impatience. 'Right about what, Tony?'

Tony beamed, teasing out what he had to say. 'About teaming you two up. One of my better decisions.'

Ellis said, 'You mean... we got it, we got the city council job?'

Tony's eyes gleamed. '"Got it" is an understatement. We killed it stone dead.'

Julia bit her lip to stop from laughing out loud. We?

Ellis joined in. 'For a minute I was sure you were going to break it to us that we'd lost out. Better luck next time and all that.'

Tony massaged his temple with his forefinger. 'On another day maybe that's how it'll be. In this business you win some and you lose some, but not today. Today we won and it's sweet.'

Tony swivelled in his chair, still laughing. He saw Julia and the grin disappeared from his mouth. 'You're a bloody success, woman. I expected you to be kicking up your heels and dancing on the desk. Why aren't you?'

To hear herself addressed as 'woman' irked Julia. She wanted to remind him it would take more than a new piece of business for Grapevine to have her dancing. Instead, she went with an unconfrontational reply. 'I'm delighted, of course, though not surprised.'

'Then, tell your face about it.'

'I'm in that space everybody's been in at one time or another – between the thrill of getting the job and the awful realisation that now we have to do it.'

Tony waved her concern away. 'That's for tomorrow and with you guys involved it won't be a problem. Stand outside yourselves for a second and appreciate what you've achieved here, Julia. This is big. Big for Grapevine and big for you. Results like this don't come along very often. It demands a celebration. Drop whatever you're working on and take the rest of the day off. I've booked a table for eight o'clock tonight in The Buttery. After that we'll round off the night at the Red Sky Bar in Finnieston.'

Ellis didn't hesitate; he was all in. 'Wow! That sounds great.'

'It will be and you've earned it.'

Julia didn't share his enthusiasm. Tony was being generous – to see it any other way would be churlish, and besting such formidable rivals did deserve recognition. She said, 'You haven't mentioned who's included, because if Ravi and Olivia aren't—'

Tony interrupted her. 'Why would they be? They haven't done anything to get us here.'

'In case you've forgotten, that's not down to them – they were expressly excluded, remember? This is just the start. There's a long way to go. By the end they'll have done their share.' She folded her arms across her chest. 'Ravi and Olivia are valued and valuable members of my team and if we're looking for them to get onboard for the hard graft...'

She let him figure out the rest. The MD hadn't expected this response and gave way. 'If you say so, but—'

Julia's response was terse. 'I *do* say so.'

'Okay, okay. From here on in we need everybody involved and, as you correctly pointed out, Julia, getting a job is one thing, delivering a successful outcome is another. Ravi and Olivia will make a significant contribution so of course they're invited.'

Tony returned his attention to the papers on his desk; the meeting was over.

14

The Buttery was among Glasgow's most enduring restaurants yet still somehow managed to stay one of the city's best-kept culinary secrets. Its location, squeezed between the motorway and the resurgent area of Finnieston, had something to do with it. As a venue for a quiet celebration it would be hard to beat; Julia approved of Tony Connors' choice though she wouldn't be telling him.

When she'd phoned, Rob had encouraged her to relax and enjoy the experience. 'Your boss is a slave driver. It's your duty to bite his hand off when he's picking up the bill.'

'Then you don't mind me out late again?'

'Mind? On the contrary. Besides, I'll be late myself so I insist you order the most expensive bottle on the wine list to wash down your lobster thermidor.'

His casual response had niggled. He wasn't bothered in the least that they'd spend yet another night apart. And what the hell? Did it never occur to him to say he couldn't work late? Apparently not.

She'd pretended there was a call waiting and said, 'Other line. Gotta go.'

Julia painted on her happy face when the taxi dropped her in Argyle Street outside the restaurant's front door. Inside hummed quietly with a dozen conversations going on at once. A waiter showed her to a table where Ravi and Olivia were nervously shifting in their seats, clearly pleased to see her. Julia hadn't told them about Ellis's objection – it wouldn't do much for their confidence and would destroy any chance of a viable working relationship. They'd made an effort for the occasion. Ravi had shaved and was wearing a tie; Olivia had her hair down and had ditched the jumper and leggings for a dress. The transformation was marked.

Julia said, 'I have a question. What've you done with Ravi and Olivia? Those two scruffy buggers I see every day. Come on, where are they?'

Olivia laughed. 'I'm so glad you're here first. We were dreading it being Ellis.'

'Dreading? Why, for heaven's sake?'

Olivia giggled as Ravi ran his hand through invisible stubble, lowered his voice, and did an impersonation of Ellis. 'Because he doesn't like us. Or, more specifically, he doesn't like me. Olivia has no idea what he thinks – he doesn't speak to her. Don't you think that's odd?'

Julia was shocked to think of them silently suffering. They deserved an apology. 'I'm sorry, I didn't realise. In spite of the impressive CV Tony banged on about, it seems our Mr Kirkbride's interpersonal skills aren't the best. You should've come to me. I would've taken him aside and spoken to him.'

Ravi shook his head. 'And what exactly would I have said? "Ellis Kirkbride is being mean to me"? No, I'd rather leave Grapevine before I let that happen. Most of what he does is small, by itself nothing that amounts to much, yet it's there.'

'How can he dislike you? You're practically strangers.'

'Yes, we are, but he's not a fool, that's for sure. When you aren't around the hostility rolls off him.' Ravi searched for the words. 'Then, he's in his element, ordering me about like he's my boss and none too nice about it, either.'

Julia wanted to tell him he was wrong and would have if she hadn't already seen for herself what Ellis was capable of. Tony thought the sun shone out of Ellis Kirkbride. Voicing concerns with him would be a waste of time. This needed to be sorted out and it was her job to do it.

Olivia chimed in. 'In a way you're lucky. I might as well not exist. I can't recall a single conversation with him. Maybe he has something against females.'

Julia's instinct was to protect her team. 'No favourites and no unfavourites' was a maxim she'd picked up somewhere and stuck to. From the moment Tony had waltzed into her office with Ellis behind him, the team dynamic had changed and Ravi and Olivia had lost out. This evening was meant to be a celebration, an opportunity to bond before they tackled one of the most prestigious commissions in Grapevine's history. Instead, at best it was a sham that might very well turn into a disaster. Once they'd all had a few drinks, the underlying friction she hadn't known about could rise to the surface and spoil everything.

Olivia whispered, 'He's here.'

Julia turned in her chair to see the source of their concern striding towards them with the camera she'd come to accept as part of him slung over his shoulder. He was stylishly casual in jeans, T-shirt and a body warmer – all in black. His hair had a 'just washed' look and his skin glowed. He dropped into the seat next to her, leaned his elbows on the table and flashed a grin.

'Thank God.' Ellis sounded as though he'd escaped some terrible fate. 'I had visions of being first here, just me and Tony. No harm to him, and maybe I shouldn't say this, but I've listened to the man sober – Christ knows what he's like drunk.' He glanced round, perhaps to check the MD wasn't standing behind him. When he came back to the table, the grin was missing; he hunched his shoulders, lowered his voice and took the other three by surprise.

'Before he arrives, there's something that needs to be said and I'm the one who has to say it. Ravi. Olivia. Julia had nothing to do with shutting you guys out. It's important you understand that. Actually, she argued against it. Put up a pretty spirited case, too. Going up against Tony Connors is no mean feat. If there's one thing I've learned in my short time with Grapevine it's that, when she gets started, Mrs Julia Sutherland is a formidable lady.'

The speech came across as insincere, something Ellis had rehearsed in the taxi on his way here. Olivia didn't buy into it. She said, 'You don't have to tell us; we know Julia. We never believed it was her idea. She wouldn't do that.'

Ellis agreed. 'Wouldn't and didn't, Olivia. Take it from me. I was there.'

He focused on Ravi. The designer made eye contact with him and held it defiantly. 'You and I have got off on the wrong foot. That was my fault. When I'm on a campaign I get too involved, too intense. I lose sight of other people's feelings and become—'

'An arse?'

Ellis smiled ruefully. 'Not quite what I was reaching for, Ravi, though thanks for the suggestion – I deserve it. The Greeks have a word: *malaka*. I'll let you dig out the translation. I'm sure you'll think it's apt.'

Ravi was still hurting; he wasn't won over so easily. 'As long as it means arsehole, I can go with it.'

Ellis met the animosity head-on. He held out his hand and Julia saw his tanned skin disappear into his cuff. 'It boils down to three things. One: I've got a nerve talking about Tony being difficult when, at times, I'm no better. All I can say is leave that with me. I'm on it. Two: we're the players – not Tony Connors, not anybody else – *us*; the ones who take abstract thoughts and half-baked notions and make them fly. And three: with this project we have a golden opportunity to do great work together, so let's not dissipate our energy on petty squabbles. What do you say, mate?'

Julia wanted to cheer; she couldn't have welcomed this more. Before the night had even begun Ellis was single-handedly pulling the team together, making it whole, undoing the damage that had been done. All it needed was Ravi to meet him halfway and they'd be back on track. Ravi didn't respond. Ellis's outstretched hand hung in the air, his eyes hardened as the warmth that had been in them a second earlier started to fade, and Julia dreaded the healing moment was about to slip away.

Everyone was watching Ravi, waiting for his response, understanding what was riding on it for all of them. He said, 'I take it you've seen the Hogmanay graphics.'

'Yeah, I've seen them.'

'And?'

Ellis didn't rush to answer. When he did his tone was measured and even.

'In my opinion they aren't quite there.'

Ravi repeated what he'd said. '"Aren't quite there" – what the hell does that mean?'

Ellis sighed. 'It means I didn't like them.'

'Didn't like them or—?'

'I think you can do better. Actually, I *know* you can do better.'

Disdain fell from every word of Ravi's reply. 'You think I can do better. Really? And who exactly do you—?'

'To be completely truthful, I have to admit I fucking hated them.'

'You arrogant bastard.'

'I'm sorry if that's how it comes across. But I've got an idea about a different approach if you're willing to listen.'

On the other side of the table, Olivia closed her eyes and bowed her head. Ravi was a sensitive guy, and he was a friend – this had to be hard for him.

'Colleagues are allowed to criticise each other. Not settling for anything other than excellence is what pushes us to be better than the rest.' He finished with a question, in the circumstances the only one worth asking. 'So, are we a team or aren't we, Ravi?'

Julia held her breath: this was it. Ravi blinked, his features slowly softening as he reached across, gripped Ellis's hand and shook it.

'We're a team.'

When Tony arrived, the four of them were laughing. He slipped into a chair beside Julia, saw their empty glasses and admonished them. 'There was no need to hold back on my account. Fire ahead; that's why we're here. Sorry, bloody roadworks on the South Side. What've I missed?'

Julia brought him up to date. 'Ellis was telling us how he came to be in the Table Bay hotel's swimming pool at three o'clock in the morning with his clothes on.'

Olivia added some detail. 'The guards escorted him, dripping wet, off the premises and warned him not to hurry back. Except he did. A week later—'

Ellis modestly cut the retelling short. 'Not my finest hour. You had to be there, although I'm very glad you weren't, Tony.'

'That makes two of us. It'll be funnier once the drugs start to work.' He made a movement with his elbow to assure them he was referring to alcohol and nodded to a waiter. 'Let's get started, shall we? What're we having? Champagne, for sure, a bit later on.'

Julia said, 'Not too late or they'll flog us Aste Spumante and charge for Veuve Clicquot.'

Tony joined in. 'By then, we won't care. And, by the way, it isn't only Ellis's jokes that get better when the audience is smashed – my speeches are masterpieces of the spoken word, as you'll discover in an hour or two.' Tony ignored their collective groans and carried on. 'Bubbles and plenty of them. What do you want to kick off with – G & T, white wine? Something with cherries and an umbrella? Don't be shy, shout it out.'

The banter relaxed them. Olivia smiled while Ravi had apparently shucked off his resentment for Ellis Kirkbride. Ellis was the biggest surprise, returned to the likeable guy he'd been in the pub, and when Tony popped the cork on the first of several bottles of champagne they raised their glasses to Grapevine and to each other.

Tony could be satisfied with his choice of restaurant; Julia realised that was exactly what her boss would be thinking. But fair play to him, the get-together was going well: Ravi and Ellis had formed an unlikely comedy double act, sparking off each other, very different from their relationship at the beginning of the evening, while the normally timid Olivia earnestly explained the track-by-track merits of Kendrick Lamar's last album to a poker-faced Tony. Julia basked in the mellow glow that came with good food and wine – the feeling all was right with the world. It could only be better if Rob was here. That thought brought her down and she was overcome with an urge to speak to her husband. It wasn't fair: here she was eating pan-fried West Coast scallops, drinking chilled white wine, while he was, most likely, slumped in front of the TV in Hamilton Drive flicking through the channels, killing time until she came home.

Julia had to hear his voice even if it was only for a few seconds. She dug her mobile out and punched in the number; his phone wasn't turned on. In the middle of so much positive energy the disappointment was crushing and Julia was suddenly desperately sad.

She turned her face away, embarrassed, not wanting the others to notice. But Ellis Kirkbride was watching. He raised his glass in a silent toast, smiling a smile that barely touched his lips, as though he understood her loneliness and sympathised.

* * *

They could have walked; where they were going wasn't far. Tony vetoed the suggestion, judging they'd had too much to drink, and got the restaurant to call a taxi that dropped them outside the Radisson RED Hotel. While he paid the driver the others waited on the pavement, then together took the dedicated lift from the foyer to the ninth floor. On the way up, Julia studied her companions. Ravi was flushed; sweat filmed his forehead and his eyes were glazed. Beside him, Tony had been adopted by Olivia, who rested her head on the MD's shoulder – tomorrow, if she remembered, she'd be mortified. Tony stared ahead, his face puffy and more lined than in daylight; he was in his fifties and it showed. Where alcohol was concerned Tony was capable of holding his own – Julia had seen him do it – but these days the booze took more than it gave. Tony wasn't obviously drunk but as the evening had worn on he'd become quieter, more of a father figure whose role was to open his wallet and make sure his younger charges didn't come to harm – a side of him she hadn't known existed.

Only Ellis appeared relatively unaffected, less involved in the jokey give and take, content to allow it to carry on without him. Once or twice she'd caught the edges of his mouth turn down disapprovingly when he'd thought nobody would notice. Julia hadn't actually seen him empty his glass and it occurred to her that, perhaps, he hadn't knocked back as much as the rest of them.

The Red Sky Bar in Finnieston was a fairly recent addition to the city and the perfect place to end an evening; Tony had organised a table at the window looking out onto panoramic views across the River Clyde. When they were seated he drew on an extra reserve of enthusiasm tinged with relief that his stewardship was almost over. 'Okay. Same question I've been asking all night. What's everybody having and, whatever it is, make it a double, otherwise you'll be using your own money instead of mine.'

Ravi read between the lines and moaned his disbelief. 'You're checking out? Surely not, Tony? We've only just got here.'

'Checking out, calling time, admitting defeat – however you want to put it, I'm done. It's a wise man who knows when he's had enough and I am that guy. In the morning I'll be busy keeping all of us in employment while you lot roll in hungover and not fit to strike a blow until the middle of the afternoon – you lucky people.'

Julia said, 'I won't be far behind you. I'm starting to see two of you and one is more than enough.' They all laughed. 'Just as well Rob isn't home or he'd be sending out a search party to look for me.'

Ellis gave her a hug and said, 'Never mind, you've got me.'

Tony gave a waitress with an Irish accent their order and finished with a few words that sounded totally genuine. 'Thanks for what you've achieved and for what you're going to achieve. I'm convinced the future of Grapevine is in safe hands. Tomorrow, the possibilities are endless: anything can happen. Take care.'

Tony took the party spirit with him; there was nothing else for it but to go home. The four of them emptied their glasses and Olivia and Ravi said their goodbyes. Ravi kissed Julia on the cheek and shook Ellis's hand. 'I didn't want to come. In fact, I almost didn't. That would've been a mistake because I've enjoyed myself more than I thought I would. Let's put our heads together on the Hogmanay stuff, Ellis. I'm keen to hear what you have to say.'

'Better wait. You might not agree.'

'It'll be coming from a good place.'

Ellis said, 'Hold it. I almost forgot: team photo. Come on, people, squeeze in. We're making history here.'

He handed the Nikon to a waiter and took his place between the other two behind Julia's chair with his hands on her shoulders. The photograph was a fitting ending to what had been a successful evening.

With Ravi and Olivia gone, Julia moved out onto the terrace where it was less noisy. Her head swam. She shut her eyes and filtered out the music the DJ in the corner was playing. When she opened them Ellis was smiling at her from behind his camera. Julia covered her face with her hand. 'No, no, I must be a mess. Please don't, please—'

CLICK.

His arm circled her shoulders. He said, 'Tired?'

'Not too tired to say how much I appreciate what you did tonight. It really helped, honestly.'

He feigned ignorance. 'I have no idea what you're talking about.'

'With Ravi. Supporting him, bringing him back into the team, and for doing it without lying to the guy. You're right. Of course, you're right. The Edinburgh graphics are off the mark and he knows it. Yet you made your point and left him feeling good about himself. That's a talent not many people have.'

Ellis edged closer; his fingers brushed her cheek. 'I'm glad you're pleased, because I did it for you.'

'Then I'm a fortunate lady.'

'I knew it was what you wanted.'

'It was. It is.'

'Don't I deserve a kiss?'

Before she could reply his lips covered hers. In the moonlight it seemed the most natural thing in the world and Julia gave herself to it. She didn't hear the quiet 'click' of the Nikon recording the moment.

15

Drinking had never been Julia's thing; even as a teenager keen to explore the adult world the idea of not being in control hadn't appealed. In fact, it had terrified her. Out on the town with her friends in the days before she'd met Rob she'd constantly been the butt of jibes for always being the sober one, the mother hen who made sure the others didn't get themselves into trouble. Towards the end of a heavy session – and there had been a few of those – they'd been glad of her. This morning, the wisdom of not overdoing it was all too clear. At first, Julia wasn't certain she was capable of getting out of bed without assistance – her head was too heavy, some unknown practical joker had glued her eyes shut, and vomiting was a real possibility.

Memories of the previous night arrived ominously, like hyenas circling a wounded animal. She dragged clothes over her stricken body and lay still. But hiding couldn't last. The fragments before the champagne corks started popping were fine; listening to Olivia and Ravi share their fears; Tony Connors breezing in and taking over in his own inimitable way; and finally, Ellis, rebuilding a damaged relationship. Nothing too awful till she remembered the terrace and Ellis Kirkbride's fingers caressing her cheek, the feel of his warm lips on hers as he pressed against her body, and knowing he'd wanted her. How long it had lasted before she'd pulled away and left him framed in the silhouette of the city skyline she couldn't say.

Julia told herself she was overreacting, that it had been one of those crazy things that happened when people under pressure and too much alcohol were thrown together. Work events, Christmas parties and the like were littered with casual flirtations fuelled by booze: par for the course and usually regretted by the people involved.

So, what was she beating herself up about?

A kiss, a harmless kiss.

Tony, Ravi and Olivia had left; she should've done the same. So, why hadn't she? The answer was obvious: so far Ellis Kirkbride had been over-bearing one minute, apologetic the next. Last night, with Ravi, he'd shown himself in a new light and Julia had been impressed by what she'd seen. A creative team needed to pull in the same direction; Ellis had gone a long way to ensuring this one would and Julia had found herself liking him for what he'd done.

He'd picked up on her warmth and misread the signs. As simple as that. When he'd moved closer to her on the Sky Bar's terrace everything about him had signalled what he was going to do. And while she wasn't guilty of encouraging his attention, in that moment she hadn't rejected it, the reason she was tearing herself apart.

Underneath the covers, shivering and nauseous, Julia cast around for excuses and found none. For a happily married woman, there was no such thing as a harmless kiss. If she confessed to Rob that was absolutely how he'd see it. Now, because of her stupidity, she had to depend on Ellis keeping his mouth shut. That put her, as team leader, in a difficult place, but as Rob's wife – it was potentially more serious. The best she could hope for was that Ellis recognised it as an insignificant indiscretion, and that her husband would never know how stupid the woman he shared his life with could be.

She took a deep breath and turned onto her side, expecting Rob to be there, for once relieved when he wasn't. Somehow, she'd managed not to wake him when she'd crept into bed.

Or maybe she had and couldn't remember.

Her clothes were scattered over the floor and Julia thanked God; it meant she'd undressed in the dark. Rob was a sharp guy who would be able to tell from the other side of the street if she was lying to him. Replying to an innocent question like 'How was your night?' would suddenly be a test of her nerve, every mention of Ellis fraught with the fear of Rob sussing something wasn't as it should be.

Just talking would be a minefield: a pity she hadn't considered that earlier. Hangovers were the unforgiving price of over-indulging, the inspiration behind the anguished empty vow of so many drinkers, 'Never again!'

Her suffering would pass; things would return to how they'd been. As for the kiss – she was exaggerating. It wasn't as though they'd had sex, and while Julia would die rather than have Rob find out, there really had been nothing to it. On the other side of the city, Ellis might be asking himself what the hell he'd been playing at moving in on his boss, dreading having to face her.

She pulled the covers away and crawled out of bed. Calling in sick was tempting, though all that would do was delay the inevitable. Her job was to get a grip on her paranoia and deliver a cracking marketing campaign. Giving headroom to anything else was wasted time.

Yet, innocuous or not, the kiss was a warning, a red flag reminding Julia she and Rob had lost their way, slowly becoming those clichéd ships that passed in the night. They should be spending time together, just the two of them, enjoying each other's company. Tonight, she'd insist they put a date in their diaries and decide where to go on holiday.

It wasn't an option any longer; it had to be done.

* * *

Rob opened the main door of the offices in Park Circus and punched in the code to neutralise the alarm. His first priority was coffee before he even thought of doing anything remotely work related. His mood was low; he wasn't proud of himself. Last night he'd heard the quiet 'click' of the front door closing, then Julia noisily coming into the bedroom, and pretended to be asleep. In fact, he'd only arrived home a couple of hours earlier from Michelle's place. Going there rather than a hotel had been her suggestion and pointed to a not-so-subtle shift in the status of the relationship. The house, like the lady herself, was stylish and well maintained. They'd started making love in the lounge and ended up in the bedroom without knowing how they got there, and Michelle wasn't the veteran of countless affairs as she'd led him to believe – that was her front, a mask worn to protect herself from the pain of disappointment and rejection. The *real* Michelle was kind, warm, fun to be with. Rob was sure she was falling in love with him. And that was a problem. Because it wasn't one-sided. Leaving Julia was something he'd never expected to consider.

An uneasy night hadn't produced a solution to the situation he found himself in. He stared out at 'the circus', the Mercs and the Jags pulling into their reserved parking spaces as the drivers got ready for another day of making money. Having a position at a firm like Galloway, Bartholomew and Figgis was something he'd only dreamed about in his uni days. His work had already been recognised and, in the fullness of time, a junior partnership would be his if he wanted it. All he had to do was keep his head down. GBF were an old established business, the very definition of conservative. A drama in his personal life would be seen as a distraction, viewed unfavourably, and impact his prospects. But none of that mattered.

What did was destroying two women who deserved better.

Julia was his wife: the right thing to do, the only thing, was to end it with Michelle and dedicate himself to becoming the husband Julia needed and believed she had – painful, yes, but if the decision got out of his hands the consequences for all of them would be a nightmare where there were no winners.

He opened his PC and scrolled through his emails; the people in Ayrshire were asking for one more onsite meeting to clarify some last-minute changes. Standing in a field with a cold wind coming off the sea wasn't something to look forward to.

Rob quietly cursed the client. 'Read what I sent six months ago, you fucking idiots.'

His exasperation was misdirected – the development on the coast wasn't the problem.

This morning's sackcloth and ashes was the response of a repentant sinner to a guilt trip in the wee small hours. Whatever he told himself, when it came right down to it, this sinner was enjoying himself too much; he wasn't ready to end it with Michelle.

16

The first thing Julia noticed when she opened her office door were the flowers: red roses, twelve of them. Tony Connors had been open about how invested he was in Grapevine winning the city-centre gig, and her immediate assumption was they'd come from him – a final generous gesture before he squeezed every ounce of blood from her and the rest of the team. They were beautiful, it had to be said. Julia forgot how she was feeling and ran her fingers through the leaves, searching for the note that would confirm her suspicions.

There was no note, which meant Tony would come bounding in spouting his happy-clappy motivational chat, expecting her to match his enthusiasm; he was going to be disappointed because she just didn't have it in her.

The emergency coffee bought on the way in tasted vile; even adding an extra Stevia couldn't save it. Julia forced it down and made a face. The two paracetamol she'd taken before leaving the flat hadn't helped, either, and it was too soon to take more. Getting to work, navigating a path through the rush-hour traffic with a brass band rehearsing in her head, wasn't an experience she was in a hurry to repeat. Julia prided herself on being well organised. Her morning routine was a battle plan honed by years of practice intended to minimise fuss. Today, her hands had trembled so badly even simple tasks like applying her make-up had been close to impossible. Fortunately, none of the team were around to see the state she was in, a small mercy but she'd take it. No, the coffee was fine, it was her taste buds – she'd probably killed them off.

Julia lifted the bouquet, carefully wrapped in kraft paper and cellophane, and smelled its fragrance. Fair play to him, Tony hadn't stinted: each stem was at its peak, the leaves a glossy green contrast to the scarlet petals. By most metrics, the MD was a success, yet during the previous evening he'd cut a lonely figure going through the motions and she'd felt for him. Tony had money, a reputation in the industry and more girlfriends than Julia could remember, Botoxed Barbie lookalikes young enough to be his daughters, so similar it was difficult to tell them apart. To her knowledge he'd never been married and had no children. Grapevine was his family.

A knock on the door startled her. Ravi came in and sat down; he looked tired and Julia guessed he wasn't faring any better than she was. He sighed. 'Olivia called. She won't be joining us. Apparently, she isn't well. Can't say I'm surprised – she threw up in the taxi on the way home. The driver wasn't amused.'

'I can imagine.'

'Yeah, I enjoyed myself, but it all got a bit out of hand, didn't it? Mixing your drinks is never a smart idea. We should've let the champagne go, or went with it because it was a celebration and stayed off everything else.' He laughed. 'Hindsight's a wonderful thing, isn't it? How are you?'

'Honestly, not good. In fact, not good would be great, if you know what I mean.'

'I do. I've been walking around the town since seven o'clock. Been here since eight. Some people claim a hair of the dog works wonders. Not in my case. Even the thought of alcohol is enough to have me running for the nearest sink.'

'Never again?'

'Ah, famous last words. No, I wouldn't go that far but not for a while, my system needs time to recover. Nice flowers, by the way.'

'Beautiful, aren't they? Tony certainly knows how to impress.'

Ravi hesitated; he didn't understand. 'Tony?'

'There isn't a note. I naturally assumed...'

'Tony had nothing to do with the flowers.'

'Really? Then, who did?'

'Ellis dropped them off shortly after I got here. Lord knows where he found a florist at that time of the morning. Unless he ordered them online and had them delivered to his place.'

Julia felt her cheeks flush. 'What did he say?'

'Nothing much, not even good morning. He put them on your desk and left.'

'That's strange. And you're sure he didn't mention the flowers?'

'Absolutely.'

'Where is he?'

'He muttered something about a day off.'

'Day off! He didn't run it by me!'

Ravi held up his hands. 'Don't shoot me, I'm just the messenger. I suppose he'd anticipated a heavy night and asked Tony. Have to admit the guy's timing is spot on. When I woke up I would've given my right arm for a day off work. Still would. I only turned up out of loyalty. Olivia's ill, Ellis is off – seems I'm in the minority.'

Julia had stopped listening, processing what she was hearing. 'Have I missed something? Let me get this straight. Ellis asked Tony if he could take today as a holiday. And Tony said yes. Tony is the boss and does whatever the hell he likes, I get that. But Ellis knows I'm his line manager and still cut me out of the loop.'

Ravi read the danger signs and didn't want to be involved. He said, 'I'm too scared of you to do anything like that.'

Julia wasn't in the mood for jokes; the designer's attempt at humour wasn't appreciated. He tried to change the subject. 'What do you want me on?'

She was still thinking about Tony Connors and Ellis Kirkbride and was distracted. 'What?'

'This morning, what should I work on?'

'Oh, right, the Edinburgh stuff until everybody's here and we can have a proper discussion about it.'

'Will do.' Ravi saw the dark clouds gather in Julia's eyes and wanted to be somewhere else when the storm broke. 'If you need me, I won't be hard to find.'

When he'd gone, Julia let her anger ebb before allowing herself to assess what she'd just learned. Twelve red roses – obviously, like her, Ellis considered what had happened on the Sky Bar's terrace a piece of silliness never to be repeated. The flowers were his way of saying there were no hard feelings, a sentiment Julia echoed, and she guessed not having to face each other while the embarrassing memory was fresh in their minds suited him every bit as much as it did her.

* * *

Whether Ravi was hard to find or not, Julia would never know, because she didn't go looking for him; she didn't have the energy. With Olivia sick and Ellis on holiday, her part of the building was unnaturally quiet. Even the incorrigible Tony Connors hadn't made an appearance, no doubt too vain to be seen at less than his best. By lunchtime the worst of the hangover was behind her and Julia felt sufficiently improved to go out into the fresh air. Eating wasn't an option, her stomach was still too delicate for food, but at a café in Gordon Street she bought a bottle of water and sat outside in the sunshine to watch an endless stream of black cabs dropping passengers at Central Station further up the street. For all the 'can do' excitement of The Buttery, the morning had been, without question, the least productive she'd ever had; frittering away an afternoon seemed pointless. Julia didn't need permission to bunk off. In that respect she was her own boss; nobody was checking up on her. Besides, bloody Grapevine got more of her time than it deserved, something she intended to remedy. As a courtesy, she called Tony's mobile to tell him she wouldn't be back. He didn't answer and the decision was made. She finished the water and started walking towards Trailfinders in St Vincent Street, suddenly feeling better than she had all day.

* * *

Julia counted the steps, all fifty-three of them, on her way down to the path and turned left towards the river. The brass band rehearsing in her head had packed up and gone home and her tummy had settled but the uneasy feeling hadn't gone. Her visit to Trailfinders had helped. She had collected an armful of brochures from a stand inside the door and was on her way out when she'd changed her mind and taken a seat until a smiling girl with an Australian accent had called her over and asked where she wanted to go: Julia hadn't been sure – she hadn't thought that far ahead – and had been surprised to hear herself say, 'Vietnam.' Forty minutes later she'd been on the pavement hailing a taxi, wondering if rice fields and temples, elephants and blood-red sunsets would fix them.

Rob didn't know it yet, but he was going to Asia.

Julia checked her laces were tied properly and started to run. She hadn't jogged in more than a week, and at first her under-used calf muscles complained, telling her to ease into her routine rather than be too ambitious. She took her usual route past the ruins of the North Woodside Flint Mill, trying and failing to keep a steady pace for the first time ever. The peacefulness hadn't worked its magic but her mind was clear – the previous night was a snapshot of somebody else's life. If she didn't want it to be become hers, things had to change now. If she'd learned anything it wasn't that champagne gave her a splitting headache – she'd already known that and chosen to disregard it, swept along in the heat of the moment – but rather that forgetting what was important had consequences.

The adage about marriage being something you had to work at had become a cliché because there was truth to it.

At the bottom of the steps a man stood under the bridge. Glasgow, like every big city, had its share of street people; this one unsettled her. He was tall, neither young nor old, not drunk or dressed in rags; vestiges of who he'd been in another life clung to him in the straight-back of a soldier and the dark-brown houndstooth coat, barely fit for a charity shop now, expensive when it was new. Julia would've preferred not to look at his face yet was drawn to it, and as she hurried by a light went out in his eyes, so obvious she almost turned to explain she wasn't carrying money.

A couple of noisy kids coming down the stairs distracted her and the moment passed.

* * *

Ellis leaned on the parapet of the Belmont Street Bridge. Glasgow had some nice spots; this was one of them. Afternoon sunshine split the trees on either side of the river but he wouldn't be taking photographs, not today; he had plenty. He was here simply as an old-fashioned admirer.

The information people gave away about themselves astonished him – ask a casual question and it came tumbling out. Julia liked to run. He knew because she'd told him in the pub, volunteering the where and when unprompted, teasing him with the prospect of seeing her sweating and out of breath. She might not have been aware of it but she'd been reaching out to him.

He'd followed her from the flat in Hamilton Drive to La Crosse Terrace and watched her go down the stone steps to the Kelvin Walkway. On anybody else the baggy grey tracksuit trimmed in blue would've been grungy. Not on her and Ellis wished he had brought his camera.

Her husband didn't run with her – another detail offered up for nothing. Well, more fool him; Rob didn't appreciate what he had. A man should support his woman in everything she did. Rob Sutherland wasn't that guy – whether he was greedy or stupid or both, Ellis hadn't decided.

She started slowly, allowing her muscles to warm up before increasing the pace. He stayed until she was out of sight – he'd seen what he wanted to see.

Julia was special; she wouldn't be with Rob Sutherland much longer.

17

Rob let the oncoming traffic pass, then steered the Peugeot into Hamilton Park Avenue. Yards from the flat he switched the engine off and sat staring at nothing. Hand on heart he could swear he hadn't been looking for an affair, though it was equally true he'd seized the opportunity when it arrived. Michelle had been everything he'd hoped for and more – exciting, liberating, an ego-boost for him as a lover and a man. Except, as he was discovering, it wasn't all upside. Rob would never get used to living a double life, terrified he'd blurt out some detail at odds with the lies he'd told.

Just how many times could he realistically claim to be working before Julia started to question him?

Plausibility wasn't something Michelle seemed overly bothered about. In the beginning they'd set the ground rules, agreeing not to take risks. There would be no demands, they'd promised each other, and absolutely no tantrums if arrangements had to be cancelled without notice. It was sex, nothing else, nice when it was there, over when it was over. Nobody was supposed to get hurt, although that wasn't how it was panning out.

When Michelle had thrown her arms around him, kissed him passionately and begged him to come to her place again tonight nothing could've stopped him. And yes, he'd known where it was heading, yet didn't care.

Rob tried to understand what had gone wrong with Julia.

The answer was nothing – it simply felt right with Michelle.

* * *

Persuading her workaholic husband to down tools wouldn't be easy, even if the destination was Ho Chi Minh City. Julia preferred its old name of Saigon. Much more romantic.

Her plan was simple: when he was on his third glass of wine and suitably mellow she'd tell him about her visit to Trailfinders, produce the brochures and an outline itinerary for their trip. His response was predictable: he'd hum-and-haw as he always did, tell her he had too much on, it 'wasn't the right moment', and all the other excuses she'd been accepting for far too long. This time she wasn't taking no for an answer.

After her run, Julia showered and sat in the lounge comparing prices and leafing through the pages of beautiful photographs, imagining the two of them kayaking down the Mekong River, wondering if perhaps you had to have a certain level of comfort in your life before you actively sought experiences that tested you physically and emotionally. The philosophical musing triggered a memory of the homeless man under the bridge. The streets of every big city were littered with people sleeping rough. This one was different: he hadn't been drunk or out of his head on drugs and she'd known that something, some personal tragedy perhaps, had taken him there. The look of total desolation in his eyes when she'd walked on had stayed with her. He'd lost hope.

She heard the front door close and hid the brochures on the bottom shelf of the TV console. Rob was pale; he looked tired. However much he protested, Julia knew they needed to get away from Glasgow to recharge their batteries. She poured a glass of the Marlborough Sauvignon Blanc she'd already opened and handed it to her husband.

'Are you hungry? Hope so.'

Rob sighed. 'I haven't really thought about it.'

'Well, dinner will be ready in five minutes. I can push it back to ten if you want to jump into the shower.'

He shook his head. 'No, that would take more energy than I've got. What is it, anyway?'

Julia grinned. 'What do you care? It's food. Why didn't you eat the casserole I left for you last night?'

Rob hesitated. 'What? Oh, I was exhausted and went to bed early. Please tell me that isn't what we're having.'

'No, it's pork with my secret sauce.'

'You mean a tin of Campbell's mushroom soup – am I right?'

'That was a lucky guess. We haven't had it for ages. I'm surprised you remembered.'

'Is this your subtle way of reprimanding me?'

She wanted to say, yes, absolutely, instead she kissed his forehead and loosened his tie. 'Nothing subtle about it. Meals are better shared and we've missed too many. Did you hear me come in last night? Sorry if I woke you up.'

Rob lied. 'No, I was sound. Was it good? Did you enjoy it?'

She took his hand and led him to the kitchen. 'Good isn't how I'd describe it and if my head this morning was anything to go by I enjoyed it too much.' She raised a glass of bubbles very different from the ones she'd been drinking in the restaurant. 'Which is why I'm on sparkling water now. Sit down. Let's eat.'

* * *

They were curled up on the sofa in what a romantic novelist would call 'companionable silence'. Rob toyed with the stem of his glass. 'This secret sauce of yours, who else knows about it?'

'Just us... and the million or so people on Campbell's social media platforms – why?'

'Because it was really tasty. Maybe you should ring the changes, try it with cream of chicken?'

'Try it yourself.'

'Where would I find the time?'

'What... to open a tin of soup?'

'By the time I'd discovered where we keep the tin opener you'd have died from starvation. Besides, you know how busy I am.'

'Exactly, too busy, and we have to do something about it.'

Julia untangled herself from him and brought over the brochures. Rob sat up, immediately defensive. 'Is this what I think it is? Because—'

'Because nothing, Rob Sutherland. We need a break. *I* need a break. And we're having one whether you like it or not. I got these today. I'm thinking three weeks in Vietnam.'

'Three weeks! Not possible. Two's the most I can get, if that.'

'Then start looking for a new job. The firm you work for has done all right out of you. Now it's your turn. Three weeks – and think yourself lucky I'm not insisting on a month.'

'Are you sure Grapevine will let you have three weeks? I mean—'

'They will if they want to keep me. This is important for us, surely you realise that? Or don't we matter anymore?'

'Of course we do, but be reasonable, how much will it cost?'

The beggar flashed into Julia's head again. She remembered the look in his eyes, the saddest thing she'd ever seen and understood. Unwittingly she'd dealt the final blow and he was done. Down as far as he could go.

She leapt to her feet. 'Put your shoes on.'

'Why? Where are we going?'

'Don't ask, just do it. And bring your wallet.'

'My wallet?'

Outside, Rob had to sprint to keep up with her and didn't appreciate it. Julia waited for him at the steps and tried to explain. 'I met a homeless man today when I was jogging and haven't been able to get him out of my mind. You asking how much it cost reminded me. Here we are, about to spend thousands, and this poor guy...'

She couldn't say the words out loud.

Rob lost it. 'I've no idea what you're talking about. You saw a junkie and felt sorry for him, so what? Glasgow's full of them. What the hell has that got to do with us?'

Julia carried on as though he hadn't spoken. 'His eyes, Rob, there was nothing in them, nothing at all. He'd totally given up. I can't begin to imagine how terrible that must feel, can you?'

'No, I can't and I don't want to.'

'Whatever dreams he'd had were gone and they weren't coming back. This was it: his life was a procession of endless days of misery and squalor, and it didn't matter. What must that be like?'

Rob didn't answer; he couldn't.

Julia said, 'How much money have you got?'

'Fifty, maybe sixty pounds.'

'C'mon. Give it to me.'

The light was fading from the sky as night settled over the city. At the bottom of the stairs Julia peered into the shadows where she'd seen the man earlier in the day. Behind her, Rob was uneasy. 'This is a job for social services, not us.'

She ignored him and spoke to the darkness. 'Hello. Is anybody there?'

When there was no reply, Rob said, 'You've missed him. He's moved on.'

Julia moved closer and asked again. 'I can't see you. Are you there?'

They heard the rustle and Julia stepped nervously forward. 'I met you this afternoon and wanted to apologise for walking by. If it's all right, we'd like to give you something.' The homeless guy pulled his coat around him and Julia edged closer. His eyes weren't empty now – they darted between her and Rob, wary and mistrusting. She saw the suspicion in them and kept going. 'It isn't much but it might help a bit. Please take it.'

Rob wasn't happy with where this was going. He whispered, 'For Christ's sake, Julia, this is madness.'

She ignored him and pressed the banknotes into the guy's hand. His fingers closed round them and, with a nod that said nothing and everything, retreated into the shadows.

Back in the flat Rob poured himself a stiff whisky. He hadn't said a word. That was about to change and Julia didn't blame him. He'd been dragged against his will into a situation he was uncomfortable with and was understandably furious. His tone was stiff and distant. 'Care to tell me what the hell that little fiasco was all about?'

'Of course. The man we've just left lives a life that, if we're fortunate, we'll never know. Flicking through those travel brochures reminded me that, while I was considering spending thousands of pounds on a trip, he didn't even have a bed to sleep in.'

Rob stared into the glass and Julia realised she wasn't reaching him. He said, 'All very admirable but I don't get what it has to do with you and me.'

'Don't you? I should've thought it was obvious. That guy didn't start out under a bridge but that's where he's ended.'

Rob finished his drink and poured a refill, angrily splashing whisky into the glass. 'What's your point, Julia – that life isn't fair? Then my advice would be to grow up. We've worked hard for what we have. I refuse to feel guilty about it.'

Sometimes Rob could be thick. 'It isn't about guilt and it isn't about possessions. It isn't even about doing some good in the world.'

He lost his temper and shouted across the room. 'Then I've no idea what you're saying to me!'

'Gratitude. It's about gratitude. Realising what's really important is nurturing each other, making the other person happy because we love them. *And*, yes, being thankful we aren't living under a bridge.'

The fire had gone out of Rob though the cynic was still there. He said, 'And that's why you had me running after you to give some poor unfortunate man a couple of quid. I feel sorry for him, of course, who wouldn't? But whether it's sixty pounds or sixty thousand you must know it'll go the same way. He'll blow it on drink or drugs. Probably both.'

'I don't believe that but, if it's what he needs right now, I'm not going to judge.'

He shook his head. 'You mean well, Julia, but what you did tonight won't make any difference.'

The put-down, arrogant and condescending, incensed her; she rounded on him. 'You're wrong, Rob, it's already made a difference. It's made a difference to me. And if you can't see that you're not the Rob Sutherland I married.'

'Julia—'

'What the hell has happened to you?'

'I'm stating facts. You may not like them but—'

'That isn't what you're doing. You've turned into a callous bastard, somebody I don't recognise and certainly don't want to spend the rest of my life with.'

The rebuke left Rob visibly shaken. For a minute they stared at each other in silence across the room. Julia's bottom lip trembled, tears welled in her eyes, but she didn't allow herself to cry.

Seeing his wife upset, knowing he was to blame, brought Rob to his senses. 'Please, I hate it when you cry.'

She folded her arms and turned away. 'Don't flatter yourself. I'm sad because you used to be a guy with a good heart – one of the reasons I fell for you.'

'I still am, of course I am, and I'm sorry, you're absolutely right – we should do anything we can to help people less fortunate than ourselves. No question.'

'You say that but do you believe it?'

'Yes, 100 per cent. It's just that I've so much on my mind these days it's easy to lose perspective.' He smiled. 'Lucky for me I have you to bring me back to the centre.'

Julia seized the opportunity. 'And that's the whole point, isn't it? I've been thinking about us a lot recently. We're in too much of a hurry to get where we want to go and blind to where we are.' She glanced at the travel brochures on the coffee table. 'Being together is all I care about. If we can't find time for that, then...'

He reassured her. 'We will, we will. And a trip is a great idea – God knows we deserve it. Let's get it booked before our diaries become impossible.'

'So, Vietnam?'

'Vietnam's fine with me. I've always wanted to go there. How much notice will Grapevine need?'

'Well, we have to finish the current project – any time after that.' Julia laughed. 'Tony would have me working 24/7. He won't like it when I tell him but it's his choice – he can let me go on a holiday we desperately need, or find somebody else to do my job. I don't mind either way because we'll be sitting on plastic seats at the side of a road somewhere eating out of a bowl.'

Rob put his arm around her. 'You know, what you did with that home-less guy tonight was fantastic.'

She shrugged the compliment away. 'Nobody deserves a medal for doing the right thing. You saw him. Did he look like an addict to you?'

'No, he didn't.'

'Yet, there he was, under a bridge. It gave me a jolt. We've talked and talked about our priorities without actually doing anything to change them. Standing there in his old coat with that look of abject desolation in his eyes was like a warning to us.'

Rob's mobile buzzed: Michelle. He pressed reject and turned the phone off. Julia said, 'You should answer. It might be important.'

'That's the trouble, isn't it? It's always bloody important. I'll deal with it tomorrow. The problem will still be there, it usually is.'

* * *

The rest of the evening was like old times. Julia quickly forgot she'd sworn off alcohol and helped Rob finish the wine. He was in great form, standing in the middle of the lounge, glass in one hand, bottle in the other, telling stories about his colleagues, doing impressions of them that made her laugh. She said, 'Actually, you spend so much time there, I assumed you liked it.'

'Like it? You're having a laugh. I can't stand it or them.'

'I'm surprised. I'd no idea. Why put up with it?'

The humour left him; Rob suddenly became serious. 'Because that's life, what you do if you want to get on.'

'Nobody's forcing you to do it.'

'You're right, they aren't. It's the price we pay for how we live.'

'Then it isn't worth it. Happiness can't depend on how much money is in our bank account.'

'Thank God for that or we'd be sharing that bridge with the homeless guy.'

'You know what I'm saying, Rob.'

'Yes, of course I do and I agree, though you have to admit, it helps. Take this Vietnam trip. When you mentioned it, practically the first thing

I asked was how much it would cost. The truth is that with our salaries it doesn't matter. I was avoiding the real issue.'

'Which is?'

'Fear. There's so much to do at work, going on holiday wouldn't feel right.'

'Okay, I get that but where does fear come in?'

'They might discover they don't need me as much as they thought they did and that would be the end of all this. Goodbye West End flat.'

'I'd still love you. "For richer, for poorer" and all that.'

He grinned. 'Well, I'd rather not put it to the test, if you don't mind. Let's go to bed while we still have a roof over our heads.'

In the bedroom, Rob had the shower he'd put off earlier. Julia waited for him. A day that had started with her feeling like death had ended with a breakthrough. Tomorrow she wasn't looking forward to telling the news about Vietnam to Tony; he wouldn't be pleased. Too bad.

Her phone pinged on the bedside table. Julia considered following Rob's example and ignoring it. Curiosity got the better of her; she picked it up and read the two words followed by a kiss.

Nite Nite x

It was from Ellis.

18

'Nite Nite x'.

Thinking about it made her shudder: the Sky Bar had been a moment of madness, no more than that; an embarrassing slip best forgotten for the sake of everyone concerned. And those bloody flowers! She'd naïvely assumed they were Ellis's over-the-top way of saying he understood the kiss had been inappropriate. Wrong. The clue had been there; she'd missed it. He'd given her roses, red roses, the symbol of love and passion. Added to the text message, a complication she didn't need.

Driving into work, Julia blotted out all thoughts of what might be waiting for her in Bothwell Street. When she arrived she took the stairs rather than the lift to postpone the confrontation a bit longer and nervously opened her office door half expecting to see Ellis.

The roses were on the desk in their water balloon where she'd left them, but he wasn't around. She sighed, made herself a black coffee and sat down to review her options: she could ignore the flowers and the text, behave as though it was business as usual, and hope whatever was going on died a natural death. Or – and this alternative certainly had appeal – given Ellis had been presented as a fait accompli and shoehorned onto the team with no input from her, she would be justified in dumping the problem on Tony to let him sort it out.

Except she had, however briefly, kissed him back and her boss would use that to return the problem to her court, where it belonged.

The disquieting truth was that somewhere along the line Ellis had misread the situation, ignored the fact that she was married and come on to her in the Radisson. As his boss it was her responsibility to put him straight without humiliating him. The guy had made a mistake. It happened. Taking him aside for a quiet word was the obvious approach, though if he actually believed she'd encouraged him the chances of it ending well weren't good.

At eight twenty-five she heard footsteps in the corridor and braced herself. It might be Ravi, Olivia or even Tony Connors, but if it was Ellis Julia had decided it was better to get the conversation they inevitably had to have over with so they could put it behind them and carry on with the day. It would be awkward, worse than awkward, excruciating for both of them. Nobody would come out of it feeling good about themselves – Ellis would stare red-faced at his shoes while she reassured him what they were discussing wouldn't go any further, that the subject would be closed.

It didn't happen.

Ellis appeared at the door with something under his arm and smiled when he saw her. Julia caught the look on his face and felt a shaft of fear pass through her. She edged back as far as her chair would let her and found she was trapped between the desk and the wall.

Ellis grabbed her wrists, whispering, 'Julia, my darling, you've no idea how much I've missed you.'

'What? Ellis! Get off me!'

She pushed him away, close to panic as words tumbled from his mouth in an insane cascade. 'When you didn't reply to my text I thought he'd read it and almost came to your house.'

'Come to my house? How dare you?'

Ellis hurried to explain. 'I was worried he might harm you.'

'Harm me? Who gave you that idea? Rob wouldn't harm me.'

'He might if he knew about us.'

Julia couldn't help herself. 'Us? There is no us! What the hell are you talking about?'

Her reaction shocked him. He said, 'I... I... don't understand. I thought...'

'What's got into you? You've just assaulted me. Do you realise that? I should call the police.'

'No, I haven't. How could you even think that? I love you. You know I do.'

'I don't know anything of the kind. This is insane!'

'The other night—'

Julia interrupted. 'Was a mistake, a silly mistake we made because we were drunk.' She appealed to him. 'Surely you realised that? You can't really think—'

'I bought you flowers.' He held out the box in his hand. 'And chocolates.'

The response was pathetic and Julia saw she was dealing with someone who wasn't right in the head. Unless she took the heat out of the situation there was no knowing where this might go. She spoke slowly, the way she would to a child. 'And I appreciate it, Ellis, I really do, but honestly, you've read more into it than there was.'

'Really? Have I? That's a surprise. You kissed me back. Don't say you didn't.'

This was crazy. The quiet word she'd imagined she'd be having with him hadn't materialised – he'd turned the spotlight on her. Julia held up her hands to placate him. 'Okay, okay. For a few seconds, yes, I won't deny it.'

Ellis lowered his head and nodded; he seemed relieved. 'At last. You felt it, didn't you? The same as I did, you felt it.'

'Then I came to my senses and left. You have to agree that's what happened.'

'Maybe, but not before we kissed. You wanted me. If we'd been alone, somewhere else...'

Julia tried to speak and couldn't; the story he was telling was fantastical and, frighteningly, he was convinced it was true. He saw her weaken and moved closer. 'Admit it. Say it.'

'I can't. We were drunk – that's all there was to it – and when I realised what we were doing, I stopped.'

A knock on the door startled them. Ravi stuck his head round the frame. 'Everything all right, Julia?'

Julia ached to reply that, no, everything wasn't all right and ask him to stay. Instead, she said, 'Fine, Ravi. We were having a creative disagreement and got carried away. Nothing to worry about.'

Ravi eyed Ellis up and down with undisguised disbelief. 'Fair enough. Remember, if you need me I won't be far away.'

'That won't be necessary. Ellis was just leaving.'

When the designer had gone, she whispered, 'Ravi was probably out there from the beginning. He'll tell Olivia, she'll tell somebody else... in an hour the rumours will be all...' Julia put her head in her hands and broke down. 'Oh, God, what've we done?'

Ellis was unmoved. 'Is that *we* as in *us*?'

'Stop, please stop!'

'Lying makes people ugly, even you, Julia. There was a connection from day one. Tell me I'm wrong. Convince me you weren't touched by it.'

'I wasn't, then or now. Would you prefer I opened the window and shouted it?'

'In the pub—'

'In the pub we were two people unwinding over a drink. You'd been very honest about what had happened in Cape Town. It was awful to hear how you'd been hurt and I sympathised. I liked you.'

Ellis gave a derisive little laugh. 'You liked me. Praise, indeed. I have to say, Julia, I thought about us and didn't see this coming. Not how I usually am at all.'

'You seemed nice, a guy who'd come through a tough time, so of course I liked you. But as a colleague – no more than that. I made no secret of the fact I was married. When I got home I even told my husband about you.'

Ellis smiled at some private joke he didn't offer to share. 'By the way, how is old Rob? Still working every hour under the sun?'

Hearing him use her husband's name pushed Julia over the line and suddenly she'd had enough of Ellis Kirkbride and his ridiculous schoolboy fantasy. 'Leave him out of this!'

Ellis pretended she'd hurt his feelings. 'I'm only asking. Where's the harm in that?'

'Don't! Don't ask anything! There isn't anything you could say I want to listen to. Leave right now and this unhinged conversation goes no further. Keep on with it and I'll tell Tony.'

'Oooohhh! I'm shaking in my shoes.'

'You should be because he'll believe me.'

'I wouldn't be so certain about that. It'll be your word against mine.'

'I'll take my chances. Advertising is a reputation business and this is the twenty-first century – sexual harassment in the workplace or anywhere else is taboo. If Grapevine's clients were to discover the founder and managing director had known a female employee was being harassed on his watch and done nothing about it they'd publicly distance themselves as fast as their PR departments could cobble a statement together and leave in their droves. Overnight, Grapevine would cease to exist. It's called damage limitation, Ellis. Tony only cares about what's good for his company. As for Rob, never compare yourself to him. He's everything you'll never be – and I love him with every breath I take. Now, get out of my office.'

* * *

From the bay window of his office in Park Circus Rob watched the driver of a black Merc struggle to find a parking space for his expensive jalopy. After three unsuccessful circuits he gave up and drove off, probably cursing his misfortune, conveniently forgetting the car cost north of £90,000. High-class problems, indeed, and he recalled the homeless man. Julia had forced him, otherwise he wouldn't have been anywhere near the guy. His reaction had revealed a side of himself Rob wasn't proud of. He'd become the kind of person he'd always hated – aloof and living in a bubble, out of touch with what other less fortunate people had to deal with, convinced whatever they'd achieved was the result of their own talents and work ethics. Tossers. For most people, the truth was too terrifying to contemplate – a fork in the road, a lapse of judgement or plain bad luck and they'd be under that bridge.

As for a lapse in judgement, why in God's name had Michelle called him at home? Julia could've overheard or, worse, taken the call and the S.H.I.T. really would've hit the fan. Dissatisfaction had made her bold – and reckless – because contacting him when he was home with his wife had crossed the line.

Rob was angry and would've preferred not to speak to her but if he didn't return her call she'd try again. Perhaps, if he still didn't answer, she'd give it one more go and assume he hadn't the guts to tell her to her face that he was ending the affair. Michelle would curse herself for being a fool – might even cry herself to sleep – but it would be over, he'd never see her again, and they could fly off to Vietnam, Cambodia, or wherever Julia fancied.

One woman would be disappointed, the other could start planning which clothes to wear in Hanoi. Except, it wasn't quite so simple. The thought of Michelle alone and unhappy didn't make him feel good. The opposite – he couldn't imagine life without her now.

Outside in Park Circus the Mercedes was back in time to compete with a blue Lexus for a space about to be vacated by a Tesla Model Y. Both drivers vied for an advantage; the macho-bullshit performance was unnecessary. Glasgow was full of parking places – why put themselves through the stress?

Shouldn't he be asking himself the same question?

His mobile buzzed. Caller ID confirmed it was her.

He lifted the phone. Before he could speak, Michelle jumped in. 'Rob. Rob, I'm sorry. What I did was... I can't explain... you must be so angry with me. What if your wife had answered? It doesn't bear thinking about. This will sound pathetic – it *is* pathetic – but I was lonely and needed to hear your voice. It won't happen again. No matter how low I feel I'll leave you in peace. Can you forgive me? That's all I need to know? Please, please, forgive me.'

At the other end of the line she was crying. He said, 'Of course, I forgive you, but you must understand we got lucky. Julia can't find out. She doesn't deserve that.'

'I do, Rob, I do. I was afraid you wouldn't want to see me again.'

'I'm trying to be straight with you, Michelle.'

Rob could hear her sobbing like a little girl on the other end of the line, a world away from the woman in the Hilton. She said, 'What I did was selfish and stupid. It could've cost you everything.'

Her regret was genuine and he said, 'People make mistakes – we all do. If we learn, we'll be okay.'

'I thought I'd lost you. Tell me I haven't.'

He sighed. 'No, Michelle, you haven't lost me. I'm here.'

'Oh, Rob, you've no idea how much that means.'

'From now on I'll ring every morning as soon as I'm in the car.'

'Really?'

'Really. A few hours at your place isn't fair on you. Let's have lunch or even coffee rather than jumping into bed every time we meet. How does that sound?'

'It sounds wonderful. And I won't call again when I'm not supposed to.'

'Promise?'

'Cross my heart and hope to die.'

The line went dead. Rob pressed his fingers against his temple, not able to process what had just happened.

He knew the answer: it wasn't about Julia or Michelle, it was about him – he loved both of them, but, bigger than that, he was drawn to the danger. Walking outside the lines, making love to one woman while thinking about another, was exciting and he couldn't let it go.

19

Ellis was standing on waste ground beside what he assumed to be the banks of the Clyde near a semi-derelict warehouse or factory, long abandoned. The structure's principal surviving feature was a brick tower with the name Glassford painted across the top third in a black-and-white band. Ellis had no idea how he'd got there; the last thing he remembered was Julia threatening to go to Tony Connors and the withering comparison with her husband. In flashes exploding behind his eyes he saw himself running towards Central Station, bumping like a drunk man into a passer-by, almost falling but stumbling on.

That had been in the morning. Now, the sky above Glasgow was darkening, the fever or whatever possessed him had broken and released him from its grasp in this forgotten part of the city. Where the hell had he been all this time?

He was wet from head to foot, strands of hair matted his forehead and there was mud on his palms, between his fingers, even under his nails; everything he was wearing was covered in the stuff. An odour thick with decay reached him. He recoiled from the stench, sickened, and by sheer willpower forced himself not to retch. He sat on a pile of bricks at the end of a collapsed wall and wiped filth off his shirt and trousers. There was an explanation, there had to be – he'd strayed too close to the bank and slipped? Probable, except that still didn't account for the gap in his memory or why he was at the river in the first place.

He shivered, folded his arms round his body, and realised he'd lost his jacket – his wallet was in the pocket, and his phone, so they were gone, too. In other circumstances, losing credit cards would be a mini-disaster. Now it hardly registered. More than anything it was not being in control that freaked him out and the agonising recognition that, yet again, he'd picked the wrong woman.

Julia had talked about her happy marriage; Ellis had had no reason to disbelieve her. But when he'd told the fairy tale about the woman in South Africa, biting back hurt, faltering in all the right places, he'd watched her expression soften and detected an attraction between them that was entirely mutual.

They'd had a few bumps but those were just the teething problems all new relationships went through. And he certainly hadn't misunderstood the Sky Bar.

Ellis revisited his memory of the confrontation in her office and anger welled inside him. After all the things he'd done, nice things like letting her take credit on the campaign they were developing when it had actually been his idea, Julia had humiliated him in front of that smug bastard Ravi of all people. Only a bitch would do that. Blaming her behaviour on alcohol and having second thoughts about the kiss weren't good enough excuses.

As for accusing him of sexual harassment – when he'd kissed her, she'd kissed him back: fact! The grand opinion of her husband she'd thrown in his face would change pretty damn quickly if she knew what Ellis knew, and the wayward Rob's reaction to his wife's little romantic interlude on the Sky Bar terrace would be interesting to say the least.

As the shadows lengthened Ellis closed his eyes. He was exhausted, more depressed than he'd been since those final few hours in Africa. In the silence, a truth came to him, so obvious it was hard to credit he hadn't seen it earlier. Her impassioned over-the-top crap about 'Every breath I take' wasn't true even if she believed it. The marriage was a sham, a faithless union he had unwittingly stumbled into. Whether they were aware of it or not, Julia and Rob Sutherland were incapable of fidelity: they deserved each other.

Why Ellis had been in the river wasn't a question he could answer and, perhaps, that was for the best – he'd blacked out and lost a day, for the moment as much as he needed to know. With no wallet, no money and no mobile, he had a long walk to his flat in front of him. It began to rain and, ridiculous as it was given the state he was in, his instinct was to look for shelter. He found it behind a pillar of the derelict building and Ellis took stock of his surroundings: the floor was slabbed in stone, cracked, overgrown with weeds and pieces of brick, the Victorian walls – what remained of them – gathered everywhere in crumbling piles. Apart from a few bent corrugated sheets the roof was open to the night sky.

In its prime, this old place had no doubt known many incarnations. In its heyday, alive with activity, it might've been used for bleaching, textiles, a match factory, even a tobacco warehouse; Ellis would never know, but at some point an attempt had been made to salvage anything of value from the dereliction including lead from the roof.

At the far side of the site, a twenty-foot steel container offered no clue. Seeing it sparked something in him. He approached cautiously, wary of what it might hide. The original grey paint had been breached, exposing the metal underneath. Ellis guessed the lifespan of these things was twenty-five or thirty years. This one looked as if it had been here for at least a couple of decades. The doors were closed, secured by a slide-bolt on each side. He hesitated before flipping up the tabs on the locking bars and pulling. Age welded them in place. It took three attempts before the rust cracked and they gave. A blast of putrid air forced him to step back; Ellis let it clear. In the poor light it was impossible to make out anything beyond the shards of green glass and old wine bottles on the floor, but he saw enough to make him smile. He'd spent weeks, sometimes months, wrestling unsuccessfully with a marketing idea only for the solution to suddenly arrive fully formed. And so it was again.

He laughed out loud at his genius. 'Every breath you take, Mrs Sutherland – well, that can be arranged.'

20

The long trek home had been uneventful. He'd kept to the shadows, ducking out of sight if headlights appeared in the distance in case it was the police, remaining concealed until he was certain it wasn't before going on; the state he was in would take some explaining and Ellis didn't need questions he couldn't answer.

When he finally arrived at his flat pink streaks flecked the sky to the east but over the city it was still dark; he hurriedly undressed, tossed his stinking clothes into the washing machine and showered. Suddenly, Ellis was hungry – and not just hungry, ravenous. Rather than make a sandwich, he cut a block of Cheddar into slices and ate them one after another standing naked in his kitchen, downed half a pint of milk straight from the carton and wiped the white from around his lips with his fingers.

He should've been exhausted, yet he'd never felt more alive.

Ellis Kirkbride was wired: high on retribution.

He felt so powerful he might never sleep again. How could he when his mind was alive with possibilities? Drugs had never been his thing – he disliked both the idea of them and the type of people they attracted. He had his drug of choice and its name was revenge.

Julia would expect a reaction from him – he wouldn't give her the satisfaction. Instead, he'd behave as if nothing were amiss, until it was time to teach her a painful lesson. First, he had to check if what he was planning was feasible rather than a pleasant fantasy.

On his way out he lifted cash and the spare car keys from the drawer in the bedside cabinet where he kept them and went to find a taxi to take him to his car – assuming it was still in the underground garage where he'd left it yesterday.

* * *

Ellis kicked a piece of crumbled brick across the stone floor, watching until it disappeared into the long grass, and silently nodded his approval. The scene that had greeted him when he'd emerged from the blackout, wet and covered in filth, was everything he'd hoped it would be. Last night it had been an alien landscape; this morning the bleak industrial wasteland was a friend. He'd walked the deserted streets to the city in the rain, barely aware of it, preoccupied with his new plan. The more he'd thought about it, the better he'd liked it and, in spite of being soaked to the skin, Ellis had smiled.

In the early-morning light what little remained of the building stood against the sky like an iron skeleton from another age. Ellis's confidence faltered; he was close to dismissing the plan as far-fetched, until he saw the battered shipping container again and knew he was onto something. What he had in mind required privacy; this place was perfect: the uneven land ran from the river to a high wall on three sides, the entrance barred by a padlocked mesh gate meant to keep people out. It hadn't succeeded – a faded 'No Trespassers' sign lay on the ground and a hole had been cut in the wire, probably by kids who'd seen this as an ideal playground. The metal gate had been there so long the youngsters who'd forced their way in might have children of their own. Ellis studied the opposite bank and saw nothing to concern him. Flats would've meant prying eyes and a problem; there were none. He'd neither seen nor heard traffic since turning off the main road – and why would there be? What was there to bring anybody to this place? Last, he checked the buildings on the far side. The windows were either shuttered or broken; whatever businesses they'd been home to had called it a day and ceased trading.

Finally, he approached what had set the whole thing off and felt a nervous flutter in his gut. It all depended on this. He paced around the container, photographing it from every angle, assessing whether what he had in mind would work or if it was too out there, even for him.

He opened the tabs and pushed the slide-bars. Last night, fused together by disuse, they'd resisted, but today they moved apart smoothly. Ellis opened the right-hand door, then the left, and assessed what he was looking at. The wine bottles and the shattered glass were where they'd been, along with the badly decomposed body of an animal – a cat or a large rat – matted on the floor. Ellis sucked air through his teeth, nodded approvingly a second time. He'd expected worse – much worse – and was glad to discover he'd been wrong. All things considered it was in better condition internally than on the outside. When the site had finally been abandoned, whoever was last to leave hadn't taken the unit with them. Under his breath, Ellis thanked them.

He hauled himself onto the roof and knelt over the edge to examine a louvre air vent set high up in a long wall. The slats were fixed, never intended to be moved – a difficulty, though not insurmountable; for what he was planning to work obstacles would have to be identified and overcome.

Ellis scanned the Clyde, wondering if the river was a complication, still not 100 per cent convinced. All it would take was some over-eager tourist with binoculars to put paid to the whole thing. The easiest solution, the smart solution, would be to forget this mad notion and quit Grapevine. Leave. Right now.

He stared across the waste ground as a new day came up over Glasgow. There was a future for him here if he could hold onto it. The lady he was searching for – the one he'd always been searching for – who wouldn't betray his trust, was out there.

The sky was brightening. His thoughts returned to why he'd come again to this godforsaken spot: Julia Sutherland and her cheating husband. Ellis had offered her a chance at real happiness with someone who'd love her forever the way she deserved to be loved and she'd rejected it. Yet, Julia and the others before her were only part of his pain. How Ellis felt went back, way back, to a hysterical child crying for his mother, powerless as she walked away from him.

His father had been destroyed by his wife's desertion. Ellis had tried to erase from his memory the woman who'd given him life. But the idea of who she'd once been remained the standard every female since had been judged against and found wanting.

He raised the viewfinder to his eye and took a shot of the rusted metal box.

CLICK.

Julia and Rob's cosy world was about to come crashing down.

As for quitting, if it had ever been an option it sure as hell wasn't one now.

* * *

Julia had decided to deal with the problem at Grapevine by herself and not share the drama with Rob, who was sure to ask questions she couldn't answer without the whole story coming out. Most of the time Rob was a pussycat, as mild-mannered as anyone you could meet, but underneath was a fiery temper he'd learned to control. Telling him Ellis had tried it on with his wife would unleash that temper and when she admitted she'd kissed Ellis back it could only end one way; Rob would go crazy. Julia didn't judge her husband – if the positions were reversed and he'd behaved like that at the Christmas party, he'd be spending the night in the spare room.

She'd been awake when he'd left and heard him moving around the flat but pretended to be asleep. Rob would only have to catch her in an unguarded moment to realise something was wrong. And it was. Very wrong. She desperately needed somebody to talk to. Without Rob, there was no one.

Her charming, handsome colleague was a sexual predator and an ambitious one at that. But she wasn't some teenage kid in a short skirt who'd only been five minutes out in the world. No! She was his boss. Any reasonable person would've seen the kiss for what it was: a drunken misstep. If Ellis Kirkbride had realised that, they wouldn't be here.

The rooftop fiasco was one thing – it was what had come later that worried Julia. She hadn't known Ellis long, yet the clues to who he was and what he was capable of had been in plain sight from the beginning. She could only speculate on how many gullible women he'd drawn into his orbit with flowers and chocolates and heartbreaking yarns intended to get their sympathy. His other targets might have handled it differently – she'd stood her ground, although the throwaway comment about 'old Rob' hadn't escaped her.

Was he insinuating something or merely tossing doubt into the equation? These days she wasn't short of that.

Either way it had failed, leaving the problem of how she could continue to work with an individual who'd shown himself to be calculated and unscrupulous. Tony should've been her first port of call, except the MD identified proudly as a dinosaur and had already proved his support couldn't be relied on when Ellis had openly bullied her over not working late.

In a he said/she said situation, her chances of being believed were zero.

Julia was understandably reluctant to make a complaint or take the matter further. By the time Tony had listened to Ellis Kirkbride's twisted version of events, Ellis would be the victim and she'd be on the wrong end of a lecture about conduct in the workplace; she could even lose her job. Try going home and telling Rob she'd been fired for sexually harassing a member of her team.

* * *

Julia saw Tony before he saw her. The MD hadn't been around since paying for the drinks at the Sky Bar and leaving early. He strode down Bothwell Street wearing a black leather jacket she guessed had cost more than she earned in a couple of months. He didn't say hello and acknowledged her with a curt nod. Julia shuddered: in the time she'd worked with him, whenever they'd met there had always been a minute or two of casual chit-chat before Tony morphed into 'the boss'. She wanted to blurt out that she could explain and what he'd been told wasn't how it had been. Instead, Julia pretended there was a problem with her shoe and let him go into the lift by himself.

Tony held the door until she was ready – this couldn't be happening.

She was used to him breezily tossing out sexist observations. When he didn't paranoia kicked into high gear: Ellis – the devious swine – had told him about the kiss, missing out all the horrible stuff he'd said and done. Everything Julia had imagined was coming true. Obviously, Tony had believed him. She expected to be summoned to his office and... Julia didn't want to think where that would go.

Tony broke into her nightmare. 'So, what did I miss?'

'Sorry, Tony?'

'After I'd gone. C'mon, spill, give me the goss. What's their names... Ravi and young Olivia... are they a thing?'

'I... I... don't know what you mean.'

'You don't...' He was unaware of the terror in her eyes and shot a quizzical look at her.

'Oh, no, for Christ's sake, Julia. Don't tell me you made a bloody idiot of yourself. You're the team leader. I expect you to be setting an example. My God, if you can't handle alcohol at your age you're never going to. My advice, for what it's worth – leave it alone. And yeah, people will assume you're an alkie and talk about you behind your back, but who cares about what they think, right?'

Julia said, 'You're joking, aren't you? This is you being funny?'

The MD was enjoying himself too much and carried on. 'What did Rob say?' Tony answered his own question. 'Though what is there to say when your wife falls in the door?'

Julia lost her temper. 'Stop! Please stop, you're upsetting me! Rob didn't say anything because there was nothing *to* say. And if you're trying to be funny it's time someone told you it isn't working.'

'Julia—'

'No, Tony. Enough with the superior humour. I'm sick of it.'

'I was simply trying to bring a little a.m. levity to the daily grind.'

'The daily grind will survive just fine without it, and so will I. Now, if you'll excuse me, this is my floor.'

In her office Julia slumped behind the desk and put her head in her hands, fighting back tears. She'd enjoyed working at Grapevine, loved it, actually: the hours were long, the clients were demanding, but there was a sense of achievement when a campaign they'd slaved over went live. Every day was different from the one before and managing her team had been a joy. All enough to ignore Tony Connors' *Jurassic Park* impersonations. And on the odd occasion when he dropped the act, underneath she'd discovered a good guy not keen to come out. To a natural-born chauvinist like Tony, all females were neurotic. Her outburst would confirm that opinion; Julia groaned at the thought. Tony was an insensitive clown, no argument, though he couldn't know how fragile she was. As for his own behaviour, Tony was just being Tony, wasn't he?

It was her husband's reaction she was most worried about. If she blamed her sacking on being unwilling to stand for the MD's inappropriate comments, it would lay the responsibility squarely with Grapevine. Rob would rave about unfair dismissal and threaten to hire an employment lawyer but, in the end, the truth would surface and he'd wonder if he actually knew the woman he'd married.

She heard voices, went to the door, and looked out. Across the hall Ellis and Ravi were bent over a Mac animatedly discussing the Hogmanay images, nodding and pointing to the screen. Julia hadn't spoken to Ravi about the scene he'd interrupted in her office, nor did she intend to – the best outcome for all concerned would be to push past it and move on.

Ellis was absorbed in what they were doing and appeared to have come to the same conclusion. He shouted, 'Morning, Julia,' as though yesterday hadn't happened and flashed a smile at her. Julia retreated to her office, nauseated. He might look normal but there was something badly amiss with Ellis Kirkbride; she was the only one who saw it. This was the same guy who'd sent a bedtime 'Nite Nite' text and referred to them as 'us'.

Then there was the comment about her husband she didn't understand.

By the way, how is old Rob? Still working every hour under the sun?

And the callous assessment of Tony Connors that wouldn't be far off the mark.

It'll be your word against mine.

She closed the door, feeling as low as she'd ever been, shaking, close to tears. It was nine-thirty in the morning; the day had barely begun. Julia wasn't sure she had the strength to get through it. Concentrating was impossible when there was a crazy man across the corridor. She longed to hear Rob's voice and fingered her mobile, tempted. What a mess. Her internal phone buzzed. Tony Connors said, 'Come up when you get a minute, will you?'

Julia took the stairs rather than the lift to postpone the inevitable, expecting to be given a written warning at the very least. If, as she suspected, Ellis had already poisoned the well she'd be lucky to hold onto her job. Tony was famous for not acting unless he was certain of the impact on his beloved Grapevine. It was possible her outburst had handed him the excuse he'd been looking for to get rid of her. Their relationship in the past would count for nothing; this time tomorrow Ellis would be in her place, while she began the search for a new job. Julia guessed his first call of the day had been to HR to establish what his options were and how much it would cost him. Julia was too emotionally drained to care. She'd said what needed to be said and didn't regret it; what happened now was out of her hands.

Whatever criticism she had of Tony, his work ethic was unmatched. The guy was a workaholic who demanded everybody else be the same – nobody in the building gave more to Grapevine than the MD. Over the years, Julia hadn't once come into his office without finding him on the phone, signing papers, head down busy with something.

Today was the exception. The expensive jacket he'd been wearing lay on a chair; he hadn't bothered to hang it up. His eyes followed her into the room. She braced herself. He didn't speak, confirming Julia's fears, and motioned for her to sit down. 'Sorry to drag you away from what you're doing. Can I get you anything? Tea? Coffee?'

'No, thanks.'

'Before the day gets started I thought you and I should have a chat.'

Julia stiffened, fearing the worst. 'A chat? What about?'

Tony steepled his fingers and stared at the ceiling, marshalling his thoughts. 'I like you, Julia, I always have. In private I tell anybody who'll listen that, if Grapevine had another dozen Julia Sutherlands, nothing could stop us; we'd rule the bloody world. What impresses me most isn't your creative ability or even your flair, it's your focus. It never falters, lasered on the current challenge and, God knows, in this business we aren't short of those.'

Tony leaned forward and made eye contact with her. 'That's why I want to ask – and I don't mean to pry – is everything all right at home? Everything okay between you and Rob?'

She hesitated. 'We're fine, Tony.'

The MD was getting to the point. 'In that case, it's me, isn't it? You seem tense lately, unhappy. I assumed it was your marriage. When Ellis suggested working late your reaction was... dare I say fiery... not something I expected from you and naturally... Look, I'm trying to apologise, Julia, and making a mess of it.' He faked a laugh. 'I'm a bit rusty in that department. Don't get too much practice.'

Julia realised she wasn't getting sacked and found her voice. 'I'd noticed, Tony.'

'Yes, yes. Look, I hope you agree, you and I rub along pretty well. We do, don't we?'

'Most of the time.'

'That'll do. I'll take it because I don't mind admitting this morning in the lift rattled me – and I'm not easily rattled. It made me think. If I offended you, I'm sorry.' Tony barrelled on. 'I won't promise to act differently – let's keep it real, eh? – but if I overstep the mark consider yourself empowered to call me out. And you can come to me any time. Any problems, any concerns, the door is always open. So, are we good?'

This was the moment, the opportunity to tell him about his golden boy. It didn't feel right and Julia let it go. 'We're good, Tony.'

The MD clapped his hands. 'Excellent. Now, what's the score with Ravi and Olivia – is he shagging it or isn't he?'

Normal service had been resumed and Julia seized the opportunity: palm trees and blue skies called louder than ever. She slipped in her announcement as an afterthought. 'Before I forget, Tony, Rob and I are taking a much-needed holiday – and don't faint, it'll be after the Glasgow project is done and dusted. I'll email HR and CC you so we don't get our wires crossed on it.'

Tony glared at her from across the desk; he'd been outmanoeuvred and knew it.

'Remind me never to play cards with you, Julia.'

21

Ellis connected the Nikon to his Mac and downloaded the latest images.

Julia Sutherland was a cool one, you had to give her that. He wouldn't be surprised to discover she'd spoken to Tony and told him... told him what exactly? That she'd led him on then rejected him? Hardly. It would take more than tears to convince an old Lothario like Tony. He would've already asked for Ellis's side of the story and he hadn't. Which meant Tony wasn't involved, at least, not yet.

Ellis had considered going to the MD himself – man to man, in strict confidence, of course – for advice on how to handle an amorous line manager with the power to make life difficult. Naming names would be unnecessary; they'd both know who they were talking about. And, yes, it would be his word against hers, though, short of resigning, what else could he do? Tony Connors believed he was a man of the world – he'd have plenty to say on the subject, and when Ellis left the MD's office his position at Grapevine would be stronger than ever.

He despised the weakness in himself that drew him to these unworthy females but not nearly as much as he despised the women. From that first morning he'd been attracted to Julia. In the pub, when it had been just the two of them, that attraction had deepened. She'd wanted him as much as he'd wanted her. Ellis couldn't forget that kiss and had been greedy for more, ready to do anything to get it. Well, she'd killed what might've been and made a fool of him in the process.

They could have been lovers, instead, they were enemies.

* * *

Julia was in shock: Tony Connors had apologised – actually apologised – not skirted around the edges or made excuses, the old war horse had said he was sorry and admitted his behaviour was unacceptable. Her outburst in the lift had stunned him into a caring human being. Wow! Okay, he'd reverted to type almost immediately with his sleazy question about Ravi and Olivia because under the skin that was who he was. Fishing for gossip meant Tony didn't know about the episode with Ellis, and Julia could've cried with relief. His open-door offer had been genuine and she'd almost taken him up on it, except there was no guarantee how telling him about Ellis would go down. The MD had noticed she wasn't right but missed what was in front of him. All she could do was make the best of it and carry on. At least she'd come out of it with no opposition to her trip. Where Tony Connors was concerned, that was a win.

Downstairs, Julia stuck her head around the door for a progress report. 'How's it going?'

Over Ravi's shoulder she saw Ellis. Ravi spoke for both of them. 'We're kicking ideas around and think we've come up with some nice stuff.'

'Pleased to hear it. This one hasn't had the attention it deserves. The client expected to have signed off on it weeks ago. Not a good look for Grapevine.'

Ellis said, 'We're pretty confident we'll have something to show you by the end of the day.'

Ravi hadn't welcomed Ellis's input, though he seemed happy with it now. 'Yeah, "two heads" and all that. Edinburgh's such a photogenic city, I'd got sidetracked on the images. Ellis brought the focus where it should be – on people having a great time in the capital at New Year.'

Julia was relieved: Tony hadn't fired her, the team was pulling

together and Ellis seemed to have come to his senses. She could concentrate on doing her job.

'When can I see what you've got? Give me a time.'

Ravi didn't commit himself. 'Hard to say. It still needs a fair bit of
tweaking.'

'What about working on to get it finished? We can't afford to get sidetracked.'

Ravi said, 'So long as it's not too late. I'm going to O'Neill's Merchant
Square to watch the match.'

Ellis hesitated, then shook his head. 'Sorry, tonight's out for me, I'm
meeting somebody. In fact, I'd like to leave early, if that's all right?
Hogmanay is Ravi's baby. All I've done is throw in my tuppence worth.
The big ideas are his and he's done a great job. From here on in, however
it turns out, I'm okay with it.'

Julia hid her surprise. Could this really be the guy who'd stormed
out when she'd said she needed more notice? He hadn't been
impressed with the Edinburgh artwork or slow to trash it and attack
Ravi behind his back. Was Ellis leading his own little war of attrition,
cooperating but only up to a point until he saw an opportunity to get
back at her?

If it was, Ravi wasn't aware of it. He said, 'When I think it's there I'll
get your take on it, Julia, and action any changes to the message. With any
luck we won't be here all night and it'll be with the client in the morning,
how's that?'

* * *

Ellis drove through the afternoon traffic pleased with how the morning
had gone. Actually, he was *very* pleased. Collaborating with the designer
had been all right, not because he brought much to the party – he hadn't;
everything remotely creative had come from himself – letting the guy
believe they were a team and his contribution was valued had amused
him. Now that he knew Ravi better, his original assessment of him had
been reinforced. If anything, he rated him even less than he had. Limited
described him to a tee. When Ellis was running the team he'd hand-pick

his own people, carefully selected for ability, and there would be no place for Ravi.

Loyalty to Julia wouldn't mean a thing; she wouldn't be at Grapevine, either.

Park Circus was quiet; parking wasn't a problem. Ellis found a space where he could see the main entrance to Galloway, Bartholomew and Figgis. Rob Sutherland's silver Peugeot sat outside, which meant he was still there. Ellis played with the Nikon and settled down to wait. He had Julia to thank for being here. As soon as she suggested working late he'd realised she'd given him the opening he was looking for: she'd phone her husband and tell him not to expect her home – great news for old Rob.

At five minutes to four Rob Sutherland came out of the building, got into his car and pulled away. Ellis followed, so close he could see him driving with one hand, holding his mobile to his mouth with the other, and guessed it wasn't his wife he was talking to.

The Peugeot travelled down Woodside Terrace, along Clairmont Gardens, crossed Sauchiehall Street at the lights and rejoined it further on. When he made a right turn into Kelvin Way towards the car park Ellis realised where he was going and instinctively fell back so he wouldn't be spotted. Coming to Kelvingrove Art Gallery and Museum – not much more than a mile from where he lived – was folly. Ellis caressed the camera on the passenger seat and thanked Rob for making it easy.

He'd been to Kelvingrove on a school trip when he was nine or ten years old and didn't recall much about it. What he did remember was every kid on the bus having a packed lunch while he'd had a packet of crisps, a can of juice and a one-pound coin left on the kitchen table by his father. Ellis had kept the money and scoffed the rest.

The museum exactly matched the images in his memory: the exhibits were different but the main gallery was huge. Ellis climbed the stairs and looked over the balcony. Rob was at a table in the café on the ground floor. He hadn't ordered, obviously expecting somebody to join him. Meeting in a public place was a new development, bold and ill advised, if what he suspected was true. Ellis heard the echo of high heels clacking on the black-and-white marble floor and turned on the Nikon's quiet shutter mode. Experience had taught him not to wait for the 'perfect moment' or better light and when Rob and his lady friend embraced he shot them at eight frames-per-second.

CLICK CLICK CLICK CLICK CLICK CLICK CLICK CLICK.

He'd got what he'd come for and could've left there and then only he was having too much fun to stop. Rob went to the counter. When he returned with two coffees the woman tenderly stroked his cheek with her fingers. Ellis zoomed in and fired off another burst.

CLICK CLICK CLICK CLICK CLICK CLICK CLICK CLICK.

He went down to the café to have a closer look at the man who was cheating on Julia. The couple were too wrapped up in each other to notice him, talking quietly like the conspirators they were. Sasha's blond Australian had been handsome. In Ellis's opinion Rob Sutherland wasn't, but two females would disagree with him and he was here risking everything for one of them. Seeing Rob's companion up close, Ellis understood why: he guessed she was late-twenties/early thirties, stylish rather than showy, with red hair and a good body – a lady who'd taken care of herself. Rob was a lucky guy; he certainly could pick them, though he didn't look lucky, glancing nervously over his shoulder while his girlfriend bit her lip and squeezed his hand to reassure him about whatever was on his mind – probably his wife. Maybe he was thinking about leaving Julia. How ironic would that be? A couple of days ago, Ellis would have cheered. Now, it didn't matter – the damage was done and there was no going back.

Rob and Julia had a future together, that much was guaranteed.

Ellis knew exactly what that future was.

At ten to five they finished their coffees and got up to leave. Ellis pretended he was reading a leaflet and stayed where he was, then followed them to the exit. As he left a uniformed attendant wished him good evening; Ellis didn't acknowledge him. In the car park, Rob's arm was around the woman, his face bent towards her; she tilted her head and leaned back. When their lips met, Ellis was reminded of Doisneau's 'The Kiss by the Hôtel de Ville'. The Paris street photographer had taken the famous shot in 1950 with a Rolleiflex. That had been staged, this was real, but the result was the same: perfect.

CLICK.

Ellis stopped outside at the top of the stairs. Julia's husband and his 'friend' were talking earnestly and for a second he thought about taking another few shots, then dismissed the idea. No, it was all there, especially that final one, hungry and demanding, explicitly revealing the passion of the relationship – the most vivid photograph he'd taken since the bodies on the moonlit beach. Ellis never tired of looking at that one.

Unable to tear themselves from each other, the couple didn't notice him get into his car. Ellis watched them through the windscreen, shaking his head: this guy had it all going on – nice wife, nice life – but it hadn't been enough. He'd made a huge mistake, bigger than he could imagine; his grand deception was about to come crashing down around him. The images on Ellis's computer and memory stick guaranteed his marriage was over, whether he knew it or not. This time next year he'd be living a very different life – *if* he was living at all.

The redhead wasn't part of the plan, yet she'd contributed massively to her lover's fate, so she wasn't exactly innocent. Ellis slipped the car into gear and when she pulled away he was right behind her. He knew nothing about the woman: that was about to change.

22

Ravi heard the door slam behind him in Albion Street and stopped on the pavement to clear his head; he was hammered and wished he weren't. His world was rocking and it had nothing to do with alcohol. In The Buttery, he'd played along with Ellis Kirkbride's heartfelt little speech without believing a word of it. Working with him had confirmed his opinion that Ellis was a superior prick who, from the beginning, had treated him and Olivia like idiots. And there was something about him, something he couldn't quite put his finger on.

Ravi had been with Grapevine for fourteen months, a year of it working with Julia. He'd even been invited to a party at her and her husband Rob's house in the West End, leading him to think his relationship with his boss was pretty good. The enmity between him and Ellis had an edge to it that ran deeper than differences over artwork and campaign slogans. Perhaps their paths had crossed in a past life because Ravi didn't like him and knew the feeling was mutual. Julia was a good-looking woman. Ravi had been attracted to her from the beginning, although he'd quickly recognised he didn't stand a snowball's chance because she was happily married.

Perhaps Mr Smooth fancied his chances. If they were both attracted to the same woman it might well be a stag thing.

But at the end of the day Grapevine was just a job he showed up to five days a week that paid the rent on his place in Dennistoun, leaving a few quid over to watch Hearts play at Tynecastle and have a couple of beers. What more did he expect? If he wanted to get rich, graphic design wasn't how it was done. Designers were the low men on the totem pole. People airily and mistakenly assumed all it involved was knowing which keys to press: the 'machine' did the work. Julia hadn't been one of them and it had been nice to be appreciated.

The same couldn't be said for Tony Connors: when he passed the MD in the corridor, Tony ignored him. Ravi would be astonished if he'd even known his name before the night out.

Tonight, after Ellis had left, he'd kept at it with Julia until half past seven when she'd said, 'Okay, off you go to your football. I'll take it from here.'

'Would it be helpful if I come in early tomorrow and get on it again?'

'Yes, it would, although it's just about there, isn't it?'

'I think so. When they open their computer it'll be waiting for them.'

'Great. If I want anything altered I'll put a note on your desk, and thanks for hanging back. Enjoy the game. Is your team playing tonight?'

He'd laughed. 'What, Hearts in the Champions League? No chance of that. Probably never will be. Goodnight, Julia.'

''Night, Ravi.'

'Julia...'

'What?'

'I have to speak to you about Ellis.'

'What about him?'

Her attention had been on what she was doing and she hadn't been listening. Ravi had seen it wasn't the right moment and let it go. 'Never mind. Don't work too late.'

The one thing Glasgow had no shortage of was pubs; it had hundreds. O'Neill's Merchant Square was his current favourite. He'd sat at the bar with a pint of Guinness and lost interest after a boring, goalless first half. Eating would've been doing his system a favour: it hadn't crossed his mind. Ravi's first mistake of the evening but not the last.

Somewhere along the line – he'd never recall exactly when – he'd switched to Southern Comfort. His last clear memory was telling the barman to make it a double, tasting its smooth fire in his mouth, ordering a refill and another after that, until he was well and truly smashed. Ravi had squinted at the TV where the players were shaking hands. The match had been over; he'd had no idea how it had ended and didn't care. His mind had been on Kirkbride. The Hogmanay ads were sharper than they'd been. Ellis knew his stuff, no doubt about that. Fair enough. Yet, no matter how impressive he appeared, the guy was odd.

Ravi had grabbed hold of the bar to support himself and knocked over somebody's drink. Voices, distant and angry, had shouted at him: he was paying the price of mixing a bellyful of booze with a head full of resentment. Now he was out on the street, cool air hit him. Instinct kicked in. Getting home was his only priority, far from easy in a world that refused to stop spinning. High Street station wasn't far. From there, a train would take him the two and a half miles to Dennistoun in minutes. He fell against a wall, grateful for its support as the pub door opened and three men came out into the night.

In this city drunkenness was considered a self-inflicted wound. He heard one of them say, 'All right, mate?' and snigger as they walked away.

Ravi knew he was in trouble and struggled to pull himself together. If a police car came round the corner his misery would be complete – he'd be arrested and spend the night in the cells. The thought of Ellis Kirkbride laughing at him behind his back with Julia and Olivia was more than he could stand and in the heat of the moment he made a decision.

Life was too short!

He fumbled for his mobile, intending to call Julia at home. She'd assume it was the booze talking and coax him to at least wait until he'd sobered up but she wouldn't succeed. Ellis, the golden boy, could be at Grapevine for another ten or fifteen years and the prospect of suffering his smug face every day was unbearable.

To add to his woes it had started to rain. He stuck the mobile back in his pocket, scraped wet hair out of his eyes, and lurched as far as Ingram Street without mishap. The reactions of the few people he passed were much the same as the men from the pub: they kept their distance and left him to it. Ravi stepped off the pavement into the road without checking.

Halfway across he stumbled and almost went under the wheels of a taxi that swerved to avoid him and only just did. The tyres screeched like a flock of startled birds while the driver blasted his horn and furiously waved his fist.

Even in his out-of-control state, Ravi understood he'd been lucky and staggered into a deserted Shuttle Street. The rain was coming down hard now, rattling off the cobbles, already forming little rivers in the gutter carrying cigarette butts and discarded pieces of paper to the drains. Ravi closed his eyes, still shaken from the close call with the taxi, sure he was going to vomit. His insides heaved, bile burned in his throat and he had to fight the desire to just lie down where he was and go to sleep. His head hurt; images of Ellis mocking him returned more vivid than before and he swore out loud, slurring the words.

'Fuck it! I don't need this shit!'

Ravi fished the phone out and pressed Julia's number. He didn't notice the man who'd followed him from the moment he'd crashed through the pub doors. The figure came towards him like a ghostly spectre, footsteps dulled by the downpour until he was right beside his unsuspecting victim. The initial strike, a punch to the back of the head, sent Ravi to the ground. Then the kicking started and didn't stop, blows heavy enough to break bone and crack ribs. His assailant grinned at his victim, raised his boot and stamped repeatedly on his kneecap.

Ravi didn't feel the final kick to his head: he was already unconscious.

PART III

23

The shrill ringing of her mobile brought Julia out of a troubled sleep. In the darkness her fingers searched the bedside table to get to it before it wakened Rob. Phone calls in the middle of the night were never good news. She propped herself up on one elbow and squinted at the number, instantly suspicious when she didn't recognise it. The accent at the other end of the line was unmistakably West of Scotland. 'Mrs Sutherland? Mrs Julia Sutherland?'

'Yes.'

'Sorry to disturb you so late. This is Sergeant Dewar from George Square Police Station. Do you know a Mr Ravi Malik?'

Julia swung her legs from under the clothes and sat on the edge of the bed. 'Ravi, yes, we work together. What's happened?'

'I'm afraid Mr Malik has been involved in an incident.'

'What kind of incident?'

'He appears to have been assaulted.'

'Assaulted! Oh my God! Is he all right?'

The policeman avoided the question and replied with his own. 'Can you come to the Royal Infirmary?'

'Me?'

'If you could. We don't have his next of kin.'

'His next of kin? He is all right, isn't he?'

The sergeant was an old hand. He said, 'I'm afraid I don't have that information. When you get here a doctor will give you an update.'

Rob was beside her. He said, 'Who is it?'

Julia covered the phone with her palm. 'The police. Ravi's been assaulted. He's in the Royal and it sounds serious. They want me there.'

She returned to Sergeant Dewar. 'I don't understand – how did you get my number?'

'His mobile was lying in the road. Your contact details were on the screen. It looks like he was about to call you when he was attacked.'

'Call me?'

'Yes.'

A quiver of dread passed through Julia. 'He's... not going to die, is he?'

The police preferred asking questions to answering them. He said, 'Please get here as soon as you can, Mrs Sutherland.'

* * *

They drove along a shuttered Great Western Road, stunned into silence by the news. Julia stared out of the window, close to tears, and thought about the designer, imagining the worst. Rob turned the Peugeot into Park Road and spoke for the first time since they'd left the flat.

'I don't understand why Ravi would be calling you at that time of night.'

'Neither do I.'

'As for the police, I mean, he's been in Glasgow a while. Doesn't he have a girlfriend, a partner, somebody?'

Julia would rather not have discussed it but couldn't stop from joining in. 'I see him five days a week, speak to him all the time, yet, and I'm ashamed to admit it, I know practically nothing about him because I'm always too bloody busy to ask. What does that say about me, about who I am?'

Rob saw where she was going and cut it short. 'However well you get on with him, you aren't friends. Not in any real sense. He's a colleague, Julia. You're his boss. Take that away and what's left?' He let what he was saying sink in and raced up a deserted Woodlands Road to the motorway before he went on. 'If somebody asked what the people where I am do when they aren't behind their desks, honestly, I couldn't tell them. It would be the same in reverse because we're ships that pass – all there is to it. Ravi's a guy who happens to be part of your team. And that's it. You aren't responsible for him. At the end of the day when he walks out of the door he's on his own. Glasgow's the same as any big city anywhere. No better, no worse. He's been unlucky.'

Julia didn't disagree. 'Except I'm so single-minded at times it scares me.'

'It's called focus, one of the reasons you're good at what you do.'

He took her hand and kept the other on the wheel. 'Look, let's wait till we know how he is before starting on a guilt trip over something that has bugger all to do with you. If you need me, I'll be here.'

* * *

The 'Royal', as it was commonly referred to, was the oldest hospital in the city, a forbidding granite building Julia had passed hundreds of times but never been inside. A uniformed constable greeted them at the front entrance and took them to the third floor. She hated places like this; the smell reminded her of things she didn't want to think about. The sergeant shepherded them to a boxroom outside the wards and asked them to take a seat. Julia preferred to stand.

He said, 'Sorry again for involving you, Mrs Sutherland. Can I get you something to drink?'

'No, I'm fine. Tell me about Ravi.'

'A doctor is on his way to speak to you and answer your questions.' He took out a notebook and opened it. 'How do you know Mr Malik?'

'We're colleagues.'

'Where?'

'An advertising agency in Bothwell Street. Ravi's part of my team.'

'So you're his boss?'

'Yes.'

'Does he have family in Glasgow?'

'No, I really don't know very much about him beyond work.'

'He was found unconscious in Shuttle Street. Have you any idea what he was doing in that part of the city?'

'He was watching football in a pub.'

'Which pub?'

'He told me, but I don't remember the name.'

'Was he meeting anyone, a friend?'

'I don't think so. We worked late and he left because there was a match he wanted to see. Ravi doesn't talk about his personal life.'

'So he could've met somebody.'

It was a statement. Julia had nothing to add to it and the policeman made a note in his book. 'When you were with him did he seem all right?'

'"All right"? Yes, of course. What do you mean?'

'I'm trying to establish if he was worried or unusually tense. If there was something on his mind.'

The sergeant was only doing his job but the questions irritated Julia. She snapped, 'You said a doctor was coming. Where the hell is he?'

He closed the notebook and put it in his pocket. 'Mr Malik was pretty badly beaten but robbery wasn't the motive. We know that because his wallet wasn't taken. It had money and a couple of credit cards.'

'And what does that prove?'

The policeman answered with his characteristic caution. 'Either he ran into a marauding gang looking for trouble – the most likely explanation – or it wasn't random.'

'You mean...'

'This was a particularly vicious assault. Your colleague may have been targeted.'

'Targeted?'

'The motive could be racial. We have to hope Mr Malik will be able to tell us when he regains consciousness.'

Julia couldn't take it in. The attack on Ravi was shocking enough without the suggestion it could've been over something as unimportant as the colour of his skin. 'He's the most easy-going person I know, always laughing, always making jokes. I don't understand. It's dreadful.'

The officer saw the confusion on her face. Years on the force had taught the sergeant that reason often had little to do with violence. The streets were fraught with danger, especially after dark. He said, 'We'll know more when we talk to Mr Malik.'

Before Julia could speak again a doctor in a white coat hurried towards them and introduced himself. He had fair hair and tired grey eyes that told the story of too many hours on duty.

'The initial X-ray showed a broken femur and cracked ribs but our main concern is the trauma Mr Malik has suffered to his head.'

Julia couldn't take in what she was hearing. 'Poor Ravi. Can I see him?'

'Not at the moment, I'm afraid. He's heavily sedated but there's no immediate cause for concern; he's stable. In the next twelve hours we'll be doing tests and a CT scan. Tomorrow I expect to have a fuller picture.'

'But he is going to be okay, isn't he?'

The doctor heard the fear in her voice and smothered a sigh. 'Believe me, the best thing you can do is go home, get some sleep and call in the morning. Mr Malik—'

'Ravi.'

'Yes, of course. Ravi's in good hands.'

* * *

The attack on her colleague had hit her hard and on the drive back from the hospital in the early hours of the morning Julia slumped lifelessly in the passenger seat, silently processing what had happened. Rob couldn't help being concerned and glanced anxiously across. His wife had a good heart, something he loved about her; she cared about the people she worked with and needed time to process the senselessness of it. The doctor hadn't allowed them in to see Ravi but his injuries sounded dreadful. Rob had met him briefly at a party in their flat and barely remembered him. Julia thought he was one of the good guys and that was enough. At the Royal, Rob had stayed in the background while she'd spoken with the policeman and the doctor, then taken her arm and led her to the car. As her husband his job was simple – concentrate on the road and say nothing, just be there.

For Julia, sleep was impossible; she tossed and turned, ashen-faced and exhausted in the morning. Rob had yet another hectic day ahead of him and was dressed ready to leave. He came in with coffee and sat on the edge of the bed. He took her hand and covered it with his. 'He really is in the best place.'

'But it's all just so horrible. He didn't deserve this, Rob.'

'Nobody deserves it.'

'Yes, but Ravi...' she searched for the words '...is such a nice man.' Julia laughed a brittle laugh. '"Nice". What an inadequate description.'

'Telling you not to worry would be stupid. I'll say it anyway. Ravi will recover from this. Stay positive, there's nothing to be gained any other way.'

Julia chased a strand of hair from her forehead. 'I wish it was that easy, I really do. I can't help worrying about why he'd phone me.'

'You've nothing to reproach yourself for. He probably doesn't know himself. He was pissed.'

'Mmmm, I'm not so sure. Ravi wasn't happy at Grapevine. I should've forced Tony's hand and didn't.'

She'd lost him. He said, 'You can't go blaming yourself. You didn't assault anyone. Ravi ending up in hospital has sod all to do with what you did or didn't do.'

'You don't get it, Rob. Maybe he got drunk because of how he was feeling. If I'd stuck up for the team instead of giving in, he wouldn't have been there and it wouldn't have happened.'

'For Christ's sake, come on, Jules. He's a big boy. He spent most of the night in the pub because he could and drank more than was wise.'

Julia's expression said she wasn't convinced.

Rob said, 'Connors is the boss. End of. He's entitled to do whatever he thinks is best for his business.'

'Yes, but—'

'But nothing, Julia. You're forgetting it turned out to be the correct decision because teaming you and Ellis together got a result for Grapevine.'

'It was handled badly. Ravi and Olivia were shut out.'

'Okay. Connors is arrogant and tone deaf – that's hardly news. I'd need both hands and feet to count the number of times you were an inch away from quitting over exactly the same kind of stuff. But you didn't; you got on with it. And supposing you're right about not taking a strong enough stand. Do you actually believe it would've made a difference? Bad things happen to good people, Julia, that's just a fact. How any of this relates to a vicious attack on a Glasgow street really is beyond me. And what about Olivia? Did she fall apart because she was sidelined?' Rob shook his head. 'Nobody twisted Ravi's arm up his back and poured booze down his throat. Like it or not, he has to accept responsibility for getting drunk and putting himself in harm's way.'

Julia heard his frustration and fell silent. He stood up. 'Look, I have to go. We'll speak later, yeah? Promise me you won't waste the day beating yourself up over this. Ravi's fortunate to have you in his life and so am I.'

He kissed her cheek and left. When the front door closed behind him Julia thought about what he'd said. Of course, there was truth in it, yet, however much Rob disagreed, she still felt at least partly responsible for Ravi's state of mind.

* * *

Rob got into the Peugeot and pulled out of Hamilton Drive into the traffic on Great Western Road. The conversation with his wife had unsettled him, though not as much as his reaction. Julia was taking what had happened to her colleague personally, holding herself to account for something she'd played no part in, and he'd come close to losing his temper.

Rob waited until he was in his office at Park Circus before calling Michelle; she answered after the first ring. 'I hadn't expected to hear from you so early. Always good for a woman to know the man in her life is keen.'

'The man in her life.' Weeks ago he would've been repelled by her phraseology and corrected it. That he didn't told Rob how the dynamics of the relationship had changed – it wasn't an affair any longer, it was... He stopped short of giving it a name; this wasn't the time.

'God, it's great to hear your voice.'

'What's up?'

'That's a long story. Spent most of the night in A & E. A guy from Julia's team was beaten up last night in the city centre. He's in bad shape.'

'That's awful.'

'Yes, it is. Julia's close to him; it's hit her hard. But listen, let's not dwell on that. Can you get away this morning? I'm thinking the car park at Kelvingrove Museum.'

'So I'm right, you are keen.'

After his wife's soul-searching this woman seemed uncomplicated and desirable and Rob desperately wanted to be with her. She said, 'Give me an hour to reorganise my schedule but it shouldn't be a problem.' Michelle hesitated before adding, 'And, Rob, I love you too.'

24

Julia got hold of the hospital before leaving home and was immediately put through to the ICU. The doctor she'd spoken with in the early hours of the morning wasn't on duty and, because she wasn't an immediate family member, the only information the nurse who answered would give was that Mr Malik was comfortable and scheduled to have more tests later in the morning.

In Bothwell Street Julia's first stop was Tony Connors. He was on the phone and gestured for her to take a seat, then he saw her expression and cut the conversation short. 'Don't tell me you're pregnant. I don't want to hear it.'

'No.'

He swivelled in his chair and clapped his hands. 'Thank God for that. So what's the problem?'

'Last night Ravi was attacked in Merchant City.'

The MD was shocked. 'Christ Almighty!'

'He's in hospital. The police contacted me.'

Tony eyed her. 'I appreciate you're like a mother to your team, Julia, but isn't that over the top even for you?'

'They found his mobile in the road next to him. My number was on his screen. They believe he was about to call me when it happened.'

'Poor guy. So how bad is he and what can Grapevine do?'

'They're doing tests and don't know the full extent of his injuries so aren't saying much. But even if the tests are clear it's still bad, Tony.'

'Have you spoken to him? Does he know who did it?'

'They wouldn't let me see him but the police are speculating it may have been racially motivated.'

'Dear Lord!'

'I'll break the news to the rest of the team and go back to the Royal this afternoon.'

'What about family?'

'They're trying to contact them.'

'Girlfriend?'

'As far as I know he doesn't have one.'

'He isn't gay, is he?'

Julia didn't answer; Tony was a throwback who couldn't help himself. Her unspoken disapproval registered and he said, 'So, you're it.'

'That's how it looks at the moment.'

'Then we mustn't let him down. Tell him not to give this place a second thought. Colin Campbell has some excellent people. I'll get somebody over to you from his group. Do what you have to do and keep me in the loop. If you need anything, don't hesitate, okay?'

Tony Connors was an enigma; with him Julia was never sure what she was going to get. Apart from his crass 'gay' comment he'd been a concerned employer – probably not how he really felt, given the pressure they were under, but he'd reacted like a decent human being, she'd give him that.

It was still only twenty past eight; downstairs, Olivia and Ellis hadn't arrived. Julia sat behind her desk and tried to reorganise her day with little success; she couldn't concentrate, remembering the fair-haired doctor's bleak assessment and his reluctance to be drawn on exactly why he'd ordered a CT scan. Of course, she knew. He was checking for the kind of injury common in cases of violence: a brain haemorrhage or internal bleeding. It saddened her to realise that hours ago in this same office she and Ravi had been finalising the Hogmanay ads, imagining what they were doing was important. Not so important now.

Julia heard Olivia's heels echoing in the corridor and let her get her coat off before she went to speak to her. Olivia and Ravi were close; she would take it hard. She'd been hurrying; her face was flushed. She saw Julia and smiled. 'Don't you ever go home? Wouldn't it be better to bring in a bed and a toothbrush? Honestly, Julia, how does your Rob put up with it?'

The smile died on her lips. 'What is it? What's wrong?'

'It's Ravi.'

Olivia's fingers gripped the edge of her desk. 'What about him?'

'He's been attacked, Olivia.'

'Attacked? What do you mean? Is he all right?'

'He's in hospital.'

'No, no, not Ravi. Tell me what's happened to him.'

'We worked late on the Edinburgh campaign and he left to watch a football match in the pub.'

'O'Neill's. I've been in there with him.'

'Yes, well, when he left, some people – the police don't know who – jumped him and beat him up.'

Olivia stifled a groan with her hand. 'I can't believe it. Ravi's the most gentle guy in the world. Why?'

'It might be a race thing.'

'What? In Glasgow? No. Catholic/Protestant, Celtic and Rangers, okay, but not colour. That isn't an issue in Scotland. There has to be another reason.'

'Has he ever told you about his family?'

'He doesn't have any. His mother died when he was a baby, his father got lung cancer. There was no one left where he was, that's what brought him to the city. I have to go to him, I have to.'

'And you will, once he's well enough. You know him better than anybody – the police may want to speak to you. I'm going to the Royal again this afternoon. When they tell us something, trust me, Olivia, you'll be the first to know.'

The news had crushed Olivia; she sobbed and stared into space. Julia couldn't leave her alone and stayed with her until she stopped crying.

'Look, if you don't feel up to working you can go home. You're Ravi's friend. Everybody will understand.'

Olivia dabbed her eyes with a tissue. 'Thanks, except what good would that do? I'd rather be with people. But there's something I don't understand – how did you find out about it? I mean, I'm assuming it was pretty late.'

'I was in bed asleep when the police called and asked me to come to the hospital. Rob drove me there. Honestly, Olivia, not knowing what was waiting for me, it was awful.'

'It must've been. Did Ravi give them your number?'

'No, he was sedated. He was trying to reach me when he was attacked.'

'At that time? It must've been important, or at least he thought it was.'

'Not necessarily. The doctor said his blood alcohol levels showed he'd been drinking heavily.'

Olivia shook her head. 'That's strange. Any time I've been with him a couple of pints is his limit. If he was drunk it has to be because something's happened, maybe in the pub. And that doesn't explain why he was trying to speak to you, does it?'

'Only Ravi can tell us. Let's hope he got a good look at the people who assaulted him.'

They heard a noise and turned. Ellis was standing in the door with his bag slung over his shoulder. He grinned. 'What's the matter? Somebody's cat die?'

* * *

Rob looked across the empty car park. Kelvingrove didn't open until eleven o'clock, an insignificant fact because, for today at least, the museum had served its purpose: this was as far as he intended to go. From Argyle Street the hum of traffic reached him as he scanned the tree-lined approach searching for Michelle's Honda, cursing impatiently under his breath when it wasn't in sight. In the hospital, hearing the details of the brutal attack on her colleague had been upsetting for Julia and he'd been glad he'd been there to support her. But while the doctor listed Ravi's injuries Rob had been thinking about Michelle. The irony wasn't lost on him: his feelings had travelled a long way since that first night in the Hilton. Now he was here and it wasn't about sex: he had to see her.

He'd told the office an overly cautious client on the South Side who needed babysitting had requested a last-minute powwow to go over the finer points of their application for a building warrant to demolish part of an old property and reckoned reassuring them wouldn't take too long – standard stuff nobody would bother to question. Michelle didn't have to resort to inventing stories. Her day was spent calling on firms like Galloway, Bartholomew and Figgis, so making time wasn't difficult and he'd detected a smile in her voice when he suggested they meet. Breaking it to her he was going on holiday with Julia wasn't something he was looking forward to, guessing how the news would go down. Admitting he'd rather be in Glasgow with her than with his wife on a tour in the Mekong Delta wouldn't lessen her reaction. Then again, maybe it wouldn't be necessary. Ravi had been badly hurt – he'd take a while to recover. Loyalty to Grapevine might persuade Julia to cancel their plans and step into the breach.

Her red Honda turned off Kelvin Way into the car park and stopped alongside Rob's Peugeot. Michelle got out of her vehicle and into his. She was wearing a black two-piece suit with a cream blouse tied in a bow. The outfit was simple but at the same time stunning, and she'd done something different with her hair. Her green eyes were bright with life, the smile he'd heard in her voice on the phone in them, and he quietly marvelled at how she always managed to be so beautiful. She blew him an exaggerated kiss from the passenger seat and Rob realised she was as happy to be there as he was.

She said, 'Your wish is my command. I'm here. How long have we got?'

'Not long, I'm afraid.'

Michelle leaned in and ran her fingers along the inside of his thigh. 'Surely there's enough time to—'

He gently lifted her slender hand and gave it back to her. 'Believe me, there's nothing, absolutely nothing, I'd like more.'

'So why not? I have a friend who claims it isn't a sin if you do it in the middle of the day.'

Rob laughed. 'We're a bit late thinking about whether or not it's a sin. If what we do isn't, it ought to be. No, as I said to you, one of Julia's people was on the wrong end of a hammering in the city last night. The police phoned Julia—'

'Julia? Why?'

'Her number was on his screen.'

'And this was, when?'

'Around one-thirty. The police were anxious to talk to somebody who knew him and I drove her to the Royal Infirmary.'

'How long were you there?'

Rob sighed. 'Long enough, but even with police and doctors and everything that was going on, all I could think about was you.'

'I'm flattered, although I only hope it doesn't need some poor bloke to be beaten up before I cross your mind. Seriously, it sounds pretty awful for all concerned. What's the latest on him?'

'No idea. Julia is trying to get more information this morning. She'll visit Ravi if they'll let her in to see him.'

'She sounds like a good person.'

'She is, a very good person, I don't want to hurt her, and...'

Michelle held her breath, certain she'd misunderstood his reasons for wanting to meet. Rob was about to tell her they couldn't carry on like this, he didn't have it in him to deceive his wife any longer; last night had shown him what a fine woman she was.

'And what?'

'She will be unless we change how we're handling this. Constantly claiming to be working late always had a limited shelf life. I mean, think about it, Michelle. At the end of the day, I'm an architect. I'm not making house calls for the Samaritans.'

'What're you proposing, Rob?'

'Mixing it up. If we don't we're going to get found out and I'm not ready for that.' He ran a hand through his hair. 'Meeting first thing would be ideal. Failing that we could get together during the day, stretch our lunch breaks. I organise my client portfolio. So long as the work gets done and enough invoices go out, nobody cares. I can free-up space by inventing places to be.'

'I can't think of a better way to start the day.'

'Neither can I.'

'But how long can that last?'

'As long as we need it to.'

She went into her bag and brought out a key. 'Okay, my place. No more hotels or skulking home hoping she's asleep.'

'Michelle, that's perfect. You're a very clever girl.'

She let the compliment pass and pressed the key into his hand. 'Listen, Rob, inviting you into my home is one thing, giving you this is another. It's a huge step for me, a giant step. I'm trusting you further than I ever expected to. Don't abuse that trust.'

'I won't. I promise I won't.'

The smile that had been in her eyes, for the moment, was gone. 'This is your last chance to walk away without completely destroying me, Rob. You have to understand that.'

He tilted her chin so he could gaze into her eyes. 'I'm already past that point but there is something I wasn't looking forward to telling you. Julia's booked three weeks in Vietnam.'

She joked to cover her pain. 'Maybe I could drive you to the airport?'

Rob replied before realising she wasn't serious. 'No, I'm taking the car. I've booked with Skypark.' He saw the tears and cursed himself for being an unfeeling fool. 'Michelle, I'm so sorry but I can't get out of it. I have to go.'

25

Ellis put the satchel on the floor and sat on the edge of a desk. He pinched his eyes. 'What a bloody stupid thing to say. I'm so sorry, I really am.'

Julia defended him. 'You weren't to know.'

He smiled a weak smile and shook his head. 'Don't make excuses for me. I need to learn to engage my brain before I speak and stop trying to be funny. It's embarrassing. How are you two doing?'

'Not good. The hospital haven't told us how badly Ravi's been hurt. Until they do, we're worried.'

Olivia said, 'Thinking about him in pain makes me feel awful.'

Ellis nodded. 'I don't know him very well yet but it's still shocking. What're the police saying?'

'Not much.'

'With CCTV an attack in a public place surely must've been picked up somewhere? Assuming they're even investigating it properly.'

Julia hadn't considered anything else. 'What makes you say that? They must be!'

Ellis stood up and paced the room. 'Not necessarily. Ravi's a colleague, a friend, for us here at Grapevine this is personal, but violence happens every day. I doubt the resources are there to properly deal with it.'

Julia wanted to dispute that statement and couldn't – that it might be true stunned her into a silence Ellis broke. 'The first thing the police should establish is why. Why it happened. Ravi isn't into anything, is he?'

The question offended the normally quiet Olivia. 'How dare you suggest that? How bloody dare you?'

Ellis held up his hands defensively. 'Whoa! Hold on! All I'm doing is trawling through the possibilities. I'm not for a minute implying Ravi was targeted because he was dealing or owed money to the wrong people. I'm doing what the police *should* be doing and probably aren't – trying to make sense of a senseless act.'

Julia took the heat out of the situation. 'Both of you, calm down. Ellis has a point, though he's wrong. The police have considered why a guy minding his own business ends up in the Royal Infirmary. Ravi still had his wallet and his credit cards, so it wasn't robbery. Nor was it just a few kicks and punches dished out for fun. Whoever was responsible intended to really hurt him. They're saying it could be racially motivated.'

Ellis's expression said he didn't believe it. 'Racial? In South Africa, absolutely, but in Glasgow that's the last rock I'd look under.'

Lack of sleep caught up with Julia; she was exhausted and didn't want to talk any more about it. 'Okay, this isn't getting us anywhere, let's leave it. Unless Ravi saw his attackers and can identify them, we'll probably never have answers.'

Ellis saw the tiredness on her face. 'You'd be better off at home, except that won't be happening, will it? Instead, you're going back to the hospital. Well, I'm coming with you... unless Olivia wants to go. I could hold the fort.'

Olivia shook her head. 'Oh, no, I want to see him but if it's bad news I couldn't handle it.'

Julia said, 'That's kind of you, Ellis, but it's better if both of you stay here. Tony's sending one of Colin Campbell's team to fill in. Bring whoever it is up to speed and get them started working on the marketing plan – we're not there with it yet.'

The shrill of her phone interrupted the conversation. Julia turned away to answer it. 'Oh, Carol, thanks for pushing it through so quickly.'

Ellis raised a questioning eyebrow and she said, 'Rob and I are going on a trip. That was HR telling me they've cleared my time off. God, I wish I hadn't booked it. Perhaps it would be better if I cancelled.'

Ellis hadn't known about any holiday and kept his interest under control. 'You'll do no such thing. If there's one person who deserves time away from this place, it's you, Julia.'

'It's not just me. Rob's been overdoing it for months.'

'He's a conscientious guy.'

'Too conscientious. The number of evenings he spends in the office is a joke. He's promised to cut back but he's got so much on he'll have to start earlier than he already does. His boss is an even bigger slave driver than Tony.'

'Where are you going anyway?'

'Vietnam. Been there?'

Ellis hesitated. 'Always wanted to, but no. How long will you be away?'

'Three weeks. I thought I'd got the timing spot on. As it's turned out it could hardly have been worse.'

Ellis swept her concern away. 'Nonsense. Don't worry about Ravi; he'll be all right. Your job is to put Grapevine aside and enjoy yourself. Somebody's coming in to help us – great! And you're right, we're not there yet but we're pretty damn close. We'll get the campaign over the line. I mean, we're a team, aren't we? I'm up for it. What about you, Olivia?'

Working with Ellis Kirkbride had no appeal but Olivia didn't have a choice. She did her best to smile and said, 'Of course.'

Ellis pressed his point. 'There you are, Julia, nothing to worry about, it's sorted. Now, no way am I letting you face the hospital on your own. I'm going with you. End of.'

* * *

Julia understood why Olivia had passed on the hospital. To her, Ravi was more than a colleague and until they knew the extent of his injuries it was wiser she stay away. Julia didn't have that luxury: there was no one else. The police might have no more to tell but the doctors certainly would, and she forced herself to stay positive. Since the scene in her office Ellis had neither said nor done anything even slightly inappropriate but

Julia hadn't forgotten how quickly he'd changed when she'd rejected his deluded advances and would rather have visited Ravi alone.

On the drive across the city if Ellis felt any lingering awkwardness he kept it hidden. He seemed relaxed, sitting quietly in the passenger seat until a red light forced Julia to stop. He shared a philosophical thought. 'One minute life is fine, the next... Poor old Ravi. We can only hope he's able to put this appalling act behind him. I wonder why he was calling you. Doesn't that strike you as strange?'

Julia didn't answer him and turned left up High Street; Ellis continued, undeterred by her silence. 'I meant it about deserving a break. You and Rob put everything you have into your jobs, though wouldn't a couple of weeks in Marbella have served the same purpose without flying halfway round the world? I'm curious, why Vietnam?'

Julia had no desire to discuss her personal affairs with this guy and kept her reply short.

'We love South East Asia.'

'Me too, I envy you. The most important thing is to enjoy yourselves. Grapevine will still be here when you get back.'

At the top of the hill Julia left the Mazda in one of the Cathedral Precinct car parks and walked across the road to the hospital. Main Reception had good news for them: Ravi was out of ICU and they were directed to a ward where a doctor would speak to them. When they got there he was waiting. Julia recognised him from the night before, still tired, but brighter than she remembered him. He nodded and gave them his assessment. 'I'm pleased to tell you your colleague has had a peaceful night.'

'You've moved him – does that mean you think he's going to be all right?'

The doctor avoided answering directly. 'After what he went through he's in a great deal of pain. We've made him as comfortable as possible.'

Julia anxiously repeated her question and he relented a little. 'For a man who was beaten as badly as he was, yes, I'd say so. We were concerned with possible head trauma. Fortunately, the scan showed nothing. As you would expect there's extensive bruising all over his body. His ankle is broken, three of his ribs are cracked and he's suffered a compound fracture to his leg. But, for us, the biggest issue is the damage to his knee. It's pretty badly smashed up. Also, because his stats aren't where we'd like to see them, we're monitoring him for internal bleeding.'

Julia thought about Olivia's reaction and was glad she'd decided not to come.

The doctor qualified his assessment. 'That's standard procedure in a case like this – it doesn't mean we expect to find anything. Mr Malik has youth on his side. Physio will help but to walk any distance he may need a stick.'

'Can I see him?'

'Briefly.' He glanced at Ellis, who hadn't spoken. 'And, please, only one of you.'

'Can he talk?'

'A little. Because of the drugs he's on you won't get much out of him, I'm afraid. Try not to act surprised – he's not a pretty sight but he's a lucky man. Believe me, it could've been very much worse.'

Julia braced herself and edged nervously into the room. The doctor's warning wasn't enough to stop her being shocked. Ravi was bandaged from head to foot, his injured leg raised in a sling suspended above the bed. Machines recording his vital signs quietly pulsed and hummed. Deep cuts and livid purple bruises covered his face; one of his eyes was swollen and closed, making him unrecognisable from the man she worked with every day. He sensed rather than heard her and the other eye blinked opened. Julia squeezed his hand, relieved when he squeezed back. 'It's okay, Ravi. You're going to be all right.'

His lips parted in a brave attempt at a smile; some of his teeth were missing. 'I bet you say that to all the boys.'

The words came out thick and mangled. 'No, just the ones I really like. Do you remember what happened?'

'That's what the police asked.'

'What did you tell them?'

'Nothing, it's a blur. I was watching the game in the pub, then I was outside and somebody was laughing, next thing I was on the ground.'

'How many were there? Did you get a look at them?'

'It happened too fast, I'm not sure.'

'You were trying to call me.'

'Was I?'

The conversation had been short; already Ravi was tiring. Julia thought she heard the doctor hovering in the background. She was wrong; it was Ellis. He came forward and touched Ravi's shoulder. 'Ravi, mate, what can I say? This is terrible. If there's anything I can do, anything you need... Christ, I wish I could get my hands on the animals who did this to you. They'd be fucking sorry.'

Ravi turned his battered face away, visibly agitated. Ellis's cheeks flushed and Julia grabbed his arm to lead him to the door. 'You heard the doctor – one of us at a time. Wait in the corridor. I'll be out in a minute. He's exhausted.'

Ellis ignored her and shouted, 'You're gonna be fine, mate! Bad news about the stick but good as new, I promise!'

Ravi raised his head off the pillow. 'Stick? What does he mean, Julia? What stick?'

* * *

Across the hall Olivia was talking with the guy from Colin Campbell's team and seemed to be coping. She'd want to know how her friend was; Julia would tell her when it was just the two of them, without mentioning a stick. What in God's name had Ellis been thinking? He'd overstepped the mark – again – and Julia was glad he'd agreed to go home. She would've liked to have done the same. That wasn't possible until she'd given Tony an update. As the MD of Grapevine he'd be concerned about the impact any disruption had on the work. Balancing concern and self-interest didn't come easily to him. He was a pragmatist; tact wasn't his strongest suit.

Tony waved for Julia to take a seat. 'Did they let you see him?'

'Yes.'

'And how is he?'

'Not good but he'll live.'

'What're the doctors saying?'

'No more than they have to, really. They've ruled out brain damage but are keeping him under observation. It was sad to see him so beaten up. If you're wondering how soon he'll be back, don't waste your time. We won't be seeing him here for months.'

'I'm sorry to hear that. He seems like a nice guy.'

'He is. It's a crying shame what they did to him.'

'Did he get a look at who attacked him?'

'Not as far as I know.'

Tony fiddled with the papers on his desk, aware how what he was about to say would sound. 'So, how close are we with the Glasgow stuff? I mean, I hate to come across as if I don't care about Ravi, but I have a business to run. The Glasgow development is a plum. Winning it was punching above our weight and we have you and Ellis to thank for that. But there are more than a few envious eyes out there. The rest of the industry is watching Grapevine, hoping we screw up. Missing a deadline would send a signal we've bitten off more than we can chew, to use a cliché. As team leader, I'd like you to reassure me we haven't. Dramas and distractions aside, tell me we're going to deliver.'

Out of sight, Julia crossed her fingers and replied with a confidence she only half believed.

'We're going to deliver, Tony.'

26

The last time Ellis had stood on the bridge he'd been crazily in love with Julia Sutherland, mapping out the glorious future they were going to have as soon as her husband was out of the picture. But that was before. Things had changed. His infatuation with Rob's wife was behind him, and when he thought of her now it was only about how slow and painful her death would be.

In the car coming back from the hospital she'd gripped the steering wheel so tightly the skin stretched across her knuckles, not speaking, refusing to even look at him, and he'd known Julia hated him. Breaking the news to the designer that he'd be a cripple for the rest of his life had been crass and cruel, calculated to provoke exactly the reaction it got: a distraught Ravi had started to cry. Ellis had felt Julia's angry breath on his cheek and tried not to laugh as she'd marched him out of the room into the corridor.

When they'd got to the underground car park in Bothwell Street he'd pretended he hadn't picked up on her mood and volunteered to get them something for lunch. 'Shall I buy a couple of sandwiches? What do you fancy?'

Julia had coldly rejected the offer as he'd known she would. 'Not for me. I'm sending Olivia home. You can go, too.'

'Home? What about this afternoon's meeting?'

'Forget it. I'm not in the right frame of mind.'

'Okay, so long as you're sure, but you are off on holiday soon and—'

When Julia turned to him her face had been white with anger. 'Is there something wrong with you?'

'I beg your pardon.'

'I'm asking if you're actually as insensitive as you appear to be, although having witnessed your performance at the hospital I already have my answer, don't I?'

'Performance? What do you mean?'

'I mean what the hell possessed you to tell Ravi about the stick?'

'I was trying to reassure him.'

'Really? Didn't you see him? Didn't you see what those evil... what they've done to him?'

'Of course, and it's terrible. All I'm saying is—'

She'd lost her temper and snapped at him. 'Oh, for God's sake, Ellis, just go, will you? Get out of my sight!'

And here he was. Where he'd been before, no more than a few hundred yards from her house, except now weighing what was in his head against the chances of being caught rather than admiring her jogging along the riverbank in her baggy tracksuit. Disappointment flashed through him. He'd been sure they were meant to be together, but his eyes had been opened; he saw Julia as she really was and knew what he had to do.

Ellis scanned the leafy scene in the middle of the city, assessing the options. Abducting her in broad daylight was bold, reckless and fool-hardy, and maybe that was its strength: pulling it off wouldn't be easy but nobody would be expecting it.

At the end of the bridge the road underneath sloped to the beginning of the walkway: a van could get down there, no problem, and anyone standing there would be hidden until it was too late. Ellis's fingers dug into the stone parapet, gripping it as Julia had gripped the steering wheel, his heart hammering in his chest. He willed himself to take his time and think it through. From the moment he'd seen the container he'd known what to do.

Three details had eluded him: where, when and how. Now, he had the answer to two of them.

In the shadow of the bridge he noticed a rolled-up sleeping bag and was annoyed; his plan had just got more risky. Well, so be it. If somebody got in his way they'd be sorry.

* * *

Ellis stood in the middle of the cramped basement and scanned the pictures on the wall where the line of anonymous Asian females had been. The images told a tale that would break Julia Sutherland's heart, and that would only be the beginning.

In the first, taken after they'd shared a Chinese takeaway, she'd made an unconvincing attempt to escape the lens. An arm round her waist effortlessly prevented her and he'd known that beneath the coy resistance she'd felt what he'd felt. The rest, in no particular order, centred on her husband and a red-haired woman, sometimes together, sometimes by themselves, at different times and locations. The shots on the museum steps and in the car park staring earnestly into each other's eyes were particularly compelling and the kiss would be difficult to explain. All good, though not quite good enough because Rob had shown himself to be a talented deceiver; inventing a story to cover his behaviour wasn't impossible.

On the bridge, he'd remembered how free Julia had been with information. And so it was again: Rob had given up working late. From now on, according to his wife, he'd be leaving home in the morning earlier than he usually did to keep up with the growing demands on him.

Ellis couldn't wait to see her face when she discovered what those demands were.

Julia had insisted on a holiday – something else he hadn't known until she'd told him. That would give him three weeks when no one would even be looking for them. Ellis had hardly been able to conceal his delight – three weeks to make her sorry for treating him like a fool.

He took the Nikon from his satchel and connected it with a USB cable to his Mac, then turned the camera on, clicked Start Transfer, and waited while the latest pictures were copied. The screen filled with the image of a man lying on the pavement, hands drawn up around his head, body curled to protect itself from the kicks and blows that had rained down on it. Ellis zoomed in on the unconscious Ravi – he'd enjoyed taking those shots and regretted that, unlike the deserted beach five thousand miles away, it had been too public to finish the job. He smiled – another time, maybe.

The printer hummed and spat out his latest work. Ellis laid the pictures on the trestle table and examined them with an appreciative eye. Quite a collection, even if he said so himself. The hours of watching and waiting had been worth it; he knew more about the bloody Sutherlands than they knew about themselves.

He set the pile of 10 x 8s to the side and turned to the plan; he'd run through every risky step and was happy with it. But he hadn't resolved the issue of where the threat would come from – because, as he'd so often said, there was *always* a threat – and the smile died on his lips. He lifted a close-up of the red-haired mistress, studying the flawless skin and the contours of her beautiful face, seeing something he hadn't noticed before. The eyes staring back held the spark Ellis Kirkbride had searched for all his life and never found.

This woman loved Rob Sutherland.

She loved him!

Ellis's pulse quickened; he whispered breathlessly, 'It's you, isn't it? You're the threat.'

His brow furrowed as he imagined the future and how it would be: this lady wouldn't accept Rob had dumped her – not in a million years. She'd be frantic; go to the police to convince them something was wrong. If she somehow managed it, where would that take them?

Ellis tacked the picture to the wall and focused on his new enemy. He'd been wrong; his work wasn't finished – there was one more piece of the puzzle to put in place and one more photograph left to take.

27

In the crisp early-morning air the key was like a tiny dagger in Rob's fingers. Michelle had made its significance clear, and while it was nice to know she'd been thinking about him – about *them* – the responsibility scared him. If he used it to open the door life could never go back to how it had been. Perhaps some men could be unfaithful without missing a beat; he wasn't one of them, although it would be hard to argue with anyone who suggested he'd managed all right on that score so far.

When he'd asked the attractive red-haired woman to go with him for an after-work drink he'd had sex in mind, nothing else; who would've imagined it would lead to this? Yet it had, they'd fallen in love, and Michelle needed a commitment he wasn't ready to give. On the steps, torn between doubt and lust, Rob cast around for reasons to turn on his heel and leave: it was too soon – they hardly knew each other; things were fine as they were, better to take what could be taken from the affair without demanding more.

And then there was Julia to consider – the innocent party in this.

The self-serving truth registered and he bowed his head, confused and ashamed at what he'd become. To hell with soul-searching. If he really was looking for a way out all he had to do was drop the key through the letterbox, drive away.

The metal glinted in the light as he reached for the flap to return the key to its owner. Suddenly, the door opened, Michelle was standing there naked, and the decision wasn't Rob's any more.

* * *

Rob had left home at a quarter to seven and driven up Woodlands Road. It was too early for shops to be open and traffic was light, a fraction of what it would be in another hour, so following him undetected hadn't been easy. He'd joined the M8 heading east, for all the world just another wage slave on his way to the salt mines. Twenty minutes further on, Ellis had seen signs for Queenslie, Easterhouse and Baillieston. Doubt stirred in his gut; he was a stranger to this part of the city – if he lost the silver Peugeot he'd have to go through the same rigmarole again on another day.

The Peugeot pulled off the motorway and continued until it entered a new housing estate. It stopped outside a smart-looking three-bedroom property with a red Honda in the drive. Ellis tucked in behind a Range Rover, rolled down the electric window and got ready to take the crucial photograph that would tell the story better than words ever could.

Julia's husband was having his cake and eating it. From nowhere, rage at what Rob Sutherland was doing overwhelmed Ellis; his hands tightened into fists. He would never have treated Julia or Sasha or any of the others like this. Women didn't value or appreciate sincere feelings, drawn instead to losers who played them at their own false game.

Rob locked the car and glanced suspiciously up and down the street. He went into his pocket and brought out something. Behind the Nikon Ellis zoomed in, his anger subsided and he laughed. 'She's given him a key! He has his own bloody key!'

CLICK.

He'd hoped to capture the killer shot, the moment that couldn't be denied or explained: the final proof of infidelity. What he saw left him speechless and pounding the steering wheel with his free hand. 'Yes! Yes! Absolutely yes! Talk your way out of this one, Mr Sutherland.'

CLICK CLICK CLICK CLICK CLICK CLICK.

PART IV

28

FOUR WEEKS LATER

Julia heard the shower hiss in the bathroom and reluctantly opened her eyes. Usually she was asleep when Rob left. Not this morning; she was too excited. Today was her last at Grapevine before they went on holiday – just as well, because she'd given all she had to give and had no more in her. She'd promised Tony Connors the Glasgow campaign would be finalised before she set foot on a plane for South East Asia. Thanks to the efforts of the team, it had been. Yesterday, she'd gone with Tony and Ellis to the City Chambers in George Square to present a detailed roll-out of it to the steering committee, a daunting experience that had drained her.

Rob had cooked dinner, spaghetti and meatballs, and surprised her with how good it was until she'd found the M & S packaging in the bin under the sink. The harmless deception had made her smile. Apart from supporting her career every step of the way he'd kept his word about not working late and most mornings somehow – she had no idea how he managed it – dragged himself out of bed without disturbing her. Rob needed a break as badly as she did and Julia had already decided to encourage him to look for a less demanding job when they came back.

She saw his shadow against the light next door and called to him. He came through, dressed and ready, and sat on the bed. 'What're you doing up? Don't you know what time it is? You must be shattered.'

'I am but it doesn't matter. Today's our last day for three whole weeks. We'll soon be sitting at a roadside café eating something spicy from a bowl, a world away from Glasgow. I honestly can't wait.' She reached out and tenderly stroked his cheek with her finger. 'Think about it, Rob. Just the two of us; the hard slog will be behind us – all we'll have to do is enjoy each other. It'll be wonderful. Just like in the beginning.'

Rob took hold of her hand. 'Not India but close enough.'

'Better. We'll appreciate it more. And I'm not letting you out of my sight, even for a minute, Rob Sutherland.'

'You'll be sick of looking at me.'

'No chance. Now, beat it and let me get back to sleep.'

* * *

Rob drove the now familiar road to Michelle's house in the slow lane of the motorway at a steady 60 mph, replaying Julia's enthusiasm for the trip in his head; he would've given anything to feel the same. Unfortunately, he didn't and there was nothing he could do except pretend. Three weeks was a long time and Julia was a smart woman. This morning she'd been too caught up in her excitement to notice, but he couldn't keep the charade going indefinitely – sooner or later she'd sense something wasn't right and the shit would hit the fan: far from being a second honeymoon, Vietnam would be a disaster. They'd fly home on separate flights, their marriage over; Julia would divorce him and who would blame her?

Was that what he wanted?

He turned into Michelle's drive, switched off the ignition and sat behind the wheel, confused and unhappy, knowing he was in an impossible situation of his own creation. Julia had done nothing; she deserved better from him. Michelle's mistake had been falling in love with somebody else's husband.

He saw Michelle at the window and his resolve melted. Inside, they kissed. Rob pushed her gently away – he'd been an idiot to come here, today of all days. She clung to him and every common-sense thought he'd had disappeared. 'I can't stay. I never should've said I'd come but I had to see you. I know this is painful, Michelle, it's difficult for me, too.'

'You've no idea, Rob, you really don't. I'm so jealous. I'd give anything for it to be me.'

She threw her arms round him desperately and started to cry. 'Don't go! I can't let you go with her!'

Rob tried to regain control of the situation; he took hold of her arms and stepped back. Seeing the anguish in Michelle's eyes was almost like a blow. 'Michelle, listen to me. This isn't helping, is it? I have to go, you know I have to, please don't ask me to stay.'

'I feel as though I'm losing you.'

'Well, you're not. I'll find a way to call you.'

'Every day?'

He hesitated, but only for a second. 'Every day.'

'Don't let me be alone. Call me tonight.'

'I will.'

'Promise me, Rob.'

'I promise. This can't go on. It isn't fair on any of us. I can't spoil this trip for her, but when I come back I'm going to tell her I'm leaving.'

Michelle smiled through her tears. 'It means so much to hear you say that, Rob. For three weeks all I'll have is your voice on the other end of the line. Don't forget about me and fall in love with her all over again.'

He kissed her tenderly on the lips. 'How could I? Stay strong. I'll phone later when she goes for a run.'

* * *

After living and breathing the Glasgow campaign, Grapevine seemed to have ground almost to a stop. The sense of urgency and purpose that had fired so many mornings was missing and a feeling of anticlimax hung in the air. Julia expected to see Tony Connors at some point even if it was only to wish her bon voyage. If he remembered. Tony wasn't a man who gave out compliments lightly but a huge thank you to all concerned for the previous day wouldn't be undeserved.

Julia, still buzzing from the meeting at the City Chambers and preoccupied with her trip, didn't hear the MD until he spoke. 'I'm surprised you bothered to show up – last day and all that.'

Her boss was leaning against the frame of the door with his arms folded. Julia fired back, 'Oh, you know me, Tony. So long as the money keeps hitting the bank, I'll be here.'

He came into the office and drew the tips of his fingers over the top of a filing cabinet, inspecting it for dust. 'You're a hero – or, in the politically correct madness we live in, perhaps that should be heroine?' Tony clapped his hands. 'Who gives a damn? After yesterday you could burn the building down and nobody would dare say a bad word about you. I've been in this business a long time – too bloody long – and can honestly tell you I haven't seen a more polished performance.'

He was obviously sincere and Julia was touched. 'Thanks, Tony, I appreciate it.'

'No need to thank me, it's true. While you were on your feet I was watching the faces. It might not be the Palace of Westminster but make no mistake – these people are career politicians who spend their lives wading through committee reports, budget cuts and the like; they're drowning in paper. Deadly dull stuff. No wonder they can't keep their eyes open.'

Tony was being nice; Julia let him speak and didn't interrupt.

He said, 'You had them in the palm of your hand from the first minute. You were great, Julia. Really great. Everything you told them was on point and they got that. Referring the campaign back to their own plans for the new-look city centre made it hard to disagree.'

He moved to the window and looked down at the traffic in Bothwell Street. 'They particularly loved the when the address matters concept of naming the four flagship properties after Scottish clans: The Buchanan, The Cameron, The Fraser and The Wallace. Super-strong identities for luxury flats. The Buchanan's my favourite. Wouldn't mind living there myself. Was that Ellis's idea?'

Julia swallowed her annoyance. 'Ellis contributed a lot. That one came from me.'

'Clever girl. It's worked out well, you and him, hasn't it?'

Tony was enjoying himself, no need to spoil it. And when she thought about it, he wasn't wrong. Since she'd spurned his advances, apart from blurting the news to Ravi about him needing a stick, Ellis had behaved faultlessly. In the car coming from the hospital she'd been angry with him, very angry, though maybe a combination of shock at the severity of the attack and the pressure at work had made her react more sharply than was really necessary.

Tony said, 'Genius. And the graphics were terrific. Was that Ellis or Ravi?'

'A bit of both.'

'How is Ravi, by the way?'

'He's at home trying to put his life back together. I went to see him a couple of days ago.'

'Can he walk?'

'Hobble would be nearer the mark. He's still in pain and, if you want my opinion, some of those heavy drugs are only adding to his depression.'

'Be sure to pass on my best wishes.'

'I will.'

'Good. So, now it's off to – where're you going again?'

'Vietnam.'

'Vietnam, of course, and we'll see you when you get back. Okay, don't do anything I wouldn't do, eh?'

* * *

Ellis said, 'Sorry I'm a bit late. Something I had to deal with.'

'Today of all days that isn't a problem. You just missed our illustrious leader.'

'Tony? Did he congratulate you on yesterday?'

'As a matter of fact, he did. He congratulated all of us and said he believed it had gone over well.'

Ellis snorted. 'Well? It went a helluva lot better than that. You smashed it, Julia. While you were talking I remembered that first session – seems like years ago – when we were kicking ideas around and you came up with when the address matters.'

'We got a takeaway from the Shanghai Teahouse.'

'That's right. Who would've thought you'd end up presenting in the City Chambers?'

Julia frowned. 'Tony asked whose idea it was. You said it was mine but I've never been sure it actually was.'

'I can assure you it *most certainly* was. If it had been mine I'd have claimed it in a heartbeat, don't worry about that. Seriously, you were terrific yesterday; they loved it. Now, go off on holiday and forget about Grapevine, Tony Connors and all the bloody rest of it.'

'I will, but before I do I have to say something. In the car coming from the hospital I was angry with you, very angry.'

'You had every right to be. What a clown. I should have kept my big mouth shut.'

'I think the shock of seeing what they'd done to him along with the pressure from work... you couldn't have known they hadn't told, Ravi. I overreacted, and I'm sorry.'

'Oh, please, that isn't necessary.'

'No, I am and it is.'

Ellis leaned across her desk; there was amusement in his eyes. 'Forget it, Julia, it was your turn to be out of order.'

29

Ellis ran into Julia in the corridor and made a show of checking his watch. 'I expected you to have left before now. What's keeping you? Didn't think leaving Grapevine would be difficult.'

'Believe me, it isn't. Two more minutes and I'm gone. Still have our packing to finish and I'm going to look in on Ravi on the way home.'

'No running tonight, then?'

'Wrong, it'll help me shuck off Grapevine. I'll be out there – tonight and every night.'

He laughed. 'You're a fanatic.'

'I prefer to think of myself as committed.'

Ellis frowned and pursed his lips. 'How was Ravi the last time you saw him?'

'Not great; he's depressed.'

'Any idea when he'll be well enough to come back to work?'

'Not any time soon, that's for sure. Physically he's a lot better, but mentally and emotionally he hasn't progressed. I feel bad about leaving him when he's so low. If only...'

'Would it help if I dropped by?'

Julia shook her head. 'No, Olivia suggested the same thing. When I asked him about it he told me he doesn't want visitors. I'm the only one he'll speak to and, believe me, I do most of the talking.'

'It's understandable given what he's been through. Tell him I said hi! What time's your flight?'

'Four o'clock from Heathrow to Singapore and on to Ho Chi Minh City.'

'I've never been able to understand how sitting in a plane can be so tiring, yet it is. Enjoy the holiday.'

'I'll do my best.'

* * *

Without question the trip with Rob was overdue, yet Ravi had no one and Julia couldn't shake the nagging accusation she was abandoning him when he needed her most. Rob had bluntly reminded her the graphic designer wasn't a friend. Of course, he'd been right. But it wasn't possible to have seen him beaten, broken and barely conscious and not want to support him until he was in a better place. She'd called before leaving Bothwell Street to let him know she was coming and got a monosyllabic grunt devoid of gratitude for her trouble. Ravi was sorry for himself: the attack had left him crippled and he hadn't come to terms with it, cursing the crutches the hospital had given him, in his eyes a symbol of his disability. The road back to a normal life would be long and hard; Julia was determined to be on the journey with him, whether he liked it or not.

The front door wasn't locked; inside, the curtains were drawn and it was dark. Ravi was in an armchair, his leg elevated on a stool. He said, 'Please excuse me if I don't get up,' and she sensed the heavy atmosphere around him. The guy she'd known had been easy-going, always with something funny to say. This was a different Ravi: his eyes were dull, his face thinner than she remembered. Since Julia had last seen him he'd lost weight and was wearing a crumpled dark-blue rugby shirt that hung loosely on him and looked none too clean; he wasn't taking care of himself.

She hadn't come to lecture him and settled for opening the windows, letting fresh air in. He watched her morosely and said, 'Thanks for coming. Don't think it isn't appreciated.'

Julia lifted a football magazine from the floor and tucked it in a rack by the fireplace. 'It's no bother. I couldn't go away without popping in.'

'Yes, well, before you start organising the place *and me* I'd prefer you leave everything as it is, if you don't mind.'

'I'm only—'

'I'm aware of what you're "only" doing, Julia, and I'd rather you didn't. When the mess begins to annoy me, I'll do something about it. Right now, I couldn't give a monkey's about any of it.'

'At least let me make you something to eat.'

'I'm not hungry.'

'Everybody has to eat, Ravi.'

His jaw tightened and Julia realised that, without intending to, she was testing his patience. He spoke with a quiet intensity that alarmed her. 'And when I'm hungry, I will. Now, stop fussing. That's all people do around me. Fuss, fuss, fuss. I tell them I hate it, but they carry on as though I don't exist. Have they no idea how that makes me feel?'

'People? What people?'

'A nurse comes in twice a week and I've got a home help until I've recovered enough to look after myself. Brilliant, isn't it? Twenty-three years old and my very own home help. Thankfully, my mother and father aren't here to witness how their only son turned out.'

His lip trembled; Ravi was in a bad place and Julia fell silent. The last time she'd been here he'd seemed in better spirits, a performance for her benefit.

He guessed what she was thinking and mellowed. 'Look, I'm sorry, forgive me. I'd prefer nobody saw me like this. You mean well but you shouldn't have come. Really, you shouldn't.'

Julia pushed back. '"Shouldn't have come"? Nonsense, of course, I should. What kind of friend would that be? Now, I want coffee. Care to join me?'

Ravi wasn't doing well and in the kitchen she wondered what to say that wouldn't start him off. When she came through he took a cup from her and sat it on the arm of his chair.

'Is there anything you need, anything at all? Because I'll get it for you.'

'No, I'm fine.'

'What about a few beers? You like Guinness, don't you?'

Ravi sighed and stared at the wall. 'I'm all right, Julia. I've decided to give up drinking. It's obviously not a good fit with who I am.'

'Are you sure?'

'Absolutely.'

'Why?'

'I should've thought that was obvious. If I hadn't been drunk this wouldn't have happened. Lesson learned. So, it's a no to the Guinness.'

Julia raised the question that had nagged her from the beginning. 'At the hospital when I asked why you were calling me at that time of night you said you couldn't remember. I thought that was strange – you must've had a reason.'

Ravi avoided looking at her. 'I lied.'

Julia put her cup down. 'Lied? Why would you? What was there to lie about?'

'I didn't feel like getting into it – it wasn't the right time.'

Ravi was depressed, vulnerable, and Julia hesitated, knowing all she had to do was press him on it and he'd tell her. She heard a catch in his voice and knew he was going to. 'After the pub is a blank. Most of it, anyway. I was drunk, drunker than I've been in my life, but I knew what I was doing.' Julia let him finish. 'To tell you I was leaving.'

'Leaving? I don't understand. I thought you were happy at Grapevine.'

'I was.'

'So what changed that made you drink yourself insensible?'

'Ellis. Ellis is what changed.'

'But he apologised publicly in the restaurant, didn't he? I was there, I heard him myself.'

'Yes, he did.'

'Didn't you believe him?'

Ravi had said more than he'd intended and closed down. It hurt Julia to see him so distressed; she tried to reach him. 'Listen to me, this isn't a conversation we should be having, especially right now. When you're better we'll discuss anything you want to discuss, calmly and rationally. I'll tell Tony we—'

Ravi produced a sheet of paper from the side of his armchair and handed it to her. 'No, we won't do anything of the kind. My mind's made up.'

'What do you mean?'

'I've resigned from Grapevine, effective immediately. This is a copy. I'm not coming back so there's nothing to discuss, is there?'

Julia was too shocked to speak – she hadn't expected this.

'Tony won't accept it.'

'Yes, he will. He can't remember my name, for God's sake.'

'I'll tell him how important you are to the team.'

'Not according to Ellis.'

'Ellis has no say in this. Have you had words with him, actually had an argument?'

Ravi gave a short ironic laugh. 'You mean, like the one you had?'

Julia had forgotten he'd overheard her heated exchange with Ellis and wished he hadn't. 'Did you hear much of it?'

'Enough to know there was a problem between the two of you, and that it wasn't just me. Don't deny it, Julia.'

Her faced flushed. 'I'm not going to because you're right, we did have an issue. I was very upset and felt the way you do now. To be fair, having said that, Ellis hasn't put a foot wrong since then. So, please, take this back. There's no need to resign, at any rate not while you aren't fit to look for another job. You're being hasty. I refuse to have any part in it.'

He shrugged. 'Look, I appreciate what you're trying to do but it's no use. I'm done with Grapevine.'

She'd lost him and it seemed there was nothing she could do about it. 'This is so sad. I wish you'd reconsider.'

'There's nothing to reconsider. I'll miss working with you, and Olivia's a nice girl. As for the rest...'

'I've let you down, haven't I?'

'No, you didn't hire Ellis Kirkbride, that was Connors' bright idea – he thinks the sun shines out of him. Listen, it's for the best. Ellis could be at

Grapevine for the next ten years. Twenty years.' He rapped his knuckles on the plastercast. 'Stuck here day-after-day with this has given me time to think things through. You're a good person and a good friend, Julia. Have your holiday with Rob but watch yourself with Ellis. He's bad news.'

30

Ellis had been to Hamilton Drive so many times it would've been easy to believe he was the one playing happy families here with Julia rather than the errant Rob: a sad, deluded fantasy he'd have done just about anything to make come true. But that had been then, not now. No! No! No! Definitely not now. The scales had fallen from his eyes and he'd seen the truth: Julia Sutherland was a heartless bitch. The world was full of them and always had been.

The Mazda was parked outside the door as Ellis had known it would be, but there was no sign of the silver Peugeot, which meant Rob was still in his office or paying a last visit to the redhead like the randy dog he was.

Ellis waited patiently for Julia to appear in that bloody awful charity-shop tracksuit, wondering how she'd got on with her sycophantic friend. Ravi had a thing for his team leader so blatantly obvious it was impossible to miss. Maybe he'd put on a brave face to impress her, cracking his bloody lame jokes and making her laugh.

That little double act had got under Ellis's skin from the very first day.

Then again, given the setback he'd suffered, perhaps it had been a more subdued affair and they'd shared a little cry. Boo-fucking-hoo; he certainly hoped so. In the midst of their blubbing had either of them twigged she was the reason Ravi would use a walking stick for the rest of his life? Probably not, but Ellis had put him in in his place, all right, sorted him good style. And now it was her turn.

The moment her front door opened Ellis engaged the gears and pulled away: it was beginning. South Africa all over again, only this time there would be no tears; this time he was going to enjoy it.

* * *

Julia started briskly along Hamilton Drive towards the Botanic Gardens, gradually increasing her pace after the first hundred yards as her muscles relaxed and the familiar sense of well-being settled over her. When she should be thinking about long, hot days and tropical nights, the disturbing conversation she'd had with Ravi was still in her head.

This would release her.

Usually, she went the other way round. Tonight she was distracted and not paying attention, for once letting her feet take her wherever they wanted to go. Rob had called to tell her he had one or two issues to deal with before he could finally close his PC and leave the office. Even if he'd been at home he wouldn't have come with her. Claims of endorphins stimulating a 'natural high' didn't convince him and he only accompanied her occasionally. The lazy sod didn't know what he was missing, especially in the evening with the heat going out of the day and shadows falling across the river. Tonight, the beauty of it would escape her as her mind returned to the concerning scene in Ravi's flat: in the aftermath of the assault he was clearly far from well, irritably refusing help, throwing out bleak warnings from his armchair prison. Making sense of his resentment wasn't difficult. From the start there had been no love lost between him and Ellis. Tony Connors had seen to that with his tactless slight, fracturing their relationship before it had even got going.

It hadn't healed and never would – a pity for all concerned because Ellis's contribution to the recent campaign had been invaluable.

Ravi was desperately low, depressed and alone. She trusted him, yet knowing he'd been on the other side of the door and overheard her conversation sent Julia's heart rate to a level that had nothing to do with how fast she was running.

Ellis was a strange fish, of that there was no doubt, and she'd tried hard to erase the bizarre experience in her office from her memory. He'd been a crazy person that day, intense and obsessed, referring to them as 'us' and 'we', grabbing her wrists, calling her darling and reminding her *she'd* kissed *him*. Then he'd coerced her into admitting to feelings she hadn't had, genuinely shocked when she'd rejected him. Ravi's interruption had been timely; she'd welcomed it.

Except... how long had he been there? How much had he heard?

Julia increased her speed, driven by anxiety, trying to outrun his voice in her head.

'You kissed me back. Don't say you didn't.'

At Queen Margaret Drive she veered right into the gardens, crossed the river and started back along the opposite bank. A grey-haired man with a black Labrador coming down 'Greek' Thomson's famous Sixty Steps ignored her as she raced past and Julia replayed Ellis's sinister enquiry.

'By the way, how is old Rob? Still working every hour under the sun?'

She hadn't understood it then and didn't now but, at the time, it had sounded strange. Was that what Ravi had meant about Ellis being bad news?

Under Julia's tracksuit her body was covered in sweat and suddenly it seemed more necessary than ever to get away from Glasgow, from Grapevine and everyone connected with it. When they got back from Vietnam she'd make a decision about her future and get Ravi the care he needed, no matter how much he resisted.

To her right, the river widened; home wasn't far and she was glad. In the distance, by the bridge, a man was waving to her, arms in the air, shouting something she couldn't make out. When she got closer she saw Ellis Kirkbride, the last person she expected, and her stride faltered.

He reached out. 'Julia, thank God I've found you!'

* * *

The plan was bold, no denying it, audacious some might say, seriously unwise a more accurate description. Each element had been weighed, carefully considered and was in place. But it was far from perfect and what he was about to do was the riskiest part. All it would take was somebody to wander along at the wrong time and... Ellis drew his mouth into a grim smile. Acknowledging weakness was one thing, dwelling on failure was something else: it would be what it would be.

He got out of the car, folded his arms across his chest and leaned against the bonnet trying to look inconspicuous; drawing attention to himself was the last thing he needed.

Julia was a self-confessed creature of habit who ran the same route at the same time every evening in life. Tonight would be different, she'd be later, helpful because it would be dark. He expected her to come down the steps – the sooner the better; the longer he spent in the open, the greater the chance of some sharp-eyed nosey old bird in the houses high above the path being able to identify him.

After ten minutes Ellis anxiously began questioning himself. This was the most problematic piece of the plan and, as such, out of his control. She should be here by now. What was keeping her? Had he got it wrong? Had she changed her mind and doubled back to her flat? If so, the opportunity would be lost, maybe for ever.

He crept forward, thinking perhaps she was on the bridge deciding if it wasn't better to let the run go this evening, but there was no sign of her and Ellis resisted the temptation to climb the stairs to the road. He peered in the opposite direction as far as he could see. The Kelvin Walkway was deserted and the irony of the situation twisted his mouth into a silent snarl: the circumstances were ideal, exactly as he'd imagined them in his dingy basement. Everything, except Julia!

He got back into his car and beat his fists on the steering wheel, scarcely able to believe what was happening. He screamed his rage. 'No! No! Fucking no! She should be here! She has to be!'

Frustration welled in his eyes. He angrily brushed the tears away, turned on the engine and tried to calm down. Okay. All right. If this was a bust it wasn't the end of the world. Julia Sutherland wouldn't get away with how she'd treated him – he'd go to his basement and come up with a new approach. He'd done it before; he could do it again.

Out of nowhere in the rear-view, a grey shape raced towards him through the gloom; Ellis's heart leapt in his chest. Could it be? Lamplight caught the runner's face as she lifted her chin. It was her.

Ellis punched the air. 'Yes! Yes!'

Julia must've gone the other way. If he'd waited in Hamilton Drive he'd have known that. Instead, through his own stupidity, he'd almost left and abandoned what he'd so meticulously put in place.

The original plan had been based on surprise, stepping out from the cover of the bridge and catching her unawares; grabbing her before she could resist and throwing her in the boot – the whole thing over in seconds. Improvising didn't faze him. Ellis jumped out of the car and waved his arms in the air, shouting as she came closer. Her cheeks were red from exertion and she was breathing heavily.

He forced panic that wasn't entirely fake into his voice. 'Julia, thank God I've found you!'

'Why?'

'We've been trying to reach you but your bloody mobile's off.'

She stepped away from him, suddenly afraid of what he was going to say. 'Oh, no, don't tell me something's happened to Rob. Please don't tell me that.'

Ellis struggled to speak and went into his act. 'Not Rob, he's fine.'

'Then what?'

'It's Ravi.'

'What about him?'

'He's tried to kill himself.'

Shock drained her colour as she processed what she was hearing. 'What? Ravi? I can't believe it! I was with him just a few hours ago.'

Ellis took her arm and led her to his car. 'I know, you told me you were going.'

'Where is he? Is he okay?'

'In hospital. And it's touch and go, I'm afraid.'

'I have to see him. Take me to him, Ellis. Hurry!'

'I will, get in.'

Ellis fired the ignition and shot a glance across at his frightened passenger. She said, 'Was it pills? Did he overdose on his painkillers?' She wrung her hands. 'Oh my God, what a terrible thing. Poor Ravi. This afternoon when I was with him he wasn't in a good place but I didn't realise...'

Ellis aggressively cut out in front of a black cab and turned right onto Great Western Road. He said, 'Don't give yourself a hard time. You couldn't know what was going on in his head. Nobody could.'

'I appreciate you saying that. Unfortunately, it doesn't make me feel better. Have they pumped his stomach?'

'No.'

'Why not? Isn't that what they do?'

'It wasn't pills.'

'Then... what?'

'Ravi slit his wrists.'

Julia covered her face with her hands; this was too awful. 'Oh, God! Oh my God! Poor Ravi.'

Ellis let the information sink in before he went on. Julia was crying. He watched her and added to her misery. 'An upstairs neighbour found him unconscious.'

'Will he...? Do they think he'll live?'

Ellis hesitated for dramatic effect, spinning it out, enjoying her pain. 'Well, the doctors haven't said but it doesn't look great. He's lost a lot of blood.'

At the traffic lights he took a left into Byres Road and smothered a smile. This conversation was an unexpected bonus, the icing on the cake. Julia sat quietly dabbing at her eyes. For the moment, at least, she'd run out of questions. Ellis joined Dumbarton Road and drove on, wondering when she'd notice they were going in the wrong direction.

She spoke and he detected the dawning of doubt. 'Which hospital is he in?'

Ellis had his answer ready and delivered it confidently. 'The Queen Elizabeth.'

'But that's miles away. Ravi lives in Dennistoun. Why not take him to the Royal?'

Ellis shrugged and overtook a bus. 'It was an emergency. Maybe that had something to do with it.'

Julia was numb with shock but she was a clever lady and he could practically hear the wheels turning in her brain as she slowly put it together. 'The Queen Elizabeth's in Govan, on the other side of the river, isn't it? Surely we should be heading for the Clyde Tunnel?'

Ellis stared ahead, his lips set in a tight smile.

Almost got it Julia, you're almost there.

'This way's faster.'

'How can it be? The only other bridge is Erskine.'

A grin spread across Ellis's face; he was as relaxed as he'd been the night they'd shared the Chinese takeaway and Julia realised something wasn't right.

'You're a remarkable woman, you really are. Why you've thrown yourself away on that loser of a husband is a mystery for the ages.' He shook his head at some private joke. 'Tony Connors told me you were smart but we both know old Tony likes the sound of his own voice. Have to admit I didn't believe him. Sold both of us short by not mentioning just how smart, didn't he? I had to figure that out for myself. Shame, really, because it didn't have to be like this.'

'I don't understand. What're you talking about and why are we going the wrong way?'

'The wrong way?' Ellis laughed. 'What makes you think that? No, this is the right way – the only way, actually.'

Julia tried to open the door; it was locked and she faced him, fear seeping into her. Defiance was all she had. 'Let me out. I'm warning you. Stop the car and let me out before this – whatever the hell it is – goes any further.'

Ellis dropped the façade – it had served its purpose – and spoke without anger or malice. 'This isn't me, Julia, no, no, no. I'm not to blame. You brought it on yourself.'

'Ellis, you need help, you're insane, you have to be. Nobody in their right mind—'

The fist struck her squarely on the jaw. She didn't see it coming; her head crashed against the window. Ellis pressed his foot on the accelerator and sat back in his seat. It had been a rocky start but the plan was back on track.

He said, 'Let's see who's in their right mind in a day or two, shall we, Mrs Sutherland?'

31

With a work schedule like Rob's there would never be a convenient time to go on holiday. If the decision had been his, he wouldn't be going. Julia had given him no choice and it was scant consolation to know when he returned it would all be here waiting for him.

On the upside, so would Michelle – the real reason he was reluctant to leave.

Outside in Park Circus it was starting to get dark. As he watched, cars parked since morning vacated their designated spaces. Lawyers, accountants and architects like him heading for home after one more profitable day at the office. Rob had too many loose ends to tie up before he could follow them and it wouldn't be Hamilton Drive he went to.

A part of him regretted his infidelity, another part rejoiced in it. When the red-haired woman had introduced herself and held onto his hand a second or two longer than necessary, he'd been aware of something passing between them. If he'd recognised the danger in it, what would he have done? Rob knew the answer: he'd have remembered he was a married man, smiled politely and let go of the gently squeezing fingers. Five minutes later he'd have called Julia to hear her voice, overwhelmed by the luck that had brought them together.

And life would've gone on uncomplicated, seemingly complete.

The frantic couplings in hotel bedrooms, the clandestine meetings in coffee shops and car parks, wouldn't have happened. There would be no demands, no hopeless expectation, nothing except him and Julia dreaming of – how had she put it? – 'sitting at a roadside café eating something spicy from a bowl, a world away from Glasgow'.

Once, that would've sounded exotic, romantic, wonderful. Now, the prospect made him feel empty. He'd made promises to Michelle, promises he intended to keep. Rob punched the number hidden amongst his business contacts and waited for her to pick up.

* * *

Winding things up had required an interminable series of text messages and emails, barely legible notes he'd struggle to read later, and brief client phone conversations in a holding pattern that kept everybody in the loop until he was able to reconnect with them.

In the Peugeot, driving down Woodlands Road, Rob resigned himself to having done the best he could and only hoped no metaphorical fire broke out while he wasn't around to douse the flames.

Who would've believed being an architect could be so stressful?

The challenge now was to clear his mind of work and dedicate himself to ensuring his wife had the trip she needed and deserved. Michelle was a separate conversation. Her he kept in another part of his brain to be visited and revisited. He was later getting home than he'd thought. Tonight, that wouldn't be a problem. Julia was aware he couldn't just shut down his PC and quit Park Circus without a backward glance. The firm paid him a decent salary, so of course they insisted on their money's worth. Being taken on by Galloway, Bartholomew and Figgis was the reason they'd been able to afford the West End, otherwise they'd still be in that outrageously expensive bedsit. Although, he couldn't deny they'd had some great times in that cramped little box.

The memory made him smile before the cold truth of how far the relationship had changed washed it away, leaving him sad and a little afraid.

The table lamp given to them as a wedding present was on in the hall;

all other lights in the house were off. He climbed the stairs to check if she was having a nap and saw the two suitcases of neatly folded clothes open on the bed. Julia always did their packing. Thank God – he wouldn't know where to begin. Down in the kitchen he made himself an espresso, took it into the lounge and sat on the couch wondering what to do with himself. After a few minutes he lifted the TV remote and languidly surfed the endless channels that always seemed to be showing repeats, reality shows or Matt Damon going up against the bad guys as Jason Bourne. Rob turned it off and silently surveyed the familiar surroundings that were so alien without his wife: this was their place, his and Julia's; every piece of furniture, every picture, even the cup he was drinking from, had a tale behind it only they could tell. Was he ready to destroy everything they'd built and break her heart in the process?

His thoughts turned to Michelle: the 'other woman'. Rob remembered the hurt on her face at the door as they'd said their goodbyes. He dug out his mobile and weighed it in his hand, uncertain what to do for the best, in his mind's eye seeing her, alone, depressed, sitting with the lights off, an almost-empty bottle of Absolut near her on the floor beside the shoes she'd kicked off. They'd spoken just a couple of hours ago – phoning when she wasn't expecting to hear from him might upset her all over again, the very last thing he wanted.

He returned to the kitchen, about to put the cup in the dishwasher, and stopped as the hopelessness of the situation he'd created came rushing in. Julia would've emptied the machine and expected it to stay empty because tomorrow they were leaving, leaving for three whole bloody weeks. Rob went back to the lounge and poured himself a stiff whisky. He put it to his lips, threw it back in one go and wiped his mouth on his sleeve like a street-corner drunk with a litre of rot-gut wine. The alcohol burned his throat and he splashed a second measure into the glass; it went the same way as the first but didn't lessen the loathing he felt for the man he'd become and the inevitable harm he would cause his wife.

At the window he looked out onto a deserted Hamilton Drive, suddenly uneasy. Something wasn't right here; Julia had never been this late back from her run.

He punched in her number and got through to voicemail. Rob disguised the disquiet gathering in his chest. 'Julia, where are you? Call me when you get this.'

Five minutes later, he tried again, less concerned about his tone. 'Julia, we've talked about this and I'm starting to lose it. Answer your bloody phone! That's the whole point of having it with you. Call me. Please.'

He paced the room, genuinely concerned, cursing himself for not objecting sooner. Running by the river was all well and good in the summer when it was still light at nine or ten o'clock. But not after dark. Julia loved the peace, claimed it renewed her soul. Well, it could be as peaceful as the grave but it wasn't wise and he should have forbidden her. Through his fear – because that was what it was now – he scoffed at the nonsense he was telling himself. The notion he had the power to forbid his wife from doing any bloody thing was ludicrous. Julia was her own woman; running was her thing and she didn't require approval from him or anyone else.

He stared at the phone, willing it to ring, frustration boiling in him, close to smashing the useless piece of crap against the wall. In the beginning she'd left hers at home and it was only after several frank exchanges that she'd agreed to take it with her. At least it wasn't turned off; a small mercy Rob was thankful for.

When his mobile pinged he grabbed it in both hands and found her message in WhatsApp. Reading the words confirmed his fears.

> I'm hurt. Can't walk. Come and get me

Rob frantically thumbed a reply, forcing his emotions under control.

> Where are you?

Thirty seconds later the phone pinged again.

> River. Near the bridge.

He dismissed taking the car because, foolishly, he'd been drinking. In seconds he was in the street on fire with resentment. This or something like it was exactly what he'd been afraid of. Being right didn't help, not while Julia was lying somewhere hurt. They'd gone running together just twice and he hadn't forgotten the route they'd taken – along leafy La Crosse Terrace, across the Belmont Street Bridge and down the steps to the walkway.

Rob was angry his wife might be injured. He anticipated a twisted ankle – what if it was worse than that? The holiday would have to be cancelled.

In the middle of the bridge he paused to catch his breath and scanned the dimly lit riverbank below, seeing the silhouettes of trees against the night sky and the black smudge of the water, but no sign of his wife. His hurried footsteps slapped the stone stairs until he got to the bottom, so focused on Julia he didn't realise anyone else was there.

Behind him, Ellis moved from the shadows and crashed the rock gripped in his palm against the back of Rob's head. Rob stumbled forward and fell to the ground, powerless to prevent his attacker kicking him in the head, rolling him onto his back and straddling his chest.

Rob's eyes fluttered open and closed as the rock found its mark again. An exhilarated Ellis raised it once more and stopped at the top of the arc. It was tempting. Here, under a bridge in the West End of the city, killing Julia Sutherland's husband would be clean and immensely satisfying.

But it wasn't part of the plan: it wouldn't be enough.

Ellis tossed the stone into the bushes. 'No,' he said. 'No, Rob, that would be too easy, mate.'

32

DAY ONE

Julia had been semi-conscious in the passenger seat when the car rolled to a stop and she'd seen Ellis get out and unlock a shiny new padlock at odds with the old gate, amazed she could notice such a stupid detail. Her jaw ached and there was blood in her mouth. Instinct warned her it was wiser she pretend to still be out of it: Ellis had gone to extraordinary lengths to capture her; there was no knowing what he'd do if she resisted. Her throat closed over, her stomach heaved and she gagged. But if she wanted to survive whatever sick plan was in his head, she had to get a hold on herself. Julia had taken deep, slow breaths and felt the nausea subside. When he'd closed the gate behind them, he'd driven over a rough surface and come to a sharp stop. Then he'd carried her from the car and dropped her on the ground while he dealt with the door of a large container. She'd lain on the damp earth, sick with fear, hearing the grate of metal against metal, wanting to scream yet terrified it would make an already horrific situation worse.

He dragged her inside the steel box and dumped her in a chair. Plastic ties tightened and bit into her skin, binding her ankles to the wooden legs. Julia sensed he was watching her and opened her eyes.

The light made her blink and she turned her face away from it. When her eyes adjusted, Ellis was leaning against the wall, smiling. He said, 'I hope you like what I've done with the place. Not a contender for *Beautiful Homes*, I grant you, though not bad in the circumstances.' He sighed. 'You wouldn't believe how hard it was pulling it all together in such a short time. So apologies if I've missed anything, though, honestly, I've done my best.'

Julia found her voice. Somehow, she had to stop this craziness, reason with him before it went any further. 'Ellis. Ellis, listen to me. This has to end. You must see that.'

He shrugged, smiled again and carried on as though she hadn't spoken, and she knew it was already too late. His tone was light, whimsical, as unthreatening as it was possible to be. 'I expect you're wondering where you are. The short answer is nowhere. Well, not nowhere, exactly. I'd guess this was a hive of industry once upon a time. There were people, lots of them, but they left decades ago and aren't coming back.' He banged the side of the container and waited for the echo to fade. 'This old relic is all that's left to show they were ever here.'

Ellis was energised, alive in the moment, as animated as Julia had seen him, behaving as though this were normal rather than frightening and surreal. 'Of course, I don't expect you to take my word for it. No doubt you'll hammer and yell until you're hoarse and your fingers are raw – I'm sure I would.' He shook his head. 'It won't make any difference. No one will hear. You may as well be on the other side of the moon.'

He paced the container from one end to the other, tossing information into the air like a tour guide. 'The lights run on batteries and will come on with movement, which may make sleeping difficult. Again, my apologies. Nothing else for it, I'm afraid. Can't have you crawling around in the dark, can I? And while we're on the subject of apologies, please understand I appreciate a chemical toilet isn't quite what you're used to, though I'm sure you'll muddle by.'

Julia spat her disgust at him. 'Do you have any idea what you've done? Do you? Because I do, and you won't get away with it.'

'Oh, fighting talk. I admire spirit in a woman, always have, but you see, Julia, it's not what I've done you should be worried about. It's what I'm going to do.'

She ignored the threat and yelled, 'You're insane, Ellis! What's this about? Why am I here?'

Ellis pointed to the table and the other chair. 'A sharp lady like you has to have noticed there are two chairs and be asking why. Well, I'll tell you. I pride myself on being a fair-minded guy and it wouldn't be right to not give you a bit of company. Someone to talk to. Somebody you know – or think you know. I refer, of course, to Rob, your husband. Who else would a wife want to spend her last hours on earth with? Although whether they are, in fact, the *last* hours depends on her.'

Hearing his name sent Julia into a frenzy, straining against the plastic ties hard enough to break the skin at her wrist, shouting, 'Whatever this fiasco is, leave Rob alone! You hear me! Leave my husband out of it!'

'You mean the way I left your pal Ravi alone on the pavement? That kind of alone?'

'What?' Julia tried to swallow and couldn't; her throat had gone dry. Bizarrely, the admission of what Ellis had done to Ravi was almost more shocking than everything that had happened and she reacted. 'You bastard! How could you hurt someone as gentle as him? You're a psycho.'

Ellis was impervious to the rebuke. He pursed his lips and tutted. 'Harsh. Very harsh, Julia. Have to say I'm disappointed. You must've been blind not to see what was going on.'

Julia was on the edge of hysterics; this was deranged. 'There was nothing going on. You conjured it out of your sick mind. Ravi's a nice guy who just happened to be on my team.'

'Ah, yes, nothing from your side, maybe, but the idiot was buttering you up, waiting for the right time to make his move.'

'Ravi? Are we talking about the same man?'

'Absolutely. Your not-so-secret admirer.'

'Don't be ridiculous. You can't seriously expect me to believe that.'

Ellis didn't reply and Julia sneered; without trying, she'd hit a nerve. 'Well, well, well. Who would have thought it? You're jealous.'

'Jealous of a cripple? A guy who'll need a stick and limp through the rest of his life? I don't think so.'

'You knew telling me he'd tried to kill himself would lure me into the car. I'd only just left him – why didn't I see through it? Is that what this is about – Ravi?'

The conversation had taken a turn Ellis didn't like. He said, 'Listen, bitch, I couldn't give a flying fuck about your designer buddy, one way or the other. But trust me when I tell you that behind the charm and the jokey façade, you were in old Ravi's sights. You've had a lucky escape. You should be thanking me. I did you a favour.'

His final comments made Julia shudder. 'I won't be long. When I come back "all will be revealed", as they say.' He blew her a kiss. 'Try not to miss me too much.'

* * *

The metal door closed behind him. She heard the muted sound of a car driving away, and in the silence Julia bowed her head and let the tears come. This was her doing. She'd been a fool: the truth had been in front of her from the beginning if only she'd had eyes to see it. At the meeting in Tony Connors' office, Ellis's mask had slipped and the ugliness behind it had flashed into the open.

From then, Ellis had cleverly waged a one-man charm offensive against her, apologising, almost making her feel sorry for him; presented her with flowers and chocolates it felt churlish to refuse. Ravi hadn't been duped. His own experience of the guy, or perhaps what he'd overheard outside the office door, had made up his mind to the point where he was willing to quit Grapevine rather than work with him.

Ravi had been on to him. And he'd paid the price. The graphic designer hadn't been set on by a gang of street thugs; Ellis, outraged and envious of his relationship with her, had attacked a man not capable of defending himself and beaten him insensible.

Despicable as it was, it wasn't important, not now. Ellis Kirkbride was a lunatic. Escape was all that mattered; her life depended on it. She didn't know where he'd gone but when he came back, for sure, the nightmare would begin in earnest.

* * *

In the chair across the table Rob slumped forward, drifting in and out of consciousness. When Ellis had hauled him in, head lolling, feet dragging on the floor, Julia was convinced her husband was dead and despair had torn at the flimsy threads of unrealistic hope that the police would already be looking for her. Seeing him had broken Julia's heart and it was only when Ellis produced the plastic ties that she'd realised her husband was still alive. Rob was an innocent casualty of Ellis's twisted infatuation with her; he had no part in this.

Ellis tightened the restraints around Rob's ankles and stood up to admire his work.

'The gang's all here. Let the games begin.'

The words got through. Rob raised his head and Julia saw the extent of the damage. She gasped. Black blood matted his forehead, more had trickled from the nose that might be broken to his swollen lips and down his chin; his left eye was glazed, the right completely closed. Ellis had enjoyed his work.

Rob saw her and tried to speak; his mouth moved but nothing came out. Ellis spoke directly to him. 'We haven't been properly introduced. I'm a colleague of Julia's and it saddens me to report your wife played a game with me, a cruel game, surprisingly cruel, actually. She thought she'd beaten me but she was wrong. Because it isn't over. Although it soon will be. You were probably too taken with your own entertainment recently to notice. It would be nice to say your secret's safe. Unfortunately, it wouldn't be true.'

Julia screamed, 'You're mad! Let Rob go! Let him go! He hasn't done anything to you. Please, let him go! Ellis, please, I'm begging you.'

'We both realise that won't be happening so don't test my patience.' His arm swept the length of the container. 'You must be wondering what all this is about. To be honest, Julia, it was you who put the idea in my head with your little speech. Can you remember it? I can. Word for word. Let me get this right... you love your husband with "every breath I take"... that was it.' Ellis nodded at the memory. '"Every breath I take". A grand statement not easily forgotten, especially from the woman I thought loved me.'

'That was inside your crazy head. You didn't hear it from me.'

Ellis carried on, speaking to himself. 'I didn't forget and when I saw this rust bucket slowly rotting away, I knew exactly how to use it.'

He fingered the envelopes on the table. 'Excuse the cliché but every picture tells a story. These ones certainly do. Not flattering, some of them, though that isn't the point.'

Julia sensed Ellis was getting to the end and blurted out the first desperate nonsense that came to her. 'If you leave us here, they'll come looking for us.'

'Really. And where do you suppose they'd begin – Saigon? As far as everybody's concerned you're in South East Asia for the next three weeks.'

Fear rocketed Julia to a new level. Her legs started to shake; her bottom lip trembled uncontrollably as she closed her eyes to block out the terrifying consequences of his statement. Ellis observed her with a cold detachment, then went outside and returned holding his camera. He crouched, focusing, lining up the shot. 'One for the album. Something to remember you by.'

CLICK.

'Excellent. Now, let me explain how this is going to work. I've given you everything you'll need. No heater, though I don't expect you'll be alive long enough for that to be a problem. Exactly how long you last is what we're going to find out, but, obviously, you can't go on forever.' Ellis produced a knife from his inside pocket and placed it on the table beside the envelopes. 'When I leave, use this to set yourselves free. Of course, you'll squander the first two or three hours yelling like excited schoolgirls and hammering on the walls. A natural reaction to your situation.' He made a sad face. 'And a complete waste of time, I'm afraid. All you'll do is use up the one thing I haven't supplied.'

The conversational tone, the throwaway casualness of it, belied the awfulness Ellis was describing. Rob was slowly coming round, not yet fully compos mentis enough to understand. A bead of sweat dripped into Julia's eye. She understood: they were in an Edgar Allen Poe horror story.

Ellis pointed to high on the container's ribbed side, still in tour-guide mode. 'That's an air vent. Modern ones often have four, apparently. This tin can is old. It only has two, six slats each.' He leaned on the table and studied his captives in turn. 'You're asking yourselves why am I telling you this, aren't you? Well, again, Rob, look no further than your faithless wife who loves you with every breath she takes – or so she says. An interesting concept. I thought we should test it.'

Rob lifted his bloodied head and Julia was overwhelmed by shame: this was her doing. If she'd gone to Tony Connors and reported Ellis when she should have, they'd be sharing a bottle of wine and toasting the trip the next day; she'd pack the last few things in their cases, they'd go to bed and make love. Instead, they were here while a psychopath cheerfully detailed how they were going to die.

Ellis said, 'It's not all bad news – you could get lucky. Actually, that's a lie. I'm going to give you a little bit of time, then start sealing off the vents.' He nodded towards the envelopes. 'When you see what's inside those you'll have a lot to discuss. I wouldn't want you to worry about suffocating too soon.'

Ellis let what he was saying sink in and spoke to Julia. 'Your reaction will be interesting – whether you want the truth, no matter how devastating it might be, or choose to keep your illusions intact. I suppose—'

She couldn't listen to any more. 'I hate you. More than any human being I've ever known. I hate you, Ellis.'

His lips parted in a snarl. 'Not nearly as much as I hate you.'

He walked round the table, eking out the drama. 'How much oxygen can these crates hold – any idea? A couple of days? Three? Let's be optimistic and go for three. With the vents, who knows? Take them out of the equation and it becomes a very different proposition.' Ellis picked up the knife and held it against Rob's throat. 'But we can assume one person will survive longer than two.'

33

Julia and Rob stared at each other, too frightened to move. Before he'd gone, Ellis had cut the tie on Julia's wrists and stepped sharply out of reach as she'd lunged for the knife. The attempt was clumsy and irritated him. He said, 'I'd never accuse you of being predictable, Julia, but that was just stupid. Please don't insult my intelligence again or you'll leave this life unaware who the man you're married to, the one you claim to love so much, really is.'

He stood behind Rob and pressed the blade against his throat again. 'If I'd only wanted to kill you, you'd both already be dead. Surely you understand that? Don't force me to prove it.'

Neither of them needed convincing. Ellis laid the knife in the centre of the table and walked to the door. 'As I said, you're not going to be short of conversation. Just remember, everything you say or do depletes the oxygen. At first, with the vents open, you won't notice, but as I start closing them off it'll become progressively more difficult to breathe and you'll think about how you can survive for another day, another hour, another minute.'

The door clanged shut, leaving them alone in their metal coffin. Julia grabbed the knife, sliced through the plastic holding them and they fell into each other's arms. She shivered, riven by panic and pent-up fear. Rob held her, gently whispering words he didn't believe. 'Hey, hey. C'mon, c'mon. Somebody will find us.'

'They won't. We're supposed to be out of the country. We've made it easy for him.'

She broke free and threw herself against the wall, pounding it with her fists. Rob caught hold of her again and pulled her away. 'Don't. Don't, Julia. You heard what he said. All we'll do is use up the air.' He took her face in his hands and tenderly kissed her forehead. 'The smartest thing we can do is stay calm. The way he took us, first you then me, shows he's telling the truth. He could've killed us yet he didn't. He wants something.'

'Yes, to make us suffer.' Julia struggled out of his arms again and hammered the wall a second time, then collapsed on the floor, defeated, sobbing hopelessly. 'No, no, I'm not ready to die.'

Rob was determined to stay strong for his wife, but he felt his resolve crumble.

'Nobody's going to die. I promise you, nobody's dying.'

'We will if we don't do something to get out of here.'

'Something, yes, not this.' He helped her to her feet and led her back to the chair. 'Look, he's given us bottled water, energy bars so we won't starve, light, even sleeping bags. Christ knows how long he's been setting this up. We aren't the victims of some random assault. A crazy man's abducted us for a reason.' Rob was talking to convince himself. He ran a despairing hand through his hair, wincing at the pain; the wound was still bleeding.

Julia forgot about herself, jumped to her feet and examined it. 'This looks deep. Let me clean it with the water.'

She took off his T-shirt and pressed it against the gash to stem the flow. Rob said, 'I don't get it. Tony Connors isn't a fool. He's a decent judge of character – why did he employ this guy?'

'Because he's plausible. Charming when it suits him. And he's clever. When people are around he acts normal. They don't suspect what he's really like, what he's capable of.'

Rob covered her hand with his. 'Why does he hate you? What does he think you've done to him?'

Julia avoided eye contact. 'Ellis Kirkbride's fixated on me, has been from the first day at Grapevine when Tony introduced him. I thought he was flirting and, though it made me uncomfortable, laughed it off. Until it got out of hand and I had no option but to put him in his place. Little did I know he was emotionally unstable. And violent. He actually admitted it wasn't a street gang who beat up Ravi, it was him.'

'For God's sake! Why would he hurt Ravi?'

'Because Ellis is obsessed with me. Insanely jealous of anybody who comes near me. Ravi was always laughing, always joking; Ellis didn't like it.'

'Did you tell anybody? Did you report him to Tony?'

'No, I didn't.'

'Why the hell not? He's your boss. Grapevine's his company. Everything that happens under its roof is his business.'

'I didn't think he'd believe me.'

It sounded weak and Rob was stunned. 'You didn't think... Why wouldn't he?'

'You have to work there to understand.'

Rob lifted his head. 'Try me.'

'Ellis is Tony's star boy. I objected to him coming onto our team. Tony's like an elephant; he doesn't forget and wouldn't want to hear anything bad about Ellis, especially from me. I'd have been accused of professional jealousy and reminded it was my responsibility as the team leader. Failing that, take it to HR and let them sort it out.'

'So why didn't you do that?'

'I was afraid everyone would assume I was trying to get Ellis sacked because I felt threatened by his ability.'

'Fucking incredible. I had Connors down as a bit of an arse but gave him credit for having more going on than that.'

Julia tried to get him to understand what it had been like. 'It came to a head one morning in my office. Ellis really overstepped the mark, talking crazy talk about "us" and our future. I put him in his place. In fact, I threw him out and wrongly assumed that would be the end of it. Ravi was in the corridor. He heard raised voices and asked if I was all right.'

'What did you say?'

'I palmed him off with nonsense about a creative disagreement.'

'Why didn't you tell him? He'd have believed you.'

Julia was exhausted; frustration got the better of her. She said, 'I don't know, Rob, but I didn't.' Her voice softened. 'I thought I'd dealt with it.'

Talking about it to Rob rekindled the resentment burning inside. Before he could stop her she angrily snatched the envelope with her name on it. 'What the hell was all that about having plenty to talk about?'

Rob put his hand on hers. 'Leave that. He's toying with us, can't you see? Getting us to play by his rules. God knows what he's set up, but for sure it won't be anything good. If we don't engage he'll be forced to change his plan. I vote we tear both of them up and throw them in the corner. Then we'll see how he reacts.'

Julia shouted at him. '"See how he reacts"? Look around, Rob, this is it! This is how! We're dealing with an irrational mind; the slightest thing could set him off. It already has. And those bloody lights going out when we stop moving is freaking me out.' She tossed the envelope back on the table and dropped to her knees. 'I don't have the energy to face whatever's inside this.'

Rob couldn't argue with her logic and didn't try. 'Okay. Just hold it together for both our sakes, Julia. This guy hasn't dragged us here by accident. If we panic, we really will be lost. Let's both of us drink water and wait for him to make his next move.'

Julia felt herself starting to shake; she couldn't control it. 'He told us what it is. He's going to cut the air off.'

Rob responded the only way he could and tried to calm his wife down. 'Look, this is insane. I don't believe that. He just wants to scare us.'

'Well, it's working.'

* * *

Ellis poured three-fingers of a twelve-year-old Glenfarclas and raised the glass to the light in a silent salute to himself. The amber, sparkling like a golden sun, persuaded him to take the bottle with him. Why not? He had something to celebrate.

In the basement, he slipped out of his jacket, put the mobiles and the watches he'd taken from them on his desk. The Anglepoise lamp illuminated the spider's web of cracked plaster snaking behind the photographs that had replaced the nameless Asian girls. Later, when he printed the shot of the terrified Sutherlands tied to their chairs, the photograph, not the last by any means, would all but complete a new collection.

Normally, Ellis would've been in a hurry to add it. Tonight, he could do better than a glossy 10 x 8. The remote-access camera installed days after he'd stumbled across the container produced a surprisingly high-quality picture.

The screen flickered, the voyeur in him awoke, and adrenaline quickened his pulse. As the image sharpened, Ellis saw Rob and Julia and groaned with satisfaction that was instantly banished by a stab of disappointment. They seemed stoically resigned to their fate. He'd expected them to be frantically searching for some means of escape – at the very least screaming oaths at each other. Instead, they sat much as he'd left them, and Ellis feared his warning about using up the oxygen had spooked them into catatonic inaction. The idea had been to scare them, not turn them to stone.

Though their hands were free, the proof of their infidelities lay unopened and Ellis guessed that had been Rob's doing. A good try but it wouldn't last; it couldn't. The moment one of them felt a catch in their chest, their imagination would go into overdrive; the metal walls would start to close in around them and the inevitable panic would begin.

Long before then, curiosity would have killed more than the cat – Ellis's money was firmly on her. Females had to know everything; it was part of who they were. Julia would insist on uncovering the mystery on the table in front of her and there would be nothing her husband could do to stop her. After that, accusation and counter accusation would follow. They might even come to blows. He'd have the best seat in the house as their marriage shredded before his eyes. The irony was it wouldn't make a blind bit of difference because they were both going to die.

Ellis edged closer to the screen, anxious not to miss a single second. He swirled the whisky in the glass and downed a third of it, wishing the spy camera had audio so he could hear as well as see their fear; in hindsight, that had been a mistake.

No matter. This was going to be good.

34

DAY TWO

Michelle woke up on the couch wearing the same clothes she'd had on the previous day. She stood up and immediately sat down again. Her head felt as though it had been used as a football and the lounge was unbearably hot because she'd forgotten to turn the heating down overnight.

With an effort she crossed the room and opened a window, grateful for fresh air, then turned to face the evidence of her unhappiness. The bottle of Absolut lying on the carpet hadn't been full, a small mercy. Michelle remembered screwing the top off and lifting it to her lips. The vodka had been tasteless and she'd gone to the kitchen to get something to cheer it up. It and her. She pinched her tired eyes and tucked a strand of loose hair behind her ear – well, she'd certainly managed the first part.

Half a bottle of Absolut and cranberry juice. No wonder she felt sick.

The thought of eating made her want to vomit so she settled for sipping a glass of water. Her mobile lay on the couch, almost out of charge. Michelle checked it for missed calls and found none. What the hell was she expecting? Rob wouldn't have left Glasgow, probably wouldn't even be at the airport. Yes, he'd promised to ring every day and there was no reason to think he wouldn't. But he'd be with his wife, not her.

And that was the point.

Promises weren't enough and never would be. She needed him here, now, not six thousand miles away. If he spent so much time with Julia, it would be easy to rediscover what had attracted him in the first place and fall for her all over again. Speculating was self-inflicted torture – she had to get a grip. He'd said he'd leave Julia after the holiday was over; she had to trust him. Meantime, life would go on. She had a job, responsibilities that required her attention. Counting the hours like a silly schoolgirl wouldn't make them pass more quickly.

Jealousy beyond her control clawed at her fragile belief. What had begun as an affair had morphed into love. Now, the thought of living without Rob was more than she could stand.

Michelle dried her eyes and forced herself to sit up. It was time to confront what was really going on. To the outside world she was strong and assured – an ambitious woman who knew where she was going and how she'd get there. The truth was infinitely more complex: underneath the confident veneer was an insecure woman and that same insecurity was tearing her apart.

She picked up the Absolut bottle and poured what was left of the vodka down the sink. The next three weeks would be agony – the price of love – but she'd survive without a crutch, thank you very much.

* * *

Ellis hadn't slept; he was too excited. It had been naïve to assume he could simply close down the drama on the computer screen and go to bed and in the early hours he'd returned to it.

The basement was colder than it had been earlier, the smell of damp more pronounced; the shadows cast by the lamp seemed strangely forbidding and he sensed a little of what his prisoners must be going through. Ellis shrugged the insight away with an unconvincing laugh, cut short when he heard floorboards creak in the room directly above and froze. Down here there was no difference between day and night. Every noise was an intruder, every darkened corner concealing an enemy ready to do him harm. Bloody nonsense, of course. He was the enemy. If there was harm to be done, he'd be the one to do it.

Adrenaline pumping through his body sharpened his awareness, heightening every sound and sensation. Added to the stress of getting through the last few super-difficult weeks at Grapevine – answering yes, Julia, no, Julia, three fucking bags full, Julia – had taken a toll on his nerves when what he'd really wanted to do was tighten his hands around her pretty neck and squeeze the way he'd done with the first one, crying until it was over.

He shook himself back to the present. No wonder he was on edge.

But he wasn't that young fool now.

He turned the Mac on and connected to the surveillance app, trembling with anticipation. Watching the Sutherlands as their world fell apart would be a pleasure. Last night he'd seen them cling to each other, desperately trying to believe they'd come through this. Credit to Rob, he'd obviously played his hand well and declared the envelopes a ploy to pit them against one another.

'Go ahead, loser!' Ellis had shouted at the screen. 'Do you seriously think I'd let you miss out on my trump card?'

Ellis was calmer than he'd been and why not? It was all going to plan. Witnessing Julia's reaction as her life and her entire belief system crumbled in front of her was not to be missed. When it did, he'd have a grandstand view – the best seat in the house. Once she saw who the man she was married to really was, her own indiscretion would be quickly forgotten. Righteous fury would take over and she'd go for him. Rob wouldn't give in without a fight. No, he'd make a half-hearted attempt to defend himself, driven to survive, but the weight of his infidelity would inhibit him.

Julia would seize the knife and stab her husband, again and again, before the fever broke and moved on leaving her spent and sobbing on the floor.

Then she'd realise the gravity of what she'd done, remember she was trapped and know it would be her turn to die next. Would she go insane?

The thought gave him goosebumps.

* * *

In the silence, Rob gingerly put his fingers to his chest and pressed, wincing when the pain arrived. He thought his ribs were bruised rather than broken, which was something, though seeing clearly was a problem. His left eye was closed as if the lids had been glued together, throbbing with a dull monotony; the rest of his body ached relentlessly from the kicking it had received.

What he wouldn't give for another chance at the bastard.

Rob didn't remember much about the attack – one minute he'd been rushing down the steps at the Belmont Street Bridge, the next on the ground with someone laying into him. Before tonight, Ellis had been no more than a name, a colleague Julia had spoken about a few times, which made this all the more confusing. Rob thought about the level of planning that had gone into pulling off a double abduction and his mouth went dry with fear. Whatever had driven him – and they might never know for sure – this guy hadn't taken such an enormous risk, first with Julia, then with him, for nothing. It wouldn't be right to accuse him of being reckless – he hadn't been. It had clearly all been carefully considered and faultlessly executed. The foot of the stairs where, even in daylight, he wouldn't be seen until it was too late was the perfect place to jump out on the unsuspecting. The violence that followed had been both gratuitous and excessive; the fight – if such a one-sided contest deserved to be called a fight – over before it had started.

The 'welcome' speech had held the hollow ring of a script written in advance. Rob scanned the container with an architect's eye, judging it to be 20 x 10 x 9 feet. What that meant in terms of how much air the box held, he had no idea but guessed they wouldn't last long; it smelled sour and damp as it was. He dragged the table over and stood on it. Up close he saw the slatted vents Ellis intended to shut off were grilled on the inside and firmly bolted, the grill holes so small even the tip of the knife couldn't get through them. Rob tried to prise it loose with the blade until it threatened to snap in his hand.

The chances of Ellis coming back into the container were slim. If he did, they needed a weapon: the knife was all they had.

He got down and furiously pummelled the doors and the panelled walls, searching for a weakness in the metal but finding none.

You had to give it to him: he'd thought of everything.

Rob shot a glance at his wife pretending to be asleep on the floor. Julia was traumatised – not fully understanding where this was going and how it would end. He understood and wished to God he didn't.

Suffocation would begin slowly, almost imperceptibly: breathing would become laboured; they'd slur their words, unable to stay awake; their bodies would close down and they'd lose consciousness. Starved of oxygen the brain wouldn't survive.

Rob had read somewhere that six minutes was the limit beyond which recovery was generally considered impossible. Indeed, their corpses might not be discovered for months, years even. The worst part would be knowing it was happening and being powerless to stop it. He looked at the knife glinting on the table. In the final hours before she blacked out the emotional and mental anguish would be unimaginable – it would be hard but he wouldn't let her go through it.

Rob forced himself back into the present. Ellis Kirkbride was on Julia's team at Grapevine.

This was about the two of them.

Julia had freely admitted Ellis was obsessed with her. Okay. It happened. Except it didn't ring true. When this lunatic's fixation had become a concern she hadn't gone to Tony Connors? Given the MD's dubious reputation, maybe that was understandable. But he was her husband – why hadn't she sought his advice?

A picture of Michelle as he'd last seen her smiling through her tears flashed across his mind and Rob wished this were a dream he'd wake from soon and not have to face the dreadful reality.

He lifted the envelope with his name on it. All he had to do to know the damning truth was open it. Could Julia have a secret as dark as his own?

Was their entire marriage a sham?

He hesitated, unsure, weighing his doubt against the contentment he'd known in the past. She'd been a good wife, sharing not only the same bed but the same hopes and dreams; they'd been ridiculously, deliriously happy. At least, he'd thought so. Now, as he remembered her working late, supposedly on this Glasgow project, sweat broke on his forehead and he felt ill. Rob understood what 'working late' had meant for him – validation he hadn't known he needed and the best sex he'd ever had. On the way, he'd put himself through hell over his affair with Michelle, unaware Julia's behaviour was no better than his own. Unjustified resentment and wild jealousy stormed his brain as he mulled the possibilities, each more sordid and outlandish than its sleazy predecessor. How long had this been going on? Was Ellis the first or had there been others? Tony Connors was a handsome guy – was he one of them? Had that bastard been her lover? Maybe. Then again, no. Tony liked them embarrassingly young – young enough to be his daughter.

Ellis Kirkbride had almost certainly been the last. Julia must have ended it and this was the result.

Imagining his wife in the arms of another man was devastating and for a moment the mortal danger they were in, even Michelle, was forgotten. In just hours Rob's life had imploded. And while every atom of his being urged him to face the truth, no matter how ugly it was, he resisted. Guessing what his envelope held was bad enough. What was in the one with Julia's name on it was almost a certainty. At all costs, it had to stay unopened.

* * *

Julia had crawled inside one of the sleeping bags on the floor and lain curled in the foetal position, exhausted physically and emotionally. Although her eyes were closed she hadn't slept; her mind raced, sifting through every conversation she'd had with her captor for a thread of hope to cling to. Ellis had proved himself capable of violence, but murder? Maybe Rob was right that he only wanted to make her believe they were going to die. Once that had been achieved his revenge would be satisfied and he'd release them.

Her terror level subsided enough to allow her to think. None of the thoughts brought comfort: Every breath – the impassioned words she'd thrown at him in her office – had inspired a sick mind and unless she somehow was able to persuade Ellis Kirkbride she had feelings for him – an unlikely scenario given their history and his reaction to rejection – he'd be back to systematically shut off their precious air. Oh, God! How long would that take?

A vision of herself clutching her throat, gasping for air while her lungs collapsed in on themselves, forced her to take a deep breath and calm down. Please don't let that be their fate. If it was, surely it was better to resign themselves to the inevitable than wage a futile war against it?

She heard her husband sigh. Poor Rob. When Ellis had dragged him semi-conscious into the container, beaten and bloodied, she'd been horrified... both horrified and relieved, grateful he was alive and that she wouldn't have to live through this alone.

Julia wanted to reach out to him but something wasn't making sense. Why was he even here?

She opened her eyes. The light was on. Rob was where she'd left him, at the table talking to himself, staring at the envelope in his hand. She bit her lip, awash with fresh guilt. Her foolishness had done this to him – to both of them. Rob had been right – as soon as Ellis had started acting weird she should've gone to Tony.

The stupid, stupid episode at the Sky Bar had been the tipping point. From then on, it had all been leading them here. She'd rejected Ellis and he wanted to punish her for it – the envelopes were part of that punishment.

There was one for each of them yet Rob wouldn't open them, stubbornly saying he refused to play Ellis's game. It sounded strong, defiant, though anybody with half a brain would see it as an empty gesture: they were in a metal box, the available oxygen dwindling with every movement, every sentence, every defeated sigh. The envelopes were important to Ellis, part of his plan. Surely it was better to understand exactly what they were up against? When they were arguing in her office he'd asked an odd question about Rob. At the time it had niggled her. Now Julia whispered under her breath, 'Oh, Rob, what does he know? What have you done?'

He was a good man and she loved him. But while protecting her was admirable, at the end of the day he was her husband, not her master. It was her envelope: what to do with it was her decision.

She marshalled her resolve and got quietly to her feet. Rob, still preoccupied, didn't notice until it was too late. Before he could prevent her, Julia dived past him and snatched the one with her name on it from the table. In the dim light, his face was a shadowy mask. He threw himself across the container, knocking her to the floor still clutching the envelope. Rob pinned her, kicking and punching, to the ground, forcing her fingers to relinquish their hold. 'Please, Julia, please give it to me. He can't beat us like this.'

'You know what's in it? For God's sake tell me!'

'I don't know. How could I? I've never met him. For Christ's sake, it'll be some faked-up crap.'

'Don't I deserve the truth before I die?'

Rob released his grip and rolled away. Julia saw defeat in his eyes and heard his voice crack with emotion. 'All right. Look at it if you have to. But it won't make any of this better.'

35

DAY THREE

Michelle woke up consumed by a sense of foreboding bordering on dread. Rob was in trouble. The certainty of it made her stomach churn. On the edge of panic, she buried her head in the pillow in a futile attempt to think rationally and block out the premonition. She was overreacting, torturing herself. Except, she didn't believe that. People laughed at female intuition – they could mock all they liked; it was real.

Rob had promised to phone. Logically, there might be a dozen reasons why he hadn't. But the voice in her head wasn't driven by reason and it was telling her to be afraid.

Possibilities, each more terrible than the last, pushed through: he'd been in an accident on his way to the airport; the plane had crashed – one 'what if' after another.

Michelle had never been in love. Not like this. All he'd need to do was say the word and she'd follow him – to any town, any city, anywhere on the planet. Looking up, seeing him near, would make her the happiest woman alive. Without him, life had no meaning. She'd been misguided to ever imagine it had.

When he'd reluctantly broken the news about the trip with his wife she'd been crushed, bitterly disappointed, but understood he had to go. Julia's time with him was coming to an end, then he'd be hers.

So why did it have to hurt so much?

Just days ago she'd had a job she liked doing, a nice house that would be paid off years before she retired and money in the bank. Her few friends were old and trusted; girls she'd met at school who were women now, mothers some of them. As for sex – if you looked as good as she did it wasn't hard to find. She'd had everything. Until she'd met Rob and discovered she had nothing at all.

When he held her close, gazing into her eyes, she'd known he felt the same. That certainty convinced her that when he'd said he'd call, he would, unless something terrible had happened to him.

Michelle snatched her mobile from the bedside table and scrolled through the headlines for something, anything, to explain his silence. She didn't find it because it wasn't there and the deep uneasiness that had wakened her morphed into uncontrollable panic.

Michelle dragged the covers away, threw on her clothes and ran to her car.

* * *

Ellis sat with his feet up on his desk humming a song he detested but couldn't get out of his head. He was alone in the office. Despite being up most of the night he felt remarkably fresh. What he'd achieved energised him; the credit for that belonged to Julia. Her insulting rejection had spawned a master plan. And the plan was working; the difficult part was behind him. Now, he could sit back and enjoy the drama. He took out his mobile and turned it in his palm – the wonders of technology, indeed! With a touch the surveillance camera fixed high in the corner of the container allowed him to look in on how Mr and Mrs Sutherland were handling their new reality. They hadn't killed each other – at least, not yet – although a few hours ago things had heated considerably.

He crossed his legs, remembering the scene he'd witnessed. Around five in the morning he'd brought a cafetière of coffee and some crackers and cheese to have while he watched the show. For a while there hadn't been much to see. In fact, it had been as dull as those godawful TV things where some guy called Jason made toast and washed his hair, waxing lyrical about the shampoo he used. Rob had tried in vain to find a weakness that wasn't there in the container. Then he'd sat at the table staring into space. Julia had appeared to be asleep and he'd been tempted to go back to bed. That would've been a pity – he'd have missed her snatch her envelope from Rob. What a scene that had been: he'd tried to grab it and they'd ended up rolling around on the floor before he'd given in.

Ellis's laugh had echoed in the basement when her eyes widened as, one by one, she'd gone through the damning photographs and anger turned to agony.

He'd punched the air. 'Yes! Yes! How does that feel, bitch?'

Julia hadn't spoken. Rob had had his explanations repelled with a wave of her hand and they'd returned to where they'd been – him to the chair, her to the sleeping bag pressing the envelope to her chest – until the sensor lights went out and the computer screen had gone blank.

For a spectator it had been hugely entertaining. Not so much for the Sutherlands. For them, it had been devastating: Rob hadn't held onto his secret and the truth had destroyed his wife.

Tony Connors interrupted the memory, startling Ellis, who hadn't heard him come in. 'What does it feel like to be the boss?'

Ellis removed his feet from the desk and instantly morphed into the charming persona he switched on at will. 'Is that what I am? I didn't realise.'

'Well, until Julia gets back you're running things. Call it a temporary promotion. We don't have anything major on, which is no bad thing after the last few months. My advice would be to relax and enjoy it without getting *too* comfortable.'

'I will, Tony.'

'Good. Julia has done an incredible job for Grapevine. She's a remarkable woman – don't tell her I said that or she'll be knocking on my door demanding more money.'

'She's worth it.'

'Oh, she absolutely is. From the outside it looks glamorous but, as you know, advertising is pressure. It gets to all of us, eventually.'

'Even you?'

Tony smiled. 'All of us. Even me. Rattling around South East Asia will be just what Julia needs. I expect her to come back reinvigorated, ready to go.' He glanced at the sheet of paper he was holding. 'Actually, it's you I came to see. This was on my desk. Arrived yesterday.'

'What is it?'

'Ravi Malik's resignation letter.'

Ellis hid his pleasure and faked concern. 'Ravi's packed it in?'

'Yes. Can't say I'm surprised but from Grapevine's point of view it's a buggeration, especially with Julia gone.'

'Not really. Graphic guys are ten-a-penny these days.'

'Normally, I'd agree and put it down to the come and go of any business. Of course, we'll give him as generous a package as we can. HR will handle the details and I'll sign whatever they put in front of me.'

'I'm hearing a but.'

'Correct, you are. And it's a big but. Julia likes Ravi. She'll be upset if she comes back and finds we didn't try to change his mind. After what he's been through it's a fair point. His confidence is bound to be rock bottom without us making it worse. To you and me this is a straightforward personnel issue. Emotion doesn't have a part to play in it. Once upon a time, graphics people were sought after. Nowadays, the industry has moved on and they're, as you say, "ten-a-penny".'

Ellis twisted the knife. 'How I feel about Ravi isn't a secret. I don't rate the guy. He's not good enough to be working at a top agency.'

Tony let him have his say before he spoke. 'You're entitled to that opinion. Unfortunately, there's a lady who disagrees with you, and I know her well enough to suspect quitting's crossed her mind more than once recently. I'm not keen to push her in that direction.'

'Nobody's indispensable, Tony.'

'So they say. The problem is some are more difficult to replace than others. Julia falls squarely in the "some" camp. As soon as word got out she was on the market she'd be snapped up. You've worked with her, surely you appreciate that?'

Ellis didn't answer him. Coming from the hard-headed MD famous for forgetting the names of the people Grapevine employed, this reaction was unexpected. Ellis said, 'She mentioned she was going to visit him on her way home. She might already know.'

'Ravi might've decided not to spoil her holiday.'

'So you want me to call him, is that it?'

'No. I want you to go to his flat.'

'Go to Ravi's flat?'

'Yes. Persuade him he's making a mistake.'

'For him or for us? I mean, loyalty's wonderful and all that—'

Tony shot him a sharp look. Ellis Kirkbride hadn't been with Grapevine long, though long enough for him to understand how it worked. Clearly, he hadn't been paying attention. Tony's lips set tight with irritation. He said, 'Don't give me an argument, I'm not in the mood. Just do it. Then I can tell Julia we tried.'

* * *

Michelle found a space in Hamilton Drive and pulled in behind a line of cars running all the way to the Botanic Gardens. She turned the engine off, took a deep breath and tried to stay calm. In the middle of the night she'd been woken by a terror without any detail. Now, it had a form. Rob's silver Peugeot sat alongside what she assumed was Julia's Mazda when it should've been in a secure car park near the airport. It was only a year old and unlikely to have broken down. If Rob was safe, why was it here? Plans changed, travel plans especially. He might have decided to take a taxi. That might account for the Peugeot's presence – it didn't explain his silence. He'd been as reluctant to leave her as she'd been to let him go, insisting he'd call, not once or twice or when he got a chance, but every day.

Rob hadn't lied to her; she refused to believe it.

She got out of the car and crossed the road to the house in the middle of the Victorian terrace, searching for signs of life. She saw none and was tempted to walk up the path and look in the window.

Except, what would that prove?

Phoning him was the obvious thing to do. She'd even invented a work-related excuse in case his wife answered, but couldn't find the courage. Back in the car, she beat her hands impotently on the wheel: what did you do if you suspected someone was missing? You'd go to the police. She caught her reflection in the rear-view mirror as the absurdity of her reasoning hit home. 'Oh, yes, and say what exactly? Excuse me but my lover's gone on holiday with his wife and hasn't called me? Could you send out a search party, please?'

If they didn't lock her up, they'd laugh her out of the door.

When she'd waved him goodbye it hadn't occurred to her she'd be outside his house paralysed with anxiety. She wasn't a starry-eyed teenager, nor was she a hysterical fool – she'd give it another twenty-four hours.

Then she was going to the police.

* * *

Ellis stood on the pavement in Duke Street eyeing the sandstone tenements built in the middle years of the nineteenth century to house the city's poor – a very long way from the villa outside Cape Town and the well-heeled elites at that party. The drunk – he couldn't recall his name – would probably have boozed himself into the ground by now, pining for the woman he'd lost to Sasha's father. She must've been special, because nothing since, political influence, exclusive golf club memberships or fancy friends, had been enough to replace her. Ellis had no sympathy for the maudlin old lush. She'd led him on, ruined his life, and he'd let her get away with it. Hell mend him.

On the buzzer system Malik was the fourth name from the top. Ellis pressed and waited for the door to spring open. It didn't. Irritated, he tried again. Tony Connors had known what he was doing when he'd ordered him to come here and Ellis sensed the patronage he'd enjoyed ebbing away: he wasn't the golden boy any more.

When Julia didn't return after her trip, the MD would hire a recruitment outfit to put together a shortlist of suitable candidates. Ellis's name would be on there but the job would go to somebody else.

He smothered a laugh. When this was done, he was finished with Glasgow. Finished with Scotland. For good this time.

A middle-aged woman pushing a pram came out of the building. Ellis helped her and she smiled gratefully. 'Thanks. Most people let you struggle.'

He didn't reply; he'd forgotten her already.

Inside, he climbed the concrete stairs to the second floor, stopping outside a solid-looking brown door with Malik etched into a brass plate above the letterbox. Ellis knocked, got no answer and knocked again, harder. Tony had sent him here because Julia had a soft spot for the designer and would be upset if he wasn't still with the company when she got back from her Asian jaunt. Appeasing her defined him: underneath the tough-guy front, the flashy suits and macho bullshit, Tony was weak. In his position, Ellis would've given the bastard whatever he was due and got shot of him.

He peered through the letterbox at the empty hall and shouted, 'Ravi, it's Ellis! Let me in!'

Nothing stirred in the flat; he tried again. 'C'mon, mate. We're worried about you!'

His voice echoed on the deserted landing and faded. Ellis gave up and went downstairs to the street. Ravi was recuperating, walking with a stick – the guy was a bloody cripple, for Christ's sake. Going anywhere would take an almighty effort; he was in there but had nothing to say, at least, not to him. Ellis didn't blame him for that. If the roles were reversed, Ravi Malik would be the last person he'd want to speak to.

As for the MD, the gutless joker could relax: Julia wasn't coming back.

* * *

With the sensor lights off, the container was in darkness broken only by the thin horizontal lines of a new day creeping through the vents on either side. If Ellis closed them as he'd said, they'd disappear, taking precious air with them.

Julia couldn't see Rob but she could hear him breathing. Maybe he was asleep, though how anybody could be at peace after...

The thought went unfinished. He wasn't worth it.

She lay on her back as she had since that awful revelation, with an arm across her eyes, empty of every emotion. All she'd believed – and it really was all – had been revealed to be a sham. Nothing in her life was as it had seemed.

Rob hadn't wanted her to open the envelope. Now she understood why: the photographs. Awful, terrible photographs of him and a woman. In one of them Julia had recognised Kelvingrove Art Gallery in the background. Ellis had captured the exact moment their lips met and burned the image of them together on her bleeding heart. There were more images of her husband with the same woman, holding her, kissing her, gazing into her eyes, but the one that had carried Julia to a place where emotion didn't exist was of Rob reaching out to touch his mistress's naked body when she opened the door to welcome her lover – a game he'd played with her.

She hadn't cried and knew she wasn't going to; the pain went far beyond tears. What hurt most in this almighty mess was the part she'd played, her own blindness – at Grapevine and in her marriage. She'd worked side by side with Ellis Kirkbride for months without realising her charming, talented colleague was a madman who'd turn on her as soon as she spurned his creepy advances. Ellis had been an oddball. Ravi had seen it. Why hadn't she?

It wasn't only her; he'd fooled Tony, as well – not the consolation it might have been.

But, more than being abducted and kept in a container, what Rob had done was the biggest blow. Because he'd been her friend; her best friend. And best friends were meant to take care of each other. Julia had complained they were spending too much of themselves on their jobs rather than each other. She'd been the one pushing for the trip. It hadn't occurred to her the problem ran deeper and wouldn't be fixed by blue skies and beaches. Again, that fatal blindness.

The woman in the photographs was undeniably pretty. But she was pretty too, wasn't she? Or had her husband stopped noticing?

Somewhere in the container Rob coughed; he wasn't asleep and the hurt Julia was blocking out returned, bringing question after question: how did he feel now his dirty secret was out in the world? Was he relieved? Had he planned to leave her and build a new life with this bitch?

Her body ached from the physical struggle, her fevered brain drawing her down dangerous roads. And in her weakness, she followed.

Was that why he'd agreed to the trip? Had he planned to tell her when they were halfway round the world away from everything she knew? Did he imagine a last holiday together would lessen the pain?

Julia couldn't help herself – she laughed out loud at the sad irony of the situation. Somewhere, a woman was expecting a call, a text, a message of some kind that wouldn't come, while she and Rob took their last breaths. As strangers.

Then, rising through her pain, the core question, the one she had to know the answer to. Why hadn't she been enough?

Suddenly, the lights came on; Rob must have moved. Julia saw him at the table and was gripped by a forgotten fear: there was another envelope, the one with his name on it, waiting to be opened.

What twisted lie had Ellis Kirkbride's demented mind invented and how would Rob react? The instinct to survive took over and her eyes darted to the knife.

* * *

Their jailor hadn't started the hellish process of shutting off the air. For Rob, it would be a mercy. When the end came he'd welcome it. In a sea of regrets the biggest was that Michelle would never know he'd died loving her and go through life believing he'd lied. Though it was far from the only one: the scene with Julia had been ugly; he'd tried to explain, except what was there to say? Sorry was woefully inadequate, so, like boxers, they'd retired to neutral corners to lick their wounds.

Rob saw the look on his wife's face and was ashamed of the hurt he'd caused.

This wasn't how it was supposed to be. Now, when they needed each other most, Julia hated him. Yet only yesterday she'd been imagining them strolling hand in hand round flea markets, stopping to haggle over an old silver ring or laughing at the price tag on an antique-jade Buddha statuette, which was actually coloured resin produced from a mould in a factory up a backstreet in Saigon. In her daydream, they'd drink local beer and order steaming plates of broken rice or Pad Thai from a painted stall half a yard from the traffic, before returning to their hotel to make languorous love into the night.

And when would he have told her he was in love with someone else? Towards the end, on the final day, or would he have waited until they were back home? The cruelty of it appalled him and Rob sneered at his cowardice: he'd said yes to the holiday without thinking it through. Had he really believed that for three weeks he could have sex with Julia while Michelle was in his head? Had he somehow convinced himself a holiday would soften the blow? The notion was childishly idiotic and dishonest – demeaning to both women and to himself.

He lifted the second envelope and ran it through his fingers as a truth that had never been far away slowly dawned: he'd been drowning in guilt, terrified Julia would find out about Michelle, willing to agree to anything to protect his secret.

But his behaviour, inexcusable as it had been, wasn't what had brought them here. No, whatever had gone on between this maniac and his wife was the root of that.

Across the container, Julia saw the change in him and felt a sliver of fear. That change reached his voice; there was an edge to it. Rob said, 'I've been sitting here for hours punishing myself, wishing I was dead, too stupid to face why this nightmare was happening without realising I'd been caught up in something that isn't about me.' He waved the envelope at her. 'Let's see what's in this, shall we? Let's see what my devoted wife has been hiding.' He snarled the words at her. 'You already know, don't you?'

Julia jumped to her feet, her anger a match for his. 'You're wrong! Completely wrong!'

'Am I?'

'Come on, Rob. This is me we're talking about. Whatever's in that thing is a lie and we both know it. It's deliberately designed to pit us against each other!' She banged her fist on the wall. 'He's probably out there listening to us and laughing.' Julia hammered the wall again and shouted, 'Are you enjoying this, you insane bastard?'

Rob said, 'Nice try. Very convincing,' and tore the envelope open. The contents dropped out and they stared at the two photographs on the floor: in the first, Ellis's arm was round Julia as they both smiled for the camera; the second was the picture he'd taken the night they'd gone to the Red Sky Bar: she was kissing him.

Rob spoke so quietly Julia almost couldn't hear him. 'Well, well. Not quite the little saint after all.'

'Don't be a fool.'

Rob picked up the images. 'A fool? Really? This is you kissing him, isn't it? It certainly looks like you.'

'Yes, it is, but I can explain.'

Rob crushed the glossy pages into a ball and threw it away. 'Oh, I don't think that's necessary.'

'Rob—'

'How can you judge me when you're no better?'

Julia ran at him; he stepped back, startled by her reaction. She grabbed his lapels, faces inches apart, hissing hatred. 'Don't you dare try to justify yourself with this. It's fake and you know it.'

Rob prised her hands away and stood his ground. 'Fake? You're denying it's you?'

'I'm not denying anything because there's nothing to deny. It looks how Ellis wants it to look and you're stupid enough to fall for it. I almost wish it was true.'

Rob sneered. 'As you so rightly remind me, I'm stupid. But not quite that stupid.'

Julia's shoulders sagged. 'You heard him. Ellis is making me suffer for rejecting him. He's a monster. What's in those pictures isn't real.'

Rob paced to the end of the container and back. When he spoke there was a hardness she hadn't heard before. 'Frankly, Julia, I don't believe you. And I don't want to die because you fucked up.'

36

DAY FOUR

At two o'clock in the morning Ellis didn't expect to be seen, though you could never be sure. Some insomniac out with his dog would be a complication he could do without. He parked in nearby Ruskin Lane and walked the short distance to the house. The Sutherlands wouldn't be coming back here, which made what he was doing pointless. Pointless, but fun! He took a last look up and down a deserted Hamilton Drive and used Rob's key to open the door.

Inside was exactly as he'd imagined it – stylish and comfortable. The beam from his torch played over the lounge and, in the darkness, three miniature African heads carved in ebony standing guard on the polished wooden floor. There was a flat-screen TV in the corner and a multi-coloured rug covered in irregular shapes, diamonds and zigzags, he guessed was from Marrakesh or Fez hung above the fireplace.

The Sutherlands had eclectic taste and a thirst for adventure. Well, they were having an adventure now, all right.

A half-empty glass of whisky and a bottle of Johnnie Walker Black Label were on the coffee table, abandoned probably when Rob had got Julia's distress message – the message he'd sent. Ellis picked up a fresh glass and helped himself to his host's booze. He sank into an armchair, recalling the nights he'd spent outside in his car watching their shadows dance on the curtains, envying them their nice life.

Upstairs he wandered into a bedroom where suitcases packed for the journey waited to be closed. Two pairs of sunglasses, Dolce & Gabbana and Tom Ford Fausto, lay side by side on the cover. Ellis tried on the Tom Fords and checked himself out in the wardrobe mirror. Nice. He slipped them into his top pocket. Johnnie Walker Black Label and top-of-the-range designer shades? Rob Sutherland certainly liked the good life.

Next door, Ellis pulled out drawers and examined the contents, rubbing Julia's things between his thumb and forefinger. Suddenly, a momentary sense of loss broke in him and he slumped against the wall. They would've made a fine couple. He would have been a good husband – if she'd let him.

But it wouldn't have worked and he knew that now.

Underneath she was no different from the others.

At the end of the landing he came across a small single room left unfurnished, perhaps with an eye to converting it into a nursery with bunny-rabbit wallpaper and furry animals in the cot.

Some unborn child had had a lucky escape because Julia would make a crap mother, a subject Ellis knew more about than most.

When he'd seen everything there was to see he went back downstairs, finished his whisky and left.

* * *

Ellis spent more time in the basement these days than anywhere else, including the bedroom; it had become his special place. He'd given up trying to sleep in his bed, preferring to doze in the chair, in case he missed something. Yesterday had been especially good. Before his eyes the Sutherlands' marriage had come apart in a welter of accusation and counter accusation. Rob's infidelity might have killed the union, but the photographs of his wife in the second envelope had buried it and Ellis congratulated himself on a job well done.

Although it wasn't all good news. He lifted Rob's mobile and reread the WhatsApp messages from his mistress, each more insistent than the one before.

> Where are you?
>
> Where are you, Rob?
>
> Is everything all right?
>
> Are you okay?
>
> I'm getting worried.
>
> Please answer me.
>
> Rob, answer me.

A quiver that might've been fear passed through him: the redhead was persistent, he'd give her that. Ellis considered replying and decided it wasn't necessary – what could she actually do? If she went to the police some grey-haired duty sergeant who'd seen it all before would politely hear her out, then remind her that ignoring lovesick messages from your girlfriend wasn't a crime. As for being missing, Mr Sutherland was on holiday with his wife, wasn't he? Had she considered this was his way of ending the relationship?

Embarrassing! Ellis should've been convinced but he wasn't.

Where will the threat come from? His frequently asked question wouldn't let him go and in his dingy basement with the shadows thrown by the Anglepoise lamp on the wall, he realised he could be looking at the answer.

What if she turned on the waterworks, played the helpless female, and actually managed to convince the jaded old copper there was something to her story?

A woman who would steal another woman's husband was capable of anything.

He wasn't worried about getting caught; his exit strategy was in place and solid. No, he wasn't concerned about that. But the thought of some white-fucking-knight coming over the horizon and rescuing the bitch gnawed at his gut.

* * *

It had to be early, not much after dawn, because the light from the vents –
the only indicator of whether it was day or night – broke the darkness in
the container in thin grey horizontal lines. Rob had tossed and turned on
the hard floor, pain all over his body, and was awake when the car pulled
up outside.

Ellis, here to make good on his promise.

The abduction had been shocking, yet the lunatic had only been
setting the stage – the worst of the ordeal was about to begin.

His eyes darted to his sleeping wife and on to the knife. Julia didn't
deserve this. Nobody deserved it. She'd misjudged Ellis Kirkbride, made
a mistake with a psycho, and they were both paying a hellish price for it.
From the depths of a nightmare she'd called her husband's name, over
and over again, and Rob cried silent tears for the pain he'd caused her. He
felt an overwhelming urge to hold her close, to protect her and keep her
safe, but resisted, knowing that, even now, she'd reject him. They hadn't
spoken since the last tormented scene between them, and had retreated
to their prisons within a prison.

What was coming would be awful – he had to be strong enough to do
what needed to be done; he wasn't sure he was. Ending her life terrified
him more than anything Ellis Kirkbride could inflict on them and
through the endless hours he'd examined every possibility of escape until
eventually giving up, desolate and mentally exhausted.

Their fate was sealed. He had to accept it.

One day, perhaps years from now, some curious unfortunate would
force the doors open and find what was left of them. Too late Michelle
would understand he hadn't deserted her.

Ellis didn't mute his arrival. He whistled while he took what he
needed from the boot, a man happy at his work. The metal ladder he'd
brought to reach the vents scraped against the side of the container. He
peered through a slat at his prisoners, shouted a jaunty, 'Good morning,
people!' and the last deluded hope Kirkbride wouldn't actually go
through with it died.

Rob had never known a greater sadness than he did at that moment: a new day was breaking over the city; soon they'd never know another one. With precious air denied them, the end wouldn't be far away.

On the roof, Ellis walked around stamping his feet, savouring the effect the noise was having on his captives' tortured nerves. He tore open the paper bag he'd brought with him and began scattering handfuls of sugar across the panels, chuckling at his inventiveness. Inside the container, Rob heard the sound like gently falling rain and he lost it completely.

This was truly insane – what had gone on between Julia and this maniac to make him act this way?

He jumped on the table and hammered his fists against the ceiling. 'You bastard! You bastard, Ellis! Just finish it! I know what you're doing! Just finish the thing!'

Julia raised herself up. 'What? What's he doing?'

Her husband shook his head and didn't respond, unable to bring himself to tell her Ellis had taken his revenge to a new level of depravity – she'd find out soon enough, and when she did, she'd be petrified.

For a minute there was nothing, then the first line of light disappeared as though it had never existed. Julia stiffened; she stared at her husband, eyes wild with fear, rocking backwards and forwards on her knees, her features twisted in anguish.

Rob went to her but their time had passed and she pushed him away.

It began as a murmur, a low moan deep in her throat, and grew to a deafening wail reverberating off the corrugated steel walls. Julia's fingers pulled at her hair like a madwoman, ripping out handfuls, tearing at her clothes.

Powerless, Rob covered his ears as the echo of her screams went on and on and on.

* * *

The officer behind the desk in Stewart Street was working on a computer and didn't realise he wasn't alone. Michelle read the posters on the wall until he noticed her. She hadn't been inside a police station before and would rather it had stayed that way. Rob's silence, along with his car parked outside the house instead of at the airport, had made the decision for her. Seeing a good-looking woman at the desk was the kind of distraction that was never unwelcome. The constable raised his head and smiled. 'How can I help?'

In the wee small hours when she'd made up her mind to come here Michelle had realised she'd be questioned and how crazy her story would seem. It hadn't deterred her. She said, 'I want to report a missing person.'

The policeman picked up a pen. 'Can I have your name and mobile number, please?'

'It's Davidson. Michelle Davidson.'

She gave her details and he said, 'Is that Miss or Mrs?'

'Miss.'

'And who do you want to report?'

'Rob Sutherland.'

He wrote the name down, quietly mouthing the words. 'When did you last see Mr Sutherland?'

'A few days ago.'

'What makes you think he's missing?'

Michelle bit her lip. 'Look, before I even start I get how mad this will seem. Trust me, I'd be a lot happier if I had something straightforward to tell you.'

Every duty officer has dealt with their fair share of cranks. Today, it looked as though it was his turn again. The policeman said, 'Try me. But first, what's your relationship with this man? How do you know him? Is he a neighbour, a friend, what?'

He rolled the pen through his fingers and waited for her to go on. Michelle almost backed away from the desk. She'd known this would be awkward and it was. Instead, she held her nerve – she'd only have one chance to make this work. This was it.

'Okay, Rob and I are lovers. He's married, I'm not. In the beginning, it wasn't meant to be serious but that's what it became. Rob was going to leave his wife so we could be together.'

Michelle watched the policeman's face for a sign she was getting through to him. His impassive expression gave nothing away and she continued. 'This thing with us came out of the blue. Julia – Rob's wife –

isn't a bad person. He didn't want to hurt her. She'd planned a trip to Vietnam for them. Rob felt he owed it to her to go before dropping the bombshell the marriage was over.' She hesitated, suddenly uncertain. 'Is this making sense?'

'Eh, not yet, if I'm honest, but don't let that put you off.'

'Their flight left two days ago. Rob promised to call me every day and he hasn't. There's been no word from him. Nothing. And that isn't like him so I drove to his house yesterday. Their cars were outside.' The policeman's expression hardened – she was losing him. Michelle rushed on. 'He'd paid for airport parking. You don't do that then take a taxi.'

He started to speak; she stopped him in a last-ditch effort to get him to take her seriously. 'Look, I'm not some lovesick teenage girl. I've been out in the world long enough to know when a man's getting ready to run, and I'm telling you that isn't what's happening here.' Michelle gripped the counter. 'Something's wrong. I'm sure of it. If you only understood what it took for me to come here...'

The officer nodded. 'I hear you and don't doubt you believe what you're saying but—'

'But, what?'

'This trip. Why would a man go on holiday with his wife if he intended to leave her? Does that sound right to you? Because it doesn't to me.'

'Frankly, no. I was afraid Rob would realise it was her he wanted. Please, I can't explain it properly, but something's wrong. I just know it.'

The officer stared at her, stone-faced, taking in the smart clothes and her unshakeable conviction. He picked up the internal phone and dialled a number, talking to himself. 'I'm going to get a right bollocking for this. DI Geddes, there's a woman at the desk I think you should speak to.' A voice rumbled down the line and he flashed a look at Michelle. 'What's it about? I think it would be better if she explains it to you herself.'

* * *

As soon as Andrew Geddes walked into Reception he understood why the constable on the desk hadn't just noted the details and sent her on her way. With her slim figure and red hair falling to her shoulders, she was striking. Smart too, because she studiously avoided eye contact, making it harder to send her packing. After a messy divorce the DI had prided himself on being immune to women. True. Until he'd met Mackenzie Darroch. She'd pierced his dour defences and now with half a dozen whiskies in him on a Friday night – or any night, for that matter – he'd stopped telling anybody who'd listen that marriage was a mug's game. So, no, not immune, but still not swayed by nice legs and a pretty face.

He raised an eyebrow at the officer that had nothing to do with personal prejudice and everything to do with wasting his time – it wouldn't be forgotten, as the uniform must've known when he made the call.

Geddes introduced himself with a smile that barely existed long enough to settle on his lips. 'DI Geddes. Please follow me.'

In his office, he listened to what she had to say, admiring her composure in spite of himself: though obviously upset, she presented her suspicions as clearly as the complexities of the story allowed and Geddes found himself liking her and wanting to help. Unfortunately, what he was hearing was far from enough to persuade him and his initial response was no different from the constable's. This lady had made the mistake of getting involved with somebody else's husband – she wasn't the first and wouldn't be the last – and was casting around for reasons why the affair couldn't possibly be over.

She said, 'I've lost count of the messages I've left Rob – a dozen, at least. When he's in a meeting he always responds as soon as he has a chance. This isn't like him. It really isn't.'

Michelle offered him her phone. 'Would you try him?'

The DI cleared his throat. 'Leave the number, by all means, but calling people unless it's an emergency isn't what we do. I'm sorry.'

Her suggestion had been naïve, an indication of where she was emotionally. Referring to her lover in the present tense as though the relationship were still alive was touching. Geddes wasn't unsympathetic, though in his estimation she was kidding herself – this Rob Sutherland character had ditched her and hadn't had the courage to tell her to her face.

Michelle saw the detective wasn't convinced and repeated her story about the car. The DI held up his hand to bring some much-needed reality to the conversation. 'I appreciate how it looks, but by itself it proves nothing.'

She held her disappointment in check. Almost. 'I knew you were going to say that.'

Geddes leaned back in his chair. 'I say it because it's true. However, I will look into it and get back to you if I discover anything. Otherwise…'

He escorted her out. At the front door, he said, 'I won't tell you not to worry, that would be stupid. I'll be in touch as soon as I can.'

She shook his hand. 'Thanks for letting me get it out.'

'No problem. That's what we're here for.'

He watched her get into her car – wherever he was, Mr Sutherland was either an idiot for letting her go, or luckier than any man had a right to be if he had better at home.

Geddes stood on the pavement considering what Michelle had told him: the Peugeot parked outside the house was odd, he'd give her that, but the real question, the only one worth answering, was whether Rob Sutherland and his wife had actually got on a plane.

He glanced up at the clouds gathering in the sky and went back inside to the desk. The constable saw him marching towards him and braced for the bollocking that was surely coming.

The DI had other things on his mind. 'You got us into this so make yourself useful. Call Border Force at the airport. Ask them if a Mr and Mrs Sutherland boarded their flight.'

'Yes, sir. And if they didn't?'

'We'll cross that bridge when we come to it.'

37

Ellis had listened to Olivia prattle away to Ravi; she had nothing to say to him and that was how he liked it. The texts from Rob's lady friend had stopped. He could relax: the mistress wasn't going to be a problem after all; she'd put two and two together and decided Sutherland had dumped her.

His early-morning visit to the container had been the beginning of the final phase and he wasn't happy – it hadn't been as satisfying as he'd thought it would be. Watching them on the screen in his basement had seemed like a stroke of genius. In fact, spying on them was dull. They hadn't delivered.

After the initial anger and storm of recriminations, they'd hardly spoken. Rob sat in the chair while she lay on a mattress curled in on herself. At this rate, the air would take forever to run out. But the little surprise he'd put in place for later tonight would get them moving. Meantime, he was tempted to speed up the process.

Tony Connors appeared at the door. Over his shoulder a leggy young blonde with a fake tan and unnaturally white teeth hovered in the corridor behind him. Ellis hadn't seen his boss and wasn't complaining about that. Tony said, 'How did you get on with Ravi? Did you tell him we'll keep his job open for him until he's well enough to come back? What did he say?'

'I didn't get a chance. He wouldn't speak to me. Wouldn't even answer the door.'

Tony shrugged. 'Then, screw him. We tried.'

* * *

Sometimes it seemed as though God was on the side of the bad guys; the wheels ground slowly and getting information took forever. Today wasn't one of those days.

Geddes put down the phone, his mouth set in a thin line, remembering Michelle Davidson in the chair opposite telling her story, 100 per cent convinced something had befallen her lover, willing him to believe her. He hadn't, because she'd lacked the one element that changed speculation into certainty: facts. Geddes gripped the receiver hard enough to leave imprints on his skin. The airport had confirmed BA had recorded a no-show for two passengers named Sutherland leaving Glasgow and connecting at Heathrow for Ho Chi Minh City.

The hours were rubbish and the salary was an insult but, even when he was at school, DS Rory Calder hadn't wanted to be anything other than a policeman. Glasgow was his town and he was determined to make a difference to it. His girlfriend was less enthusiastic, but then she hadn't worked beside Andrew Geddes. If she had, she'd have understood. Geddes had a well-earned reputation for not suffering fools. Anybody who forgot it deserved everything they got. Unlike some, the detective inspector's bark wasn't worse than his bite; he was demanding, obstinate and never forgot a friend or an enemy.

He poked his head round the squad room door and spoke to Calder. 'Whatever you're doing, leave it and come with me.'

'Where're we going?'

'The West End. I'll fill you in on the way.'

* * *

The silver Peugeot Michelle Davidson had described looked okay. Nothing obvious like a flat tyre. Coming to the station on no more than female instinct and a broken promise had been gutsy. But if the Sutherlands had decided to bump their foreign trip and were strolling arm in arm along the North Shore at Blackpool discussing how they could mend a broken relationship, they were all going to look pretty bloody foolish and he'd have some explaining to do.

He scanned the length of the street, walked up the path to the front door and knocked. When no one answered, he knocked again. The redhead wasn't the only one with instinct; after twenty-odd years in the service he had his own, and it rarely let him down.

'Calder, go round the back. Look in the windows. Shout if you see anything.'

Geddes took a couple of steps away. He loved Glasgow and knew the history of the city. This A-listed property would've been built around the 1860s, sometime after Great Western Road had cut a broad swathe to Loch Lomond and the Highlands. The 'dear green place' would've looked a whole lot different, though underneath the surface not much would have changed.

He followed his sergeant to the small garden and the rear entrance. 'Anything?'

'Nothing, sir.'

'Okay, we could get a warrant from the PF or we could leave them out of it and deal with this ourselves.'

Calder couldn't tell if it was a statement or a question but didn't hesitate. As far as he was concerned, DI Geddes was a legend; among his many achievements he was the copper who'd put child-killer Richard Hill away for life. The young DS considered himself fortunate to be working with him. He said, 'I'm okay with whatever you decide.'

'Right answer. If you're asked, this is how we found it.'

A legend and an enigma – on one hand an uncompromising officer with the moral compass of Calvin, on the other a maverick frequently proving the shortest difference between two points was through red tape and departmental procedures. No surprise it had taken him years longer than it should have done to make detective inspector.

If Geddes had regrets about his career's trajectory, he kept them to himself. He smashed his elbow against the glass and waited for the familiar wail of an alarm. When it didn't come he reached in and opened the window. Calder said, 'Shall I call it in?'

The senior detective replied without looking at him, already on his way to the rest of the house. 'Absolutely. As soon as we establish the intruders aren't here.'

'So, when?'

'I'd say in about twenty-five minutes.' He stopped and turned. 'Look, feel free to object. This is your career I'm messing with. If you're not comfortable you have my permission to stay in the car. And we never had this conversation.'

There was nothing to think about. Calder had joined the service to do real policework, not fill out forms and make sure nobody had their toes stood on. He said, 'I've no idea what you're on about, sir. Twenty-five minutes, it is.'

Geddes nodded. 'Great minds. Now, let's see what we have here. Check upstairs. Be ready for anything. Could be his wife found out he was cheating and he's lying up there in a pool of blood.' He lowered his head and looked directly at Rory Calder, making sure he understood. 'And since this is now a crime scene we need to be careful not to contaminate it. Let's not toss all the rules out of the window and only hold onto the ones we like. Get the suits, the overshoes and the gloves from the car.'

Geddes left him and went into the lounge. Town houses from the Victorian age typically had high walls edged by a cornice to disguise unsightly joints. These were almost certainly part of the original building. He took in the handmade multicoloured rug above the fireplace, a stark cultural contrast to the flat-screen TV in the corner, and imagined Rob Sutherland stretched out on the couch mindlessly watching some reality show after a hard day at the office. On a coffee table, an opened bottle of Black Label sat beside two glasses, one empty, the other holding a measure someone had neglected to finish. A serious drinker wouldn't have left it.

Other than that the room was neat and ordered, very different from Geddes' flat where his clothes all somehow ended on the floor. He went out to the hall and saw DS Calder on the landing. The sergeant's voice was flat, his expression giving nothing away; he was learning. 'You need to see this, sir.'

If Geddes had had a tenner for every time he'd heard those words, he would've retired long ago. Asking what he needed to see was unnecessary, he'd know soon enough.

At the top of the stairs, he said, 'Where?'

Calder pointed to the room on his left. 'Their briefcases and coats are in there. This one's more interesting.'

The DI followed him inside. Whatever Andrew Geddes had been expecting, it wasn't this: Michelle Davidson would've made a better officer than many of the numpties he'd been saddled with over the years. At the risk of being ridiculed, she'd come to them with no evidence and a tale that made her look like a deluded neurotic female, yet her instincts had been uncannily accurate.

Border Force at Glasgow Airport had confirmed Rob and Julia Sutherland hadn't taken a plane. Geddes would've put his pension on them not taking a train, or a bus, either. The open suitcases on the bed suggested they hadn't gone anywhere.

As for the designer sunglasses, if Mrs Sutherland was still in the city she wouldn't need them.

* * *

DS Calder said, 'The twenty-five minutes are up, sir. Shall I call it in?'

Geddes was standing in the middle of the lounge, arms folded behind his back like a member of the royal family on a walkabout in a factory.

'Already? Time flies when you're enjoying yourself, doesn't it? Give it another five minutes. After that, this place will be crawling with uniforms and we won't be able to think.'

He rubbed his latex-covered hands together. 'The suitcases upstairs tell a story. What is it?'

'I'm not sure, sir.'

'And neither am I, DS Calder, neither am I. Bear with me while we examine the options. Rob Sutherland – the guy who lives here – is playing away from home. We have this from the woman he's been having an affair with. He intends to split with his wife and tell her at the end of the trip they're about to take, but, for reasons we can't hope to know yet, he doesn't get the chance: what if the whole sordid mess comes out the night before they're supposed to leave? The wife storms out. The marriage is over. Only it must've been the most civilised break-up in marital history because – apart from Julia Sutherland's heart – nothing got broken. There's a whisky glass handy yet she didn't fire it, or anything else, at her husband's unfaithful head.'

Rory Calder wondered if he was expected to make notes and decided against it. Geddes pointed to him. 'If that had been you, what would your next move be? Don't say you don't know. I'm encouraging you as a detective to do a bit of detecting.'

DS Calder nervously licked his lips. 'I'd call whoever I was involved with. In fact, I'd probably go to her place and deliver the news in person.'

Geddes smiled. 'Good lad, so would I. Then, how come Rob Sutherland didn't? Still hasn't?' He walked to the bay window and looked out at Hamilton Drive. 'Because that isn't what happened.'

He turned to face his younger colleague. 'Look around, Calder. Tell me what you see.'

The DS scanned the room, anxious not to disappoint. 'It's smart, stylish, though the rug above the fireplace is a bit bohemian and hippie for me. No sign of a struggle. A bottle of whisky and two glasses on the coffee table. That's about it.'

'No, it isn't. The glasses, what about them? Give me more.'

'One's empty, the other has whisky in it.'

'How much – a full measure?'

'Not where I come from.'

'Nor me. And?'

Rory shook his head. 'Sorry, sir.'

'Let's assume it was Mr Sutherland on the couch with the bottle an arm's length from him, suggesting he was settling in for a nice wee session before his holiday. Whoever else was here was standing. Why aren't both glasses empty? Did Sutherland leave in a hurry? And who was the other person? I haven't met a woman happy to stand while you're sitting, have you? Especially if she's having a drink.'

'With respect, sir, that seems an awful big stretch to me.'

'Does it, Detective? Get creative. Try to imagine it. We forced our way in. Somebody else didn't have to.'

Calder joined in. 'Because they had a key or Sutherland opened the door to them.'

'You're catching on, Sergeant. And why did the visitor – if there was a visitor – have time to down their whisky but Sutherland didn't? Somebody dominant enough to interrupt your plans and make you go with them?'

The DS was out of his depth. 'Not sure. If you say so, sir.'

Geddes snapped, 'I don't "say so". We're following up a reported missing person – it's a possibility. One of many to try to explain why the Sutherlands' cases are on the bed upstairs, why they didn't get on the plane and why they haven't been seen in days. If all we have to work with are a couple of whisky glasses, so be it.'

He got his irritation under control. 'Call this in. Say we need Forensics here asap to collect fingerprints and DNA. If Charlie MacAllister's in charge, emphasise the urgency of the situation. Tell them to request the record for Rob Sutherland's mobile, and contact Michelle Davidson – we need to eliminate her prints. Oh, while they're at it start checking the hospitals – these people might've been in an accident. I'll go through the briefcases upstairs, see if they throw up something. And, Calder, gloves or no gloves, don't touch a bloody thing.'

38

Geddes pulled in along from the advertising agency in Bothwell Street where Julia Sutherland was employed. Letter-headed stationery in her briefcase had supplied that information and on the other side of the city, as soon as Forensics arrived, young Calder would be doing the same at Galloway, Bartholomew and Figgis in Park Circus.

Rob's wife wasn't known to them so Geddes had opted to talk to people who worked with her on the off chance somebody could shed light on the situation. The DI had been involved in investigations that had dragged on, sometimes for decades. This one was moving at the speed of light – in one day he'd interviewed the girlfriend of a married man who hadn't responded to her WhatsApp messages, broken into his house in the West End and requested a forensics team on the strength of two whisky glasses, a parked car and a couple of suitcases that hadn't gone anywhere.

Geddes didn't relish trying to convince the chief super he was onto something. He hoped his instinct was right. If it wasn't, he'd be hauled upstairs. Again.

The public didn't know the half of what went on: an astonishing fifteen thousand missing people incidents were reported to Police Scotland every year; it was accepted that many more went unrecorded. Fatal outcomes outnumbered the victims of homicide, a sad and shocking statistic. Quoting that to his boss wouldn't save him if he'd wasted police time and resources on a couple in a troubled marriage who'd taken a train to South Ayrshire rather than a plane to South East Asia.

Rory Calder was a good lad – in another five years he'd make a detective the service could be proud of – but he was green, still learning his trade. The young DS had patiently listened to him explore his theories because he hadn't had a choice. But he wasn't a believer.

That left the voice whispering in Geddes' head, the one that had brought him here.

He flashed his warrant card at a receptionist with 'Turkey teeth' – they were all over the bloody place; had folk stopped looking in mirrors? – and false eyelashes. 'DI Geddes, can I speak with whoever's in charge?'

She smiled – Geddes guessed she did that a lot – and directed him to the fourth floor. Going up in the lift, he tried to remember how many missing person cases he'd been on in his career and gave up. The stats said it all: if he was in a hurry, they were the reason why.

When the lift stopped he got the warrant card out again and showed it to a stern middle-aged woman behind another desk, who barely glanced at it.

She sniffed. 'Mr Connors is Grapevine's founder and MD.'

'Please tell him the police are here.'

'He's in a meeting. If you care to wait—'

Geddes felt his temper snap. 'Well, get him out of his meeting. And do it now.'

Two minutes later he was in the MD's office ready to go through the same dance with the warrant card. Tony Connors was wearing a white open-necked shirt rolled up at the sleeves and was on a different page from the dragon on the other side of the door. 'It isn't often we have a visit from the police. I'm not sure I'm comfortable with it.'

Geddes used his stock reply. 'We have that effect on most people, Mr Connors, and long may it continue. It doesn't necessarily mean you've done something wrong.'

Tony replied with a breezy cliché. 'I'm as pure as the driven slush. How can I help, Detective Inspector?'

Geddes kept it simple. 'We're trying to establish the whereabouts of one of your people and would like to speak to her colleagues.'

Tony sat forward in his chair. 'Her? Who're we talking about?'

'Julia Sutherland.'

'Julia! She's on holiday. Probably halfway up the Mekong by now.'

Geddes stroked his chin. He wasn't keen on giving too much away. 'Well, that's what we're trying to confirm.'

The MD put his hands palms down on the desk. 'I'm not getting this. Why would you be looking for Julia?'

'At this moment we're not sure she's anywhere near where she was supposed to be going.'

Tony was visibly shocked. 'I assume you have a reason for thinking that?'

'Yes, unfortunately we do. But it's far from conclusive. That's why I'm here.'

Suddenly, the MD was falling over himself to be helpful. 'How do you want to handle it? Would in here be okay?'

'Here would be perfect and thank you for offering.' Geddes took out a notebook and a pen from his inside jacket pocket. 'I'll start with you, if that's all right? Tell me about Julia – what's she like?'

Tony straightened in the chair. 'Julia's a star, an absolute star. I'd have to check with HR how long she's been here, though I can say the people on her team adore her. This agency won a major piece of business right here in Glasgow recently largely because of her. If anything has happened...'

Geddes raised his eyes from his notes. 'And how well do you actually know her?'

The question surprised Tony. 'How well do I know her? You mean... outside Grapevine?'

'Yes, how well do you know her socially?'

'Socially? I don't. That isn't the relationship I have with any of the people here.'

'And her husband?'

Tony made a face. 'Rob? Never met the guy.'

* * *

After Tony Connors, Geddes had spoken to a relatively new employee called Ellis Kirkbride, a tall, handsome, arty type with a trace of an accent. The detective was hopeless with accents. This one sounded South African but might just as easily have been Australian. Though he'd frowned in all the right places there had been an arrogance to him; Andrew Geddes hadn't taken to Ellis Kirkbride. Kirkbride had praised Julia's marketing talents but hadn't had anything to add about the woman or the state of her marriage.

The last member of Julia's team was Olivia. At first she kept her head down, answering so quietly he couldn't make out what she was saying. Where she differed from her colleagues was on who Julia Sutherland was when she wasn't impressing everybody.

Geddes asked, 'What did she do after work? Did she go to the pub? To the gym?'

'She ran.'

'Really? Any particular place?'

'Yeah, every night along the Kelvin Walkway. Made a big thing of it. We thought she was mad but she loved it.'

When the policeman asked who Julia was closest to, without hesitating, Olivia replied, 'Ravi.' Tony had mentioned him in passing, saying he'd been involved in an accident and left.

Geddes pulled his chair closer so he didn't miss a word as the voice in his head that would, no doubt, cost him his pension some day kicked in.

'Did they meet each other outside work?'

Olivia dismissed the question with a vigorous shake of her head. 'No, no, it wasn't like that. Ravi made her laugh.'

'Why isn't he here?'

'He left.'

'You were close to him, too?'

She whispered, 'Yes.'

'Why did he leave?'

Olivia blinked. 'He got beaten up. After that he didn't want to come

back to work. They hurt him pretty badly. He's young. I guess he didn't
fancy being seen like that. I mean, would you?'

'No, I wouldn't. Have you visited him? How's he doing?'

She turned away, embarrassed, and her voice became still quieter. 'I
don't know, I haven't seen him.'

The inquisition started before he could stop it. 'But you're friends,
aren't you? Surely, a friend would check?'

This time there was no reply, not even a whispered one. Geddes saw
tears in her eyes and regretted the part of him that didn't let go, even
when it made a young girl cry.

* * *

At the traffic lights at the bottom of St Vincent Street, Geddes rolled
down the window, still thinking about how it had ended at Grapevine.
Sometimes he didn't like himself very much.

He swore at nothing in particular and turned his ire on the traffic.
Driving in Glasgow was a hassle. Once upon a time it had been
possible to get from A to B without taking a detour round X, Y and Z.
Not any more. The bright sparks who'd thought the new systems up
obviously had a guiding principle they stuck to religiously – shunt
every bugger onto the motorway and let them sort it out for
themselves.

He reached across to the passenger seat for his mobile. DS Calder
had expected to hear from him and had his story ready. 'Forensics took
their time. When they arrived at the house it was too late. I'll go to
Galloway, Bartholomew and Figgis tomorrow.'

Geddes had other things on his mind. 'Did you stress to them this is a
hurry-up situation?'

'I told them, sir.'

The DI repeated the words slowly. 'You told them. And?'

Calder didn't have to guess how what he had to report was going to go
down. 'There's a queue.'

Geddes slammed his fist against the steering wheel. 'That's rubbish!
We're in the twenty-first century, for Christ's sake! Haven't they heard of

rapid DNA sequencing? Two and a half hours max. Latent prints should take about an hour to identify if they're on the database. These people—'

Calder's next statement was akin to throwing a lit match on paraffin. 'We aren't a priority, apparently.'

'Really? Well, we bloody will be when I get a hold of them! Of course we're a priority! The Sutherlands haven't been seen in days. The whole thing stinks to high heaven and some Noddy's telling us to wait our turn. God Almighty!' His attention jumped back to the road and a Renault.

'Indicate, you tosser! Indicate!'

Calder smothered a laugh at the DI's outburst; delay with Forensics was an old chestnut. On another day, another case, Geddes would take it in his stride and pull a few strings if need be.

The sergeant moved to safer ground. 'How did you get on, sir? Anything useful?'

'Hard to say at this stage. Julia Sutherland liked to run the Kelvin Walkway – see if anything out of the ordinary has gone down there recently. And while you're at it, have a think about this. Somebody in her team at Grapevine has just left – a guy called Ravi Malik – I'm on my way to speak to him now. Julia's missing and this Ravi guy was beaten so badly he's crippled. Maybe it's me, but that's a lot of action for one small company.'

'Could be a coincidence, sir.'

'Don't believe in coincidences, DS Calder. Never have, never will.'

He hung up and pressed Charlie MacAllister's number on quick dial. They weren't friends – with few exceptions, Andrew Geddes didn't do friends – but their paths had crossed many times and between them they'd killed the odd bottle of The Famous Grouse.

MacAllister was stout and grey-haired, going through the motions until retirement. He wouldn't be sorry to go and his wife wasn't short of ideas about how to spend his pension. When it finally came, Geddes would go to his leaving party, raise a glass and wish him well.

In the meantime, he needed him to do what he was paid for.

MacAllister was on his way home and didn't welcome the call. Like half the police officers in Glasgow, Andrew Geddes only contacted him when he was looking for a favour.

'Whatever it is, the answer's no.'

On the other end of the line he heard Geddes laugh. 'How's it going, Charlie? Still fooling some of the people all of the time?'

In spite of himself, MacAllister chuckled. 'A bit like yourself, then. Spare me the social chit-chat. Before you ask, I'm fine, the wife's fine, the grandkids are fine; everything's fine. Now, spit it out, what're you after?'

Geddes appreciated straight talking – he did enough of it himself. 'You ran the rule over a house in the West End this afternoon.'

'Yeah, Hamilton Drive, I remember it. Give us a chance, Andrew, we're snowed under.'

'I get that, Charlie. Believe me, I'm not trying to add to the load.'

'Really?'

'What my young colleague didn't impress on you was the urgency of the situation.'

MacAllister was losing interest already. 'Everybody's case is urgent. Thought you'd know that by now.'

'True, and I do, except this one really is. I won't bore you with the details but we need whatever you find right away. Tonight, if it isn't asking too much.'

MacAllister sighed. 'It is and you know it. Sorry, man, the days when I'd drop everything for a good cause or a pretty face are long gone. And I don't miss them. Either of them. The best I can do – and trust me, if you tell anybody you can forget jumping the line ever again – is first thing in the morning.'

Geddes kept the smile out of his reply. 'Thanks, Charlie, your secret's safe with me.'

'It better be.'

'Just to clarify, when exactly is "first thing" in your world?'

'The results will be there before you are, how's that?'

It wasn't perfect but it was a result. Geddes was delighted. He said, 'How can I thank you? Will a bottle do it?'

MacAllister had an answer for him. 'Not this time. If you really want to thank me it's easy – don't call me again.'

* * *

The detective had said he'd contact her as soon as he knew anything, but hadn't. Instead, Michelle had been summoned to the station to have her fingerprints taken. When she'd got the call with a request to come in she'd feared the worst and prepared herself for bad news. Rob hadn't answered her messages and, much as she hadn't wanted to, she'd stopped sending them.

The constable who'd offered her a coffee had given the same answer as every other officer she'd asked. 'It's standard procedure.'

Michelle had tired of hearing it and pressed him. 'But why? Why is it necessary?'

He seemed puzzled by the question. 'So we can eliminate you.'

The words terrified her. 'Eliminate me? Eliminate me from what?'

The constable realised he'd said the wrong thing and backed off. 'As I say, it's standard procedure.'

'Let me speak to DI Geddes.'

'The DI isn't here at the moment. When he—'

Michelle wasn't listening. 'You've found Rob, haven't you? Is he all right?'

'Again, honestly, I—'

She cut across him abruptly. 'Oh, God! He's dead, isn't he? That's why you want my prints – you think I'm involved. That doesn't make sense – I've never been to Rob's house. Never!' The panic she'd been holding in check spilled over. 'I was the one who reported him missing and now you're taking *my* fingerprints. I don't understand. Surely I've a right to be told what's happening?'

The officer didn't try to stop her leaving and outside she leaned against the station wall, confused and afraid. Driving herself home was out of the question, she was too upset to even consider it, so in Hope Street she hailed a taxi, told the guy behind the wheel where she wanted to go and slumped in the back seat.

Her love affair had turned into a bad dream and it still wasn't over.

39

Ellis was in the toilet on the second floor where he'd cut his hand smashing the glass; it had healed but the marks were still on his knuckles. That had been the beginning. He'd lost it with Julia and was close to losing it again. Ellis had only himself to blame – he hadn't taken his own advice and now the police were involved. Whatever Sutherland's intentions the camera had caught the light in the redhead's eyes on the steps of Kelvingrove. She was in love with him. So much she hadn't let it drop. Rob's bit-on-the-side had used her obvious gifts to convince some dope of a policeman into believing her story.

Ellis balled his fist but stopped short of punching the wall; he'd underestimated her. Whatever unlikely tale she'd told, nobody had actually laughed out loud. If they'd been to the house and seen the suitcases they weren't just looking for Rob Sutherland – they were looking for his wife, as well, and that had inevitably brought them to Grapevine.

The detective – Geddes – hadn't been impressive. The questions had been routine, uninspired. Just a middle-aged guy going through the motions, killing time 'til retirement. If he was the best Glasgow had to offer, Ellis had nothing to worry about. That said, the visit had spooked him more than he wanted to admit and he checked the real-time images from the container on his phone.

As usual, there wasn't much going on: Julia was lying on the ground with her face buried under the sleeping bag, Rob was in the chair. They were as far from each other as it was possible to get. The photographs in the envelopes had destroyed them as he'd known they would.

The end was coming. Ellis intended to hasten that end. When darkness fell there would be plenty to see and he'd be in his front-row seat to enjoy it.

* * *

Geddes pressed the buzzer and got no answer. He tried again with the same result. This late in the afternoon traffic on Duke Street was heavy; it was rarely anything else in the East End. Not far from where he was standing the last woman in Scotland to face the death penalty had been hanged in Duke Street Prison. On that grim day a hundred years ago, these tenements had been here.

According to Olivia, Ravi Malik had been badly injured; he should be home. Geddes was about to give up when a male voice as scratchy as a three-day beard crackled through the speaker. 'Who is it?'

'It's the police.'

After a moment, there was a 'click' and the door sprung open. Malik was waiting for him on the second-floor landing and it was immediately obvious Olivia hadn't been wrong. He was on crutches, his weight off the injured leg, and he didn't ask why the police were at his flat: he either knew or had no interest in knowing. Malik led them inside. As with most rentals, the furniture had seen better days; a TV with the sound turned down hummed in the far corner. The air was stale and the policeman resisted an urge to open a window as he watched Malik manoeuvre himself with difficulty into an armchair, his face twisted by the effort.

He glanced for the first time at the detective. 'They say you get used to it. Don't believe them, it isn't true. Sit anywhere you fancy.'

'*They* say a lot of things that aren't true.'

Malik was young – Geddes guessed mid-twenties – but the attack had aged him and the scars weren't all on the outside. Olivia had mentioned Julia had liked this guy; he'd made her laugh. He wasn't likely to be cracking jokes any time soon. He had the look of someone who hadn't slept properly in a long time, his eyes sunken, hooded with resentment. Taking proper care of himself wouldn't be easy and wasn't a priority. Clearly, he'd chosen the line of least resistance – his jaw was covered in thick stubble, his dark hair hadn't seen a comb in a while and there was dandruff on the shoulders of the maroon Heart of Midlothian top he was wearing. Geddes doubted he would've been bothered, even if he'd noticed – he had more pressing problems. Spending day-after-day in this room would give him plenty of time to wonder where his life was going and where it had gone. Resigning hadn't been his smartest decision; finding another job wouldn't be easy, especially if the prospective employer sensed what Andrew Geddes was seeing.

Ravi Malik was sorry for himself and he had every right to be.

Small talk wouldn't be welcome and the detective got right to it. 'I'm told Julia Sutherland's a friend of yours. Is that correct?'

Ravi was instantly defensive, a symptom of where he was in his head.

'You're "told". Who by?'

'Your colleague, Olivia.'

'Ex-colleague.'

Geddes stifled a sigh – this was going to be challenging and it had already been a long day. 'How would you describe your relationship with her?'

Ravi shrugged. 'She's my boss.' He corrected himself. 'Was my boss. I suppose it would be fair to say we're friendly. Why?'

'It appears she's missing.'

Geddes anticipated a reaction and wasn't disappointed. Malik shot forward in the armchair, suddenly animated. 'What the hell are you talking about? Julia isn't missing, she's on holiday with her husband.'

'No, she isn't. They didn't get on the flight.' He let Malik process the information. 'When did you last see her?'

'What? See her? She came here the night before they left.'

'And how did she seem to you? Was she uptight, agitated, anything out of the ordinary?'

'No, she was fine. She'd been working hard, driving a project as usual, and was ready for a well-earned rest. I can't believe this. Are you certain they haven't changed their minds and gone off somewhere else?'

Geddes answered honestly. 'At this moment we're not certain of very much. When she visited you, did you tell her you were leaving Grapevine?'

'Yes.'

'So you liked her but were okay about spoiling her holiday. What about the rest of the team?'

'What about them? There's only Olivia and Ellis.'

'Were they on good terms with her?'

'Isn't this line of questioning a bit away from the point? I mean, if she really is missing shouldn't you be trying to find her?'

'That's why I'm here, Mr Malik.'

Ravi was outraged. 'You think I had something to do with this? Me? Are you serious? Do I look like a man capable of abducting someone?'

'That's a strange word to use, isn't it?'

'It's what you're implying.'

'You're wrong, I'm not implying anything. I'm here to ask a few questions that might help lead us to Julia, nothing more. How well do you know her husband?'

'I've only met Rob once, at a party in their house.'

'What did you think of him?'

'I can't really recall. It was a while ago, not long after I started with Grapevine. There were a lot of people there. Rob and I can't have talked for more than a couple of minutes. Get to the point, Detective Inspector.'

Despite the misfortune that had befallen Malik, Geddes was finding it hard to like him. It seemed the feeling was mutual. 'I asked you how the other team members got on with Julia. You haven't told me.'

Ravi wasn't keen to revisit a past that hadn't been kind to him and baulked. 'I really don't see how any of this is relevant.'

'Please answer the question.'

'All right. Originally, it was just the three of us and it was great. Then, Connors brought in that arrogant bastard Ellis.'

'What changed?'

'Everything. We – Olivia and me – suddenly our faces didn't fit. Grapevine was invited to pitch for a big commission and we were cut out.'

'Was that Julia's idea?'

Malik dismissed the suggestion with an irritable shake of his head. 'Of course not. None of it came from Julia. We were a team. Tony Connors breezed in and destroyed what she'd built. Ellis tried to have me sacked. Told her I wasn't good enough because he wanted her to himself – the guy was infatuated, buying her chocolates, giving her flowers.'

'So she didn't have a problem with him?'

'That's what I thought, until I heard them arguing.'

'Arguing about what?'

'I'm not sure but it was full-on. She was shouting at him to back off. I went in to see if she was okay.'

'And was she?'

'Said they were having a creative difference of opinion.'

'Did you believe her?'

A sad half-smile appeared and was gone. 'No, no. Julia gets passionate about her work, not angry.'

'When was this?'

'Weeks ago.'

'And how were they afterwards?'

Malik considered the question and his answer. 'Difficult to say. I picked up some vibes.' He slapped his leg with the palm of his hand. 'Then I got this. When she visited me she admitted she felt the same as I did.'

'Okay, about the attack on you – the report says you didn't see who did it. You've had time to think since then.'

'Look, I was drunk so I can't prove anything, but I know. Of course, I know.'

He didn't offer more and Geddes pushed. 'It would be helpful if you shared your suspicions.'

'They're not suspicions, it was him.'

'Who? Kirkbride? Why would he attack you?'

'Because he was jealous of my relationship with Julia. Bastard even came to gloat at the hospital.'

Geddes let what he was hearing sink in; it sounded like the ranting of a bitter man. 'It would've been wiser to wait until you've recovered before you left Grapevine. I assume that was because of your... differences.'

The distrust that had never been far away was back in Ravi Malik's eyes. 'There's no way I was going to have him mocking me behind my back. Julia had had about as much as she could take of Tony Connors. Sooner or later she'd quit and Ellis would be my boss. I couldn't have that.'

40

Ellis was conscious of a tightness across his chest and a tingling sensation in the fingers gripping the steering wheel. This was supposed to be the fun part; it didn't feel like fun.

He glanced over his shoulder at the rolls of duct tape and the Nikon on the back seat. There was a way out if he needed one. He could tape all of the vents up, take a few pictures and go home. By morning, Mr and Mrs Sutherland would be dead and he could stop worrying. Except, that would be too easy. All he had to do was keep his nerve, stick to the plan and remember why he was doing this.

At the entrance to the waste ground he opened the gate and drove to the container. It had been only hours since he'd been to the site; it seemed longer. Throughout the day, while the good people of Glasgow went about their business, Rob and Julia were here. Ellis tried to imagine what that would feel like and couldn't, but the mental anguish had to be intolerable.

He knocked on the corrugated side panels to announce his arrival, knowing they were already aware of it. 'Hello! Anybody home?' He smiled, pleased with his joke, and started to enjoy himself. 'How're you doing in there? What's new?'

Ellis leaned the folding ladders against the container, climbed to the vent and spoke into it. 'Change of plan, folks. The "every breath" stuff is a nice idea but it's too slow so I've decided to let you go.' He laughed. 'Just kidding. No, here's the deal. This is boring. I'm speeding things up. What you do is up to you but don't forget that knife. One person will last longer than two – not much longer, admittedly, but still. My money's still on you, Julia, even though, so far, you've been a disappointment to me. After what your husband's done, cheating on you, lying to you; telling you he's working late when he was with somebody else, nobody would blame you. He doesn't deserve to live. Sorry, Rob, it's true.'

There was no sound from inside the container. Ellis shrugged – the little surprise he'd lined up for later would see to that.

He taped one slat, pressing on it to seal the edges, moved on to the other side and did the same. When he was finished he got back into his car and drove away. He'd just reduced the air getting in by 50 per cent. It would be interesting to watch how soon they felt it.

* * *

Rob looked over at his wife. Julia was on her feet clutching the sleeping bag to her like a comfort blanket, her bottom lip trembling uncontrollably, the fear she was drowning in written on her face. She wasn't far from cracking completely – the wonder was she'd lasted as long as she had. Rob went to her and took her in his arms, gently rocking until he felt her calm; this time she didn't resist him.

He whispered, 'I know I've hurt you deeply. Please believe I'm not your enemy.'

'I feel so alone. I'm scared, Rob, scared of dying in this miserable place, but I don't want to live.'

He kissed her forehead. 'Nobody's going to die, Julia, trust me.'

'How can you say that? Look at where we are.'

'Something isn't right. Suddenly he's rushing, hurrying to get it over with. We should be asking why. What's changed?'

Julia gazed into the eyes of the man who had been her rock, and Rob said, 'The only reason I can think of is if somebody's out there looking for us.'

'Who?' She pulled away from him. 'Her? You mean her?'

He'd lost her again and there was nothing he could do about it. 'Seriously, does it matter?'

'Yes, actually, it does. I'd rather it ended here than have to see you with your slut.' She raised her fist to attack him, then let it fall to her side as the sad irony hit home. 'You're not worth the breath any more.'

* * *

Ellis had had better days, no doubt about that, but it would end on a satisfying high once it got dark. He popped the ring-pull on a can of beer, put his feet on the desk and watched the people on the Mac screen. South Africa had been spontaneous, this one he'd intended to savour. If he was honest, it hadn't lived up to his expectations so far. But there was still time.

Ellis drank from the can and wiped his lips on his sleeve.

Now! Showtime!

* * *

Julia was in the sleeping bag at the other end of the container. She wouldn't be asleep, though in the darkness it was impossible to know.

Rob studied the vents and the closed-off slats, barely managing to resist the overwhelming urge to scream. With a super-human effort he held it together – he owed her that much. After his inspiring little speech, losing control would be the final betrayal in a long line. Her world had ended with the photographs of him with Michelle and he'd seen the wild look in her eyes as she'd retreated into herself, child-like, fragile, close to losing her sanity.

It wouldn't take much to finish the hellish process her insane colleague had set in motion.

They'd hardly touched the boxes of power bars Ellis had left. Charged with adrenaline, scared out of their minds – eating hadn't been a priority. Suddenly, Rob was starving. He read the ingredient list and the maker's extravagant claims about health, then devoured one in three bites. It didn't ease the gnawing in his gut and he longed for a fish supper so badly he could almost smell the salt and vinegar.

He put the image out of his mind: how long had they been here? It felt like weeks although it could really only be days. His joints were stiff, sore from lack of movement and lying on the metal floor, and his ribs hurt like hell. The only good news was his head had stopped bleeding, but he suspected the wound had become infected.

His fury exploded and he yelled, 'Damn you, Kirkbride! I refuse to die like this, do you hear me?'

He went to Julia and shook her. 'On your feet. C'mon, Jules, we can't give him the satisfaction of destroying our spirits as well as our bodies.'

From under the cover her defeated voice answered. 'What's the point? We'll just use up the air.'

'No, we won't, there's still plenty coming in. We need to eat. We need to drink. And we have to get on our feet and move around. Our survival could depend on it.'

'You have more to survive for than me.'

The comment stung. Rob felt his face flush and turned away. He said, 'I'm sorry, Julia, you'll never know how sorry. But I'm serious. There's a good chance the police are looking for us. Being strong enough to last even a few more hours could be the difference between leaving here on our own two feet or being carried out with a sheet over our heads.'

Rob didn't mention that his affair was their only hope of being rescued. Slowly, Julia dragged herself up. He handed her a couple of energy bars and a bottle of water, ignoring the pain in his head, and began stretching, praying she'd join in. She unenthusiastically followed his lead until the runner in her surfaced and she started to power walk round the cramped space.

Rob fell in at a slower pace behind and, over her shoulder, she said, 'You know this is crazy, don't you?'

'It's better than the alternative. Anything's better than that.'

They were talking – communicating for the first time since they'd opened the envelopes. Julia had shaken off her despair and as the light that had been absent returned to her eyes the guilt her husband had been carrying lifted and Rob remembered why he'd fallen in love with her.

She faced him. 'Thank you.'

'For what?'

'Making me try. Please don't spoil it by lying. It's too important. Do you really believe they're looking for us? I mean, really?'

Rob took her hands in his and answered honestly. 'Yes, I do. I absolutely do, Julia.'

'Why?'

'Because there's nothing else. It's all we have.'

They both heard the scratching at the same time. Julia said, 'There's someone on the roof. I didn't hear a car, did you? There's someone there, Rob.' She started shouting and banging on the walls. 'Help! Help us!'

Rob put his arms around her and held her close, whispering, 'Stop. Stop. Stop, Julia.'

She pushed him away. 'But there's someone there.'

'No, there isn't.'

'Then, what is—?'

He hesitated, wishing he didn't have to break it to her. 'It's rats. The bastard's put stuff down to attract them.'

'Rats!'

Dozens of tiny feet scurried across the metal and in that terrible moment everything that had been gained disappeared. Julia stumbled backwards, sobbing uncontrollably, covering her ears against the sound.

'Ellis! Ellis, please, please stop this! I'm sorry if I hurt you. Please, Ellis, I'm begging you!'

In his basement Ellis Kirkbride was on his feet, cheering as he watched her come apart. The drama he'd longed for had finally ignited and he was loving every second of it. He clapped his hands like an excited child.

'That's it, Julia! That's what I want! Cry! Cry for me!'

Rob tried to get through to her. 'They can't get in, Julia. He's messing with our heads.'

It was too much for her. Just when he'd thought they were drawing closer, he'd lost her again. Rob hammered on the walls, trying to scare the creatures away. When he turned, Julia was in the sleeping bag with her back to him. The scratching stopped. The rats had gone – for now; the only sound was his wife's muffled moans.

Rob didn't notice the knife wasn't on the table.

* * *

Summoning the loathsome scavengers was the sickening product of a diseased mind and Julia realised it was over; she had nothing left to fight with. In the folds of the sleeping bag she stroked the cool blade in her hand, aware of what it would take to use it, not sure if she was strong enough to actually end her own life. Ellis had won because without Rob her life was empty. What was there to go back to? A desperate feeling of being alone overcame her and she buried her head under the bag. They'd been wonderful together – that much had been real – yet, as the hellish pictures in the envelope proved, it hadn't been enough for him. She looked across at his drooping head; he couldn't stay awake much longer. When he fell asleep she'd finish this quickly and cleanly on her own terms.

41

DAY FIVE

It was still dark outside when Andrew Geddes got out of bed and hauled himself into the shower. Three cups of coffee later he was in the car on his way to Stewart Street. Geddes wasn't a morning person. Those who knew him had learned it was better to let him ease his way into the day rather than engage in conversation that was unwelcome and sure to be gruffly rebuffed. He hadn't slept; his mind was too active. Yesterday had been crazy. Today might be more of the same.

The missing person crisis was a silent epidemic – in the UK somebody was reported missing every ninety seconds. Over the years, he'd been involved in his share of them, most famously the one the press had labelled the 'Baby Lily Hamilton case'.

This one smelled different.

He nodded to the desk sergeant and went to his office, expecting the fast-tracked forensic information Charlie MacAllister had promised to be on his desk waiting for him; it wasn't. Geddes was about to phone to find out what the hell was keeping him when his mobile pinged. The message was from MacAllister and it was short.

CALL ME.

The DI pressed redial and couldn't get through, left it for five minutes and tried again: MacAllister's phone was turned off. He'd said, 'The results will be there before you are, how's that?' Geddes could count on one hand the people he could depend on. Apparently, MacAllister wasn't among them. He said, 'So much for promises, Charlie.'

Through the night he'd gone over everything in his head and knew his next move. It was ten minutes to eight. Grapevine wouldn't open until nine. Ellis Kirkbride hadn't appreciated being interviewed by the police the first time. He wasn't going to like it again.

* * *

Geddes had been right; Ellis was pissed and didn't care who knew it. He sat with his legs crossed, one elbow resting on the arm of the chair, glaring at him. The DI began with the usual empty pleasantries, making no effort to infuse them with sincerity.

'Thank you for coming in at such short notice, Mr Kirkbride.'

Ellis concentrated on a mark on the wall behind Geddes, clearly unhappy. 'Did I have a choice, Detective Inspector? I hadn't noticed.'

'Well, if you put it like that, no, not really.'

'That's what I thought. On the phone you said there was something you wanted to speak to me about. I'm a busy man. How can I help you?'

The detective remembered why he hadn't liked this guy; he was too confident, too abrupt, too sure he was the smartest person in the room.

'We're all busy, Mr Kirkbride. Yesterday, I asked about Julia Sutherland. Can you recall what you told me?'

Ellis drew a finger reflectively down his cheek. 'I said she was talented – which she is – professional, hard-working...'

'Indeed, you were very complimentary.' Geddes leaned towards him. 'What interests me is what you didn't say.'

'You've lost me.'

'You left out the heated argument you had with her. And I'm wondering why someone would do that.'

If Geddes had hoped to spring it on him he was going to be disappointed; Ellis Kirkbride was unfazed. He blinked but didn't speak, then his lips parted in a slow smile.

'Ah, you've been talking to our friend Ravi, Detective.'

'Detective Inspector. Are you denying you argued?'

'Absolutely not. Your information's accurate. We had words, yes.'

'A shouting match?'

Ellis laughed dismissively. 'Julia's too much of a lady to shout. I'd call it a frank exchange of opinion.'

'Not a creative dispute? That's what she told Ravi.'

'I know, I was there. She was being kind. We were arguing all right, about him.'

'About Ravi?'

'She had a blind spot where he was concerned. I didn't. His work wasn't good enough – he didn't have it to be with a top marketing agency. Julia couldn't see it and we both got pretty steamed up. Ravi's given you the edited version and you've swallowed it.'

Geddes held his stare. 'Really? He claims you were infatuated with her, bought her chocolates and flowers. Is that an edited version, too?'

'No, it isn't. I was rude to her in Tony Connors' office. I owed her an apology so I said it with flowers. I'm sure Tony will remember; it was embarrassing.'

'And the chocolates?'

'Were for everybody in the team. Now, if you're satisfied, can I go?'

'Yes.'

Ellis stood but he wasn't finished. 'Ravi Malik was a lucky boy to be at Grapevine. Somewhere else he might've bluffed his way through. Not here – the standard's too high. Did he bother to mention I saved the campaign he was working on? Or that I apologised publicly for criticising him? No, I didn't think so. As for infatuated, the guy's projecting. He was the one with his tongue hanging out, not me. For all I know he might even have been in love with Julia. I'm reluctant to tell you how to do your job, but you could do worse than have another word with him... Detective Inspector.'

* * *

Ellis Kirkbride was arrogant and unlikeable, but he'd defended himself and his explanations rang true. He'd been worth a second look; Ravi Malik might be too.

Geddes turned his mobile on to discover he'd missed a call from Charlie MacAllister. The DI redialled the number and listened to it ring. He didn't have to wait long and MacAllister wasn't best pleased. 'The last time we spoke I asked you not to call me on the mooch again. You thought I was joking and maybe I was because we go back a long way. But I'm not joking now. This is the last, the very last, favour I'm doing you or anybody else. Am I making myself clear, Andrew?'

The veteran crime scene investigator was furious; Geddes didn't understand why. Until he knew what had inspired this outburst it was wiser to tread carefully. He took his medicine and said, 'Crystal, Charlie. Now, what've I done to rattle your cage?'

MacAllister calmed down. 'After we talked last night I took an executive decision for auld lang syne and had your Hamilton Drive evidence shunted to the top of the heap. Not as straightforward as it sounds when every detective in Glasgow is hammering on the door demanding their results. You said it was urgent. You're a good copper and I haven't forgotten what you've done in the past.'

'Nice of you to say so, the same goes for you, Charlie, though I'm not sure why you're so angry.'

'Aren't you? I'll tell you. Because of me, some poor bugger had to cancel his plans last night to work on your stuff. To keep my promise about the information being there first thing I contacted the Scottish Crime Campus at Gartcosh and said we needed the results asap. They got me out of bed at three o'clock this morning to tell me what he'd found.'

'Thanks for going the extra mile. It's appreciated.'

'Is it? Well, can you explain why you didn't call me back?'

'I tried and couldn't reach you.'

'You should've tried harder.'

'What've you got?'

'You're the detective. I'll let you figure it out.' Geddes felt the hairs on the back of his neck stand up. 'No match on the prints.'

'So the DNA—'

'Should be a bust. Except, it isn't. It belongs to a Peter John McMillan.'

'Great work. Who is he?'

MacAllister had been made to wait to break the news and wouldn't be rushed. 'Well, it's not so much who he is but *where* he is that's interesting.' Geddes held his breath as MacAllister enjoyed his moment in the sun. 'For the last twelve years, Peter John McMillan has been serving a life sentence in Shotts Prison.'

42

A DI in the field had a fair measure of autonomy but there were limits. Geddes had left those behind and knew it was unwise to proceed further without having his actions officially sanctioned.

He called his boss, Detective Chief Inspector Leitch, from the car, driving with one hand, holding the phone with the other, and laid out the case. The DCI was a by-the-book policeman and no fan of Andrew Geddes; the two had butted heads more than once. Leitch preferred more biddable officers and would've been happier not having to deal with this one. He listened as Geddes gave the details of a missing couple.

Before he could finish the DCI cut in. 'I hear you, although it occurs to me that this might be an appropriate time to pause and consider before rushing on, don't you agree?'

Andrew Geddes didn't agree. 'With respect, no, the DNA—'

The DCI ignored him. 'Because, for all your admirable – shall we call it 'zeal'? – you haven't conducted an investigation as such, followed lines of enquiry, thrashed out the possibilities of the evidence with your team.' He sighed. 'What I'm saying is, it's all a bit off the cuff, isn't it? Your commitment isn't in question, most certainly not, but I'm not convinced an actual crime has been committed – do you see what I'm getting at, Geddes?'

Geddes saw and bit down a reply that would've got him suspended.

Predictably, Leitch stayed with his standard approach of 'if in doubt, do nothing' and was about to tell him to pull back when Geddes threw Charlie MacAllister's bombshell into the mix. 'We found DNA on a glass in the house.'

The DCI hesitated as interest stirred in him for the first time. 'And do you have a match?'

'That's what I've been trying to tell you.'

'Sir.'

'Sir. We do, a guy in Shotts Prison.'

That little nugget changed the pen-pusher's mind. He said, 'Okay, I'll call the governor and tell him to expect you.'

Geddes thanked him and neglected to mention he was already on the M8 heading east.

At Stewart Street, on his way out of the door, he'd shouted to Calder, 'Get me everything you can dig up on a Peter J. McMillan convicted of murder. He's in Shotts.'

'What's he got to do with us, sir?'

'That's what you're going to find out, isn't it, Sergeant? Give it to me in bullet points. Come on, man, move yourself! We haven't got all day!'

Shotts was a relatively new maximum-security prison nineteen miles from Glasgow. Geddes had been responsible for putting a few of the inmates behind its bars. He was passing the Eurocentral Industrial Estate and the Dakota Hotel when he got the call from a breathless Calder. The DS sounded as though he'd been running. He said, 'I'll put what I got in an email and send it to you.'

'Do that but give me the top line.'

'All right. The woman McMillan murdered was his ex-wife, Marion. He strangled her to death, beat her with a half-brick and dumped her body in a wood. In the dock at the High Court he didn't offer a defence and pled guilty. The whole thing was done and dusted in a day. The judge sentenced him to life and he's been in Shotts ever since.'

'Anything else?'

'Background stuff. Nothing that stands out.'

'What about family?'

'A son who seems to have cut his father out of his life when he killed his mother.'

'Somebody left that DNA in Hamilton Drive and for sure it wasn't the guy I'm going to see. Find out where the son is and pull him in.'

* * *

The governor was an imposing man, broad shouldered, tall even sitting down, and it was easy to imagine him confidently striding through the halls holding the most violent criminals in the country. He had only good things to say about Peter McMillan, describing him as a model prisoner.

'We've told him you're coming but if it's his ex-wife's murder you want to interview him about, then I wish you luck. In all the time he's been here he hasn't spoken about it to anyone.'

'He can't be in denial, he pled guilty.'

'I wouldn't call it denial. Prisoners talk – there's not much else to do in a place like this. Peter has always refused to be drawn.'

'And, in your experience, that's unusual?'

'Good God, no. In the early years of a long sentence 90 per cent claim they're innocent. Later, when they've come to terms with the reality of their situation, they admit the truth. And with a few exceptions that truth is almost always, yes, they did it.'

'But not McMillan.'

'Correct.'

'Can I see the list of his visitors?'

The governor shuffled the papers on his desk. 'That won't be possible.'

'Why not?'

'He hasn't had any.'

'In twelve years?'

'Not one.'

'How has he coped?'

'The same way he's coped with everything else. He's completely resigned to things as they are and doesn't talk about it.'

Geddes hid his disappointment and started to believe this was a wasted journey.

'What about friends – somebody released in the last six months who shared a cell with him?'

The governor wasn't hopeful. 'Nobody comes to mind. Shotts is a maximum-security prison. Most prisoners will spend a third, a half or even the rest of their lives in here. Leaving doesn't happen very often.'

'Well, you never know, maybe he'll speak to me.'

'He's remarkably well read. He'll speak to you, all right – about politics, history, literature; every subject under the sun except one. You'll leave no better informed than when you arrived. He won't tell you anything about killing his wife.'

He pressed a buzzer on his desk. Thirty seconds later the door opened and a warden came in. The governor said, 'Please take the detective inspector to Peter McMillan.' He turned to Geddes. 'It's a strange thing to say about a guy who strangled a woman he'd loved and covered her body with leaves, but you'll like him.'

* * *

A cold, hard wind blew across the fields through the trees lining the approach road to HM Prison Shotts and rain fell in heavy drops, spattering the windscreen, exploding against the glass – a portent of the coming storm Andrew Geddes didn't notice as he got into the car. The interview had lasted exactly eighteen minutes and Peter McMillan had been everything the governor had warned him to expect, sitting with his arms folded, relaxed and only mildly curious about why the DI was there. Geddes' training had taught him how to read body language and guessed McMillan was putting up his defences, assessing him with the guarded interest of a man who hadn't had a visitor in over a decade. Prison had been kind to him: the skin around eyes bright with intelligence was unwrinkled and his recently washed hair was thick and long.

By now, McMillan would be back in his cell, confident he'd kept his own counsel as he'd done for so many years and revealed nothing about the murder of his ex-wife, but one look at him was all it had taken for the detective to see the resemblance.

In Glasgow, DS Calder answered his mobile on the first ring; Geddes' shrill voice came down the line. 'Forget the son, I need everything you can find on Ellis Kirkbride asap. Get everybody available onto it.'

* * *

The rain was coming down in sheets, so hard the wipers struggled to clear the screen. Andrew Geddes peered into the deluge and gripped the wheel; the bones of his knuckles poked through his skin. On the motorway, a white van in the inside lane drifted towards him. He swerved to avoid it, loudly cursing the driver's incompetence. Near the Blochairn Interchange at Junction 14 his mobile rang and an excited Calder blurted out his news. 'DVLA will take a bit longer but we've searched the databases and come up with four Ellis Kirkbrides.'

Patience had never been a virtue of Geddes and wasn't now. He barked, 'Is our guy in there?'

Unwisely, the DS drew out his reply. 'I'll let you make up your mind about that, sir. One's an eighteen-month-old baby, another's a disabled pensioner and two are deceased.'

It was what Geddes wanted to hear. He said, 'Right, lift the Ellis Kirkbride we know and bring him to the station. I'm ten minutes away from Stewart Street.'

* * *

Ellis had studied the policeman's ruddy face for telltale signs of distrust as he answered his questions and found none. The rest of the meeting had gone well and he'd left the station pleased with himself, confident the plod was satisfied with what he'd learned about Ravi's motives. Yet, the more Ellis had thought about it, the less he'd liked it. He'd been interviewed twice now. Too close for comfort.

Suddenly, he'd felt uneasy. Instead of going to Grapevine he'd driven out of the city to the container and taped up more of the vents, expecting to hear the Sutherlands pleading with him to let them go. When they didn't, Ellis was tempted to open the door. He changed his mind: why take the chance? In a few hours he'd seal the last of the vents, crack a few beers at his flat and watch the finale play out.

He didn't lie to himself: his revenge on Julia had been meticulously and elaborately planned, but it hadn't delivered. The rats had been genius, the absolute highlight, and he'd been elated with her reaction until the husband had calmed her down and spoiled the fun. The rest had been a let-down – he'd made mistakes. Roping in Rob, exposing his infidelity to increase her pain, had been too ambitious, he recognised that now. It would've been better to keep it to Julia and watch her slowly go mad.

His mobile showed he'd missed a call from Tony Connors. No doubt the MD had come down from his ivory tower to discover nobody except Olivia in the office. Fuck him! He'd show up when it suited him, not before.

A leisurely lunch in a café bar in the Merchant City not far from where he'd sorted out Ravi Malik mellowed him, and he wandered around the Gallery of Modern Art in Royal Exchange Square trying to make sense of what was on the walls. An hour later, he'd given up and headed for Grapevine, certain Tony would be at lunch with one of his Barbie doll floozies. As he turned into Bothwell Street it started to rain and he saw two police cars screech to a halt outside the Grapevine building. The doors flew open and four uniformed officers rushed inside. Ellis immediately understood but refused to allow himself to panic.

Without breaking stride, he dropped his mobile into a rubbish bin and kept going.

Apparently, the detective hadn't believed him after all.

* * *

Geddes pulled his coat over his head, slammed the car door and ran to the station with rain drilling the road; in seconds he was soaked. An anxious Rory Calder was waiting for him in Reception. Geddes didn't need to ask; the detective sergeant's face told the story.

'Kirkbride's not there. He's not there, sir. He texted his boss he was on his way, but he never arrived. Could be he's onto us.'

The DI's reaction was instant. 'Get officers to his house and arrest him on suspicion.'

'They're already on their way. We got his address from his employer – we should hear from our guys any minute.'

Geddes thought about going to his office and settled for shaking water off himself and pacing up and down. Calder wanted to speak but he'd worked with the DI long enough to realise the smartest thing was to keep his mouth shut. When the call came, Calder took it. His hand dropped to his chest and Geddes realised it wasn't good news.

'No sign of him, sir. What do we do?'

'Go in. Now!'

'Without a warrant?'

Geddes shot Calder an evil look. 'Are you serious? Really? Are you? We've reason to believe the Sutherlands are being held against their will in that property and you're on about a bloody warrant?' He sneered. 'With that attitude I see a bright future for you, son. But not in the service I'm in.' Geddes lost his temper and shouted at the sergeant. 'For Christ's sake, this is the real world! We worry about filling in forms when we've got nothing better to do. Tell them to break the fucking door down! Break it down!'

43

Ellis was angry with himself. The plan shouldn't have gone wrong but it had; the new life he'd created in Glasgow and everything that went with it was behind him. All that remained was to finish what he'd started and disappear. He was confident – he'd done it twice before and he could do it again.

Coming out of the blackout to find himself staring at the container seemed a long time ago. He'd immediately recognised its usefulness, a usefulness still to be fully realised, although it would be – a few hours from now, while the police were scratching their heads, Julia Sutherland and her husband would be dead. He laughed. The detective would be in the basement, his eyes narrowed on the Mac screen. When he finally figured it out, Ellis wondered if the plod would appreciate his little joke.

He got the ladder from the boot and the last two rolls of duct tape from the glove compartment. Standing on the roof, he remembered the consternation the rats had caused and wished he could do it again. Ellis peered through the grill, saw her staring up at him and spoke, his voice tinged with genuine regret. 'When you're casting around for who to blame for this, Julia, remember it could've been so different if only you hadn't been like the rest.'

* * *

Police vehicles had closed off the street and Geddes braced himself against what he might be about to confront. Ten years in the job or twenty – when it came to this, time served didn't matter. Officers were human beings who liked dancing with their wife or husband and taking their kids to the latest movie, then Pizza Express. Going home to their loved ones with images of some inner-city atrocity still playing behind their eyes while they pretended they were okay took a toll. Telling yourself it was a job only worked for so long. Andrew Geddes had been lucky. He had no children. There was no wife, at least, not these days. In his opinion, policing and marriage were a combination better avoided.

He got out of the car and walked past the uniform stationed at the open front door to a sergeant waiting in the hall, who immediately launched into his report. 'We approached from front and rear securing both exit routes. We knocked. When we got no answer we obeyed your order and forced entry.'

The sergeant was dotting the I's and crossing the T's. When the report was written he wouldn't be on the wrong end of breaking in without a warrant. Geddes pretended to be interested; he wasn't. 'Okay, good job. What've we got?'

'The place is empty. Wherever our man is, he isn't here.' Geddes nodded and the sergeant continued. 'The basement's interesting.'

'Basement? Didn't know these places had them. What's in it?'

The sergeant didn't commit himself. 'Not sure I can give it a name, sir. I think you'll understand what I mean.'

Geddes followed him down a narrow staircase, their footsteps echoing in the confined space. As they neared the bottom the air became stale and the detective braced for another grisly addition to the gruesome collection in his head.

In a twenty-odd-year career he'd witnessed plenty of things he'd rather forget; this could be one more.

The sergeant moved aside to let him past and Geddes understood his reluctance to describe it: the space, lit by an Anglepoise lamp, was no bigger than a store cupboard, one wall covered with photographs, so many that they overlapped. Julia Sutherland took centre stage in most of them – on the street, getting into her Mazda outside her home and in the city; smiling unconvincingly at the camera with Ellis's arm round her.

In another image alongside a shot of Ravi Malik's broken body, a man and a woman lay on a beach, the female obviously dead. Malik had claimed Kirkbride was obsessed with his boss – he hadn't been wrong. A section separate from the rest proved it – she was on a path beside a stretch of water dressed in a grey tracksuit, her blonde hair held back with a sweatband, running along the Kelvin Walkway as she did every evening according to young Olivia.

Unbeknown to her, he'd been watching. And apologising with flowers was a lie; there had been more to it than that. Geddes was discovering how much more.

He addressed the sergeant without taking his eyes off what was in front of him. 'Kirkbride's mobile will tell us where he is. Get onto that, then double-check if there's been a report of a disturbance in the last few days near the Kelvin Walkway.'

'What kind of disturbance, sir?'

The DI bit back his irritation. 'Any kind, Sergeant. Any bloody kind.'

'Why the walkway?'

Geddes answered with certainty. 'That's where he lifted her.'

He scanned the line of glossy images, aware of his heart beating faster in his chest. Towards the end, one photograph caught the DI's attention. Taken at night and obviously rushed, the picture was different from the others and had all the polish of a drunken selfie.

In it, two people locked in a kiss. Andrew Geddes recognised both of them – the woman was Julia Sutherland, the man Ellis Kirkbride.

After Ravi Malik had revealed the tension between them, this was unexpected. Geddes whistled quietly. 'Well, well, well. Apparently, Rob isn't the only one playing away. Have a forensics team go over this place. Kirkbride may have held them here at some point.'

A policeman slipped into the chair and turned on the computer while Geddes focused his attention on the other side of the wall. Michelle Davidson and Rob Sutherland starred in a dozen shots of them kissing or holding hands. Why Ellis Kirkbride would be interested in the lovers was a mystery; Geddes didn't get it but, for sure, there was a reason. His eyes moved slowly to the middle of the sinister montage and two grainy monochrome 10 x 8s secured by brass tacks, the sole black-and-white shots in the group. One of them, the picture of a battered old sea container, couldn't have been more incongruent. The other showed Julia and Rob Sutherland beaten and tied to chairs.

The detective pointed to the container. 'Find that thing and who the dead girl on the beach is. This guy—'

He was interrupted by the man at the computer. 'Sir, you need to see this.'

Geddes felt the familiar mix of excitement and anxiety of adrenaline pumping into his bloodstream. On the screen, Rob Sutherland sat at a table studying his hands as though he'd only just noticed he had them. At the far end of the room an arm stuck out from under a sleeping bag. Julia wasn't moving. Whether she was dead or alive it wasn't possible to tell.

'Can they hear us? Can we speak to them?'

'No, we haven't got audio.'

'Damn it!'

'How long can someone survive in that thing, sir?'

Geddes didn't have an answer for him; he was asking himself the same question. The detective angrily stabbed the picture on the wall with his finger. 'Kirkbride's holding them in that container. See if some bright spark can get a fix on that spy camera.'

The man seated in front of the screen shouted, 'Something's happening, sir!'

Rob Sutherland was on his feet, Julia beside him, faces taut as they hammered the corrugated panels with their fists. High up on the wall a horizontal line of daylight flickered and died and the sergeant spoke in a voice that had dropped to a whisper.

'Christ, it's him. He's outside.'

Geddes finished the sentence for him. 'And the bastard's shutting off the air.'

* * *

Rob's brain sensed his body's need for oxygen. He coughed, his chest tightened and he glanced over to his wife, wishing it weren't true yet knowing it was: the air was already running out.

The light that came on whenever they moved wasn't as strong as it had been – the batteries were dying – and in its fading glow Julia's face was ghastly pale. She'd moved her sleeping bag underneath one of the vents and lay in it with her eyes closed to shut out reality and the hopelessness of their situation. Rob's feelings were more complicated.

They both heard the car approach. Julia tensed and got to her feet, her voice a monotone edged with anxiety. 'Why is he back, Rob? Why so soon?'

Rob rose from the table but didn't answer until they heard the scrape of the ladders against the container. 'Stay quiet. Don't react. Don't give him what he wants.'

Ellis casually whistled fragments of a tune; through the grill he saw the woman who'd diminished him. 'When you're casting around for who to blame for this, Julia, remember it could've been so different if only you hadn't been like the rest.'

There was a finality to the statement. Julia recognised it and instantly forgot Rob's words, dredged defiance from deep inside herself and shouted, 'You're a sad, pathetic creature, Ellis! Nothing you do can change that! As for you and me...' she forced a bitter laugh '...there could never have been anything between us! Never! Even after what he's done, Rob's ten times the man you are and always will be!'

Ellis ignored the insults. He cut a piece of tape, stuck it over the first of the remaining slats and followed it with another. Asking his wife not to react suddenly seemed ridiculous and together Rob and Julia threw themselves at the corrugated panels, pounding on them, pleading with Ellis to let them out.

Ellis worked systematically on both sides until the last strip of daylight vanished. Julia slumped against the wall. She had nothing left to fight with. Rob put his arms round his wife and held her to him and for a moment the past was forgotten as she clung to him.

After a while she calmed down and pinched her eyes with her fingers. Rob thought she was going to cry but he was wrong. She said, 'It's all right, Rob, there's no need to lie to me any more. Nobody's coming and we both know it. We're going to die here.'

He wouldn't allow her to go down that road without a fight. 'No, no, you asked me why he was back so soon. Well, I'll tell you... and this is the truth. I think he's scared, Julia, I really do.'

She pulled away. '*He's* scared? Take a look at where we are.'

'Why else would he come back?'

'Because he's sick and enjoys making people suffer.'

'So what's the rush all of a sudden? He has us where he wants us, doesn't he? What's preventing him from taking his time?'

'Is this her again? If it is I won't listen to it.'

'It isn't anybody again. All I'm saying is something's put a fire under whatever this guy had planned, and it isn't you and me.'

'Okay, please God you're right, but he's been clever. How could anyone find us?'

Rob would've preferred to have an answer but settled for the only truth available to him. 'I don't have a clue, Julia, but we need to stay calm, keep movement and talking to a minimum. From now on, every breath counts.'

* * *

Ellis heard them banging desperately on the walls, begging him to set them free, and imagined the terror of knowing each anguished cry, each pitiful sob, brought the end that little bit closer. How much longer Julia and her husband had, he couldn't say. Hours or minutes, it didn't matter; for him it was done.

He walked across the stony ground towards the river remembering the time, not long ago, when he'd emerged groggy and half mad from the blackout near the abandoned unit. In that awful moment, despite his pain, fate had allowed him to recognise he was staring at the instrument of his retribution.

And so it had been. Glasgow was a bust – the future he'd longed for wouldn't be here – though the dream lived on because the woman he'd been searching for since his childhood was still out there somewhere.

The noises from inside the container had stopped. Ellis wondered if the Sutherlands were already dead and hoped not – he wanted them to suffer and keep on suffering. Getting rid of his phone meant he wasn't able to connect to the camera and witness their last moments – a pity, because that would've been sweet indeed. But he mustn't be greedy. It was enough to know that in the basement the police would have a grandstand view of their failure from the best seat in the house.

Ellis was about to turn away when another idea struck him. He laughed out loud because he was going to meet the very man for the job.

44

The unmarked CID car wasn't equipped with a blue light or sirens so Calder used the horn to bully vehicles out of their path – a risky manoeuvre in any conditions, doubly dangerous now. In the passenger seat, Geddes was in radio contact with the control room in Motherwell demanding constant updates on progress. They assured him an ambulance was standing by and every available police car in the area was searching for the container he'd described. Behind the wheel, DS Rory Calder peered through the windscreen as the wipers worked overtime to clear it. He had only one job – to get them to the village on the fringe of the city as fast as possible without crashing. He was nervous, his palms were sweating, but the breakneck speed they were travelling at wasn't the reason. The spire of the old Bargeddie Church on Manse Road was a local landmark. Growing up in nearby Baillieston, he'd seen it almost every day of his life, yet, in the short time since he'd identified the tapering stone needle of the 150-year-old building and told his DI, doubt had crept in. Like everyone in the basement, the detective sergeant had watched the horrific pictures of Rob and Julia Sutherland pleading for their lives as Ellis Kirkbride sealed the vents and knew the consequences of getting the location wrong.

Across from him the senior man didn't share what he was thinking, preferring to keep his own counsel as they bombed along the motorway towards their destination. The silence was too much. Calder had to voice his uncertainty; he couldn't help himself. He said, 'I hope to God I'm right about this, sir. Those people... If I'm mistaken—'

Geddes heard his anxiety and replied without moving his head to look at him.

'Relax, you're not. It's Bargeddie. I should've remembered it.'

'Why would you remember it, sir?'

Geddes spoke slowly, reluctantly confessing why he'd been so quiet. 'Because I've been out here before, Sergeant. A long time ago, admittedly, though the moment I saw the spire lurking in the background of that photograph it should've clicked.'

The subject was closed and DS Calder knew his boss well enough to leave it and settle for listening to him check back in with the control room.

'Anything yet?'

'Nothing, except they've traced the mobile you wanted them to locate.'

'Where was it?'

'In a rubbish bin in Bothwell Street. The man you're after, he's smart – he knew the phone could lead us to him and dumped it.'

Calder threw in his tuppenceworth. 'He must've seen our guys going in.'

Geddes massaged his eyes with one hand while the fingers of the other tightened round the radio, barely able to control his frustration. 'Every criminal thinks they're smart. Smart won't save this guy. I'm going to get him.'

They left the motorway at the Coatbridge turn-off with the church visible ahead of them on a hill. The DI spoke out loud to himself. 'So where the hell is it?'

The sergeant would've loved to have an answer for him. Suddenly, the radio crackled and a voice broke the news they'd been aching to hear. 'They've found it. They've found the container. Where exactly are you?'

'Coming off the M8 at Bargeddie.'

'You're less than a mile away. Turn left at the second roundabout and keep going until you're on Gartcosh Road. You'll see a dirt track, again on your left. We've got two cars already there and the ambulance is on its way. What do you want us to do?'

It was a stupid question. Andrew Geddes didn't hesitate. 'Get it open. Get those people out.'

Calder pressed the accelerator to the floor and overtook a Transit van. The car surged forward, slewed left and he whispered, 'Please, God, let us be in time.'

The track had been gouged by heavy lorries, muddy and eroded by the torrential rain. They bumped over it and stopped beside three marked police vehicles. The doors of the container had been prised apart and in the distance the telltale spire of Bargeddie Church, shrouded by mist, seemed to sway in the grey sky like the mast of a phantom ship.

Geddes pushed past the group of uniforms huddled in twos and threes dressed in high-vis yellow waterproof coats, staring straight ahead into the prison that had held the missing couple, for the second time that day dreading what was waiting for him. But something was off. At first, he wasn't sure what, then he got why the policemen were standing around, doing nothing.

Because there was nothing to do: Rob and Julia Sutherland were dead.

An officer held onto his hat and introduced himself. Focused on the container, Geddes didn't register his name. The DI swallowed, struggling to believe what he was seeing. From far away he heard the policeman say words torn from his lips by the wind and felt his stomach heave.

'There's nobody here, sir. It's empty.'

* * *

The words fell like stones, each heavier than the one before; Geddes heard them and was devastated. He wasn't the first copper to have been in a room with a murderer and let him go: that knowledge was no consolation. He'd interviewed Ellis Kirkbride, stared him in the face – not once, but twice – and failed to read the signs.

Aware of the others looking to him for direction, he jolted himself back into the moment, firing orders to the group. 'Somebody find out what kind of time these people have got so we understand what we're dealing with!'

He called the sergeant at Kirkbride's flat. 'What's happening in the container? Are they still breathing?'

The officer would have loved to give the DI a more encouraging report; it wasn't possible. He said, 'It's dark. The screen's a blank. We can't tell. Without somebody moving around inside the container to trigger the lights, they won't come on.' The silence at the other end of the line registered and the policeman added, 'I'm sorry, sir. Best we can do is pray they hold on until we get to them.'

The call ended and the corners of Andrew Geddes' mouth set hard. He wasn't religious; praying wasn't an option. 'Kirkbride's messing with our heads. Dragging us out here, making fools of us.'

'But why, sir? I don't get it.'

Geddes shook his head. 'Because he can, Sergeant, because he bloody well can. It's part of who he is. Somebody said he's smart and they were right. He abducted the Sutherlands the night before they were going away so nobody would notice they were missing for three weeks. Rob Sutherland's neglected mistress going to the police spiked that. And, in case you haven't noticed, he's leading us a merry dance.'

He shot instructions at the DS. 'Get me Contact Force Overview, then get one of those pictures cropped and get Kirkbride out to the media.'

'Will that help, sir? I mean... given the time.'

The senior man knew what he meant. 'Listen, son, whether we find the Sutherlands alive or dead won't alter the fact there's a maniac out there. Just do what you're told, will you?'

A minute later a chastened Rory Calder handed him the phone. Geddes pressed it to his ear, introduced himself with his characteristic brevity and ploughed on. 'We're trying to find two people being held in a sea container and there's strong reason to believe the oxygen supply has been cut off. Unless we get to them and soon, the chances are they won't make it. We need everybody you have on it – every car, every beat officer, anybody with local knowledge of Bargeddie. What we're searching for is somewhere outside the city, too big an area to cover from the ground.

We're standing in a field close to the old parish church so you don't have to tell me the conditions are bloody awful. Believe me, I get it. But without air support we may not find them in time. How feasible is getting a chopper up in this? Talk to them, or let me talk to them. Explain the situation. If it's on, start here, where we are.'

Geddes wiped rain from his brow and waited impatiently for the response. 'Tell them we're looking for an isolated container, probably abandoned. The suspect got rid of his phone when he spotted our men arriving in Bothwell Street. Approximately twenty minutes later he closed off their air vents – that should give you an idea of radius.'

Calder hadn't learned his lesson. He said, 'There's nothing here, sir, why not start nearer the city?'

The DI drew a stubby finger down his cheek and scanned the blackening sky over the Clyde Valley. 'Because, as we've agreed, this guy's smart. He doesn't do anything without a reason and he's already played us for fools. This area's important to him. For all we know, the real container could be over the hill.'

'Why is it important?'

'Less than a mile from where we are his father murdered his mother and dumped her body in a wood near the Monkland Canal. Bringing us to this place isn't a coincidence, Calder.'

Geddes scanned the clouds gathering in the south and knew what the answer to his request would be. This was only the prelude; the actual storm was chasing towards them like an angry mob and it was going to get rough. No pilot could fly safely in this. Even if they were mad enough to try, visibility was against them.

A violent gust bent the trees, rocking the group of officers where they stood, blowing the hat off one and dousing the flickering hope in Andrew Geddes' heart that they might still get to Rob and Julia Sutherland in time.

* * *

The incessant beating on the metal roof was a sterner test of their already shredded emotions than even the rats had been because, eventually, they'd stopped scratching and scurried off, whereas the sound of the rain drumming in their ears seemed to dull their senses, sapping what remained of their fragile resolve. There were eight or nine power bars and a few bottles of water left but they had no appetite to eat or drink. At the beginning, the light inside the container had been bright. Now, days later – although Rob had no idea how many days – the batteries had very little juice left in them. At any moment they could be plunged unbelievably into total blackness and a new level of terror. Rob's eyes had adjusted sufficiently to notice the missing knife before Julia could use it; he'd intervened and gently taken it from her.

The tenderness they'd shared when she'd given up the blade without a fight had been short-lived. Watching her curled up on the floor in the sleeping bag, hiding from the end closing in on them, listening to her struggle for air, Rob considered turning the blade on himself as Ellis Kirkbride had foreseen. In Kirkbride's fevered brain the choice would be both stark and clear – one would perish, the other survive a little longer, praying for help that wouldn't come, dying alone and terrified.

Rob couldn't and wouldn't let that happen to Julia. He rose from the table, acutely aware of his fingers gripping the weapon. This was the hardest thing he'd ever do and, even as he moved silently towards the bundle on the ground, he wasn't certain he could do it.

Julia sensed him and rolled round. She saw the dull glint of the blade in his hand and jumped to her feet. Rob had no words. 'Julia... Julia... I know...'

She screamed, 'Get away from me! Get away, you bastard!'

'You... Julia, you don't understand.'

In the poor light his features were blurred and shadowed, the face of a stranger. Julia was breathing heavily but her voice was calm. She overcame her fear with a mocking laugh that wounded him more deeply than she'd ever know. 'Going to explain why you were creeping towards me with a knife, are you, Rob? Don't bother, I understand perfectly.'

'No, you don't, you don't. It isn't how it looks. I'm doing it for you.'

'My God, there really is no bottom to you, is there? Since when is killing somebody doing them a favour?'

Rob fell to his knees, frantically begging her to listen to him. 'This isn't about me! I don't want you to suffer. Please believe me!'

Julia took a step away, her blazing eyes not leaving her husband, lips formed in a sneer. 'Believe you? Are you fucking serious? You'd stab me if it gave you ten more minutes of air. Five more!'

'How can you say that? I'm telling the truth. I'm trying to save you.'

'What, after months of lying day and night, deceiving me with another woman, *now* you're telling me the truth?' She spat at him. 'Christ, you're pathetic, you really are. What did I ever see in you? As for protecting me, forget it! You forfeited that privilege the second you even *thought* about breaking your vows and lost the right to make any decision that concerned me. I don't need you, Rob. And I don't want you anywhere near me.'

The force of the outburst stunned him; his head bowed and the knife fell from his hand to the floor. Julia picked it up and hurled it to the other end of the container. 'And know this. Ellis Kirkbride can't kill me, neither can you. Because, thanks to you, I'm already dead.'

45

DAY SIX

The previous time he'd come to this place it had been a twenty-minute drive. Today, it had taken Geddes more than twice that, gripping the steering wheel with both hands while strong winds tried to force him into the side. Flooding at Newhouse reduced traffic to a single lane hugging the inside of the motorway and the DI hoped he wasn't on a fool's errand. The storm was not expected to blow itself out for another thirty-six hours. Too long; Andrew Geddes couldn't wait.

He'd sent Calder back to Stewart Street where the hunt for Ellis Kirkbride would go nationwide once the Procurator Fiscal issued an arrest warrant. When that was in place, Kirkbride could be picked up on sight. Geddes had come alone, unsure exactly what he expected to achieve, but with no concrete leads this was the only option. According to the governor, Peter John McMillan hadn't had a visitor in all his years of incarceration. But prison was a strange place; inmates had ways of communicating with the world beyond the walls.

The son McMillan had fathered was a stranger to him.

Or was he?

* * *

The man across the table was set to replay Geddes' last visit. He raised an eyebrow. 'Well, this is a surprise.'

The DI wasn't in the mood for mind games. He said, 'Is it? Let's start the way we mean to go on – with the truth. Has your son been in contact with you?'

'As I told you the last time you were here, I haven't seen Jonathan since before the trial.'

'These days he calls himself Ellis.'

A strange look shadowed McMillan's features as curiosity morphed into concern. 'Ellis was his mother's maiden name. He must have...'

Geddes hadn't been certain what had brought him here – a feeling, a hunch, something in his bones – but he knew now. 'You pled guilty and didn't offer a defence. When I read the report of the trial, that stuck with me. Your lawyer could've put forward any number of circumstances to merit a lighter sentence – provocation, diminished responsibility – yet he didn't. Why not?'

McMillan folded his arms and didn't reply. Geddes said, 'I couldn't work it out because it didn't make sense. But now it does. You were protecting someone. Confessing to a crime you didn't commit so they wouldn't be caught.'

The edge of Peter McMillan's mouth twitched and the detective realised he was right. He shook his head. 'You've spent a dozen years of your life in here for something you didn't do. Jonathan killed his mother and you let him get away with it.'

McMillan had invested too much to give in easily. He shifted in his chair and unfolded his arms. 'It's a nice theory. This many years down the line, good luck proving it.'

Geddes leaned forward and closed the distance between them. 'I couldn't care less what you've done or haven't done. All I'm interested in, the only reason I'm here, is in case you're in contact with him and know where he is.'

'I don't. I haven't set eyes on him in over a decade.'

Geddes pressed him, unconvinced. 'You've lied your freedom away, why should I believe you?'

'Because it's true.' McMillan had waited a long time to unburden himself. He said, 'The marriage was a disaster. We fought, fought all the time. Jonathan was just a child. We damaged him. The night his mother left him to be with another man he watched her go, begged her to take him with her.' McMillan hadn't spoken to anybody about this or the aftermath; his voice cracked and for a moment Geddes was afraid he couldn't go on, but he rallied. 'He was too young. He couldn't understand it wasn't him she was getting away from. After she'd gone he cried for weeks – and I really mean weeks. He was destroyed. Christ, it was heart-breaking.'

The DI gave Peter McMillan time to recover, then said, 'What happened?'

He shook his head as though he didn't have an answer. 'She promised to come back for him but she never did, and Jonathan changed. He formed instant, deep relationships with people. One-sided commitments he fixated on. Then, when somebody rejected his friendship, another child, a girl, anyone at all, he went into a violent rage. I'd calm him down, remind him it was *me* she'd abandoned, not him.' He shuddered. 'For a while he kept a picture of her underneath his pillow but seemed to have got over it, until one day – I wasn't there – by sheer chance he saw his mother having a picnic with two kids. She'd abandoned him and had a new family. It was too much for him. He snapped.'

'And you put your life on the line to allow him to get away with it.'

'No, not to get away with anything. He was a victim. What I did was give him a chance to put it behind him and make a fresh start.'

'And because of a decision you took thirteen years ago, somewhere on the outskirts of Glasgow two people are running out of oxygen and might already be dead. We also believe he's killed at least one other person. That's what he's done with his fresh start.'

The DI rose to his feet. 'Marriages fail, Mr McMillan. Sometimes the children get hurt. Except that isn't what went on here. Jonathan murdered his mother because he's sick. Your son is a psychopath – he was then and he is now – and I intend to catch him before he can harm anybody else. Now, where the fuck is he?'

* * *

On his way back to Glasgow gale-force winds rocked the car; there was worse to come. Geddes concentrated on the road in front of him, his mood as low as it had been in a long time. Asking a pilot to go up in this weather was madness and, understandably, wasn't happening, but without that support the chances of locating where Rob and Julia Sutherland were being held captive were zero. In HM Shotts he'd heard an all too familiar tale with no winners and the DI wasn't unmoved. Peter John McMillan had been a loving father who'd given years of his life to redress the damage the toxic relationship with his wife had done to their only son. But protecting him from the justice he deserved had prevented him from getting the help that might or might not have changed his course. No one would ever know.

McMillan hadn't committed the crime he'd been convicted of, yet he was far from innocent.

* * *

The grizzled worthies drinking bottled Guinness in the corner were too engrossed in their conversation to notice the stranger at the bar. The pub in Finnieston would normally be doing fairly brisk early-evening business. Storm Hilda had put paid to that – it was close to empty.

The red storm warning issued by the Met Office the day before was still in place. With as good an excuse as they were ever likely to have, people had heeded it and not gone into work. On the TV high on the wall BBC News Scotland was playing a mash-up of the havoc Hilda had caused and was still causing across the country. Huge waves lashed the esplanade at Largs where a man walking his dog had been washed into the sea – his body hadn't been recovered and wouldn't be until the weather abated. In George Square outside the City Chambers, an overturned double-decker bus lay on its side blocking the road surrounded by shards of its shattered windows. The report cut to a chimney in the Ibrox area blown from the gable end of a sandstone tenement onto a car parked in the street below. No one had been injured though the vehicle was a write-off.

The barman watched, mesmerised by the images, only losing interest when a picture of a man Police Scotland were hunting flashed onto the screen. He reached for the remote control, turned the sound down and spoke to nobody in particular. 'Yet they tell you global warming isn't real. Who're they kidding, eh? It's about money. It's always about money.'

The guy at the bar finished the whisky in front of him and signalled for a refill. While he waited his eyes darted between the TV and his reflection in the mirror behind the gantry: the shoulder-length hair had been replaced by a No. 1 buzzcut and instead of designer stubble, he was clean shaven. The finishing touch was the round vintage eyeglasses.

Ellis Kirkbride – the man on the screen – had been erased; he didn't exist.

The barman was in the act of putting the drink on the counter when the door opened and a blast of cold air rushed in. He shouted angrily over his shoulder. 'For Christ's sake! Shut that thing! In case you haven't noticed, it's a bloody gale out there.' He saw who was responsible and immediately regretted his outburst. 'Oh, it's yourself, Tommy. Didn't expect to see you out on a night like this. Come in, man, come in. What're you drinking?'

Tommy Shaw shot him a look that said he couldn't believe anybody would be foolish enough to speak to him like that and deliberately held the door ajar for longer than necessary. He was stocky and short, not more than five feet two. Nobody reminded him of his lack of height if they valued their smile. The collar of his coat was up, his hair matted to his skull, and he accepted the hospitality of the house gracelessly. 'You know what I'm drinking, Maurice, and make it large. As for the weather, thanks for pointing it out. I might've missed it. That explains why I'm fucking soaked, doesn't it?'

Tommy was the older brother of Ambrose, a Glasgow hardman with a city-wide reputation for violence. Tommy didn't do the heavy stuff – he was the brains – but he was related to somebody who broke bones for fun, so it was unwise to disrespect him. For twenty years the siblings had sold used car parts from a scrapyard in Haghill, not far from Celtic Park – the first place Ellis Kirkbride had gone after leaving Grapevine in Bothwell Street for the last time. Finding what he'd wanted had been easy. Now it was being delivered and he was here to collect.

Shaw dropped an envelope on the bar. 'I took an executive decision and lost the glasses. If you're smart, you'll do the same.'

Ellis let the envelope stay where it was. This wasn't what they'd agreed and the edge of his mouth curled in irritation. He said, 'I like the glasses.'

Tommy Shaw didn't give him an argument. 'So do I, the glasses are fine, but John Lennon suited them better than you. All I'm saying is they draw attention to you, which isn't the idea. Or am I wrong?' He picked up the drink the barman had discreetly left near his hand and swirled the contents. 'Listen, I'm doing you a favour, giving you the benefit of my professional experience, but if you want to go with the other picture, fair enough, I'll get it changed.'

'How long will that take?'

Tommy Shaw shrugged. 'Three or four hours. You'll have it tomorrow.'

Ellis removed the specs and slid them into his inside jacket pocket. 'No. You're probably right about the glasses.' He tapped the envelope with his index finger. 'Tomorrow's too late. I'll go with this.'

He passed the other half of the money to Shaw, who put it away without bothering to count it. 'You've made the right choice if you don't mind me saying so. Anything else I can do for you, Mr... Sutherland?'

Hearing his new name made Ellis smile. 'As a matter of fact, there is if you think you can handle it. I want something crushed – no questions asked. That's your line of country, isn't it?'

Shaw pursed his lips and didn't reply.

'Can you arrange it or should I go somewhere else?'

The scrap dealer threw back most of his whisky and scratched behind his ear. 'This "something" you want crushed, what is it?'

'A sea container. I'll tell you where to collect it.'

'Sounds interesting. What's in it?'

Water dribbled off Tommy Shaw's head; scum like this guy had their uses but Ellis Kirkbride despised them. 'Which part of "no questions asked" don't you understand? Don't mess me about. Yes or no?'

Shaw was reluctant to let the opportunity slip away. 'Very well, yes – for cash the answer's always yes – only what you're asking for... it'll cost.'

'How much?'

'Not sure. I'd have to think about it. A lot?'

'How much is a lot, Tommy? And talk sense.'

Shaw dipped a finger in his whisky glass and traced a number on the bar. Ellis read the figure – expensive. Then again, it was only money. 'Okay. Half now, half when it's done.'

'No. For this I need all the cash up front.' He caught the reluctance on the other man's face and pressed his point. 'It's non-negotiable. Take it or leave it.'

'Okay, I'll take it. Tell me how the crusher works.'

Shaw grinned. 'Imagine a pasta machine flattening dough. When we're finished your container will be six feet long and six inches high.'

'Then what?'

'It'll get shredded and the metal content recovered for recycling.'

'That's the metal, what about the rest?'

Tommy Shaw laughed. 'A machine sorts the glass and plastic, the "rest", as you call it, ends up in a landfill. Satisfied?'

Ellis liked what he was hearing. 'I want it done. Put your best man on it.'

'Easy, that's me. Where is this thing?'

Ellis told him and handed over a key. 'This opens the padlock on the gate.'

Shaw weighed it in his palm as though it had a deeper significance. 'And when do you want it done?'

'As soon as.'

Shaw shook his coat, shedding rainwater onto the floor. 'If the storm breaks we'll take care of it tomorrow. Good enough?'

'No, tonight.'

The other man made a sucking sound through his teeth. 'You're joking, aren't you? In this weather? Can't see it, mate, I honestly can't. Tomorrow's the best I can do.'

It wasn't ideal but it was better than nothing. Ellis couldn't quit Glasgow without knowing Julia Sutherland had got what she deserved. He said, 'All right. So long as you tell whoever's on the crusher not to look inside.'

Tommy Shaw realised he was staring at a guy with more secrets than his brother and him put together and there weren't too many of them in Glasgow. 'As I said, I'll handle it myself. And don't worry, I won't peek.'

* * *

Michelle Davidson stared out into the storm and mouthed, I love you, Rob. Please come back to me.

It had been six days since she'd seen him and two since the detective had promised to contact her if he found something. She'd been called in to give fingerprints; if nothing had happened, why did they need to eliminate anyone, especially her? Something was seriously wrong, she could feel it deep within her and was deciding whether to go back to the station to demand answers when her mobile pinged.

She grabbed it and spoke before checking caller ID. 'Rob... Rob, is that you? Are you okay? Where are you? I've been so worried when you didn't call.'

At the other end of the line DI Geddes caught his breath before responding. Unable to tell her what he'd discovered, he hadn't been looking forward to the call. Now he dreaded it. 'Apologies for not contacting you sooner, Miss Davidson. We've—'

She cut across him, frantic for information. 'Please tell me you've found him, that he's okay.'

'Unfortunately we haven't been able to locate Mr and Mrs Sutherland. We do know they didn't fly to Vietnam. A full investigation is under way to determine their whereabouts.'

It sounded wooden and rehearsed – police speak.

'But he's okay, he's alive?'

Geddes pushed the images of the two people begging for their lives to the back of his mind and answered as honestly as his position allowed. 'Until we locate them, I'm afraid I can't answer that. But I promise I will be in touch as soon as we know anything. I'm sorry I don't have something better to tell you at this moment.'

Michelle thanked him and he ended the call. She stared blankly out of the window and didn't notice the storm had picked up pace in the short time it had taken the DI to tell her almost nothing.

* * *

Julia lay on the sleeping bag listening to the never-ending rain. If she let her mind drift, astonishingly, she'd found she was able to filter it out. The moment she allowed herself to return to the present, the relentless cacophony kicked back in, wearing her down until she put her fingers in her ears to make it stop. The howling wind shook their steel prison. From time to time, something crashed against the side. But the bad news, the really bad news, was that the batteries had finally packed in. Now the blackness surrounding her was permanent and absolute.

Rob hadn't spoken since she'd accused him of trying to kill her. In the dying light Julia had seen the livid bruises and the dried blood on his face from the beating he'd taken and realised she'd overreacted: this was Rob, her husband, who didn't have a violent bone in his body, the man who'd gently taken the knife away from her so she couldn't do anything stupid.

She called his name quietly, expecting to hear a voice almost as familiar as her own. 'Rob. Rob. I shouldn't have said what I did. I'm sorry.'

He didn't answer and she tried again, louder this time. 'Rob. Rob. Speak to me.'

Her words echoed in the void but there was no reply. Julia crawled across the metal floor, her chest on fire, trembling hands feeling the way.

If they were going to die, let it be together.

Her voice was a hoarse whisper. 'Rob! Don't do this! Don't leave me alone! Not now! Please don't shut me out!'

Julia managed to haul herself a few yards but the effort left her weaker and more exhausted than if she'd run a marathon. She changed her focus, a trick she used to get through the pain barrier when her legs were lead weights and wanted to quit on her, picturing the familiar worn stone steps from Belmont Street down to the Kelvin Walkway, counting them off in her head as she'd done so many times. The mental distraction helped and she was able to carry on but she was spent. An overwhelming desire to be with her husband spurred her on until her fingers touched his arm and travelled to his cheek. She whispered, 'Rob? Rob, speak to me.'

She pressed her ear to his cold lips. He wasn't breathing. 'Please come back to me, Rob, please. I can't do this without you. I can't be alone.'

Julia needed to cry but couldn't. She lay beside him and held his hand, closed her eyes and gave herself to the darkness.

46

DAY SEVEN

And the rain came down.

Geddes had left Stewart Street sometime after nine o'clock and gone home because there was nothing else to be done. Everything he'd been wearing was soaked through and in his flat he'd pulled his clothes off and stepped into the shower. The hot water had worked its magic, he'd relaxed, though not enough to forget the images from inside the container or his conversations with Peter John McMillan and Michelle Davidson. That second one had been hard; she'd deserved better than he'd given her.

The detective was saving the Macallan eighteen-year-old single malt sherry oak for a special occasion and considered opening it to cheer himself up. He changed his mind; while Rob and Julia Sutherland were in danger, it wasn't the time. Instead, he poured three-fingers from a bottle of Bell's and took the glass through to the bedroom – no matter how much he fancied it, there wouldn't be another one.

Dawn found him on top of the covers, arms folded behind his head, wide-eyed and restless. It had been a long night; the detective was too wired to sleep. During the seemingly endless hours he'd listened as Hilda hammered Glasgow, rattling window frames across the city from Barmulloch to Blythswood Hill, ruffling roof tiles with the swagger of a Mississippi river-boat gambler cutting a new deck, knowing that, eventually, it had to blow by and the search would be back on. The early-morning TV news channels carried the story; Ellis Kirkbride's smiling face appeared on the screen – appeals to the public attracted plenty of phone calls, but in the DI's experience little in the way of solid information.

He was dressed and ready to leave when the news arrived from Air Support. 'Detective Inspector Geddes?'

'Yes.'

'This is Ronnie Baxter. I'm piloting the helicopter this morning. I have a police observer with me. The storm's clearing, heading away from us, although we'll, no doubt, get the odd rogue gust. But it's on. We can search a square mile of open ground in about twelve minutes. Do you still want me to check the area around Bargeddie?'

Geddes could've cheered. 'Absolutely. The guy we're after likes to play games so the container could be in the next field.'

'Okay, we'll start in the east and work our way round. What colour is it?'

'I've no idea.'

'Well, that's a great help, eh? I'll stay in touch.'

On his way in the DI called his sergeant. 'Get yourself to Stewart Street.'

'Already there, sir.'

'Already... Have you been home, Calder?'

Rory Calder hesitated. 'I slept in your office on the floor.'

Geddes hid his admiration. 'Don't make a habit of it. Anything on Kirkbride?'

'Yes, his car's been found in Whiteinch. No sign of him. The satnav's been disabled and his mobile's been wiped.'

'What about the appeal?'

'The phones are busy. There's a team on it. And, sir...' the hesitation was back 'and, sir, on the screen, there doesn't appear to be anybody moving.'

It was what part of him expected but didn't want to hear. He said, 'The chopper's in the air so be ready to move the second they spot something.'

* * *

Tommy Shaw used the key he'd been given to open the gate and drove the boom truck through. He got out and eyed his surroundings. His whole life had been lived on the streets – there wasn't much he hadn't done or wouldn't do for money. This job had the stench of serious jail time yet he hadn't considered turning it down. The order not to look inside the container was a temptation but one he'd resist. In a couple of hours it would be flattened, ready for shredding, and when the pub opened he'd be first over the door: a nice thought.

The sound of the helicopter coming over the tower didn't register with him.

* * *

Geddes heard the radio static and held his breath. The pilot understood what was at stake, how much depended on what he was about to say. 'We've been north as far as Stepps and covered from Milngavie to Strathblane and across the river to Inchinnan. Now, we're over Hillington, coming back full circle. There's a lot of open space around Carmunnock and Thorntonhall. Worth a look.' He imagined the disappointment on the ground and tried to lift the mood. 'Time isn't a problem – this thing can stay up for two hours. What do you want us to do, Detective Inspector?'

The DI didn't hesitate. 'Go round again. The container's out there. We have to find it.'

The line went dead; the wait continued. Every officer in Stewart Street was aware of what was going on; a few crowded into Geddes' office and stood, tense and silent. Calder shot a glance at his boss and decided not to speak. Twenty-two minutes later the radio crackled. Baxter sounded calm – the only one who was. 'I see it. Right on the river, tucked in at the old Glassford tower. It's being loaded onto a haulage truck.'

'For fuck's sake, stop it! Can you land?'

'No, but I'll buzz him. Let him know he's been spotted.'

Andrew Geddes was on his feet and racing for the door, DS Calder behind him. Geddes shouted, 'Get everything we have down there! And an ambulance!'

* * *

Tommy Shaw had rejected Kirkbride's half-now-half-later offer and insisted on the full amount up front but it wasn't enough to justify getting caught.

He dropped the container the minute he saw the chopper and dived out of the cab to disconnect the chains. Some jobs were easy, others were dogs better left alone, no matter how much money was put on the table – a simple lesson he'd been in the game long enough to remember. So why hadn't he?

The helicopter hovered feet from the ground blocking his escape route, beating the scrubby grass flat, tearing at his overalls, the noise deafening in his ears. He shielded his eyes as a police car came through the gate – others would be on their way. Four officers ignored him and ran to the steel box. The scrap man tried not to think about what might be inside. As the policemen pulled the handles and stepped away he saw their faces, and whatever curiosity Tommy Shaw had had evaporated.

Suddenly, he'd rather not know.

* * *

Geddes wasn't first to arrive. Later, he'd conclude perhaps that had been for the best. On the way through the early-morning city traffic, Rory Calder had broken every rule of road safety but had got them here.

On the waste land, the DI counted a crane truck, an ambulance and four police cars – five if you included theirs. A plain-clothes officer recognised Geddes, hurried towards him and launched straight in. 'We found two people inside. A man and a woman.'

'And?'

'I'm afraid—'

Geddes' patience snapped. He barged past and took in the scene. The policeman waited a moment before he continued. 'He's gone and she's unconscious though she's alive, by my reckoning, only just.' He turned to the senior officer. 'How could anybody lock another human being in there?' He shook his head. 'They'll stabilise her in the ambulance then take her to hospital. Queen Elizabeth's nearest. They've been notified to expect her and are standing by. The driver's in custody. Shaw. Tommy Shaw. A small-time East End villain. Owns a scrapyard with his brother. Claims he was collecting a disused container that's been here for years and saw an opportunity for scrap. Says he knows nothing about what was inside. Surprise, surprise. We haven't charged him – thought you'd prefer to question him first.'

The clouds were clearing, revealing patches of blue sky. Soon, the sun would shine. It would seem as if the storm had never happened and the good people of Glasgow would go about their business unaware of the drama taking place in their city. Geddes recalled an agitated Michelle Davidson and her conviction something was wrong when everybody – including him – had thought she'd been used by a married lover and jilted. The DI felt a stab of regret – if Julia Sutherland pulled through she'd have Michelle to thank for saving her life, although it would be a long time before grief allowed either of them to see it like that.

'Do you want to see her?'

'I'll wait until the doctors say she's well enough.'

'Then, it's back to Stewart Street to start writing your report?'

'No, we still have a manhunt going on and before the media splashes this all over the place, there's somebody I have to speak to.'

47

FIVE WEEKS LATER, LAMBHILL CEMETERY, BALMORE ROAD, GLASGOW

The car followed the hearse under the graveyard's stone entrance arch. In the back seat, Julia hid her face behind dark glasses, still processing the fact that Rob, the love of her life, was gone. An autopsy had found he'd died from head trauma sustained in the attack, not a lack of oxygen. It didn't matter; without him nothing mattered.

Running had been her salvation, her high level of fitness had helped her survive, but the thought of going to the Kelvin Walkway or anywhere her freedom might suddenly be threatened made her feel sick. So she didn't run.

Physically, she'd made a good recovery. Mentally and emotionally was a very different story. Julia shunned the therapy route the doctors had urged her to go down. She couldn't talk about the ordeal and probably never would. Within seventy-two hours she'd put Hamilton Drive on the market. Wherever she looked there was a memory of Rob, plunging her into a deep depression that left her washed out, despairing and afraid – wanting to be alone, unable to handle it when she was. Keeping the lights on in every room in the house twenty-four hours a day was a symptom of her terror; darkness had too many ghosts.

The abduction had been on the front page of every newspaper in the country. Going to the shops sparked her latent paranoia: she imagined people were watching her, talking about her behind her back, pitying the poor woman who'd been snatched by a maniac and locked in 'that' container.

And through it all the terrible truth that haunted her day and night.

Ellis Kirkbride hadn't been caught.

After she'd left hospital the police had stationed a car in the street outside. Just seeing it, knowing it was there, had been reassuring, though it couldn't stay forever and the DI in charge had personally apologised to her when it had been recalled.

The detective inspector had sounded confident. 'Kirkbride will be as far from Scotland as he can get. Now Interpol are on it he'll struggle to put roots down anywhere.'

Julia had longed to believe him but couldn't. The policeman's motives were honest but he was wrong. Ellis had wanted... no, needed her dead. In his diseased mind... She couldn't finish the rest. Ravi saw her shoulders shake and took her hand. 'It's over, Julia. I promise he won't ever hurt you again. I won't let him.'

She turned and saw his other hand resting on the brass ball of his solid-chestnut walking stick. What a great friend he'd turned out to be, visiting her every afternoon and night. Without his support she wouldn't have been able to face this.

He hadn't known Rob in any real sense. He was here because she'd asked him.

The funeral had been delayed. After today, it would be behind her, although there would be no black-tie-steak-pie repast in a local hotel, no drinks for a select few back at the house; none of that 'celebration of his life' stuff. Her husband had been taken from her in his prime. Julia didn't want to hear it.

A subdued Tony Connors opened the car door and Julia stepped out into the sunshine. Ravi took her arm and helped her, silently admiring her courage. Michelle was already there, pale and thin, quietly weeping in the background. She'd come to the hospital and had been overcome with gratitude and surprise when Julia had invited her to the funeral.

'I assumed you'd hate me. I didn't think...'

'We both loved him. Rob would've wanted you there, that's enough.'

DI Geddes saw the two women bound by common loss acknowledge each other with almost imperceptible nods. Julia Sutherland had needed his reassurance she wasn't in danger. Reluctantly, he'd given it. The detective hadn't told her that every line of investigation relating to the whereabouts of the man who'd taken his dead mother's name and called himself Ellis Kirkbride had come to nothing. Even the East End villain, Tommy Shaw, had stuck to his story claiming he was doing the city a service by getting rid of an eyesore.

The graveside service was brief. The humanist's solemn eulogy drifted on the breeze and into the world. Later, Julia wouldn't be able to remember a single word.

One hundred yards away a figure behind a tree raised a camera to his eye – a Nikon, exactly like the one he'd lost – and waited for the moment the woman wearing black shades dropped a handful of earth into the grave.

He smiled, ran his fingers over stubble that wasn't there and shook his head. 'My money was always on you, Julia.'

CLICK.

* * *

Julia locked the door and took off the dark glasses, relieved to have got through the most difficult hours since she'd found Rob on the floor of the container. The horror of that moment would stay with her forever. Finding his body still and cold in the awful darkness had felt like being buried alive. During the service she'd been aware of what was happening, though most of it had seemed like a dream she'd wake up from to discover none of it – Ellis Kirkbride, Michelle, the horrendous time in the container, Rob dying – had been real.

Her husband would be waiting and they'd go on with their trip.

The final goodbye when the earth had fallen through her fingers onto his coffin – that had been hard. Ravi had sensed her distress and put a supportive arm around her. Without him she would've collapsed and ended up in the hole in the ground herself. As she'd walked from the grave, people had stopped to shake her hand and comfort her with words that had sounded stilted and hollow to their ears as well as hers.

Julia had always been a sound sleeper. Not any more. She couldn't remember when she'd last had an undisturbed night. There was life before the container and life after the container. A doctor had written a prescription for something that would force her body to close down and rest but losing control of herself, even for a few stolen hours, wasn't an option. She'd deal with her new reality knowing even if she managed to drop off, invariably she'd wake again, sweating and petrified.

It was two in the afternoon and the sun was shining. Drained, totally spent, Julia double-checked every light in the house was still on, then climbed the stairs, barely able to drag one foot after the other. She left her mobile in the kitchen so she wouldn't be disturbed. Anticipating a sale, the estate agent had left three messages on her phone; she'd call him tomorrow if she could raise the energy.

She left her clothes in a heap on the floor, slipped into bed and lay staring at the ceiling, too numb to think or feel. At some point she must've dropped off because the distant sound of glass breaking disturbed her and Julia felt the fear that had become such a familiar part of her life slither in her gut.

She threw on a dressing gown and went to the top of the stairs. The hall lights were out. Before she could scream, Ellis Kirkbride stepped from the darkness, looking very different from the day Tony Connors had introduced his bright new star to the Grapevine staff.

He gently scolded her. 'You didn't really think I'd gone, did you? Is that what they told you? Surely you know me better than that?'

Julia was so scared she could hardly breathe. Somehow she managed to speak and blurted out an unconvincing lie. 'The police are outside.'

Kirkbride corrected her. 'No, they *were* outside. You're going to have to do better than that, Julia.'

'You killed Rob. He's dead because of you, isn't that enough?'

He ignored the questions and started to climb the stairs. 'You've no idea how many times I've sat in the car watching you, watching him, wondering why you betrayed me.'

Julia's voice rose hysterically as he came closer. 'You're insane. I haven't betrayed you. I haven't betrayed anybody.'

He continued as though she hadn't spoken. 'This isn't the first time I've been inside and it certainly is a nice house. For sale, isn't it? Perhaps I'll buy it. What a delicious finale that would be, eh?'

She kicked out at him. He stood aside, grinning. Julia ran to the bedroom with his pitying laughter ringing in her ears. 'You're a sad, pathetic woman, Julia, you really are. I don't know what I ever saw in you.'

She slammed her back against the door, panting with terror, searching for something, anything, to fight with. Ellis threw his weight against it and it opened; he wasn't laughing now. He lunged at her. She lashed out at him again. This time she didn't miss. Her nails bit into his face and he screamed, 'Bitch! You bitch!'

His fist caught her full on the jaw and Julia tasted the metallic tang of blood in her mouth. Ellis pinned her to the floor, his hands round her neck, mercilessly squeezing the life from her. Her throat was on fire, her arms flailed helplessly. She'd known it wasn't over: Ellis Kirkbride had been determined to kill her and was about to succeed.

Suddenly, his grip loosened.

She pushed him away, struggling to make sense of what she was seeing. Ravi was standing over Ellis, holding the shaft of his cane. Blood stained the brass handle. He didn't look at Julia; his eyes were on Ellis. 'The stick seems to be working out okay, *mate*.'

Ellis was confused. 'You?'

Ravi raised the cane to strike again, paused and smiled. 'Should've taken your own advice. Know where the threat will come from.'

Julia scrambled to her feet and prised the stick away from him. She straddled the monster who'd taken everything she'd held dear from her, smiling as his eyes registered what was about to happen, and delivered the death blow.

ACKNOWLEDGEMENTS

The Wrong Woman is the latest book on my writing journey. Publishing can be a hard road and it would have been if not for the many readers, bloggers, reviewers and fellow authors who have loaned me their support along the way. I thank them all.

Closer to home, I am indebted to the team at Boldwood Books, which has grown so much in such a short time; any writer would be happy to be a part, albeit a small part, of such spectacular success. But a special thank you to Sarah. Her faith in me kept me going when it would've been easier to give in. Without it I would have. Indeed, before we met I almost did.

It's only fair to give an appreciative nod to my other editors, Sue Smith and Paul Martin, for bringing their gifts to my work and making it better. Also, DS Alasdair McMorrin, who gave his time so generously and answered my seemingly never-ending questions about what would happen in different situations from a police perspective.

And lastly, my wife Christine, unsung hero and a talent in her own right. As I have acknowledged many times before, the book you have in your hand wouldn't exist without her. No doubt about it, I'm a lucky guy.

Owen Mullen
Glasgow, April 2024

ABOUT THE AUTHOR

O. J. Mullen is a highly regarded crime author who splits his time between Scotland and the island of Crete. In his earlier life he lived in London and worked as a musician and session singer.

Sign up to O. J. Mullen's newsletter to read an exclusive extract of her upcoming rom-com, It's All Sun and Games

Follow O. J. Mullen on social media:

X x.com/OwenMullen6
f facebook.com/OwenMullenBooks
⊙ instagram.com/owenmullen6
BB bookbub.com/authors/owen-mullen
♪ tiktok.com/@owenmullenauthor

ALSO BY O. J. MULLEN

Three Sisters

The Wrong Woman

Mackenzie Darroch Series

The Marriage

Nowhere to Run

O.J Mullen writing as Owen Mullen

Out Of The Silence

So It Began

The Glass Family Series

Family

Insider

Hustle

Thief

PI Charlie Cameron Series

Games People Play

The Wronged

Whistleblower

The Accused

THE *Murder* LIST

THE MURDER LIST IS A NEWSLETTER DEDICATED TO SPINE-CHILLING FICTION AND GRIPPING PAGE-TURNERS!

SIGN UP TO MAKE SURE YOU'RE ON OUR HIT LIST FOR EXCLUSIVE DEALS, AUTHOR CONTENT, AND COMPETITIONS.

SIGN UP TO OUR NEWSLETTER

BIT.LY/THEMURDERLISTNEWS

Boldwood

Boldwood Books is an award-winning fiction publishing company seeking out the best stories from around the world.

Find out more at www.boldwoodbooks.com

Join our reader community for brilliant books, competitions and offers!

Follow us
@BoldwoodBooks
@TheBoldBookClub

Sign up to our weekly
deals newsletter

https://bit.ly/BoldwoodBNewsletter

Milton Keynes UK
Ingram Content Group UK Ltd.
UKHW042351010724
444980UK00001B/1